Florence Morse Kingsley

Paul

A herald of the cross

Florence Morse Kingsley

Paul
A herald of the cross

ISBN/EAN: 9783337257088

Printed in Europe, USA, Canada, Australia, Japan

Cover: Foto ©Andreas Hilbeck / pixelio.de

More available books at **www.hansebooks.com**

PAUL

A HERALD OF THE CROSS

by

Florence Morse Kingsley

Author of "TITUS," "STEPHEN," etc.

with Illustrations by
J. E. McBURNEY

GROSSET & DUNLAP
PUBLISHERS : NEW YORK

PREFACE.

IN "Titus," the first of this series, I endeavored to make new "the old, old story," to depict a real, a living Jesus, not enthroned in some far-away inaccessible glory, but "with us alway, even unto the end."

In "Stephen," I showed the bereft disciples, comforted with the comfort which streamed down into their sad hearts in abundant measure from the Master who had gone away because it was "expedient" for them, joyful with the joy which he had given them, and serene in the midst of trial and persecution with the peace which he had bestowed upon them, a last precious legacy.

In "Paul," I have carried the story further, and with it I have interwoven some account of the great world without the confines of the Holy Land; the world which lay in misery and sin, and into which Christ had bidden his disciples go forth to carry the Glad-tidings of the Cross.

Saul the persecutor, the relentless Pharisee, the learned rabbi, has become Paul, the herald of the Cross. We see his heroic figure starting out into the night alone, in that darkest hour which comes before dawn, proclaiming in trumpet-tones the glorious tidings of the coming day. We see the brood of evil creatures, that loved darkness rather than light, bestir themselves to do him battle. We see the conflict joined, never to be given over for a moment till the worn conqueror lays his armor down to receive the crown of victory from the hand of the Lord, the righteous Judge.

To fully understand the life and labors of the great apostle, it is necessary to also comprehend something of the hopeless degradation of those in high places, to look for an instant into the frightful abysses into which the decadent religions were hurrying mankind. I have therefore endeavored to portray the Christless world —the world as it was in the "fullness of time," as well as the divine remedy applied.

It seems scarcely necessary to give the long list of authorities consulted in the preparation of this volume. It will be noticed, however, that I refer most frequently in my occasional notes to Farrar's " Life and Work of St. Paul," and to " The Life and Epistles of St. Paul " by Conybeare and Howson. And, indeed, while I had in my possession many of the authorities to which these authors in their turn refer, I would acknowledge my great indebtedness to their scholarly works. I should also mention Guhl and Koner's " Life of the Greeks and Romans," to which I referred continually for information relating to dress, customs, etc.; and to the ancient chronicles of Josephus, where I found the stories of Agrippa, of Caius, of Herodias, and of the other historical personages who figure more or less largely in these pages.

If in these scenes from the life and times of St. Paul, I have succeeded, in some small measure, in enabling the reader to see for himself not merely Paul, the theologian; Paul, the setter-forth of " the scheme of salvation ;" Paul, the stern ascetic, thundering forth reproof and denunciation against evil-doers—but Paul, the fearless herald of the Cross, pouring out his life like water, that he might save the lost; Paul, the tent-maker, laboring with his hands that he might minister to the necessities of others; " Paul, the aged ;" " Paul, the prisoner of the Lord Jesus," healing the sick, cheering the oppressed and down-trodden, the father of all the churches, the friend of sinners and of God—if we shall look upon him thus, we shall read the Epistles with new eyes, seeing in them the outpourings of a great loving heart which beat divinely for all humanity ; and so reading, we shall long to be numbered among the saints and faithful brethren to whom he writes.

FLORENCE MORSE KINGSLEY.

WEST NEW BRIGHTON, Feb. 6, 1897.
STATEN ISLAND, N. Y.

CONTENTS.

PART I.

"*The Night is Far Spent.*"

CONTENTS.

PART II.

"The Day is at Hand."

PART III.

"An Ambassador in Bonds."

CHAPTER I.

"GIVE the little one to me, and rest thou, queen of my soul, while I show him the new moon yonder."

"He is ill because of the hot wind," said the woman wearily. "See the roses also, how they hang their heads; the breath of the wilderness is death to such tender things."

"Ay," said the man, "it is an evil spirit which the mountains yonder war against continually. But be of good cheer, it hath again been driven back into the fiery torments of the desert. Hark, littlest, hearest thou the voice of the fountains, the song of many birds also, and the rejoicing of the green leaves?"

He paused for a moment in his slow walk and the child hushed its fretful wail to listen; as for the mother, she sat quietly, her back against the parapet, her eyes fixed upon the slender horn of the new moon which hung above the low western horizon. Through the silence came the musical gurgle and rush of water, and the rustle of foliage from the little garden below.

"Look thou at the great mountain, son of mine," continued the man; "he hath put on his robes of rose

(13)

that he may say farewell to the sun. Anon, he will be clothed in violet, then in sad garments the color of ashes, afterward he will sleep. Sleep thou also, little one; to-morrow there will be no wind from the desert. Sleep thou, and the good Shepherd will watch thee."

"I hear some one knocking," said the woman. She arose and advanced to the parapet which overlooked the street. "It is our neighbor, Simon; he hath returned from his journey to Jerusalem and will tell thee of it. Give me the child; he will sleep now," and taking the little one in her arms she descended to the terrace.

A slow step on the stair presently announced the new-comer. He was a stout man and breathed heavily as he set his foot on the roof level. He was also grumbling aloud. "Had I a garden below, such as thine, friend Ananias," he said, "I would not climb to the roof."

"Greetings, friend, and a welcome," returned Ananias with a quiet smile. "Jehovah grant that thy ways have been prospered. My garden is indeed good, but this is better, for here one can feel the breath of the mountains, the fragrance of the eternal snows on Hermon yonder."

Simon replied with a shrug of the shoulders and an inarticulate grunt, as he settled himself upon a bench. "There are tidings of evil," he said abruptly. "Hast thou heard?"

"Nay, I have not heard; what hath befallen?"

"As thou knowest, I have been in Jerusalem ; there hath been there a great persecution of them that believe on the Crucified One. Many are slain ; others are in prison, and others still are fled."

The face of Ananias grew white in the fading light. "Who hath caused these things to be done?"

"They that slew Jesus of Nazareth, and who will yet accomplish the destruction of all that believe on him," answered Simon bitterly.

"Hast thou forgotten that the Christ is set down at the right hand of Jehovah?" cried Ananias. "Surely he will not suffer our foot to be moved."

"He hath already suffered Stephen to be killed with stones. He hath suffered others of the disciples to be scourged and imprisoned. He hath suffered babes also to be left desolate, and little children to wail for food. But the destroyers wax fat and flourishing ; they are not moved."

"So hath it ever appeared," said Ananias. "Yet is the Lord mindful of his own." Then, after a pause, he added, "We are at peace, thanks be to Jehovah, for there is no one in all Damascus who would lift up a hand against us—who also walk blameless according to the law. Let us send word to the smitten ones that they come hither ; here shall they find refuge."

"I have not yet told thee the worst," said Simon, dejectedly. "A certain Saul of Tarsus, a Pharisee taught of Gamaliel, and most bitter against the Christ, hath come hither to Damascus with the intent to carry away in chains to Jerusalem every least disciple of the

Crucified One. He is without mercy, and will slay and spare not all that resist him. When I heard of his purpose, I made haste to return to Damascus, that I might warn the brethren. Surely it were better to flee into the desert than to perish miserably under the scourge."

His voice died away into silence, and in the hush the voice of the mother singing to her babe floated up to them.

Ananias moistened his dry lips. " Didst thou say that the man laid his hand also upon women and babes ?" he asked huskily.

" More than once hath he seized the mother and left the little ones desolate in the house—for so it was told me in Jerusalem," replied Simon. " Yet it may be that the Lord hath had mercy upon us. I heard a strange thing concerning the man as I came hither to-night ; it was told me by Ben Ethan, one of the keepers of the Eastern Gate. Yesterday, at about the ninth hour, a company of men approached the city, some riding upon beasts, others walking. In the midst was a man, whom also two of his comrades led by the hand. When the head keeper questioned them, saying, ' Who are you and whence do ye come ?' One made answer, saying, ' The chief man of our company is Saul, a worshipful rabbi from Jerusalem. He beareth letters from the Senate and Council of Israel to the governor of this city.'

" ' Let him appear then and speak,' quoth the keeper of the gate. To whom the other made answer, ' The man Saul hath been grievously smitten in the way by a great and terrible light which blazed suddenly out of heaven as we journeyed; and lo, he is blind, and we have brought him hither leading him by the hand, even as thou seest. Grant us an entrance speedily, I pray thee, that we may fetch him to a resting-place, for he is in a desperate strait.'"

"And as Ben Ethan looked earnestly upon the man Saul, he perceived that he trembled exceedingly as he stood, and seemed not to hear what was passing about him, but continually did moan within himself, and also that his face was as the face of one stricken with death. Furthermore, he told me that when the business with the chief officer of the gate was finished, that they led the man, still trembling and moaning, into the city. God grant that death follow hard after, and that it overtake him speedily."

Ananias shook his head. "Thou knowest not what thou art saying, friend. God's ways are not man's ways, nor are his thoughts their thoughts. There is something here that we do not understand."

"If he be smitten that he die, then shall we live—we and our little ones," said Simon obstinately. "Therefore shall I continue to pray to God to remove him out of the land of the living. Surely he hath deserved to die."

"Pray, rather, that God's will may be done concerning the man and us. Even should he rend my child from my bosom I could not pray for his undoing. Vengeance belongeth to the Lord, and in his hand also is the breath of every living thing."

" Pray as thou wilt, friend," said Simon, rising, "and I will pray, even as did David, for the destruction of mine enemies. The Lord heard him and gave him his desire upon them that sought his hurt, as thou mayst read in the Psalms. Farewell ; Jehovah keep thee and thine."

Ananias seemed hardly to have heard the parting words of his guest ; he also had risen and was walking slowly up and down. His heart had grown heavy within him, and it was heavier still as he saw his wife approaching from the adjoining roof-terrace.

" Our son sleeps, my lord," she said, with a low laugh of content. " Thou shouldst have heard him pray to the ascended One ; he repeated the prayer that thou didst teach him, and afterward, ' Good Jesus, let not the wind from the desert blow to-morrow. Amen.' I could not chide him, and to-morrow the wind will continue to set from Lebanon, thou wilt see ; for I believe that the Ascended heeds the little ones whom he so loved when he was on earth."

" Teach him, then, to pray that our faith be not shaken," said Ananias with a sigh.

" Assuredly, that is a good thing to ask. But what said our friend Simon of his journey ? And why hath he made such haste to be gone ? I would fain have heard of the wondrous sights he beheld in Jerusalem."

" He brought tidings of evil, heart of mine. The brethren which dwell at Jerusalem are suffering many things at the hand of them which believe not, scourging, imprisonment, and even death."

The woman shuddered. "Nay, then, I am glad that we do not dwell there," she said quickly. "It is a wicked city and doubtless the vengeance of Jehovah will yet overtake it, even as Sodom perished at his word. But come, my lord, let us sup, for the hour grows late. I had the intent to have bidden our neighbor also, for to-night we shall taste the first of the white figs from the young tree by the fountain. They are fine, I can promise thee; I plucked them myself."

"Go thou and eat, little one; I shall fast to-night for the peace of the brethren," said Ananias, turning away his head.

"And what will it profit them, my lord, if thou dost fast? Wilt thou not eat of my figs even?" and the woman laid her hand persuasively on her husband's arm.

He looked down at her with a melancholy smile. "Dost thou love me, rose of Lebanon?"

"What shall I answer thee, my lord? I love thee even as the thirsty earth loveth the streams which flow down from the mountain; the desert laughs aloud because of the abundance of waters."

"'Tis well, life of mine. Go thou and rest in peace; but as for me, I must fast and pray this night, both for the brethren that be in peril, and also for our own souls that they faint not in the hour of trial."

The woman looked at him, her eyes misty with vague alarms. "Let me fast with thee, my lord. I also will pray."

"Nay, I would be alone.   Go."

She lingered yet a moment, looking wistfully at the
averted face, then she turned swiftly and went away,
but not before an angry little sob had escaped her.

Ananias aroused himself at the sound.   "I must
have spoken roughly to the child," he murmured peni-
tently.   "What if I tell her all—but no, I cannot.
To-morrow I will look into the matter further, and if
a persecution be imminent I will send her away into
the mountains together with my son ; they will be safe
there."   Then he fell again into a reverie, but this time
his thoughts busied themselves with the day when he
had first seen the rose of Lebanon, blooming in a
remote nook of the barren hills, and of how, saddened
and grown old before his time, he had plucked the
flower to fill his desolate home with fragrance and
beauty.   "Nay, my God, I cannot again suffer as I
have suffered," he said aloud, clenching his strong
hands.   "I will die for the faith if need be, but spare
thou these."

The long hours of the summer night crept slowly
by, the slender young moon, shamed by the golden
radiance of the thronging stars, hid herself behind
the rim of the desert.   The breath of roses floated
spirit-like on the breeze, and in the silence the voice
of myriads of fountains cried aloud, the small silver
tinkle of the jets about the basin below, the gush and
babble of water-wheels in the neighboring gardens,
and above all dominated the solemn murmur of the
river, Barada, mother of all the waters.   "From the

eternal snows I come, to the unchanging desert I go : there is no variableness, neither shadow of change in the God that hath set my course."

To the man, who still watched and prayed on the housetop, there came at length peace. He knew that the Lord had heard him, and that the blessing was not far away, that it was even at hand—as was also the day, for all the snowy heights of Hermon were flushed with heavenly color. He wrapped himself in his mantle and lay down, and immediately a deep sleep fell softly upon him. As he slept, it seemed presently that the roseate glimmer of the dawn had deepened and brightened into a splendor of light ; in the midst of the light he saw the figure of a man, a man into whose face he looked with awe and yet with an overwhelming sense of joy and love, for it was the face of his ascended Lord.

Then was there the sound of a voice, it called him by his name. He made answer, saying, " Behold, I am here, Lord."

Again came the voice and these were the words of it : " Arise, go into the street which is called Straight, and enquire in the house of Judas for one called Saul of Tarsus ; for behold, he prayeth, and hath seen in a vision a man named Ananias coming in, and putting his hand on him, that he might receive his sight."

To Ananias it seemed that without fear he answered of all that was within his heart, " Lord, I have heard of this man, how much evil he hath done to thy saints at Jerusalem, and now he hath authority from the chief priests to bind all that call on thy name."

But the Lord said unto him, "Go thy way : for he is my chosen herald, to proclaim my name before the Gentiles, and kings, and the Children of Israel : and I will show him how great things he must suffer for my name's sake." Then the glory faded, Ananias awoke, and behold, it was day.

CHAPTER II.

IN THE HOUSE OF JUDAS.

"'TIS a strange case, and most untoward, I would gladly have aided the holy council of Jerusalem in suppressing this deadly heresy; but in a heathen city and unsupported by outside authority, what could we do? If the man do not speedily recover his wits, we must report the matter."

"Thinkest thou that he will recover?"

Judas shrugged his shoulders. "Nay, how can I tell? There was a light, sayest thou? Lightning perchance, and yet how could that be out of a cloudless heaven?"

"There was a light," said the other vehemently; "I myself saw it, as did the others of our company; there was also a sound, as of a voice—a terrible voice, but the sound was void of meaning."

A slight incredulous smile flitted across the attentive face of his listener. "If there chanced to be a cloud overhead, we should say that the sound was thunder."

"There was no cloud, I tell thee," said the other hotly. "The heavens were as clear as they are at this moment."

"Well, what was it then?"

The man, who was called Silas Ben Ezra, dropped his eyes in silence, seemingly intent on nothing more important than the pattern of the rich Persian carpet beneath his feet.

"It is evident that thou hast an opinion, friend," continued Judas. "Come, explain the matter according to thy thought concerning it, thou wast an eye-witness."

Ben Ezra raised his head and looked squarely into the face of his host. "I will tell thee what I think hath befallen the man," he said, and there was a shade of defiance in his low tones. "He beheld the cruci- fied Nazarene and was rebuked of him."

"What sayest thou?" cried Judas angrily. "Art thou also apostate, who wert chosen by the holy San- hedrim to perform this sacred mission?"

"If it be heresy to believe the evidence of one's senses then am I apostate," declared the other boldly. "Saul answered the voice; twice answered he and after this manner; first he cried out as one greatly astonished and afraid, 'Who art thou, Lord?' And afterward, 'What wilt thou have me to do?'"

"The man was crazed by the heat," said Judas, with an easy wave of the hand. "'Tis no less than the act of a fool to travel at midday in this clime."

Ben Ezra's black eyes flashed angrily. "Think as thou wilt, my worshipful host," he said coldly. "And I also, who was eye-witness, will hold to mine own opinion of the matter."

"Nay, but—friend," said Judas softly, "hast thou

duly weighed and considered the matter aright? Thou
hast as yet spoken of this to no other save myself;
but and if thou shalt return to Jerusalem and say to
the most holy and reverend high priest, Saul hath
had a vision of the Nazarene whom ye lately slew, and
hath been smitten with blindness because of his
glory, what then will befall thee? Will it not be
better to say, Saul was smitten with the fierce heat of
the sun, insomuch that he fell to the earth blind and
senseless; for because of his zeal in thy service he
was traveling at midday. If it was in truth a vision,
then let the man declare it for himself, and bear the
consequences thereof—that is, if ever he recover his
lost wits, which I myself doubt."

Ben Ezra stroked his beard in silence for a time,
then he said slowly, "Thou hast spoken words of
wisdom; and I have heard and understood; also it is
an evil thing to be an apostate, and a foolish thing to
interpret a vision which hath appeared to another.
For the present I will not return to the Sanhedrim.
The others of the company may report the matter as
seemeth best to them."

"As to the man himself," pursued Judas, "if indeed
he be mad, or if an unclean spirit hath entered in and
taken possession of him, he must needs go forth into
the desert; so shall he recover himself, if it be the will
of Jehovah."

"Thou wouldst not thrust him forth, blind and helpless as he is!" said Ben Ezra, aghast.

"If Jehovah hath smitten him, or if the evil one

hath obtained the mastery over him, it signifieth one and the same thing according to the law," said the other judicially. "He hath gravely sinned, and it ill becometh man to strive against unseen powers ; besides all this, he that hath disordered wits is unclean and polluteth the house of a righteous man.—How now, Malluch ! What wouldst thou ?"

" I kiss thy feet, most worshipful master," replied the slave, who had noiselessly entered the apartment. "There is a man without who desires entrance, one Ananias, a Jew. He would see Saul of Tarsus."

" Admit him at once, and conduct him to our presence ; I would fain know his errand with the man."

The slave bowed himself before his master and withdrew, to return a moment later followed by a man, upon whom both Judas and Ben Ezra fixed their eyes with some curiosity.

" Greetings, friend," said Judas, "thou art known unto me by reputation as one that is zealous for the law and also for the peace of Israel ; I am glad, therefore, that thou hast sought my dwelling. Most welcome in these troublous times is the converse of holy men."

Ananias bowed his head courteously in response to these greetings. " My errand is with one Saul of Tarsus, who is abiding under this roof," he said gravely. " I pray you to conduct me without delay into his presence."

" Thou art not aware, then, that the worshipful rabbi met with a lamentable mischance on his journey hither," replied Judas suavely. "He hath continually remained upon his bed, neither eating nor drinking, nor holding converse with any man since he arrived in Damascus, this being also the third day. I myself have visited him a score of times and have sent for divers wise men and physicians. Some hold that he hath been smitten by the power of the sun, others that an evil spirit has entered into him; for myself I know not what to think, but I am the more grieved concerning the matter, since the man had come hither on a most godly errand, that of purging the synagogues of Damascus of them that blasphemously declare a certain Galilean, named Jesus—lately crucified in Jerusalem because of his crimes—to be the Christ foretold of the Prophets."

The sensitive face of Ananias flushed and his eyes burned with righteous anger. "Beware, lest thou also ignorantly fall into the grievous sin of blasphemy," he said sternly. "Because thou hast not known the Christ, thou mayst be forgiven; but I have both seen him and know him; and I know furthermore that that which I declare unto you is true, Jesus of Nazareth is the Christ of God, the Savior of Israel, whom also with murderous hands the chief priests and elders at Jerusalem put to death. But, thanks be to Jehovah, he hath overcome the grave and is set down at the right hand of eternal power. It was this living Jesus that appeared unto the man Saul by the way, when he would have brought chains and death into Damascus to them that believe. And behold, I am sent unto him to deliver him out of his blindness, and to declare unto him the word of peace. Make haste, therefore, and show me where he lieth."

Judas regarded the speaker with open disdain. "It is sad indeed to see a righteous man the victim of such an unlawful and unholy delusion," he said icily. "If there be many such in Damascus, the wisdom of the Sanhedrim of Jerusalem is abundantly proven. I only regret that their erstwhile able emissary hath been prevented from performing his duty. In the meantime I will conduct thee to the chamber of the stricken man, if only to prove that thou art miserably deceived. As I have declared to you, the man hath been blind and dumb for three days."

"So likewise did the Christ remain during three days in the tomb, and on the third day he arose into newness of life," murmured Ananias as if to himself.

Ben Ezra regarded the pale face and shining eyes of the stranger with awe. Instinctively he drew away a little from Judas, who had risen to lead the way to the chamber of Saul.

"He is here," said their host briefly, drawing aside the heavy curtains which served to shut out the light of day from a small chamber on their right.

Ananias paused on the threshold, signing authoritatively to the two men that they should remain without, then he entered the chamber, which, in truth, was the tomb of a fruitless life. Upon a couch in one corner lay the motionless and apparently rigid form of Saul, his face turned toward the wall, his hands clenched.

Ananias advanced without hesitation ; kneeling down at the bedside, he laid his hands upon the prostrate man and said in a clear voice :

" Brother Saul, the Lord—even Jesus, that appeared unto thee in the way as thou camest—hath sent me, that thou mightest receive thy sight and be filled with the holy Spirit."

" Blasphemy !" cried Judas, starting forward. " Mine house is polluted !"

" Let be, man, lest the curse that hath been lifted from him fall upon thee," said Ben Ezra, grasping him by the arm. " Dost thou not see that a miracle hath been wrought ?"

Judas drew back, and stared as if spellbound into the chamber. Saul had turned himself upon his bed, he raised his trembling hands to his eyes. " Thank God," he cried aloud, " I see." Then he looked steadfastly upon Ananias, as if he would fain remember to eternity that face shining with love and joy.

" The God of our fathers hath chosen thee," said Ananias softly, " that thou shouldst know his will and see that Just One, and shouldst hear the voice of his mouth. For thou shalt be his witness unto all men of what thou hast seen and heard. And now, why tarriest thou ? Arise, and be baptized and wash away thy sins, calling on the name of the Lord."

And when Judas heard these words, and when he saw that Saul was risen from the bed whereon he had lain, and that he had indeed been restored, he was greatly amazed, also he was angry.

" Fetch food and drink," he commanded his servants, " and set before the man that he may eat; and
fetch him fair raiment that he may be clothed—for he
is my guest." But he himself withdrew to an inner
chamber of his house.

Ananias perceived that he was offended, nevertheless he baptized Saul straightway in the water of the
fountain, and afterward he urged him to take some
meat.

" Come, I pray thee," he said, " sojourn at my house
for a space, and the brethren shall strengthen thy
heart."

So the two went away together, but Silas Ben Ezra
remained in the house of Judas. Of all men in
Damascus he was that day the most miserable, being
divided betwixt a longing to seek Ananias and to
declare to him, I also believe in this Jesus, of whose
glory I have been witness, and a desire to stand well
in the eyes of the rich man Judas and before the Sanhedrim, in whose service he had come thither. When
it was evening he arose and went away out of the city,
and was seen no more of them that were in his company, nor yet of Judas. And when after the seventh
day he returned not, they concluded that he had fallen
unawares into the river, or that a beast from the desert
had devoured him.

" These matters must be reported to the Sanhedrim
at Jerusalem," said Judas to Ben Ahaz, one of the
temple officers who had been deputed to accompany
Saul.

"The man should himself be fetched back to Jerusalem that he may answer for his madness before the high priest," said Ben Ahaz frowning, "for I hear that he hath even been baptized in the accursed name."

They went therefore to the house of Ananias, but it was told them, "Saul hath gone away into the wilderness to be alone for a space ; but whither he hath gone we know not."

"He is assuredly mad," said Ben Ahaz. He returned back to Jerusalem therefore, and declared before the Sanhedrim that Saul had fallen into a state of grievous madness, and that he had fled into the desert no man knew whither. As for Ben Ezra, he forgot to make mention of him.

CHAPTER III.

THE SOOTHSAYER.

"HAVE a care, Ethiopian dogs, that there be not so much as a fleck of dust upon the beasts, else shall ye taste the lash. Look to that hind leg there, Sechu. Eyes on your work, idle devils."

The slaves, who were engaged in rubbing down the glossy flanks of a pair of spirited Arabians, looked up apprehensively, then bent to their task with redoubled vigor.

The man who had spoken passed on to the inspection of a gilded chariot which was being cleansed of dust in the courtyard.

Here he was presently joined by a curled and perfumed youth wearing the livery of the Caesars.

"Thou art in good spirits to-day, my Codrus," remarked the new-comer, languidly adjusting his girdle.

"Why not?"

"It was told me that thou hadst the misfortune to spill a drop of wine on the robe of his worshipful highness, Agrippa, at supper last night, and that thy master had thee scourged for it."

"Thou hast heard a lie, slave," returned Codrus with a black look.

The other laughed and beat the palms of his hands

softly together. "I am a slave, verily ; but what art thou, good Codrus ?"

"In mine own country I was the owner of an hundred such gilded chattels as thou art," said Codrus contemptuously ; "by the fortunes of war I became what I am, a slave, yes—a brute, if thou wilt, but—" and the speaker showed his white teeth in a savage grin, "I am able to avenge an insult even as a man."

"Spoken like an orator!" exclaimed the other, with a gesture of fervid admiration. "Nay, like a prince, the owner of a hundred slaves, ha, ha ! And yet, alas, thyself a slave, beaten at a nod from thy master."

He fled away, with a mocking laugh, just in time to avoid a part of the harness which the other in his exasperation had flung at his head.

"May the gods smite him with madness !" growled the slave angrily, as he turned his attention to the harnessing of the horses. Presently, the last strap being adjusted, he sprang into the chariot and, standing erect in the driver's place, guided the prancing animals through the narrow passage which led into the great outer court of the palace, drawing up with a skilful flourish at the broad flight of steps before the principal entrance.

From this doorway presently issued two men. One of them was dwarfish, misshapen, pallid, red-haired, yet he was by no means insignificant looking ; in his cold crafty eyes and about the corners of his thin colorless lips lurked a curiously inhuman expression. He resembled some dangerous beast imperfectly disguised in human form, but whether this animal would turn out to be a swine or a wolf when once unmasked, was not clear to the thoughtful beholder. For the rest, he wore the showy scarlet and gold trappings of a general in the Roman army.

His companion was a singularly handsome man of the Jewish type ; his dark regular features and broad-shouldered athletic figure were set off to advantage by his toga of white wool bordered with a narrow tracery of the imperial purple.

"To the springs, Codrus," commanded the Roman. "Ha, the Arabians are in good spirits to-day ! A pretty pair, sayest thou not so, prince Agrippa ?"

" There is not their equal at the palace, my Caius," returned the man in the white toga, regarding the flying horses approvingly. " The emperor is perchance too deeply absorbed in matters of statecraft to notice the occupants of the royal stables."

Both men laughed softly at this. " I must secure a pair for myself, and at once," continued Herod. " Canst thou commend me an honest dealer ?"

" Nay, I will do more ; if these animals please thee, my Agrippa, they are thine, together with the chariot and the slave."

" By Apollo ! Thou hast a more than royal generosity ; I have sojourned a month in the imperial palace and have not seen the like. Alas ! our divine Tiberius is grievously beclouded by age and infirmities ; haply the gods will soon release him from the burden of his mortality, and when that shall come to pass the sceptre of the world shall fall into a worthier hand. Then let the ruler of the universe remember his friends with the same royal favor."

Caius made no reply, but a fierce light leapt up in his eyes.

"Jehovah hasten the day!" added Herod with fervor.

Caius laughed aloud. " There speaks the Jew !" he exclaimed, "and yet thy Jehovah, for aught I know, is every whit as powerful as Jupiter."

Agrippa's dark face flushed. " I fear neither Jove nor Jehovah," he cried scornfully.

" Beware how thou dost provoke the gods to anger," said Caius, with a superstitious shiver.

" Thou art right as usual, son of Germanicus," said Agrippa gaily. " I will offer a hecatomb of victims in the temple when next I visit Jerusalem, and thus appease my countrymen as well as their God ; as for the gods of Rome, thou art the last man to deny that I am a devotee of Bacchus."

The rythmic feet of the horses and the clank of the silver harness-chains filled the silence that followed. They had neared Puteoli by this time, and were skimming swiftly along the smooth road which bordered the shore at that point. Below them lay the exquisite bay of Cumae, its blue waters flecked with the white sails of numerous fishing craft ; while within the shelter of the gigantic mole, which stretched its piers of solid masonry far out into the waters, lay a swarm of merchantmen busily discharging their cargoes. Not far away, a group of royal galleys reflected the dazzling beams of the sun from their carved and gilded sides, and with their sails of silken stuff half furled reminded the beholder of a bevy of gorgeous birds from some strange far-away clime. On the right loomed the dark form of Vesuvius, the walls and towers of Pompeii and Herculaneum gleaming whitely amid the masses of verdure at its foot. Nearer at hand, and overlooking the bay, was the town of Puteoli with its baths, amphitheatres, temples, and its avenues lined with the palaces of Roman nobles.

"There is a certain spring within the shelter of this grove of olives, which I would have thee taste, my Agrippa," said Caius at length. "In my opinion it surpasses all the fountains of Baiae yonder; thou wilt find it a wondrous spur to the appetite."

"Let us taste then," said the Jewish prince languidly. "A feast with no stomach for it is worse than the bumpers of Tantalus. I have tried both," he added with a grimace.

The two now dismounted from the chariot and entered the shadow of the grove. From betwixt the gnarled roots of an ancient olive, a fountain clear as crystal gushed into its basin of golden-hued pebbles, and thence with a musical rush and tinkle fled away toward the sea.

"A veritable haunt of dryads," said Agrippa, looking about him. "And, by Bacchus," he added with a laugh, "we have stumbled upon the presiding genius of the place."

Caius drew back with a smothered oath and laid his

hand upon the dagger in his girdle. Upon the soft earth at their feet, well-nigh hidden by the luxuriant branches of laurel lay the half-naked figure of a man. He had evidently been asleep, but at the sound of the voices he raised his shaggy head and fixed his savage eyes upon the intruders; then he slowly rose to his feet.

"Begone!" commanded Caius with a gesture of disgust.

"I must needs obey the words of one on whom the gods have set the seal of an awful majesty," answered the man in a strange hollow voice. "Emperor of Rome, yet destined to die by an assassin's dagger, I salute thee." Then he turned to Agrippa. "Hail, King Aprippa! for thou shalt be king, and thy son after thee. Yet, beware the day when thou shalt again behold the bird of Minerva; in that day thou shalt surely die."

Agrippa involuntarily raised his eyes in obedience to the wild gesture of the man, and saw, perched in the leafy branches above his head, a small brown owl of a sort common enough in the neighborhood of Puteoli.

Caius was the first to recover himself. "Where is the fellow?" he cried, "I believe by Apollo, that he hath taken wings to himself. I did but lift mine eyes for an instant and behold the place is empty."

"He is hid within the laurel thicket," replied Agrippa hurriedly. "But let be; the man is mad perchance, and we have no guard."

The slave, Codrus, wrapped in his gloomy thoughts, stood holding the bits of the horses. He was scarce conscious of a swift shadow that flitted past him, but he fancied that he heard a sound as of mad laughter echoing from the hills beyond. " I will do this thing," he muttered, his eyes glowing fiercely ; "the gods have willed it. I am a slave ; I will be a slave no longer."

CHAPTER IV.

THREE PRINCES AND A SLAVE.

"FETCH more Falernian, slave ; 'tis too seldom that I sup with thee for sole company, my princess. I will drink to thee who art to be queen. Ay, look not startled, sweet one, the gods have willed it."

The princess Cypros lifted her dark eyes to the handsome flushed face of her husband, then she glanced apprehensively at the attendant slaves. "It pleases thee to jest, my lord," she said in clear low tones. "It also pleaseth me to listen. Hast thou been with the emperor to-day?"

"Nay, beloved," said Agrippa, lying back upon his purple cushions, and regarding with half-closed eyes the delicately-wrought cup of gold which he held betwixt his fingers. "Nay, I have been in better company. Truth to tell, princess, I find but sorry cheer with our emperor of late. He lieth all day on his couch, a huge bloated mass, but half alive, and unpleasant to look upon as if he were already dead."

"Thou art again jesting, prince Agrippa," said the lady, a shade of sternness in her voice. "The countenance of the divine Tiberius yet irradiates a power which is prosperity or adversity, life or death to his subjects. To me hath he granted the privilege of an audience this day; he is graciously minded to restore to thee the ædileship of Tiberias."

"He is minded to restore to me the ædileship of Tiberias?" said Agrippa with a mocking laugh. "What divine condescension! What royal munificence! Thou art my guardian spirit, princess.—Nay, now I am in earnest, sweet one, but for thee I should perchance be wandering among the disconsolate shades."

"May the immortals avert the hour!" exclaimed Cypros, growing pale. "But tell me truly, my lord, wouldst thou not rejoice to return to our own land? We have wandered far of late; would that we might find some quiet spot where we might abide with our children, and where—" she paused a moment as if her thoughts were too painful for utterance, slow tears gathering in her dark eyes.

"Dost thou not enjoy the splendors of Caprae, sweet one? Nay, there was a time when I should scarce have dared to leave so fair a flower unguarded in any one of the twelve palaces of Tiberius, but the candle hath been well-nigh burnt out; I am minded to see what will happen when its last expiring flicker shall have disappeared. Something more alluring than a paltry ædileship of Tiberias may come my way then. I tell thee I shall be a king. Ay, it will come to pass. —What sayest thou, slave? Caius and Claudius are without? Admit them; we will have a merry night. Nay, princess, do not remove the light of thy countenance."

"I cannot remain longer, my lord, Berenice hath been ailing to-day; I must see her once again before I sleep."

"Best of wives and mothers, peace go with thee!" said Agrippa, rising and escorting the lady to the door which led to her own apartments.

She lingered yet a moment to whisper imploringly, "Have a care, I beseech thee, my lord; speak no word against the emperor; if he be dying, as thou sayest, he is yet alive to a breath of treason. I like not the face of the strange slave, who attended thee to-night."

"What, Codrus? He was given me by Caius this day. Fear nothing, my princess, our star is in the ascendant," replied Agrippa, kissing her hand.

The Princess Cypros sighed as she flitted along the dimly-lighted corridor. A premonition of coming evil was heavy upon her, the remembrance of past trials and dangers only serving to make more dark the uncertain future. In truth, her position was such as to make the stoutest heart afraid : married to the Asmonean Herod at an early age, herself a princess of the same house, she had suffered all the vicissitudes of a capricious fortune during the years of her married life. Expelled from the splendors of the imperial court because of his unparalleled excesses, Agrippa had dragged the unfortunate Cypros through a series of debts and disgraces, culminating a few months since in his arrest for an enormous sum of money which he had borrowed from the treasury at Rome. In his

despair he had been about to take his own life, urging
his unhappy wife to follow his example. Cypros shuddered as the ghastly scene forced itself back upon her
remembrance. She had finally succeeded in persuad-
ing him to abandon his purpose for the moment, then
in tears and despair had sought the assistance of the
governor of Alexandria. Not unmoved by her entreaties, the gallant Lysimachus had advanced to her,
on little better security than the smile of a beautiful
woman, the goodly sum of two hundred thousand
drachmæ.

Once more at liberty, Agrippa, at the entreaty of
Cypros, set sail for Puteoli, where he was received with
certain marks of favor by the aged Tiberius. One of
the magnificent villas of Caprae had been placed at his
disposal, with tacit permission to remain a guest of the
emperor as long as it might please him.

"May the gods guard his incautious lips," murmured the anxious wife, as the sounds of revelry from
the banquet hall reached her from time to time. "A
word against yonder dying brute and we are undone."

Then her thoughts wandered to her children ; rising,
she glided softly into the apartment where the two little
maidens Berenice and Mariamne lay asleep. With all
a mother's pride in their rosy loveliness she moved
lightly here and there, smoothing a crumpled pillow,
or drawing a stray coverlid over restless limbs.

Passing on she entered the adjoining chamber. Her
heart leapt within her as she shaded the light from the
sleeper's eyes with slender tremulous fingers. " My

Agrippa," she murmured, looking down upon the handsome boy, " surely thy pathway in life must be a happy one. Would that I knew how to pray for thy future. At least I may implore that the gods will pour upon me all their hoarded wrath. I have already suffered, and little or much, all will soon be forgotten in the black night of the grave. But for thee, son of my heart, I must pray, Jehovah spare thee !" Secretly she vowed a sacrifice in the temple at Jerusalem, but the thought of the holy city, of the priests in their snowy robes half terrified her. " We are neither Jews nor Romans," she thought bitterly, " for us there is no God that cares ; of what use are sacrifices to Jehovah or to Jupiter?" And with these dark thoughts for company she returned once more to her lonely vigil.

Left to himself in the banquet hall, Agrippa welcomed his guests with the hilarious abandon of a man who had already drunken too deeply. He commanded the slaves to bring more wine.

" I would drink to thee, son of Germanicus," he cried, with a reckless laugh, " because thou art to be—"

" Hold !" growled Caius, scowling. " Forget the insane ravings of a witless fool. I have commanded that search be made for the man ; if found, his treasonable tongue shall be cut from his head."

" What unhappy wight hath had the misfortune to offend thee, my Caius," inquired the third man, leaning forward to pluck an olive from the crystal dish before him.

"A mad soothsayer," responded Caius, briefly, "who dared to speak a word against the majesty of the world in my hearing."

"If he be mad, why afflict him further? The gods have already smitten him."

Caius fixed his dull gray eyes on the speaker, while a malicious smile curled the corners of his lips. "I shall cut out his tongue, most sapient Claudius, because it pleaseth me to behold blood."

Claudius shivered; he made no reply.

"Come!" broke in Agrippa, impatiently. "Drink and forget—forget and drink! Hail to Bacchus, the god of pleasure!" and he drained the cup which the attentive slave at his elbow had just filled.

"There are no gods and no pleasures," said Caius, sullenly. "We only befool ourselves by thinking so."

"There be pleasures of the mind—" began Claudius, eagerly, but Caius interrupted him with a burst of loud laughter.

"What canst thou know of the mind, who wast born without one," he cried. "The gods gave thee a body, but even that is inferior to the body of the slave yonder."

Again Claudius was silent. He seemed either unwilling or unable to answer the man, who now lay back among his cushions with an expression of malignant enjoyment upon his pale face.

"Let him alone," said Agrippa in a low voice. "Poor Claudius, his own mother hath no good word for him; but he is not without wit, he is even writing a history which would do credit to Livy himself, I give you my word for it. Yesterday I listened for an hour while he read to me. I advised him not to show it to the emperor; 'tis too true to be pleasant reading."

"Writing history, is he?" said Caius, with another loud laugh. "Look at him now, he is going to sleep; that last bumper of Falernian was too much for him. Nay, for myself I shall make history; 'tis labor worthy a witless slave to toil with the stylus, no one save a fool would attempt it. More wine, slave."

"Thou wilt indeed make history, my Caius," replied Agrippa, confidently. "Was it for naught that thou wast born son of Germanicus, Rome's bravest soldier? that thou didst first behold the light amid the clash of arms and the bray of trumpets? that thou hast been reared amid all the magnificence of the court of Tiberius?"

The face of the man to whom these flattering words were addressed underwent a frightful change. Plain almost to ugliness at his best moments, the countenance of Caius now assumed such an expression of unbridled ferocity and hate that even his hardened companion shrank back; the pale skin grew ghastly, the gray eyes gleamed dully beneath the furrowed brow, the reddish hair, which but scantily covered the ill-shapen head, seemed to rise into bristles.

"Thou hast forgotten in thy enumeration of the blessings which the gods have bestowed upon me," he said in a smothered voice, "the fate of my father, my mother, my sisters, my brothers." * After a pause he added, with a reckless laugh, " If I myself remember, 'tis only that I may glut myself with the blood of— But stay, I may no longer enjoy the pleasures of thy hospitable board. I have an appointment with Macro which must not be broken. Come, thou dolt, thou addle-pated monstrosity, wake up!" and gathering up a handful of olive pits he discharged them full in the face of the unfortunate Claudius.

Agrippa half started up, " Do not carry thy jests too far, I beseech thee," he said soothingly. " Leave him to me, I will send him away presently."

"As thou wilt, Prince Agrippa ; farewell." With a leer of mock humility he bent before the couch of Claudius who, suddenly awakened by the shower of olive stones, sat up, rubbing his eyes with the expression of a sulky child.

" Fare thee well also, Tiberius Claudius Drusus Caesar Germanicus, thou art a prince of princes, the historian of all historians, the most amiable of an amiable and pious family."

---

* Caius Caesar, called also Caligula, was the son of Germanicus and the elder Agrippina. Germanicus was a nephew of Tiberius, and a brave, wise and virtuous man, as well as the most successful general of his day. He was poisoned by the jealous Tiberius in Syria. Agrippina, his wife, a model of a Roman matron of the highest stamp, was starved to death in the island of Pandataria. His eldest brother, Nero, was put to death, and Drusus was kept close prisoner in a secret dungeon of the palace. His sister was banished. Caius, the youngest of the family, was summoned by Tiberius to Caprae, and there only saved his life by the most abject flattery and submission.

" Nay, I will go with thee, my good nephew, since thou art come to thy proper senses!" exclaimed Claudius, his broad face beaming with delight. "And I will read to thee my history of the Roman wars this very night; thou shalt see, my Caius, if it be not meet to amuse the leisure of our emperor, who should now delight to review the triumphs of his reign."

" Thou wilt read me thy history? Nay, I will see thee choked with thy parchments first," growled Caius. " But come, thy excellent wife will be chiding thee for thy absence."

Left to himself, Agrippa looked about the empty hall disconsolately, his eye fell upon the disordered table. " Pah!" he exclaimed in a tone of dreary disgust, " Caius is right after all; there are no gods and no pleasures."

" Wilt thou not take a fresh flask of wine, my lord?" said Codrus, humbly.

" Pah!" repeated Agrippa, with an impatient gesture, " I am sick of wine." He rose slowly and unsteadily to his feet. " I will sleep," he growled, "and to-morrow—to-morrow I will see the emperor. Galilee—Jerusalem—anything is better than this accursed island."

Codrus followed him to his chamber, and deftly performed all the necessary offices. Agrippa, scarcely noticing that his usual attendant was missing, sank onto his couch, and almost immediately fell into a sodden slumber.

The slave Codrus stood at his bedside and stared at

the handsome flushed face on its silken pillow. "To-morrow thou wilt see the emperor," he said, scornfully; "to-morrow thou wilt again drink, and again be drunken, and I shall be thy slave." He stooped, and lifting the nerveless hand of the sleeper, drew from it softly the signet ring of the Herods. "To-morrow!" he repeated, with a low laugh, "to-morrow, thou shalt again remember that there are no gods and no pleasures "

CHAPTER V.

IN THE DESERT OF SINAI.

"GOD, if I must die, let me die in the land of my fathers! Slay me not in this wilderness, I beseech thee."

The voice that had spoken these words faltered, died away into silence, then broke forth anew in a stifled wail, "I have sinned—I have sinned, but have mercy upon me according to thy loving kindness and the multitude of thy tender mercies!"

Again there was silence, the silence which beats in upon the brain with the awfulness of eternity.

The man who had ventured to break the terrible stillness with his petty clamor sat up and looked about him with wild eyes. On either side towered vast precipitous heights of naked rock, blood-red where the sun smote them, purplish black where the shadows fell. In the narrow valley where he crouched, sand also the color of blood lay in wrinkled waves about the huge fantastic boulders, splintered off from the crags above by some Titanic hammer. Overhead the fierce blue of the sky, unsoftened by fleece of cloud or fleck of wing, closed in the narrow space between the jagged cliffs. Stay, there is a black speck high above yonder crag! The wretch on the sand stared at it with unwinking eyes. The black speck resolved itself into a body with wings.

"A bird," muttered the man.

Another speck appeared from behind the highest of the blood-red crags, then another, and another.

" More birds," repeated the man, still staring stupidly. " One, two, three, four, five, six. They are—"

He burst into a ghastly shriek, and tottering to his feet ran blindly down the narrow valley.

The six vultures, circling on motionless wing, looked down unmoved. What matter if the thing below them crawled yet a little further. The word had gone forth, they must feast to-night. They followed him patiently ; seeing him stumble and fall, they settled heavily down at a decent distance and watched him. They saw him tear at the sand with his claw-like hands. They saw him struggle again and yet again to rise—and fail. They saw him draw the corner of his ragged robe across his face, and their red eyes glistened with a solemn joy. They drew nearer.

> " Lord, Thou hast been our refuge from age to age,
> Before the mountains were brought forth,
> Or even the earth and the world were born,
> From everlasting to everlasting, Thou art God."

The vultures paused, then with hoarse croakings of disappointment arose and flapped heavily away. A man had issued from one of the cave-like apertures of the rock, and was walking slowly along the valley.

His head was bent; he looked neither to the right hand nor to the left.

> " Thou turnest man to dust,
>   And sayest, Return, ye children of men,
>   For in Thy sight a thousand years
>   Are like yesterday as it passeth,
>   Or like a watch in the night.
>   Thou destroyest them ; they fall asleep—"

The sound of the chanting ceased suddenly ; the man stopped in his slow, meditative walk and stared at the shapeless heap which lay across his path. He knelt beside it and drew away the ragged cloth.

" In the morning he groweth like grass ;
In the morning it is green and groweth ;
At evening it is cut down and withered—cut down and withered."

The new-comer shook his head sadly as he looked with keen eyes at the emaciated face and swollen purple tongue of the lifeless figure before him ; then, fancying that he detected a slight quiver of the muscles, he took the water-flask from his girdle and poured a few drops into the half-opened mouth. An hour or more the stranger persisted in his apparently hopeless ministrations ; at the end of that time he was rewarded by a low moan, the sunken eyes opened, and an indistinguishable murmur issued from the livid lips.

" Drink—drink, friend ; the breath had well nigh gone out of thee, but thou art saved. Be comforted and take of the water, for it is in truth the water of life."

" The vultures !" gasped the other, faintly.

" Nay, there are no vultures. Be comforted. God hath had pity on thee and hath saved thee out of all thy distresses. Canst thou stand ?"

By way of answer, the man struggled to his feet, leaning hard upon the shoulder of his rescuer. The sun was sunken behind the blood-red cliffs, and solemn shadows filled the little valley. The savage blue of the sky had softened to an infinitely tender opalescent hue ; no longer did it appear to close in above the rocky heights like the lid to a tomb, but rather to recede into remote and mysterious distances ; no trace of cloud or fleck of wing sullied its purity.

" Be comforted and walk yet a little way ; there is shelter and food near at hand."

And so, by slow degrees, the two came to the cleft in the rock, which in truth was not far distant. And there the starving man ate and drank like a child from the hand of him that had saved him, and when he had eaten he immediately sank into a deep sleep.

Strange dreams visited the desert cave that night ; they clustered thickly about the heap of dried shrubs whereon lay the man whose feet had passed quite through the valley of the shadow of death, only to turn back again. At the first, there came to him a vision of many men and beasts traveling along a stony wilderness, the burning desert flint under foot, the burning Syrian sky overhead. On and on they toiled, and as they went the pitiless sun climbed its appointed way till it stood in mid-heaven and looked down at them with red murderous eye. Then, suddenly—for so it seemed to the dreamer—the sun fell, enveloping them with sheets of awful splendor.

The scene changes. He is in a great city now, walking down a long street lined with stately colonnades; past him hurries a great multitude of every nation under heaven—Arab merchants, laden with their precious wares; Egyptians, with their dark faces and gay robes; Roman soldiers, fair-haired Greeks, Syrians, Jews, Phœnicians, Edomites—mingling and intermingling in endless confusion, amid a deep, monotonous humming as of a gigantic swarm of bees. He himself—so he fancies—is leading a blind man, and with infinite difficulty keeping him from falling beneath the feet of the reckless crowd. Suddenly the gay street vanishes, and in its place stretch long vistas of yellow desert. He is riding again beneath the fierce eye of the sun, riding swiftly to escape something that pursues him from behind; through long ages, it seems, he flees onward, ever faster and faster. His mysterious pursuer gains upon him; it is clutching at him from behind; his beast is falling. Ah, he is alone now, staring up vacantly into the brazen sky, shut in on either side by walls of naked rock. What is yonder black speck against the unanswering heaven? God! the end has come at last; but not this—not this!

"Turn, Jehovah !—How long ?—
And pity thy servants.
Fill us each morning with thy love
That we may rejoice and be glad all our days.
Give us joy for the days that thou hast afflicted us,
The years we have known adversity."

The dreamer turned on his rough couch and opened his eyes. The cool light of the early dawn streamed into the narrow opening of the cave, and rested like a benediction from heaven upon his burning forehead.

"Thank God !" he cried aloud, "Thank God !" His eyes fell upon a gourd of water placed within his reach ; he grasped it with trembling fingers and drank long and deep. "Thank God !"

"I also thank God in thy behalf, and for myself that I was able to save thee," said a grave voice at his side. "But come, break thy fast that thou mayest recover thy strength more perfectly ; thou art as yet weak and fevered."

"Who art thou that hast saved me ?" cried the other, trembling. "Surely, thou art Saul of Tarsus !"

"Even so, and thou art—"

"Silas, the son of Ezra, of all men most miserable."

"Nay, call not thyself miserable, who livest to thank God for thy life."

"But I have sinned."

"Have not I sinned, who of late made havoc of them which believed on the Anointed of Jehovah, pur-

suing them even unto strange cities in my fury? Yet
hath God had mercy upon me in that he hath revealed
to me the truth."

"Thou wast honest in thy wrath against the disciples," groaned Ben Ezra, "but I—what canst thou
say to me? I knew Jesus of Nazareth while he yet
lived, I saw his miracles, I heard his words. Nay, I
was convinced that he was the Christ of God, and for
a time I was numbered with the disciples, but when
he was seized by the chief priests I was afraid lest I
also should suffer. I fled from Jerusalem till his death
was accomplished, and afterward I denied him, not
twice nor thrice, as did Peter, but daily—hourly. How
can I be forgiven when not content with denying the
persecuted Christ, I also denied him risen, ascended,
glorified? For all of these things were known unto
me, and not once did I doubt the truth of them, yet
because of my cowardice I even joined myself with
them which hated Jesus, and when persecutions arose
against them that believed, I made common cause
with the chief priests, insomuch that I received position and advancement at their hands. For this cause
also was I chosen one of them who should accompany
thee to Damascus. Again, I beheld the glory of the
Lord when he appeared unto thee by the way, but for
me he had no word. I have sinned beyond forgiveness. Would that I had died yesterday, and that the
vultures had devoured my polluted flesh."

"What wast thou doing in the desert alone?"

"I fled from Damascus beneath the scourge of an

accusing whisper which pursued me from behind," groaned Ben Ezra, hiding his face in his hands.

" What said the voice ?"

" Nay, I know not; but it was death. Why hast thou saved me? I must again go forth."

Saul was silent for a space ; he put forth his hand and touched the other upon his bowed head. " Silas, son of Ezra," he said solemnly, " I cannot speak unto thee with the authority of a holy man, bidding thee put thy sins behind thy back and rejoice in the Lord, for I myself have sinned too grievously. I came forth into this desert place that here I might commune with the Eternal One in solitude, for he hath showed to me this much, that I am set apart for his service. Now, therefore, I will withdraw myself into the mountains to fast and pray this day in thy behalf, and I will entreat the Lord to reveal his pleasure concerning thee. Do thou remain here and cease not to humble thyself before him till I shall come back unto thee." With these words he turned away, and Silas Ben Ezra, remaining behind in the cleft of the rock, heard his retreating footsteps growing fainter and fainter, till at last the silence of the desert settled down once more over the little valley.

All that day did Ben Ezra remain upon his face in the shelter of the cave, but at evening he arose and drank of the water and ate of the bread which Saul had placed ready at his hand, then he sat down in the door of the cave to wait. When at length the first faint stars shone in the depths of heaven he heard afar off on the mountain the sound of solemn chanting, the sound drew nearer, until the measured words were distinctly audible.

> " With waiting I waited on Jehovah,
>   And he inclined to me and heard my cry ;
>   He raised me from a pit of destruction, from the miry clay,
>   And set my feet on a rock, making firm my steps,
>   He put in my mouth a new song, praise to our God."

Like the song of an angel fell the familiar words upon the sore heart of the listener. He arose to his feet and stretched out his arms toward heaven.

> " And I—distressed and needy—
>   The Lord careth for me ;
>   My help and deliverer, Thou,
>   My God, tarry not !"

Ben Ezra cried aloud in his joy. He knew that he was forgiven.

The day following Saul journeyed with his guest till they were come to the borders of the wilderness ; there they parted, for Ben Ezra was minded to return to Jerusalem.

" I must confess my sins before the disciples," he said, " and before the chief priests also, that I may witness how great things the Lord hath done for me."

But Saul returned again to Sinai that he might be alone with God.

CHAPTER VI.

THE RECLUSE OF CAPRAE.

"I MUST see the emperor, and that without delay."

"Thou art a madman—begone!"

"Thou shalt pay dearly for it, if thou admit me not; 'tis a matter of life and death, I tell thee."

"Who art thou?"

"Codrus, the slave of Agrippa; I bear his signet ring in token that I must be admitted to the emperor's presence."

The porter stared suspiciously at the solitary figure, which waited below in the half darkness. He scratched his head reflectively. "Who is with thee?"

"I am alone; canst thou not see, knave?"

"Knave, am I?" growled the other. "I know thee not, dog of a slave; get thee gone, or I shall have thee seized and thrust into the stocks."

"Ah, very well. I was ordered to give thee a golden cup, but now I shall come to-morrow, and thou wilt receive, instead, a scourging. Farewell."

"Stay yet a moment, fellow; how didst thou pass the guard?"

"By this token of the signet, blockhead.—I am going."

"Nay, I will open. One must be cautious, as thou

knowest, in these days, or lose one's breath beneath the cord. 'Tis an ugly death is strangling—ugh !" He was undoing the heavy bolts as he spoke, and presently flung open the door. Codrus stepped in.

"What is thy message ? I will carry it."

"Thinkest thou that my master would have me bruit his words in the ear of every slave in the palace ? Lead on."

"Not so fast, slave of a Jew ; there is yet the inner guard to be passed, and the officers of the bed-chamber. Where is my cup? Um—yes, a very pretty bauble, stolen, I dare swear, from thy master."

Codrus turned pale with anger. "May the gods smite thee for a chattering fool," he said violently. "Show me the way to the emperor."

By way of answer the porter lifted a small silver whistle to his lips. Two armed men instantly appeared.

"Here is a man," said the porter, "who insists upon being admitted to the presence of the emperor."

"Impossible, at this hour of the night," exclaimed the centurion, flashing the light of his torch full into the face of Codrus. "Return to-morrow at the proper time ; then, if thou art rightly credited, thou shalt be admitted."

"I will be admitted now," said Codrus boldly. "To-morrow will be too late. This is the token that my business is urgent." He displayed the signet. The two soldiers exchanged glances ; they withdrew to a little distance and whispered together for a few moments.

"Follow me," commanded the centurion with an authoritative gesture. Codrus obeyed.

Through long corridors paved with costly marbles, past terraced gardens, where the moonbeams played brightly on sparkling fountains or lingered on the white beauty of countless statues, across spaces of velvet lawn glistening with dew, went the three, the centurion leading the way, Codrus following, while the third man brought up the rear. Presently the centurion paused before a large doorway, in front of which stood four armed men. A word to these and the door swung open, revealing a large dimly-lighted apartment.

"Pass in," commanded the centurion, briefly.

Codrus trembled; great beads of moisture started out upon his forehead. He fancied that he could detect a scornful smile upon the face of the soldier. "What is this place?" he said, looking about him fearfully.

"The ante-room of the emperor's bed-chamber, knave," replied the centurion, in a half whisper. "If thou hast lied concerning thy errand, thou art a dying man, for Tiberius will cause thee to be strangled on the spot."

Codrus made no reply; he could not, his tongue clave to the roof of his mouth. He fixed his eyes on the imposing personage who had advanced to challenge their presence.

"Who is this person, and for what reason is he here?"

"A slave belonging to the Jew, Agrippa, and bearing his signet. He demands audience with the emperor," replied the centurion. "I have brought him to thee that thou mayst judge whether or not to admit him. What sayest thou, shall I put him in guard till to-morrow? It is not impossible that this is some plot to assassinate—"

"Hold thy peace!" cried the other, sharply. "Art thou not one of the slaves of Caius?" he added, turning to Codrus.

"I was formerly, worshipful Stephanion," answered the slave, who had regained his courage by this time. "At present I am the property of Agrippa. I hold his signet in token—"

The chamberlain shrugged his shoulders indifferently. "It matters little what thou art and what thy errand. The emperor is awake; thou shalt enter. It will serve to while away the hours of the night." He drew aside the heavy curtains of crimson stuff interwoven with silver, which hung before the arched opening at the end of the room, and signed to Codrus to enter.

Upon a low couch of carved ivory, heaped with cushions, lay the figure of a man, huge, bloated, the livid face hideously disfigured with purple blotches. This much the slave saw at a single glance.

Stephanion advanced noiselessly and knelt at the foot of the couch. "A messenger from the Jewish prince, Agrippa, would deliver to thee important tidings, divine Tiberius. What is thy pleasure concerning him?"

The huge bulk stirred with difficulty, the swollen lips moved. " Fetch him hither."

" He is here, illustrious master of the world."

Codrus fell on his knees ; he felt, rather than saw, that a pair of terrible eyes were fixed upon him. Again his tongue refused its office.

" Speak, slave."

" Thy life is in danger," faltered the trembling wretch.

Tiberius laughed harshly. "And does Agrippa send me this word ? By the gods, 'tis a good word, a word of cheer to send at midnight to a man weighed down by years and infirmities. What does the fellow mean ?"

" Nay, thou dost mistake ; I will tell thee all ; it is not the word of Agrippa, but—"

" What then ? Say what thou hast to say quickly. Thou art the slave of Agrippa ?"

Codrus crawled a little nearer the couch. " Be· pleased to look in mercy upon me, divine majesty, who am a slave owned by Agrippa ; two days ago I was the slave of Caius. I drove his chariot, Agrippa being in his company. They talked of many things. They spoke the name Tiberius, emperor of Rome. The Jew Agrippa declared that—but how can I speak the base words in thy hearing ?"

" Declare them instantly, knave, or thou shalt die !"

" The Jew Agrippa declared that the illustrious master of the universe, the god of the whole—mercy ! have mercy !"

The emperor had thrown the contents of a cup of
wine, which stood at his elbow, full into the face of the
kneeling man. Stephanion smothered a laugh.

"Now, canst thou speak?" growled Tiberius, raising himself unassisted to a sitting posture. "Thou
hast had wine—royal wine. Speak!"

"Agrippa declared that thou wast too old to rule
longer," muttered Codrus sullenly, "and said that he
hoped the time would not be long before a worthier
should occupy thy room."

"And what said Caligula?" *

Codrus hesitated a moment. His former master
was at his mercy, should he ruin him with a word?
Nay, he would even spare him for the present. He
smiled triumphantly. "Caius made him no answer,
master of the world."

"He can afford to keep silent, black-hearted
wretch," muttered Tiberius, as if to himself. "I know
him—I know him. But what if I cause him to be
poisoned or sent into exile, the Romans would exe-
crate my memory. Let them have the son of Germanicus to rule over them. When it shall come to
pass they will cry out in their misery that Tiberius was
a god, that his reign was a reign of happiness. Ay—
he will avenge me."

The emperor's great head had sunken upon his
breast, his eyes grew fixed and glassy, a low gurgling

---

* Caligula signifies "a little shoe," or "bootling." It was a
pet name given to Caius by the soldiers in the camp of his father
where he was born, a name which clung to him ever after.

sound issued from his lips. Stephanion sprang forward in alarm and caught him in his arms. "Hand me yonder silver flask!" he said to Codrus. The slave obeyed. "Now chafe his feet—so, while I bathe his temples with wine, ah—he is reviving."

Scarcely had he uttered the words before he was hurled violently to the floor. Tiberius had caught the last words. "Reviving!" he cried in a terrible voice, his eyes flaming, "Dog of a slave, how often must I tell thee that I am not ill. I am strong enough to strangle thee. Ay, and I will do it yet. I am old— yes, so also are the gods. I am mighty—I am terrible. I am the lord of the whole earth." Then on a sudden he sank back on his cushions, sobbing weakly like a sick child.

"Wilt thou not be pleased to take a swallow of wine, divine master?" ventured Stephanion humbly. "It may serve to refresh thee?"

Tiberius seized the cup and raised it to his lips. "Pah, it is not wine," he muttered, "it is blood—blood. But no matter, I will drink it—blood is life." He handed the empty cup to Stephanion, his manner once more calm and composed. "Send this slave away. —Stay, let him remain in the palace for the present. Call Sejanus hither."

Stephanion touched a silver gong. Instantly a number of liveried servants entered the apartment; to these he repeated the orders of the emperor in a low voice.

Codrus found himself unceremoniously hurried

away. "Stop!" he cried. "I have had no reward. I must ask the emperor for my freedom."

"Be thankful that thou hast faced Tiberius and live," answered one of the men who had seized him, with a low laugh. With this scant comfort he was forced to be content.

Left to himself in the slave quarters of the palace he gave vent to his rage and disappointment. He tore his hair and his tunic; he bit at the wooden bench upon which he had thrown himself. He cursed the fates, he cursed Agrippa, Caius and even Tiberius himself; he cursed them eating, drinking, sleeping, dead and wandering on the hither side of the gloomy Styx. He besought the gods to torture them, as he himself was tortured, with perpetual chains and servitude. In the mad delirium of his anger his voice rose to a loud scream.

"May they lie upon beds of flame!" he howled. "May they quench their thirst with molten brass! May they feed upon scorpions!"

"Ay!" interrupted a deep voice from out the gloom. "Very proper and pretty wishes, friend; but if thou art not presently silent, thou shalt arrive first upon the banks of the Styx, for I myself will immediately choke thee, and that as convincingly as a professional handler of the bow-string."

"Who art thou?" said Codrus, turning cold in his terror.

"I am Narcissus, like thyself, a slave. With delight have I listened to thy ravings; each malediction have

I echoed; but thou hast overstepped the bounds of prudence in raising thy voice. A whispered curse, good friend, will reach the ears of the furies quite as surely as one shrieked forth, and 'tis far less likely to recoil upon the head of him that utters it. Besides all this, I am weary and must sleep, therefore hold thy peace."

"I cannot sleep," answered Codrus, sullenly. "Nay, if I sleep, let it be the sleep that knows no awakening. I will no longer live a slave."

"The slave of to-day may be the freedman of to-morrow and rolling in gold," replied the other oracularly. "Fortuna delighteth to perform such miracles. Best remain alive yet a little while; many things will happen, and strange things, too, before the year is out. Moreover, I carry the keys of the wine vaults; hold thy peace that I may sleep, and to-morrow thou shalt taste the emperor's vintage."

To prince Agrippa the light of morning brought an unwonted sense of satisfaction. He lay for awhile watching the play of the sunbeams amid the silken draperies of his couch, then languidly stretching his strong limbs he admired the manly beauty of their proportions.

"Ha, ha," he chuckled to himself, "what a miserable, bandy-legged specimen of humanity is our friend Caius Caligula; a surly dog, too. But I must flatter him and keep him friendly to me, for, unless I mistake, he will one day be master of the civilized world. He will make me a king—if his humor sud-

denly change not to a fancy for strangling or poisoning
me. By all the gods—if there be any gods—there is
no such thing as true friendship in earth or heaven !
And yet there is Cypros, poor little woman "—a touch
of tenderness crept into his hard black eyes. " What
now if I do as she asks, return to Galilee. By Apollo,
I will do it. I am weary of all this myself, and as for
yonder dying brute, Tiberius, he is as dangerous as a
wounded lion ; I had best put myself out of reach of
his claws."

An hour later, fresh from his bath and arrayed in
robes of royal purple, he sought his wife. He found
her in the garden where she had bidden the slaves
prepare breakfast.

" Greetings, wife of mine," he cried gaily. " Thou
art as lovely as Aurora herself, and more sweet than
the roses beside thee."

Cypros blushed with pleasure. She did indeed present a fair picture in her filmy robes of white, bound
at the waist with a girdle of gold and pearls. Fair
and golden-haired as a daughter of Greece, her dark
fiery eyes yet reminded the beholder of her Idumaean
ancestors. The dark eyes were tender and loving
now, as they wandered from the tiny maiden who was
clinging to her robe, to the face of her husband.

" Thou wilt breakfast with us, my lord ?"

" I will breakfast with thee, princess," replied
Agrippa, throwing himself carelessly upon the marble
bench at her side. " And afterward I will see the
emperor. If, as thou hast said, he will restore to me

the aedileship of Tiberias, I am minded to accept it, though 'tis a beggarly enough place for a grandson of Herod the Great."

"And what is our present position?" said Cypros bitterly, a dark flush staining her pale cheeks. "Dependent on the bounty of a man whom we can neither love nor honor."

"Love and honor are strange words to use on the island of Capraе, princess," said Agrippa, with a mocking laugh. "What, love Tiberius! honor Tiberius!"

"Hush—I beg of thee," whispered Cypros. "I heard a strange sound, a sound as of the clash of weapons."

"Nay, little one, 'tis only the clink of silver dishes; the slaves are bringing in the breakfast, and I am right glad of it, for truth to tell I have an appetite." Agrippa rose as he spoke and with a light laugh turned toward the entrance of the court; through the open door he saw, to his intense astonishment, a quaternion of Roman soldiers.

"Fly!" gasped Cypros. "They will seize thee!"

"Nay, I will not fly; here is some stupid blunder." He raised his voice angrily. "What mean ye, knaves, by intruding upon our privacy? By the gods, but some one shall smart for this!"

"In the name of the emperor," said the centurion, laying his hand on the shoulder of the angry man. "Soldiers, do your duty."

The soldiers advanced stolidly, the foremost man

Paul—3.

"WHAT MEANS THIS OUTRAGE?"

producing an ominous-looking chain. But he paused open-mouthed as Cypros with a wild cry darted forward. "What means this outrage?" she demanded, fixing her blazing eyes upon the centurion. "Surely thou art out of thy senses."

"I am commanded, princess, to deliver the body of Herod Agrippa, prince of Jerusalem, to the governor of the Tullianum. I must do my duty."

"On what charge? Surely he may first plead his cause before the emperor—the meanest citizen hath the right."

"The rights of his position, princess, will surely be extended to him; do not doubt it. In the meantime he will be treated with the well-known clemency and justice of the divine Tiberius."

Agrippa burst into a loud contemptuous laugh. "'Tis enough," he said with a shrug of the shoulders; "content thyself, my princess, with the glad assurance. Farewell, till some happier fortune shall unite us." Turning to the centurion, he added, "Spare me that chain in presence of my children. I will go with thee without resistance."

CHAPTER VII.

THE ROSE OF LEBANON.

"WHAT thinkest thou, my lord, hath become of the strange rabbi from Jerusalem who tarried with us for a space? The moon hath waxed and waned six—nay, seven times—since he departed into the wilderness alone." As she spoke, the wife of Ananias was busily pulling the buds and young leaves from the blossoming rose sprays which swung from the wall above her head. These she gathered into the skirt of her robe, and settling herself upon the marble bench at her husband's side, began to plait them into a wreath.

Ananias looked up thoughtfully from the scroll of the prophecies which he was studying. "Thou art speaking of the man, Saul of Tarsus," he said, after a pause. "I have thought of him often of late. He spoke of returning to Damascus; I have feared lest some evil fate hath overtaken him in the wilderness, yet he is in the Lord's hands, and the Lord hath work for him to do—even as it was revealed to me. He will surely perform it."

"He may have gone to Jerusalem," said the woman, whose name was Myra, eying her garland with a pleased smile. " Look, my lord, is this not beautiful ? I will crown thee with it when it is finished."

Ananias frowned. " Nay, beloved," he said, laying his hand upon hers, " the weaving of garlands is a pastime of the heathen women all about us. Thou art a mother in Israel and shouldst train thy hands to soberer tasks."

Myra burst into a ringing laugh. " Is not this a sober task?" she cried. " See, I have pricked my thumb. As for the heathen women, as thou callest them, they are far more beautiful and pleasant than the Jewish women."

" What knowest thou of the godless abandoned creatures?" demanded Ananias with some sternness. " They are not fit—"

" Nay, do not wear that frowning brow, my lord," interrupted Myra, dropping her unfinished garland. " I but spoke kindly to our neighbor across the roofs. She is fair to look upon, and sweet-voiced as any thrush."

"A fair face and lying lips, with a heart full of all iniquity and uncleanness," broke in Ananias harshly. " Listen ! thou shalt not again speak to the woman, she is an accursed Gentile. Hear and understand, for in mine own house I will be obeyed."

" Thou art unkind ! thou dost not love me !" cried Myra, her voice shaking with sudden passion. " Have I not ever given thee my obedience ? but if thou lovest me not, I will return to the house of my fathers ; I have said it."

Ananias looked up in sorrow and amaze at the beautiful angry face before him. Surely his rose of Lebanon was set about with sharp thorns. After a long silence he spoke, slowly and with frequent pauses. "There is no need, life of mine, that I again say to thee, I love thee. Thou knowest that I love thee— love thee as a pearl of great price, as a star set in the blackness of my sorrow, as a spotless flower that blooms in innocence and grace. Could I bear to lose my pearl? Could I see my star quenched in eternal night? Could I see — God help me — my flower crushed in the mire of the streets? Thou art but a child and knowest not what Damascus is. I tell thee it is more wicked than Sodom, which the Lord destroyed with fire from on high ; it is abominable with the abominations of the pit. What canst thou know of the shameless worship of Baal and Astoreth, of their temples reeking with blood and lust? Couldst thou know, beloved, surely thou wouldst be content with the women of thine own nation—nay, thou wouldst rejoice because God hath chosen to number thee with Israel—even though Israel be oppressed and afflicted."

Myra dropped her eyes to the ground, her lips trembled. "But the woman is a Greek," she murmured, plucking ruthlessly at the half-finished garland. "Surely, the Greeks—"

"The Greeks are not better than the Syrians," said Ananias, his brow darkening. "They are all alike idolaters, hateful unto God and accursed. Speak no further of the matter. Thou wilt obey me." And with this he returned to the study of the prophecies, albeit sadly disquieted in mind.

Turning to the books of the Kings he read concerning the ancient warfare of his people against the Syrians, and again in the prophet Isaiah how that the Lord had spoken against Damascus ; and his heart burned within him. "Surely," he said aloud, "the Lord Jehovah hath given the sign even as it is written, ' Behold a virgin shall bear a son and shall call his name Immanuel !' Surely the end is nigh at hand ; the Gentiles shall stumble and fall ; their cities shall be made desolate, and the temples wherein they defile the land shall become as heaps. Immanuel hath visited his people, let Israel rise up and call him blessed." The scroll fell from the reader's hands, the memory of that awful death on Calvary flashed before him, a picture of unutterable woe and ruin. He groaned aloud. " Slain, slain ! the Prince of peace, the Saviour of Israel, slain by the Israel he came to save !"

Myra had stolen away to her chamber, her heart still sore and defiant. Truth to tell, the mountain maid had received little training to fit her for the grave responsibilities of a Jewish matron. Nurtured amid the wild fastnesses of Lebanon, she had been as free and almost as wild as the birds that flitted among the branches. The sudden transition from the careless out-of-door life of a mountain peasant to the grave decorous household of Ananias, had proved more trying to the seventeen-year-old Myra than she had ever owned even to herself.

She was certainly very, very happy, she assured herself. Was it not a wonderful thing for a man so great, so wise, so beautiful as was her husband, to single out from among all women a humble maid of the mountains like herself? And if that were not almost beyond belief, there was the little Jesse, a small sweet copy of his father, to be loved and played with through the long hours. There was the garden also, and the house to be looked to.

Assuredly, there was nothing more to ask of the good God. Her cup ran quite over. And if, occasionally, she longed to see more of the great city in which she lived—strange fascinating glimpses of which she caught in her jealously-guarded walks to and from worship—she kept it to herself, or confided it to the safe keeping of her two-year-old son.

The grave Jewish matrons whom she met in the synagogue, and even visited at discreet intervals, wearied her with their perpetual talk of religious rites and household economies, though occasionally they indulged in solemn gossip concerning the Gentile women. With bated breath they told how the Syrian wives deceived their husbands, and beat and neglected their children ; of the shameless and open way in which the Greek and Roman ladies went about in public without even so much as a veil over their painted and perfumed faces. With darker whispers of the mysterious and dreadful worship going on night and day in the gorgeous temples and groves of the heathen gods.

To all these things Myra listened with large grave

eyes. It was all very strange, she thought; but not
more strange than the story of Jesus of Nazareth,
which she had first heard from her husband's lips.
She had accepted it without question or comment,
because he had told her that it was true, obediently
adding to her morning and evening prayer a petition
to the ascended One. Indeed, there were many
strange things which were also true things. Her
thoughts wandered to the terrible Saul of Tarsus,
struck blind in an instant by a fiery vision, and healed
by the hand of her husband. Because of this she had
looked with awe and curiosity at the man during the
days of his sojourn at their house. He was sad and
silent, she decided, as well as dark and ugly to look
upon, with never a smile for the little one nor a word
of praise for her excellent housewifery. She was
heartily glad when he had departed.

"I hope that he will not come back, pearl of sons,"
she whispered in the rosy ear of the little Jesse. "Thy
father hath no eyes for us when he is here. Heigho,
little one, the heathen are merry folk—merry, merry
folk. They laugh and feast, they wear gay robes and
jewels, and if they weave garlands of roses no one
chides them, for they may fetch them to their temples
for offerings. Our God looketh not upon rose garlands. He is too great and wise—too terrible also.
And our synagogue—it is not beautiful, is it? Tell
not thy father, littlest, but I should like to be a Gentile, just for a little while—a day—a week. Would
not thou, son? Then could we see the strange tem-

ples, all rose color and scarlet and blue, with pillars
of marble set with gold and jewels, as beautiful as
heaven. What harm could it be? Nay, thou art
frowning at thy mother; thou art a man—an Israelite.
Go thou to the good Rebecca; she may sing to thee
a psalm."

The foolish little mother sprang up and surveyed
herself in the quiet pool of the fountain; dimpled
cheeks, flushed with the color of a ripe pomegranate,
long lustrous eyes, veiled with curling dark lashes and
shaded by heavy masses of blue-black hair, a flash of
white teeth through scarlet lips, such was the picture
that smiled back at her from the cool depths.

"Heigho!" she sighed, "I can never be a Gentile
—never, I am far too dark." Then she fell to thinking of the forbidden neighbor, of her pink cheeks and
golden hair, of the melting eyes the color of hyacinths,
which had looked so innocently into hers. "She is
not wicked," she murmured defiantly, "I know that
she is not; and how can I hate anything so beautiful?
She asked me to come to her house to-day, and promised to show me her jewels and dresses, pink and
blue, ah—and silver tissue. If only I might see them!
Why did I speak of her at all; my husband would
not have known. Nay, I will go if only to tell her
that I may not tarry—'tis but courtesy. Afterward I
will obey."

CHAPTER VIII.

A FORBIDDEN VISIT.

WRAPPING herself in her veil, Myra stole out into the narrow street, and in another moment with timorous hand was pulling the bell-rope that hung from the adjoining doorway. A Nubian slave admitted her; he had evidently received his instructions, for at the first faltering word, he smiled broadly and beckoned her to follow. Myra shrank back a little before the man's bold gaze, being half-minded to slip away again to the safe shelter of home. As if reading her thought the slave shut and locked the door, then with many bows and grimaces, which were evidently intended to reassure her, he again motioned her to advance. With a beating heart she followed her guide through a long dimly-lighted passage way, emerging at length into a large apartment, which opened directly upon a terrace, gay with masses of brilliant flowers. Curtains of green and white looped between the twisted columns of colored marble cast a cool light within upon the broad divans heaped with gay embroidered cushions, upon the gorgeously-colored walls, upon the carved and gilded tables, laden with cups and vases of jade and ivory, which stood about in odd nooks and corners.

The little Jewess in her dark robes seemed as much out of place in the midst of all this richness of color and ornament as a sad-colored moth within the petals of a crimson rose. She stood looking about her in a maze of bewilderment scarcely daring to move.

"Ah, my little neighbor, thou art come at last! Thou art welcome even as the breeze from yonder mountain."

Myra turned quickly with an involuntary cry.

" Nay, did I startle thee, little one?" and her hostess broke into a light ripple of amusement. " Come, lay aside thy veil, and sit by me on the divan."

" But I may not tarry," faltered Myra, drawing away a little from the touch of the white fingers. " My husband—"

" Thy husband hath forbidden thee? Yes, it is so. I am a Gentile, and worse therefore than an evil spirit. But tell me, do I look like a devil, little neighbor?"

Myra looked seriously into the fair smiling face, at the soft blue eyes, at the melting rose of the smooth cheeks, at the rippling waves of hair gathered under a coif of gold thread set with pearls; then her eyes wandered to the strange and graceful dress which fell in long folds of pale rose-hued tissue about the slender figure. She sighed.

" Thou art like—an angel," she said slowly.

"An angel?" said the Greek woman, "And what is an angel, little neighbor?"

Myra's eyes opened widely, "An angel is—Why, angels dwell in the heavens, knowest thou not?"

"A goddess then? Nay, I have often been called so."

" Not a goddess—Oh no," cried Myra in horror. " There is but one God in heaven ; there are no goddesses."

" That is what the Jews believe," said the Greek, lifting her eyebrows. " But now in truth, little neighbor, hast thou ever visited the heavens ?"

Myra shook her head, " Wise men and godly have written it in the Scriptures," she began, then she paused and twisted the corner of her mantle into a little knot. "Also Jesus, the Christ, hath declared it. He came down from heaven and therefore he knows," she finished triumphantly.

" Who is Jesus ?"

" He was the son of David—the Messiah."

" And what may that be ?"

" The King—to deliver Israel."

"Ah, yes," murmured the lady, indolently twisting the jewels on her white fingers. " Where is he now ?"

" They killed him—crucified him, because he was so good, so wonderful, healing the sick, opening the eyes of the blind, and even raising the dead to life."

" But I do not understand, little one ; who killed him ?"

" The Romans—yes, and the chief priests of the Jews, who hated him."

" Hated their king—and killed him ! Nay, that was folly ; now he cannot deliver them."

"My husband says that he will save us from our sins."

"But he is dead, saidst thou?"

"He became alive again and went up into the heavens."

"And dost thou believe this tale, little neighbor?" said the Greek lady, admiring her perfectly moulded foot in its jeweled sandal. "Why is it better than the stories of Jove and of Venus, of Minerva—the good and wise goddess, of Apollo, of Mercury, and—"

"They are heathen gods," cried Myra. "It is a sin even to speak of them!"

The Greek shrugged her fair shoulders. "Dost thou pray to this crucified man, who became alive again and went up into heaven?" she asked, a mocking smile curling the corners of her lips.

"Assuredly, thrice every day," responded Myra, with fervor.

"Then thou hast two gods in the heavens; and but now thou didst declare—"

"Nay, there is but one God," declared Myra, positively. "I—I cannot tell thee how it is," she added confusedly. "I am not wise and holy, like my husband." At the thought of her husband she sprang up from the divan. "I must not stay longer, my husband will—"

"He will not beat thee, child—though stay, I am not so sure of that. Will he beat thee, thinkest thou?"

"Beat me! Ah, no," said Myra, with a little smile and sigh; "he loves me far too well for that, but he

will be displeased and sorrowful because I have done
that he forbade."

"He will not know, child, if thou hast thy wits
about thee. Now for myself I do not carry my heart
in my hand, and bring it to my lord and say, 'Look
thou, my master, here is my heart, doth it please thee?'
Then, if he be displeased with aught that he sees there,
sit me down to weep and bemoan myself. What know
I of his life? I am but a fair plaything—a beautiful
image on which to hang soft tissues and sparkling
jewels; there are a thousand more fair to be had for
the asking."

"Then thou dost not love him?" cried Myra, a
world of pity in her dark eyes.

"Love?" echoed the lady with a light laugh of
scorn. "What is love?—But come, we grow very
dull, and Diana knoweth when I shall again behold a
human being other than a slave.—I am alone here,"
she added in response to the inquiring look in the eyes
of her guest. "My husband is in Greece, and when
he is absent I am kept like a prisoner by yonder black
wretch who admitted thee. Thou shalt taste my conserve of rose leaves, if it please thee; afterward I will
show thee my jewels." She clapped her hands,
instantly the heavy curtains parted to admit several
female slaves laden with silver dishes containing various cakes and sweetmeats, together with tall crystal
flasks of yellow Chian wine.

Myra flushed scarlet, a confused remembrance of
Pharisaical laws and rabbinical precepts suddenly over-

whelmed her. "Thou shalt not eat—unclean—polluted—accursed!" sounded the voice of her accusing conscience. She drew back and motioned away the tempting dish which her hostess was pressing upon her. "I—cannot," she said faintly, "I have already sinned, but—"

"Wilt thou not eat with me?" said the Greek, flushing in her turn. "Nay, we live under the same sky, breathe the same air, drink and eat the fruits of the same earth, but thou art blessed and I am accursed. Know then that my people also despise the Jews, and yet—I could have loved thee."

Myra's warm heart was touched. "I will eat with thee," she said stoutly. "Afterward—well, I care not for the rabbis—except my husband." And she tossed her head defiantly.

Her companion leaned forward and laid her white jeweled fingers caressingly on the little brown hand of the Jewess. This time there was no shrinking from her touch. "Because thou hast done this thing for me," she said softly, "I will go with thee to the temple of thy God, and fetch an offering, and who knows but that I may also believe on him; I would fain believe something—I am weary of unbelief."

Myra's face grew bright. There were many Greek and even Syrian women who attended the worship at the synagogue. They were called proselytes, and although they were regarded with but scant favor by the native Jews, still they were numbered with Israel and were believed to be looked upon with toleration by Jehovah. "Then thou wilt no longer be accursed," she cried joyfully, "and I may see thee without fear."

She thought almost with pleasure of the confession she must make to her husband. "He can scarce be angry with me," she said within herself, "if I have saved a soul from death."

"It will be very pleasant to be no longer accursed," remarked the Greek lady, lowering her eyelids with an inscrutable smile. "But before I shall become one of the chosen, I must even pay one vow at the shrine of Diana. Thou shalt go with me; 'tis but to drop a garland of roses at the feet of the goddess, and to give a silver lamp which I have ordered fashioned into the hand of the priest. See, here it is; a pretty trifle, is it not?"

Myra looked with a certain awe at the mysterious figures which adorned the rim of the bowl. "Is the temple very beautiful?" she asked timidly.

"Very, very beautiful," replied the other, her eyes kindling. "White marble without, as white as snow; within the columns are veined with green and rose; then there is the statue of the goddess, ivory overlaid with gold. But surely thou hast seen it?"

"Never," said Myra sadly. "It is a sin for us to look upon a heathen temple, much less to enter one. One must lift one's eyes to the heavens and repeat the Kadish often in Damascus."

"There is a vulgar saying among my people," said the Greek, a merry light dancing in her blue eyes, "that a thief might as well die for a bullock as for a calf; thou hast already eaten bread with a heathen, now come and behold the glories of a heathen goddess. Thou shalt return anon and purify thyself according to thy law, and all will be well with thee."

"I should like to see it," acknowledged Myra hesitatingly. "And after all, what harm—"

"What harm indeed?" broke in the other triumphantly. "Eglah, my mantle and veil; Rissah, command my litter to be brought."

Within the hour Myra had looked wonderingly upon the glories of the Greek temple. She had shrunken back a little and drawn her mantle more closely about her face when her companion paused before the shrine of the goddess, and she had closed her ears resolutely to the chanting of the white-robed priests, but now they were in the open air once more and she drew a long breath of delight. The slow motion of the litter borne by four slaves, the stolen glimpses of the gay streets through the fluttering silken curtains seemed to intoxicate her. She laughed aloud.

Her companion, who was attentively watching the flushed sparkling face, sighed and then smiled. "Was it so very evil, daughter of Abraham?" she asked.

"It is an evil thing to pray to an image," said Myra unhesitatingly.

"But suppose I did not pray to the image at all, little neighbor, only to the goddess herself, of whom the image is but a token and visible sign."

"But there is no goddess," persisted Myra. "As for the image, the commandment of Moses says, 'Thou shalt not make unto thee any graven image of anything, either in heaven above or in the earth beneath, or in the waters under the earth.'"

"What! no pictures? no statues? Nay, but this Moses is too hard—too severe ; one must have beauty. But holy immortals! what is this ; is it that the furies are let loose?"

A wild clamor of shouts and fierce yells mingled with the shrill screaming of women and the wails of children broke harshly upon their ears. At the same instant the litter came to an abrupt standstill. The lady drew aside the curtains and leaned out. "Proceed!" she cried angrily to the bearers, "what mean you by stopping here?"

"It is impossible to proceed, my lady," said the Nubian slave who walked beside the litter. "We must wait till the god has passed."

"What god?"

"The god Baal; to-day is the Feast of Torches. Draw the curtains closely, and there is no danger."

"Diana and all the immortals defend us!" murmured the Greek under her breath. Then she glanced apprehensively at her companion. The Jewess was peering out from betwixt the silken curtains with a look of childish curiosity.

"Look!" she cried, "See the children wreathed with roses ; are they not beautiful? But why do they look so frightened? And the woman yonder is weeping."

"They will make them pass through the fire to their god," answered the other coldly, "'tis a part of their worship. I saw it once ; I do not wish to see it again. But hush, the god is near at hand."

Myra trembled, the scarlet flush faded from her round cheeks. "I—I am frightened," she faltered. "I want to go home. I must go home," she repeated, her eyes brimming over with large tears.

The white fingers of the Greek closed like a vise upon her arm. "Fool!" she whispered. "Be quiet, or we are lost."

The words were drowned in the horrid tumult of sounds that now broke forth, the clash of cymbals, the harsh braying of trumpets mingled with the beating of a thousand palms, while a thousand wild voices shrieked, "Baal! Baal!—bow the knee to Baal!"

The litter shook violently as the crowd surged back against it, then with a sudden sound of rending silk the daylight flared in, followed by a rough towsled head.

"By the shrine of Ashtoreth!" cried a voice, "here are two fair ones, who have veiled their beauty from the light of day, but they shall come forth and bow the knee to Baal—to whom belongeth all beauty and excellence."

"Dog!" cried the Nubian, felling him to the earth. Then he seized his mistress by the arm. "Come, there is no time to lose. There are five of us—we can save you."

Instinctively Myra had thrown herself into the

crowd from the opposite side, and not a moment too soon, for the litter torn from the shoulders of the bearers was instantly trampled into a shapeless mass beneath the feet of the mad multitude.

"Baal! Baal! Bow the knee to Baal!" shrilled the rabble of yellow-robed priests, and with loud answering cries the great struggling mass of men, women, and children sank to their knees, all save Myra, who stood looking about her with a vacant glassy stare, like one who dreams a frightful dream and strives in vain to awaken.

CHAPTER IX.

IN THE TEMPLE OF BAAL.

"KNEEL, woman, kneel!" whispered a voice in her ear, at the same time a powerful hand upon her shoulder forced her down to the ground.

Myra was not a coward; she neither struggled nor cried out. For perhaps the first time in her short life she really prayed. Her eyes were fixed upon the monstrous figure of the idol beneath its canopy of scarlet and gold, yet she did not see it. "My God!" she murmured, clasping her hands in an agony of supplication, "I have sinned, but forsake me not; help me, who am helpless! Restore me for I am lost."

"Come now, pretty one," continued the harsh voice still in a half whisper, "that is better, thou hast prayed to the god; now shalt thou learn still further how to do his pleasure."

Myra turned her head and looked at the speaker who still grasped her firmly by the shoulder; to her great relief she perceived that her captor was a woman, old, bent, and shriveled.

"I must go home, good mother," she said. "I pray thee to release me; the idol has passed and the crowd is moving on."

"I must go home, good mother!" said the crone

mockingly. " Hi—yes, that is a comely speech as thou art a comely wench. Know that I am a mother of devils, girl, thou shalt be my daughter." Her tone changed to a coaxing whine, " Come, come, pretty one, do not shrink from me, I was once beautiful even as thou art. Dost thou know that I saved thee from death a moment since ? The priests of Melkarth would have slain thee, Jewess, where thou wert standing."

" I—I am beholden to thee," stammered Myra trembling, " if thou wilt come home with me I will give thee—"

" Gold ?" broke in the old woman eagerly. " Wilt thou give me gold ?"

" I will give thee my necklace," said Myra, turning away her face from the hot fetid breath, which was like, she thought, to the breath of a wild beast.

" Thy necklace ? Yes, I see it. Well, that is mine already. I must have gold ; hast thou gold at thy house ?"

Myra burst into tears. " Let me go," she cried desperately, " thou art hurting my arm."

The old woman laughed silently by way of answer ; she tightened the grasp of her muscular bony fingers. " Gold," she mumbled. " But yes—I know how to get it. Come, thou shalt go with me to the temple, there will be merry sights there to-night—merry, merry sights. Thou shalt see them, Jewess ; dost thou hear me ?"

Myra's heart sank ; she remembered her foolish

wish of the morning. "Dear good Jesus," she murmured, "wilt thou not hear me? I have sinned, but do thou forgive me, and restore me to my husband and my babe— Oh, my little babe. Have pity on me, thou who wert crucified. Never again will I disobey ; never again will I weave rose garlands, nor speak to a Gentile. I promise thee."

In her wild terror she scarcely noticed that the old woman was dragging her forward as briskly as the throng permitted. No one appeared to notice them. Myra looked from one to another of the wild brutal faces that surrounded them, and her heart sank lower still. The tumult increased moment by moment, so likewise did the heat and the pressure of the multitude. She reeled, a mist gathered before her eyes, she would have fallen but for the old woman who promply thrust a wine-flask to her lips.

" Drink."

" I cannot," faltered Myra faintly, "it is unclean."

" Unclean !" screamed the hag with a frightful imprecation. " Drink, or I leave thee to be trampled by the crowd !"

At that moment Myra remembered her husband's words : " Could I bear—God help me, to see my flower crushed in the mire of the streets?" His pale serious face seemed to rise before her, the large loving eyes full of tears. With the vision came a sudden mysterious strength. I must save myself for his sake, she resolved. " I do not need the wine," she said aloud firmly. " I am quite strong now."

"Hi—i, my pretty dove, thou art thinking that presently thou wilt plume thy wings in flight," snarled the old woman with a suspicious look; "but thou art mine—a gift of Baal; thou shalt not escape me. Now look you, we have reached the temple enclosure, presently we shall see some merry sights, as I have said; if again I say to thee, drink, then do thou drink from my flask, for this is no place for swoonings."

"I shall not swoon," answered Myra steadily. It is my punishment, she was thinking, I wished to see these things, now I must see them. She looked about her with a shudder. Twilight was already gathering, and the vast columned court in which they were standing twinkled with countless lights. Away at the further end of the enclosure she could dimly see the colossal image of the god, and the lofty altar set with flaring torches. Above in the infinite spaces of the tranquil heavens shone the first faint stars of evening.

"We are too far away," grumbled the old woman. "We cannot smell the sacrifices from here. Come!" And without relaxing her hold on Myra's arm she again began to elbow her way through the multitude.

The altar stood in the midst of a large open space floored with beaten earth, from which, Myra observed, the surrounding throng of worshipers shrank back with manifest tokens of fear. Into this place, issuing it seemed from beneath the shrine itself, there streamed a long line of priests. With low monotonous chanting they paced slowly backward and forward, bowing at intervals before the hideous image which towered above them. Presently their pace quickened almost to a run; the chanting grew louder; they had formed a double circle now about the shrine, the circles revolving in opposite directions, and with inconceivable velocity. After a time these circles resolved themselves into a wild and seemingly meaningless maze, yet in some mysterious manner a great heap of faggots, laid in regular order, was growing upon the altar.

"Ha! there will be fire in abundance to-night," chuckled the crone. She gave vent to an eldritch shriek; it was echoed by a thousand shrill voices throughout the enclosure, a wild inarticulate wailing cry that seemed to pierce to the distant stars, dying away into silence as the mad whirl about the altar suddenly ceased.

After a long pause one of the priests advanced and seizing a torch applied it to the heaped-up faggots; instantly a great billow of flame darted upward, the red light casting a hideously life-like glow upon the dark grinning visage of the idol. " Baal ! Baal !" shrieked the multitude, " god of fire ! god of light !"

Again there was silence, broken this time by a sound of sweet treble voices singing somewhere at a distance ; the sound drew nearer, till presently from the same hidden door from which the priests had issued there came a procession of children, their naked bodies wreathed with flowers, their heads bound with golden fillets. Round and round the altar they marched, the dancing fire-light gleaming on silken curls and satin-smooth dimpled limbs.

" How beautiful !" cried Myra involuntarily, half forgetting where she was.

" Beautiful—yes," snarled the old woman. " But they will tread a brisker measure before many moments."

Myra trembled at the old woman's tone and gesture. " What will they do with them ?" she asked, remembering with sudden horror the words of the Greek lady.

"Art thou also impatient for the sacrifice ?" said the crone, showing her long yellow fangs ; " the god hath waited this hour through the long year ; it ill becometh a mortal to chafe while Baal waits unmoved. See the pretty dears how daintily they trip it, they have been promised sugar cakes and honey wine, together with a gold coin, if they shall please the god this night. Ay ! there is never a lack of the lambs on any year, Baal be praised !"

Round and round, faster and faster flew the children in obedience to the wild gestures of the priests, the leaping flames rising and sinking fitfully, till at last they drowsed with a low purring sound upon a bed of glowing scarlet. The feet of the little dancers were lagging now, and the curly heads drooped piteously in the fierce heat. One by one the brave sweet voices died away into silence, still the priests urged them on with loud imperative cries. From somewhere out of the throng sounded a woman's low wail, but it was instantly drowned in the noisy beating of thousands of palms.

"The god waits!" cried the old woman, dancing up and down, "Shall he wait in vain?"

"The god waits!" echoed the multitude with a vast discordant roar.

Two priests darted forward, armed with brazen shovels.

"The fire! the fire! Praise be to Baal, the fire at last!"

The priests hastily spread the glowing coals in a thick bed directly in the path of the dancing children.

"Ay! sugar cakes and honey wine—and gold, red gold, see it gleaming before thee! Now dance my pretty ones, dance!" shrieked the hag in an ecstacy.

The children drew back with loud frightened cries; but now the watching priests sprang up and the gleam of a hundred knives flashed in the ruddy glow.

"Dance, my lambs, dance to the god!" screamed the old woman madly, "So danced my pretty ones to their rest long years ago. Ay! thou shalt dance!" And relaxing her hold on Myra's arm she darted into the sacred enclosure.

Myra stood as if turned to stone staring at the horrible sight before her. Before the angry priests could seize the intruder, the flames from the waiting fire leapt up and enfolded the gaunt figure with a scarlet shroud.

"The god hath chosen! The god hath chosen!" shrilled a woman's voice. "The children are saved!"

Then Myra turned and fled away through the crowd, the shrieks of the dying woman echoing in her ears. The veil was torn from her face, but she knew it not;

mad with horror, she eluded the hands outstretched to grasp her, neither hearing nor heeding the hellish tumult which pursued hard after her.

"My God!" she cried aloud, "My God—my God!" And faster and ever faster she fled on through the darkness, led by that mysterious something which we mortals call instinct; a something, we say grandly, which serves the lower creation in the place of the God-like reason which is denied them. A something which is perhaps both below and above reason, fit attribute for beast or angel, but which God grants in its fullness only to the most helpless of his creatures. Straight as a homing pigeon to its mate, so fled this wandering one through the black night into the heaven of home.

CHAPTER X.

THE PHYSICIAN AND THE EMPEROR.

THE physician Charicles stood near the large open window of his library, his hands folded behind him. He was apparently intent upon the scene without, and indeed a wiser than he might look again and yet again from that lofty window with both pleasure and profit, for in a manner the kingdoms of the world and the glories of them lay spread out before him. Rome, the undying city, in the full strength of her mighty youth, gleaming with palaces, temples and statues, her yellow Tiber shining like a veritable river of gold in the clear morning sunlight, Rome sat like a throned queen upon her seven hills, inviting the homage of the gazer.

But Charicles was not looking at the haughty mistress of nations ; his eyes were fixed upon a spider's web which hung from a coping not ten feet from his window, the owner and maker of which, equally indifferent to the grandeur of the imperial city, was casting line upon line of his filmy thread about the body of a fly. The luckless insect struggled valiantly, and the physician stretched forth his hand as if half minded to release it, then he gave vent to a short laugh.

" Nay, if I save the fly," he said aloud, " I shall ruin the domicile of the industrious spider, besides depriving him of his morning meal : moreover, the fly will have derived no wisdom from his experience which will serve to keep him from to-morrow's web ; also he must in any event perish soon, therefore let him die now. In like manner do the Fates watch unhappy mortals entangled in the web of life ; in like manner also is the prosperous spider spared and the foolish fly devoured, and so doth death and oblivion sweep away all." With a single motion of his hand he destroyed the web.

" I am called the wise Charicles," he continued, turning away from the window with a sigh, "yet I know little more than yonder insect concerning these wondrous human bodies which I profess to understand. Understand ?—Who then can understand the fountain of the heart, the rivers of the blood, the mysterious alchemy which takes of dead flesh and transmutes it into living flesh ; the eye, that globe of living fire, set in a cavern of bone which defies corruption. Nay, these things are too wonderful for me, and there is no voice that explains in all the empty heavens. Man is a question to which their seems to be no answer, and yet some unseen power compels us to labor as beneath the lash to solve the problem."

Seating himself at his table he began to make diligent study of a portion of human vertebræ, stopping from time to time to add a line to the closely-written parchment which lay before him.

His labors were presently interrupted by his favorite slave, who with many apologies announced a visitor.

" Have I not told thee, knave, that I must not be disturbed by visitors during the morning hours? Nay, I am too merciful, I should command thee to be tortured once for disobedience."

" But a messenger from the emperor, my good lord," began the slave cringing.

" Why didst thou not say so at once, fool. Admit him instantly. Ha, 'tis the praetorian prefect. Greetings, my lord ; I trust there is nothing amiss with the emperor ; does he send for me?"

" The master of the world is apparently in his usual health," responded the new-comer with a cautious air. " Yet there are those of us who feel much anxiety concerning him. He steadily refuses to see a physician ; but if by chance a physician should see him—"

" I think I understand," said Charicles gravely. " But how may that be?"

" He has left the island of Caprae, and is established in the villa of Lucullus at Misenum," continued Macro. " The distinguished Charicles could perchance pay a friendly visit without offence."

"Ah—yes," said the physician, glancing thoughtfully at his parchments, " next month, perhaps, when I shall be more at leisure, I—"

" Now, to-day," interrupted the other quickly. "Thou shalt return with me. There is no time to lose."

Charicles lifted his eyebrows inquiringly.

" Here is thy fee," said the other impatiently, depositing a small leathern bag upon the table. " There are horses below. Come, I pray thee, make all possible haste."

The physician lifted the bag deliberately. " I shall be able," he said with an air of animation, " to continue my experiments on—"

" The furies fly away with thy experiments!" cried the prefect with a stamp of his foot. " Make haste, I say."

" But there can be no possible doubt as to the succession, my good Macro," remarked the physician, beginning to gather his parchments together with an air of manifest reluctance. " Tiberius Gemellus, the grandson of the emperor, will of course—"

" But if the Fates have willed otherwise, there is no ' of course ' about it."

" And the Fates in this instance are represented by the illustrious prefect of praetorians ?"

Macro smiled as if not altogether displeased. He drew himself up proudly. " In any event we must know, and at once, the probable extent of the present reign," he said decidedly. " Art thou ready ?"

The emperor Tiberius was dragging out the last wretched remnant of his days. There could be no possible doubt as to that. For three and twenty years he had sat upon the throne of Rome, " hated of all and hating," the fountain head of that flood of crime, bloodshed and lust which had swept over Rome in devastating tide, reducing it to " a frightful silence and torpor as of death." During this reign of terror, in a scarce-noticed province of his realm, a mightier One than he had begun a never-ending reign, Maker of countless worlds yet the humble Burden-bearer of humanity, his cradle a manger, his roof the stars of heaven, his death-bed a Roman cross, Jesus of Nazareth, the Prince of Peace.

Tiberius had heard of this man in his wicked seclusion at Caprae,—a Jewish soothsayer, he was told, a mad fanatic, a dangerous fellow, well out of the way when out of the world—had heard and forgotten long ago. Of what possible interest was the life and death of a Jewish peasant to this mighty emperor of mightiest Rome, and yet to-day it would be hard to find a slave in all the palace who would exchange places with Tiberius. Tiberius himself knew this; he knew himself unloved, unpitied, tortured with the pains of swift-coming death, loathsome with the corruption of the tomb while yet cursed with breath. He watched his attendants with a terrible intentness, reading his sentence of death in their averted eyes. Clothing was torment, yet he forced himself to endure a kingly toilet every day. Food and wine palled upon him, yet he ate and drank with dogged determination. Sleeping and waking, he was haunted by the faces and forms of his countless victims; mingling with his attendants, their ghastly blood-stained faces hung over his couch at midnight; with withered fingers they beckoned to him from behind the shoulders of his counselors in the morning hours. He longed to shriek aloud of his misery, to wail and lament even as a slave beneath the lash, but who would listen ? Who in all the world of mortals or of spirits was there to whom he could unburden himself?

" The physician Charicles desires an audience with thee, divine master." And Stephanion bowed low before the royal couch.

" The physician Charicles," repeated Tiberius, rousing himself with difficulty from a frightful reverie. " Who is there here who needs or desires the presence of a physician ?"

" Praise be to the gods, all are in health," replied Stephanion. " The wise Charicles comes not to exercise his craft, but only to look upon the face of his royal master, since there is no greater joy or privilege in all the world."

" Fetch me a mirror," commanded Tiberius. " But no—how do we seem to-day, Stephanion ? The truth, knave—if thou hast a grain of truth in thine entrails."

"As ever, divine master, the wisdom of the ancients and the majesty and beauty of the gods irradiate thy glorious countenance."

Tiberius made an impatient gesture. " Chattering parrot !" he muttered. He drew his gold-bordered purple mantle close about his shoulders. " Drop yonder curtain ; the sun glares in impertinently. Now admit the man to my presence." He composed his countenance into an artificial smile.

" Nay, good Charicles, do not kneel, it rejoices me

to receive thee, and to see that the passing years have used thee not unkindly."

" It is needless for me to ask after the health of the illustrious master of the world. It needs but a glance to assure me of it," responded Charicles, kissing the proffered hand of the emperor.

" Ha, sayest thou so ?" said Tiberius, drawing his hand quickly away. " Yet there are those who profess to think me ill. I am no leech, but it seemeth to me that a man can scarce be ill who eats, drinks, and sleeps with the appetite of youth."

"A truer word was never spoken," assented Charicles, cautiously studying the face before him. The swollen purple visage, the livid lips, the heaving breast, all repeating to his intelligent eye the story of the laboring pulse which he had managed to touch as he kissed the royal hand.

Tiberius was not looking at his visitor now, his eyes were fixed upon the space directly above his head ; the expression of his face grew frightful.

" To eat, drink, and sleep well," continued Charicles in a somewhat louder tone, " the body must needs be in perfect accord with the indwelling spirit, all the parts of the machine working harmoniously. Thou hast in thy wisdom seized the whole meat of the matter."

Tiberius dropped his eyes with a hollow laugh. " If thou wast asked to prescribe for a man, good Charicles, who was constantly plagued by visions of the dead," he said, pulling at his pillows uneasily, " what

wouldst thou do for him ?   There is in the palace a—
a slave who constantly beholds the faces of murdered
men, ay, and of murdered women—livid, ghastly, some
with dagger-thrusts in the breast, others with swollen
faces as of those strangled, and most terrible of all, a
woman—" here his voice dropped to a husky whisper,
"a woman whose discolored skin scarce covers the
bones of her frame, and whose skeleton hands are
ever outstretched as if to seize him !"*

"A most unfortunate slave—a most unhappy slave,"
said the physician gravely.   "Nay, I can do nothing
for such an one ; death is the best remedy."

"A wise man, art thou, O physician,   I also have
said it.   But be the hour of dissolution far from us,
who have reached the age of wisdom, and who after
many follies are at last prepared to enjoy the serene
pleasures of a riper age.   Thou shalt sup with me this
night, good Charicles, that thou mayest drink to the
prosperity of the four and twentieth year of my reign."

At midnight of that same day the prefect of the
praetorian guard received the anxiously-awaited report
of the physician.

"The emperor," declared Charicles solemnly, "cannot at the longest survive more than two days ; he is
even now a dying man."

"Sayest thou so?" cried Macro with manifest
delight.   "Art thou sure ? They tell me that he
remained long at table to-night, and ate and drank
more than his wont."

---

* Agrippina the elder, see note, page 45.

The physician shrugged his shoulders. "That is also true," he said. "So might the mariner, who knows the hull of his vessel to be gnawed by the tooth of the hostile rock, hoist sail to the wind, as if by any chance he could cheat the hungry deeps that await him. The emperor is dying. I, Charicles, have said it ; and yet it is not I that have said it, but the Fates, who have spun and measured the thread of his life, and whose shining blades are even now uplifted to sever it."

Macro turned away abruptly. "There is no time to be lost," he said, "I must away." Then as if struck by some new thought he paused a moment at the door, to say with an authoritative gesture, "Thou wilt remain, my Charicles, till all is over."

Left to himself, Charicles allowed a quiet smile to look out of his eyes. "If now I cared to meddle in the affairs of state-craft I might make or mar many a fortune," he said to himself. "There is Tiberius Gemellus, against whom the tide appears to set strongly ; if at this moment I should seek the emperor and say to him, Thou art dying, and there is naught to save thee ; his last moments of time might suffice to seat his grandson securely on the throne. I, Charicles, moreover would not fail of my reward, gold, estates, perchance an high office in some distant province, and —Macro and Caius Caligula for mine enemies. May the immortals avert the hour ! Nay, an I get back to my parchments, let who will rule Rome. Nevertheless I am minded to see the end of the play."

All that night the thud of swift hoofs resounded

from the wooded avenues of the villa; messengers were being despatched to the distant provinces and their armies. All the next day whispering groups of courtiers stood about the corridors. Caius Caligula was not to be seen, he was closeted with Macro in the chamber of council. As for the dying Tiberius, he lay at last unresisting upon his couch, scarce conscious of what was passing around him. Twice during the day Charicles, moved by genuine pity, endeavored to administer a potion which he thought might serve to ease the labored breathing, but perceiving that his presence was a source of positive annoyance to the royal sufferer, he finally withdrew, leaving him to the care of his attendants.

For more than three hours now Stephanion had stood motionless at the bedside of his master, watching the irregular heaving of the broad chest; now he turned to a slave who stood near, "Let in more light," he commanded in a whisper. A flood of yellow sunshine darted into the chamber and rested full on the ghastly face beneath the purple canopy. Stephanion raised his head; his eyes sparkled with joy. "He is dead," he said in a hard measured voice. Without another word he turned and left the apartment.

Advancing on tiptoe to the couch the slave, who was now sole occupant of the chamber, gazed for a moment in silence upon the livid mask on its silken pillow. Raising his clenched hands high above his head he laughed aloud. "Dog!" he cried in a terrible voice, "for the dishonor of my child, for the murder of my son, I am at last avenged." With that he smote the dead face twice—thrice with the palm of his open hand. Then he too fled away, leaving the door of the chamber wide open.

CHAPTER XI.

THE MASTER OF THE WORLD.

" I SAW him move, I tell thee."

" Nay, thou art blind, man ; 'twas but the sunlight flickering athwart his pillow. He has been dead this half hour, and already the son of Germanicus has gone forth to assume the imperial authority.. Dost thou not hear the shouting of the guard ?"

" I hear ; but I would that it were the other."

" What Gemellus ? Not so, say I. I have had enough of the name Tiberius, and the people can stomach it no better than I. This golden cup now shall be thine. I will take the chain."

" I am afraid to do it ; Stephanion will return, and— Ow ! Didst thou hear that ?"

With eyes starting from their heads the guilty slaves hid themselves behind a fold of the bed-curtains.

A low gurgling sound had issued from the lips of the supposed corpse, now the heavy lids lifted. " Stephanion—Narcissus—" called a hoarse weak voice, " hither knaves ! Call Sejanus—What, no answer, where are the dogs ?" The huge bulk stirred, raised itself upon one elbow. " Ha ! they are gone ; they think me dead, but they will find their mistake. I am alive. I am strong again. I will feed their bodies to slow flames. I will torture them—as I myself am tortured."

To the horror of the hidden witnesses, the man who was to have stirred no more actually staggered to his feet and advanced into the middle of the floor; here he stood for a moment as if irresolute, then with a low despairing cry threw up his hands and fell heavily to the floor.

" Caius ! Caius !" shouted the voices outside. " Master of the world ! Emperor of Rome !"

At this one of the men behind the curtains started forward suddenly. " Call a physician," he cried. Then as the other still drew back, he whispered impatiently, " Dost thou not see, dolt, that this is the chance of a lifetime for us ? If we save Tiberius now he will make us free and rich and powerful, as for the distinguished prefect of praetorians and his tool, the bandy-legged Caligula, to say nothing of the overbearing Stephanion and his crew, what think you will befall them ? Make haste, I say !"

The other slave stroked his chin reflectively. " It is a chance, as thou sayest," he said slowly, staring at the prostrate figure of Tiberius which still stirred feebly. " 'T would be for a day, I am thinking; the man here is all but dead, as for Caius—" he paused and looked heavily down upon the floor.

" Thou art a slow-witted fool !" exclaimed his companion violently, " and dost deserve thy chain. Stay thou here, I will call a leech."

" Hold !" growled the other with a fierce look. " I

may be slow-witted, but I am no fool. Leave this matter to me and I will bring out of it both freedom and fortune. Keep him alive for half an hour yet, and we are slaves no longer."

Left to himself his companion bent over the body of the emperor and listened anxiously at his breast; he picked up the golden cup from the floor where he had let it fall in his fright, and pouring into it a draught of wine raised the heavy head and carefully dropped a small portion of the liquid into the half-open mouth.

"My signet," groaned Tiberius, rolling his head from side to side, "My Gemellus."

To Caius, the son of Germanicus, it seemed that the goal of his ambition was finally reached. He was emperor of Rome at last. Smiling courtiers were thronging about him, the joyful shouts of the praetorian guard rent the air, distinguished generals and deputies were arriving to do him honor. Truly he had climbed to a dizzy height, but his nerve was steady and his heart was strong. They feared him already, this glittering throng, he could see that. Well, they should fear him yet more.

"They do not know me," he said within himself. At the thought a sneering smile crept about the corners of his pale lips.

At the right hand of Caius stood the prefect of the praetorians clad in the full panoply of his office. He also was flushed and triumphant. All had gone smoothly and well; there had been no opposition to his plans, scarce a mention of the unfortunate Gemellus, who, through the machinations of the prefect, was absent at this time. And all this without bloodshed or show of violence. Of this the worthy Macro was on the whole glad; too long had Rome been nauseated with blood, from henceforth matters should be conducted on a different plan.

"If I am not emperor," he thought complacently, "I am that which is far greater, a maker and ruler of emperors. As I have moved this puppet, Caius, in the past so will I control and direct him in the future."

He expanded his chest with a deep breath of enjoyment and triumph; his tone and gesture, as he responded to some trifling remark addressed to him by the newly-made emperor, suggested that of an indulgent master to his favorite slave.

Caius perceived this; his face grew dark. At that moment his eye fell upon a man who was endeavoring to make his way through the throng of courtiers and soldiers. "'Tis my old slave Codrus," he said, "the fellow will crave a boon of me, but I have a score to settle with him first," and he drew his brows together with an ominous look.

"No violence to-day, I beg of thee," whispered Macro hastily. "There has been too much of that in days past. Do what thou wilt in secret, but—"

"And is it thou, Macro, who art emperor?" said Caius, with an insulting smile, "or is it I, Caius Cæsar? Nay, I like not thy tone and manner, good prefect."

Macro bit his lip, his face grew red with anger. "I

must venture to remind the emperor," he said coldly, "that had it not been for—"

"Nay, thou must not venture to remind the emperor," interrupted Caius arrogantly. "The emperor, like the gods, can both remember and forget at his pleasure ; for thee there is but forgetting—as far as the past goes ; this thou mayest remember," and he burst into a loud laugh at his own sorry wit.

Macro did not join in the laugh, but none the less his face lit up marvelously.

The slave Codrus had thrown himself down before them, with a loud cry. "Tiberius is alive ! he hath recovered himself by the mercy of the gods, and both speaks and sees."

The effect of these words was amazing ; the crowd of flattering courtiers dissolved away and vanished, even as a bank of mist before the rising sun ; the shouts of the soldiers were instantly silenced by some one in authority. Caius stood as if turned to stone, the arrogant laugh frozen upon his lips. He tottered and would have fallen but for the prompt arm of the man at his side.

"What—what shall I do ?" he gasped, turning his white face upon the prefect. "I—must fly !"

"Hadst thou asked me the question an hour since, son of Germanicus, I might perchance have answered thee," sneered Macro. "Thou, who alone canst remember, wilt perchance remember that for me there is but forgetting. I have, therefore, forgotten my wisdom ; I cannot advise thee."

"Nay, I did but jest, good Macro—I did but jest."

"And thou wilt again jest, if I restore thee to power," said Macro, regarding him gloomily.

"I swear that I will not," gasped Caius, his teeth chattering with abject fear. "Look, they are already coming to drag me before him!"

"Who is with the emperor?" demanded Macro, turning to Codrus.

"The slave Narcissus, no other," replied Codrus, looking straight into the eyes of the prefect. "Tiberius," he continued, in a lower tone, "rose from his couch unassisted, and is fallen upon the floor of his chamber."

"Desirest thou thy freedom, slave?" said the prefect.

"The gods be my witness that I do," responded Codrus fervently.

"Go then, deliver the soul of Tiberius from the flesh which hath too long irked him, and thou shalt have thy freedom, together with a thousand drachmae of gold. Stay—he lies, sayest thou, upon the floor of his chamber; heap upon him the clothing of his couch, and leave him alone; the gods will take care of the rest."

"I will do this thing for my freedom," said the slave, slowly raising his right hand above his head. "But the father of the gods is my witness that thou hast commanded it. I but obey—as the javelin obeys the hand of him that hurls it." With that he was gone, swift as the murderous weapon to which he had likened himself.

And so on that day perished miserably, Tiberius, in the seventy and eighth year of his life, and Caius Cæsar, son of his brother's son, reigned in his stead.

Among those who presently thronged more thickly than ever about the newly-made emperor—Tiberius having been at last officially declared dead, to the great joy of all concerned—there came a woman, pallid and sorrowful, yet bearing herself with a right queenly grace. "A boon, my lord, the emperor, a boon," she cried, throwing herself at his feet. " Herod Agrippa was thy friend, and because he was thy friend he hath languished now for many months in a foul dungeon, laden moreover with a chain of iron which cankers not his flesh more than the thought of it hath tortured me, his wife."

The foul and sluggish current of Caligula's blood was flowing more swiftly on this memorable day than was its wont, he therefore sprang to his feet with a flush on his cheek that in another might have argued the generous indignation of true friendship.

"Agrippa! and in a dungeon!" he exclaimed, "Fetch him forth instantly; and for the iron chain that hath bound him, let a golden chain be made of equal weight. For with blood will Caius Cæsar quench the fires of hatred, and with chains of gold will he bind to him the hearts of his friends."

All that heard applauded him for the god-like wisdom of his words. Macro applauded with the rest; he had begun to understand the nature of his royal master.

And Charicles, the wise physician, having seen the play to its end, went back to Rome content to have been only a looker-on. "Verily," he said aloud, thoughtfully contemplating the grinning skull which served to keep his parchment leaves from fluttering away in the breeze from the open window. "Verily, this world must present a strange spectacle to the immortal gods—if there be any gods, for in it we mortals, emerging from the black night of nothing-ness, crawl for a little in the light, sleeping and waking, burden-bearing, fighting, eating, drinking, loving perhaps and loved, of a surety hating and hated, clutching madly at a robe of sheep's wool dyed with purple—the purple, but the blood of a miserable shell-fish, empty emblem of a power that exists not—and at the last scourged again by some invisible hand into the further blackness, to emerge no more. If we be what men call wise, what is our wisdom save the power to know our unspeakable ignorance?"

CHAPTER XII.

THE CHOSEN AND THE ACCURSED.

JUDAS of Damascus was a just man ; not only was he held so to be by his fellow-countrymen, but he was respected aud even feared by all the Syrians, Greeks, Romans and other Gentiles with whom he had dealings in a commercial way. No one could regret more sincerely than did Judas the hard necessity of coming into contact with "the accursed" in even the most casual manner ; but business was business in Damascus as elsewhere, and if holiness unto the Lord was the best thing in the world, certainly the next unto it in point of desirability was to be possessed of shekels in abundance. A man might be never so holy, and yet be clothed in rags—which was assuredly an evil thing. To be holy, to be blameless after the law, and at the same time to be rich, was to be like Abraham, Isaac and Jacob, like Saul and Solomon and David ; not that Judas openly compared himself with the patriarchs and kings of old, but the thing was obvious even to the dullest comprehension ; if a man was prospered in his business, God was with him. The Scriptures taught it ; and Judas, being rich and prosperous, thoroughly believed it.

Why then was it that the face of this good man

should be downcast and gloomy. He had just
brought to successful issue a transaction which, while
it would assuredly impoverish the short-sighted Gentile
with whom it had been concluded, would just as assuredly bring a goodly sum into the strong box of the
astute Judas. Moreover he had since thoroughly
cleansed both his conscience and his hands by a vast
deal of ceremonial washing; even the robe which he
had worn had been duly purified, according to the law,
from all polluting contact. Clean without and within,
triumphant over lawlessness and idolatry, why did not
peace irradiate the countenance of the just and prosperous Judas? Alas! in this present evil world there
is ever some trial to buffet even the very elect. In
accordance with his comprehensive yet simple code of
ethics Judas was wont to set down all such mental and
bodily disquietude to the active interference of the evil
one.

"All was well with man," he would say piously,
"till the devil tempted the woman in the garden of
Eden. Through the deplorable folly of woman came
all manner of evil into the world; and so, alas, hath it
ever remained, for the devil having once obtained favor
in the eyes of woman, hath not ceased through her to
plague all the sons of Adam unto this present day."

These reflections, which he had heretofore indulged
with the peaceful calm of a philosopher, had been
brought to his mind with unaccustomed poignancy on
this very morning. He had come upon his wife in the
great court of the household just in time to see her

bestow a goodly loaf of barley bread upon a ragged
unkempt woman, whose speech and countenance but
too clearly betrayed the accursed Gentile.

"May the father of all the gods bless thee," cried
the woman, the tears coursing down her thin cheeks.
"My little ones are starving, another evening would
have seen them lying stark and cold ; but now, thanks
be to the merciful Diana—who hath softened thy heart
according to my prayer—they shall live and not die."

"Nay, good friend, say not so," replied the wife of
Judas, her dark eyes glistening with sympathy. "It
was for the love of Jesus of Nazareth, who also gave
himself for the sins of the world, that I have had compassion upon thee. Pray no more to the false gods, I
beseech thee, but unto Jehovah, the eternal One, and
to Jesus Christ his well-beloved son."

Judas stood as if turned to stone. He could scarce
believe the evidence of his unwilling ears.

"I will pray to thy god, lady, if only to please
thee,"cried the beggar woman, sinking to her knees ;
"but I will also kiss the hem of thy garment, since
thou art blessed even as one beloved of the gods."

"Hold, dog !" cried a rancorous voice from behind.
"Lay not thine accursed hand upon a daughter of
Abraham." Then quite forgetting himself in his holy
wrath, Judas advanced with uplifted hand towards the
beggar, who pallid and trembling, still clasping the
precious loaf to her breast, cowered before him, as
abject and wretched an object as could perhaps be found
within the four walls of Damascus.

"Get thee gone, vile heathen," he continued in a tone which caused the half-dozen maids and men who were staring open-mouthed at the spectacle to glance apprehensively at their mistress. "Drop the loaf— no morsel of mine shall nourish the viperous brood of a Gentile."

But at this his wife laid her hand upon his arm. "I gave the bread, my lord," she said in a low voice. "It shall not be taken from her. Go, my poor woman, and peace go with thee."

Judas turned upon the speaker, his breath coming short in his fury. "I have also somewhat to say unto thee, woman," he said; "attend me in the inner house."

The beggar released from the spell of his wrathful eyes made haste to slink away through the open doorway into the street, followed by the contemptuous glances of the servants. "Good Diana!" she gasped, "if yonder man be a worshiper of the god of the Jews, I cannot pray to him as I promised, he is too awful; but do thou have mercy on the lady, for she hath need of succor at this moment."

If there was either terror or remorse in the heart of the lady Rachel as she followed her husband into the inner court of the mansion, it was not evident to the curious eyes of the servants. The mild serenity of her gracious brow remained quite unruffled, and if her eyes still glistened with tears, they were but the tears of angelic pity with which she had regarded the wretched object of her compassion. The wife of

Judas was a tall woman, tall and large, with a certain gracious and majestic amplitude of figure. All of her movements were deliberate; she spoke little, smiled less, and laughed not at all. Yet there breathed forth from her presence such a sweet and tranquilizing serenity, such a tender and soul-satisfying warmth, that I know not unto what to liken her. She was most, perhaps, like the brooding light of a day in August, when all is complete, finished, all the sharp anxiety and stress of spring, all the lusty haste and laughing tumult of early summer; the harvest fields rest in golden peace, the clusters purple slowly in the shade of the drowsy leaves, and over all the silent sunshine lies like a benediction.

Judas was forced by reason of the smallness of his stature to look up when he addressed the stately Rachel, an attitude little suited to towering fury and scathing denunciation; on this occasion therefore, he bade her sit, that he might the better pour out upon her the vials of his righteous indignation. For some moments he kept silence, pacing rapidly up and down, and plucking savagely at his scanty beard.

The lady Rachel regarded him steadily, her large eyes beaming with anxious affection. " Thou art dis-quieted, my lord," she said at length, " because I have bestowed an alms upon the Gentile woman."

" Disquieted!" snarled Judas, stopping short and fixing his ferret-like eyes upon her. " Disquieted!" and his voice rose to a shrill wail. " God of Abra-ham! in what have I offended, that the flesh of my flesh, the bone of my bone hath presumed to rise up against me? Mine house is polluted! Mine ears have listened to wicked words! Fetch ashes that I may strew them upon my beard, and bitter waters that I may drink thereof." Then his tone changed suddenly, "Of whom hast thou learned to prate of Jesus of Nazareth? Who taught thee the foul blasphemy of calling a crucified malefactor the son of Jehovah? and when didst thou see the righteous give alms to an idolater? Answer."

"I will answer thee right gladly, my lord," replied the lady, a shadowy smile touching her lips with sweetness. "I learned the things whereof thou hast spoken, of the rabbi Saul, who also was a guest in our house, when first he came up from Jerusalem. To thee also is it known how that he was rebuked of the Lord in a vision as he approached Damascus for to make havoc of them which believe. Surely thou art not ignorant that for many months now he hath spoken both in the synagogue and elsewhere, convincing many—"

"I have known—yes," broke in Judas rudely, "that the man Saul, who was smitten with an evil spirit, and driven by it into the wilderness for a space, hath returned, and that he hath plagued the synagogues with his foul ravings."

"But hast thou heard—"

"Nay, I have not heard. I will not hear. Nor shalt thou again listen to the devil-possessed. He shall be dealt with after the law. Alas, I have been remiss in my duty, and because of it I am made ashamed in mine own house. Thou art a woman, and therefore Satan hath had easy mastery over thee ; but a sin-offering shall be made for thee, that thou mayst yet be restored."

"But I declare to thee, my lord, that I believe in my heart what the man hath proclaimed. He is not mad ; he hath convinced many—not women only, but Reuben, and Isaac the son of Nun, and—"

"What is it that thou are saying?" exclaimed Judas aghast. "But hold, I must look into this matter. Go thou into thine own apartments, put sackcloth upon thy body, and ashes upon thine head, and humble thyself before Jehovah. Neither eat nor drink, nor have speech with thy maidens, till I shall give thee leave ; for I am a just man, and holiness to the Lord is written upon the lintels of my doors."

The lady Rachel bowed her head. "Behold!" she said, solemnly, "I will fast and pray for the peace of Israel, and for the salvation of this house."

The day following Ananias sat in the garden of his house, reading as was his wont at the noontide hour from the books of the law. His face was troubled, and he sighed now and again as he read.

"I fear me that we do evil in the sight of God in that we remain within the walls of this place," he said at length, lifting his eyes to the face of his wife who sat near him, her hands peacefully employed with the distaff. "It is not enough that we keep ourselves a separate people ; we ought to come out from among them, even as it is commanded. The women of the

accursed come into our synagogues, and their children
mingle with the children of the chosen in the market
places and in the streets."

"But if by reason of so doing, some be turned unto
life, beloved, surely thou wilt rejoice," said Myra
gently.. "It may be that God hath placed Israel even
as leaven among the nations, till all shall be leavened
with the righteousness which it hath pleased him to
reveal alone to us, his chosen." Then her eyes filled
with sudden tears, "It is a year," she said in a half-
whisper. "Again they will force the children to dance
before Baal. Why, oh why, can we not do something
to save them? Surely a little child, whether born of
Jew or Gentile, is but a little lower than the angels."

"Not so is it decreed in the law and in the prophets,"
said Ananias sternly. "Behold it is written that our
God is a jealous God, visiting the iniquities of the
fathers upon the children unto the third and fourth
generation of them that hate him. And this word of the
law was spoken to Israel ; if then God spare not the
children of a sinning Israelite, how think you doth he
look upon the offspring of idolaters, who for countless generations have not ceased from their abominations. And what also did the Lord command Israel
concerning those nations which dwelt in the land of
Canaan ; was it not to drive them out, and to destroy
them off the face of the earth? Both old men and
maidens, children also and women were our fathers
commanded to put to the edge of the sword. Listen,
while I read to thee from the law. 'When the Lord

thy God shall bring thee into the land whither thou goest to possess it, and hath cast out many nations before thee—even seven nations greater and mightier than thou, and when the Lord thy God shall deliver them before thee : thou shalt smite them and utterly destroy them ; thou shalt make no covenant with them ; nor show mercy unto them. Neither shalt thou make marriages with them ; thy daughter thou shalt not give unto his son, nor his daughter shalt thou take unto thy son, for they will turn away thy sons from following me, that they may serve other gods : so will the anger of the Lord be kindled against you, and destroy you suddenly. But thus shall ye deal with them ; ye shall destroy their altars, and break down their images, and cut down their groves, and burn their graven images with fire.' "

" Amen and amen," said a deep voice from the entrance to the garden. " This shall be ; yet must the purifying fire come from on high, even as it came in answer to the cry of Elijah, consuming the burnt sacrifice, and the wood, and the stones, and the dust, licking up the water also that was in the trench."

" Enter thou in brother Saul, and may the blessing of Jehovah with which he hath blessed thee, rest also upon me and upon my household," said Ananias rising. " I would also speak with thee of something that concerns thee and thy welfare ; and of this I am persuaded to speak with all boldness because of my love for thee. For many months now, hast thou dwelt in Damascus, and thou hast without ceasing preached

Jesus of Nazareth in every synagogue, convincing men
that he was in deed and in truth the Christ of God.
But in so doing thou hast raised up for thyself fierce
enemies among the Jews." He paused a moment as
if he scarce knew how to proceed.

Saul who had listened attentively to the words of
his host, looked up with a quiet smile. " Thinkest
thou that I am not aware of it?" he said. " It is meet
that I should suffer the things which also I laid upon
others in times past : if I be persecuted, scourged,
stoned even, as I preach the Christ, I shall count it but
glory, since if I bear these chastenings in my body
with patience I shall not only receive the reward of
them hereafter, but now also in the flesh ; for if in the
flesh we do show forth the death of our Lord we shall
also show forth his life."

" I have read this day, what thou art assuredly not
ignorant of," continued Ananias, looking more and
more troubled, " how that all idolaters are an abomination unto the Lord of Hosts, and yet thou dost declare
that salvation shall come to the Gentiles. How then
can this be ? Was not the Christ foretold as the Savior
of Israel ? And can God who is the same yesterday,
to-day and forever, change ? If yesterday he hated
the uncircumcised, and pronounced against them
anathema, how can he receive them to-day ? How
can his anger against them cease to burn ? Nay,
brother, it is because of these things that murmurings
have risen against thee—and that even among them
that believe on Jesus."

"It is written that the Lord regardeth not man," answered Saul gravely. "All nations are the work of his hands. Moreover it hath been shown me, not by flesh and blood but through the revelation of God, that I am called to preach Christ to the Gentiles. All that hath happened in days past, and all that hath been written, both in the prophecies and in the law, shall be reconciled in Christ, for in him is God made manifest. The fire of God shall descend upon the heathen, and their altars shall be broken, and their groves shall be laid even with the ground, and their graven images also shall be utterly destroyed, for the fire of the spirit shall be poured out upon all flesh, and in it shall all that is unworthy and unclean be purged away."

"Would that these things might be," murmured Ananias, turning over the leaves of parchment. "But what dost thou say of the command, Thou shalt make no covenant with them, nor show mercy unto them?"

"That word was spoken unto the Children of Israel, children indeed, in that they comprehended not the glory of God nor the magnitude of his mercies, for they did continually turn unto strange gods, even making unto themselves a golden calf at the foot of Sinai, the mount that could not be touched because of the presence of the Almighty. But now we are no longer children, for unto us hath been plainly shown the wisdom and glory of God in Jesus Christ his son, of whom also it is written, 'And there shall come forth a rod out of the stem of Jesse, and a branch shall grow out of his roots which shall stand for an ensign of the people; to it shall the Gentiles seek; and his rest shall be glorious.' And to Abraham did God promise, 'in thy seed shall all the kingdoms of the earth be blessed.' Also in the book of Daniel it is written 'I saw in the night visions, and behold one like the son of man came with the clouds of heaven, and he came to the Ancient of days, and they brought him near before him. And there was given him dominion, and glory, and a kingdom, that all people, nations, and languages should serve him. His dominion is an everlasting dominion, which shall not pass away, and his kingdom that which shall not be destroyed.'"

"All nations are kindred," said Myra softly, "for all claim a common father, even the first-created."

"Ay," assented Saul, with a grave yet singularly beautiful smile. "In Adam did all sin, and through sin came death into the world; yet there is one, even Christ, who hath conquered death, and in him shall all that believe be made alive again."

At the mention of that name the face of Ananias grew bright. "I have heard that he himself declared this saying shortly before his death, and that also in the presence of certain Gentiles who had sought him, 'I, if I be lifted up from the earth, will draw all men unto me.'"

While he yet spoke, there came a sound of loud knocking at the outer portal, and one entered in who bore tidings of evil.

"There hath a plot been made to put Saul to death," cried the messenger when he had found his voice. "Moreover there be men posted at the city gates who will watch night and day that he escape not."

"And how is it that thou knowest of these things?" asked Saul, his quiet voice betraying neither fear nor anger.

" I am of the household of Judas," answered the man, " and I stood without the door as my master and certain others of the Jews talked together. When I heard what things they plotted against thee, I hasted to bring thee word lest thou shouldst fall into the pit which these have digged for thee. But alas, I know not how thy safety shall be assured."

" Nevertheless, I shall live and not die," said Saul confidently; " for I have not yet accomplished that whereunto I am set apart."

And when after sunset the thing became known unto others of them that believed, they gathered themselves together in the house of Ananias to consult as to what should be done. Some advised one thing and some another, and they were all afraid, neither could any think of a way out of the danger.

" Could he not escape by way of the walls?" whispered Myra timidly in the ear of her husband; " even if the gates be guarded."

" But how may that be, little one, since the walls are high, and moreover, we have learned that there be men posted without who patrol the city?"

" The night is dark," persisted Myra, " and Ben Eli, thy kinsman, dwells in a house whose windows overhang the wall."

" But how—"

" In this perhaps." And as if half ashamed of her thought, she displayed a large basket made of rope, the like of which was used for carrying heavy burdens. " It is strong," she whispered, " and if there be no other way—"

This suggestion Ananias made known to Saul, where he sat apart, his face quite serene and untroubled, though many of the others were weeping aloud and lamenting.

" Yes," he said with a quiet smile, looking at the basket of ropes, " it is a good thought ; so doth God choose the foolish things of the world to confound the wise, and the weak things of the world to confound the things that are mighty."

Then he called them all together, and prayed with them, and blessed them, and bade them farewell. Afterward with Ananias and one other for company, he made his way across the intervening roofs to the house of Ben Eli. When it was now the dark hour before the dawn, and the sentries dozed at their posts, with all caution and secrecy they lowered Saul in the basket of ropes from a window which overhung the wall. The silence and the darkness received him, and there was neither sound nor motion. After a little they pulled gently upon the rope and felt no weight thereon, then they knew that he was gone.

CHAPTER XIII.

SAUL IN JERUSALEM.

FOR many days the fugitive journeyed on, in weariness and painfulness, in hunger and thirst, scorched by the burning heat of desert noons, wet with the cold dew of lonely midnights, over the same tortuous and difficult road which he had traversed not many months since in all the pride and arrogance of Pharisaical zeal. Past the spot where the dazzling splendor of the heavenly vision had smitten him to the earth, past pools and streams where he had sought in vain to cleanse his blood-stained conscience with ceremonial washings, past the sea of Galilee, where the lowly Christ had walked with his disciples, till at length the mountains round about Jerusalem crowded the near horizon. Past Gethsemane, past Calvary, past that other spot outside the walls, where Stephen had fallen asleep beneath his rough coverlid of murderous stone.

If it be given to the souls of mortals to visit again the scene of this earth-life, how must their eyes, touched with the finger of eternal truth, look upon the well-remembered places. Here I laughed, while angels wept. In this place I wailed aloud and refused to look upon the light, and for what—nay, I have

9

already forgotten. Yonder, like a tortured beast of burden, I stumbled and fell, cursing the God that gave me breath.

O blind, lost, ignorant and demon-haunted children of men! O pitying God, who hath from the beginning looked down upon the unutterable ruin and woe which sin hath wrought in the earth! Angel after angel didst thou send down on radiant wing into the blackness, and the blackness devoured them and gave no sign, but at the last came He that shall be called the Strong Deliverer; He that shall yet draw all men unto himself, being the likeness of the Father, and the express image of his person; with Him came light unto the world, but as yet the darkness comprehendeth it not.

Saul, who had died in Christ and was now made alive again, entered into Jerusalem where in that other life of his he had lived and walked about, long, long ago—it seemed to him. In a maze of strange thoughts he looked upon the familiar streets, upon the schools where he had stood up in all the pride of his learning and eloquence to argue some hotly-disputed point of the Jewish law; upon the synagogues where he had presided at many a bloody scourging; upon the prisons which he fancied still echoed with the groans of the tortured Nazarenes; and yonder was the temple, within its council chamber at this very moment the Sanhedrim may be convened. Should he enter in, and like a visitant from another world proclaim the **amazing truths of heaven?**

"Not yet," he said within himself. "I must seek the disciples."

No one knew better than Saul where the followers of Jesus were to be found. Into this humble street he had entered twice, thrice, bringing sorrow and crying with him ; from the courtyard of yonder dwelling he had dragged the wife and mother, leaving the little ones wailing behind.

"My God! Canst thou forgive me ?"

His tear-dimmed eyes scarcely discerned the two little figures which were playing in the warm dust by the shadow of the wall. At the sound of his voice one of them sprang up. "Jesus save us !" she murmured, pushing the curls out of her startled eyes. "'Tis the man—the awful man ! Come quickly, little brother," and the two hurried away like frightened mice.

A woman, with a water-jar poised upon her head, turned the corner by the fountain singing softly to herself; her eyes lighted upon the stranger. "God of Abraham ! he is not after all dead !" The jar fell with a loud crash upon the stones at her feet, but she heeded it not. Catching up the child which clung to the fold of her robe, she too fled away with uneven steps in the opposite direction.

Still the wayfarer walked slowly forward, wrapped in his half-painful, half-joyful thoughts. "I have sinned, alas !—I am forgiven, thank God ! I have grievously injured—I will make amends. A year did I persecute the Christ and his elect—through all the years of my life will I serve him, and cherish those whom he loved." He paused, a man walking rapidly was coming toward him down the street. "Canst thou tell me——" he began, but the man broke into a run, and passed him with averted eyes. Saul looked after him a moment in troubled silence, then his head dropped upon his breast. He understood.

"I should have brought letters from the brethren in Damascus," he said with a sigh. "I scarce know what to do—Hold, this is the house of John, I will inquire here."

A half-grown lad opened the door in answer to his knock. "Canst thou tell me if either of the sons of Zebedee are within?" The boy stared at his questioner with open mouth. He made no reply. "I would see the man John, if he be within," repeated Saul, passing his hand across his burning eyes. For the first time he became aware that he was wearied almost to the verge of exhaustion, and that he had tasted neither food nor water for many hours. "May I enter?" he asked humbly.

"Who is it?" queried a woman's shrill voice from the courtyard; a decisive footfall followed the voice. "Who art thou, and what dost thou want? Stand out of the way, Marcus, till I shall see," and the speaker laid hold upon the door with a threatening air. "I know who thou art, Jew," she continued raising her voice, "but there is no one in this house who believes on the Nazarene; my husband is a Roman."

"Where then is John, who formerly lived here?"

said Saul with a shadow of his old authoritative manner.

The woman laughed aloud and tossed her head. " Dost thou ask me that question ? By the gods, there is no one who should know better than thou thyself." With that she shut the door in his face.

The wayfarer turned away. "I will go," he said, "to their synagogue." Then straightway he remembered that one of the first acts in his reign of persecution had been to destroy the humble edifice in which the Nazarenes were wont to gather. "A stronghold of iniquity," he had called it, "a breeding-place of foul heresies." A sudden faintness overpowered him, and he sank heavily upon a doorstep near at hand, that he might recover himself. "It is just," he murmured, "just. Nay, I must yet drain to the dregs the poisoned cup which I have forced upon innocent lips." He sat there a long time thinking and praying, till at last somewhat refreshed, he arose and went on. It was growing dark now in the narrow streets, and he was conscious of a feeling of thankfulness because of this. Pausing before a little stall whereon cakes of bread, and white and purple figs were displayed for sale, he laid a coin before the vendor.

"Sit down whilst thou art eating," said the man hospitably enough, pushing two of the leathery cakes and a handful of fruit toward his customer. "Water? Yes, there is water in the jar there ; but I must have another farthing if thou drink. 'Tis no easy task to fetch the jar from the fountain thrice a day.—No

matter if thou hast it not, drink if thou wilt ; thou hast
the look of an honest man.   Thou hast traveled far,
perhaps ?"

"I have traveled far, and I have learned many wonderful things," answered Saul gravely, "but most
wonderful of all things in this thirsty world, it seemeth
to me, is a fountain of living water, that floweth for
every one that would drink—and that without money
and without price."

"There are such fountains in this very city of Jerusalem," cried the merchant boastfully ; "if one can learn
nothing more wonderful by travel, what need, say I, to
blister one's feet."

"But there is also bread which came down from
heaven," continued Saul steadily, "on the which he
that is hungry may feed and faint no more."

"Why then buy of my loaves?" asked the other
with a short laugh and a sidelong glance at his customer.   "I once heard talk of the like—a long time
ago," he added meditatively, "when the man from
Galilee fed five thousand people in the fields upon five
barley loaves and two small fishes.   I saw the thing
done moreover, and tasted the bread myself.   By the
ark of the covenant, that were a marvel worth the
telling !   How the man accomplished the thing I know
not ; 't was a pity they killed him ; he wrought no ill
to any living mortal, and what an one to have in the
city in case of a siege or a plague—for he could also
heal all manner of diseases."

"Thou art a believer?"

The man pushed back his turban and wiped his forehead with the corner of his robe. " A warm evening," he remarked, shifting his position a little. " I cannot well abide the heat because of an ailment in my head. Wilt thou eat another cake? thou art welcome if thou wilt, since to-morrow they will be stale."

" I have satisfied my need, but I thank you, good friend.—Thou wast speaking of the Nazarene ; didst thou believe on him ?"

" The man had some compact or other with the powers of the air," answered the merchant shrugging his shoulders, " else how could he have worked his miracles. But I am not one of the Nazarenes—no, no. I had enough of that the year after the man Jesus was slain, when a great persecution broke out against them that professed to believe on him. I had consorted with them myself for a time, since they gave away money and food freely to every one that asked— a good thing for a poor man with a large family. But all that was put a stop to, and scourgings, prisons, and even stonings were on a sudden meted out to them at the hand of one Saul of Tarsus. I had no stomach for such things, and I soon left them."

Saul sighed. " Knowest thou not that thou mightest have laid up for thyself eternal glory, hadst thou remained faithful ?"

" Sayest thou so ? Thou also art one of them perchance. There is one thing that I do know, and that right well ; 'tis this, a live man is as much better than

a dead one, as a full belly is better than an empty. I
should have been dead—or as good as dead, and what
glory or profit can there be in the grave?"

"There is a life beyond the grave for all them that
believe on the ascended One."

"So they say, so they say," cried the merchant,
somewhat impatiently. "But I know not how we
shall be assured of it." Spying two men approaching
he lifted up his voice—

"Fresh sweet figs! Fresh-baked loaves! Come
ye, buy and eat. Buy of an honest man, that ye faint
not by the way. Fresh sweet figs!—honey sweet and
wet with the dews of heaven! Fresh-baked loaves!
Come buy and eat!"

One of the strangers paused at the sound of the
shrill summons, and approaching the stall stooped to
inspect the wares. "Fresh figs, sayest thou? Give
me a farthing's worth, good merchant. For the little
ones," he added with a mellow laugh, turning to his
companion.

"Ay!" replied the other with a shrug, "thou art
ever thinking of the children."

"Did not the Master say, 'Of such is the kingdom
of heaven?' And also, that if we ourselves would
enter in we must become as little children. 'Tis a
good thing to think much of the little ones. But
come, let us make haste or the preaching will have
begun."

The merchant looked after the two as they went
away. "Those be Nazarenes," he said with a wave of

his hand; "harmless enough, mayhap, but touched
with a certain madness one and all; now I could tell
thee—" he paused with his mouth half open, then
laughed under his breath. "By the beard of my
father, the fellow is off after them like an arrow from
the bow; 'tis a good thing to have a cool head and a
shrewd judgment in these times—yes, and a long eye
for the future. As it was with the master, so is it like
to be with the disciples; and God knoweth the man
came to no good end.—Fresh sweet figs! white like
milk, and purple as the dawn! Fresh-baked loaves,
brown and crisp. Come buy! Come buy!"

The Nazarenes had reached the corner of the street
ere Saul overtook them. He touched one of them on
the shoulder. "A word with thee, good sir," he said,
his voice trembling a little in his anxiety.

The man to whom he had spoken turned quickly.
"What will thou, friend?" he said, fixing his grave
eyes upon Saul.

The red glow of the evening sky shone full upon
him as he stood thus, and Saul instinctively drew back
into the shadow of the wall.

"A beggar!" quoth the other with an impatient gesture. "But I have nothing to give, and we may not
tarry."

"Sir, I am not a beggar," said Saul boldly, "save
as I crave from thee love and fellowship in our Lord
Jesus Christ, for truly there is naught else upon earth
that I desire. Look steadfastly upon me," he continued, turning his face upward toward the rosy sky,

"and behold Saul of Tarsus, aforetime the persecutor of them that loved Jesus. Not content with
making havoc of the flock in Jerusalem, I was pursuing them that believed even unto strange cities. But
thanks be to God for the riches of his grace and glory,
I was not suffered to continue in my madness, for even
in the way as I journeyed—being come nigh unto Damascus at the noon-tide hour—suddenly there shone
from heaven a great light, and I fell to the earth and
heard a voice saying unto me, 'Saul, Saul, why persecutest thou me?' and I answered, Who art thou?
And the Lord said, 'I am Jesus whom thou persecutest; it is hard for thee to kick against the pricks.'
Afterward he commanded me to arise and go into the
city, where also I remained without sight, neither eating nor drinking for the space of three days—Nay,
hear me, I pray thee to the end!" For the two men
had drawn back, and were regarding him with cold
suspicious looks.

"Dost thou not believe me?" he cried passionately.
"Did not your Master—nay, my Master also—did he
not declare that he could save unto the uttermost?
And why dost thou doubt the power of his grace for
even such an one as I."

"A strange story," said one of his listeners hesitatingly. "I would fain believe it, but—"

"Over-strange to be true," said the other, turning
away with an air of decision. "Either a devil hath
entered into the man for the purpose of deceiving the
elect, or—" and he lowered his voice to a whisper,

"he doth feign to be one of us that he may the better entrap us."

"I had not thought of that," said his companion, turning his troubled eyes upon Saul, who stood with drooping head as if awaiting sentence.

"Come, let us leave him ; we can speak of the matter to the brethren, but who are we, that we should receive him, and by so doing bring fresh distress upon the innocent ?   Go thy way," he continued, raising his voice, "until we shall have reported this matter which thou hast declared unto us to them which are in authority."

"But why may I not go with thee, that I may speak for myself?" said Saul eagerly.   "What hast thou to fear at my hands ? behold, I have spoken truly unto thee of all that hath befallen me."

"So also did we speak truly unto thee in days past, and for the truth of God thou didst recompense us with scourgings and chains ; forty stripes save one received I at thy command—not once only, but twice, thrice, and my wife—Nay, I cannot speak further with thee, thou art hateful in mine eyes.   Get thee gone."

"For the love of the crucified One—"

"Nay, we will none of thee.   Go thou unto thine own."   And the two strode rapidly away, not without many a fearful backward glance at the lonely figure of Saul, who stood still in the place where they had left him, his face bowed upon his hands.

An hour later they spoke to the brethren of the matter.   "The man Saul," said they, "who formerly scourged, imprisoned, and put to death divers of our number, and with the rest dealt even as the strong wind dealeth with the chaff of the threshing-floor, hath returned, and we have had speech with him. A strange tale told he us of a heavenly vision, whereby he was rebuked and turned from the error of his ways. He would have come with us to this place, but we suffered him not, fearing lest it should be a device of our enemies to spy upon us in our worship."

And of them that listened was there found not one to speak any good word for Saul; for they were all afraid of him. But as they talked together, Joseph, called also Barnabas, which is being interpreted, the Son of Consolation, came among them, and to him they repeated their story.

And when he heard it he praised God with a loud voice. "Behold," he said to them, "I have known this man from his youth; he hath ever feared God, truth and verity also hath his tongue spoken. When he persecuted them that believed, it was because the light had not been revealed unto him; terrible was he in his blindness even as the strong man Samson, who also destroyed and spared not, but now shall he greatly glorify the name of the ascended One." Straightway he went forth to seek Saul, and when after nearly an hour he found him at the place where the cross of Christ had stood—which place is called Golgotha, he brought him to Peter and James and declared unto them how that he had seen the Lord in the way, and that he had spoken to him; and how he had preached boldly in Damascus in the name of Jesus. Then they received him with gladness.

And he was with the brethren certain days in Jerusalem, speaking boldly in the name of the Lord Jesus in the synagogues of the Grecians, where also he himself in former days had striven to overthrow the young man Stephen. Moreover, he was not afraid, but the rather rejoiced when he heard that he had made enemies amongst them, and that these were minded to accomplish his death. "It is just that I die in this place and for this cause," he said.

But Peter reasoned with him, "It is not expedient that thou die for the faith at this time, for behold the fields are white to the harvest, but laborers be few. Go, therefore, in peace."

That same day Saul was in the temple praying, for he desired with a great desire to remain in Jerusalem. And as he prayed, all that was earthly faded from before his eyes. He saw again the form which had appeared to him on the Damascus road, again he heard the voice which had once smitten him to the earth in an agony of contrition—

"Make haste, and get thee quickly out of Jerusalem; for they will not receive thy testimony concerning me?"

Then did Saul answer out of the fullness of his heart, "Lord, they know that I imprisoned and beat in every synagogue them that believed on thee; and when the blood of thy martyr Stephen was shed, I also was standing by, and consenting unto his death, and kept the raiment of them that slew him."

"Depart!" commanded the solemn voice, "for I will send thee far hence to the Gentiles."

When he was come to himself he returned to the brethren and told them of the vision. And certain of them accompanied him as far as Caesarea; from thence he went to Tarsus.*

---

* We have no means of knowing what took place during this period of the Apostle's life. It is only known that he remained in Cilicia for a number of years, the length of time being variously estimated according to the date of his conversion. This date is not exactly known, but the year 37 A. D. is generally accepted by authorities.

CHAPTER XIV.

HERODIAS.

THE city of Caesarea-Philippi was in full gala dress, every road and by-way leading to the open gates was thronged with sightseers. Haughty Roman officials caracoling on their mettlesome Arabians, keen-eyed inhabitants of the desert, mounted on swift dromedaries, turbaned Hebrews, ambling decorously on slow-stepping mules as sleek and solemn-looking as themselves, mingled with the still greater throng of pedestrians, of almost every nation under heaven, which was crowding into the little mountain city. Eight thousand feet above their heads towered Hermon, his ancient crest white with the snows of countless winters; his scarred and rugged shoulders veiled in mystic robes of floating mist, pierced with the flashing splendor of many a milk-white torrent. But the age-long miracle of eternal snow, of unfailing flood, of evanescent vapor, attracted no second glance on this morning of all others.

"The day will be fair," quoth the weather-wise, wagging their heads in the face of the mountain. "So much the better for us." Then they fastened their eyes the more eagerly on the gay banners which streamed and fluttered from every tower and battlemented wall of the city. Within the gates, the houses, theaters and temples were decked out with a wondrous profusion of wreaths and garlands, intermingled with gay hangings of scarlet, of blue and of yellow; the streets resounded to the tread of marching columns and the loud cheerful blare of golden-throated trumpets.

All day long in the great square before the splendid temple of Augustus, liveried servants stood in long lines and distributed to the people heaps of loaves, mountains of roasted flesh, cheeses without number, fruits without limit. As for the central fountain, it no longer gushed the pure sparkling water of the mountain, for by some cunning device it was made to pour forth red wine. About it surged a throng of revelers who drank till they could drink no more, lifting their dripping mouths from its purple flood to shout themselver hoarse in honor of the founder of the feast.

"The king! The king! All hail to Agrippa, the king—the king!"

In honor of the king also were magnificent shows in all the theaters, and not so much as a farthing's charge to see the best of them. Nor were the temples forgotten; with a splendid impartiality sacrifices were smoking on Roman and Syrian altars alike, and at Jerusalem, it was rumored, in the great temple of the Hebrews, no fewer than a thousand beasts were to be slain on this day of rejoicing.

In the midst of the banqueting hall of his palace, surrounded by throngs of gaily-attired courtiers, was Agrippa himself. Arrayed in royal purple, his dark

curls bound with a diadem of gold, the newly-made
king lay at his ease on his elevated couch surveying
with a smile of triumph the scenes of revelry about
him. By his side reclined his wife, the fair Cypros,
her delicate face flushed with joy and pride ; a little
below and at the right hand the boy Agrippa, robed
like a Roman prince, was devoting himself to the delicate sweetmeats and fruits with all the zest of unaccustomed appetite. On the left of the royal couch
reclined a magnificently-appareled woman, in whose
dark jewel-like eyes, pale olive complexion and haughty
aquiline features could be traced a sufficiently strong
resemblance to Agrippa to betray their kinship. Her
companion, a man apparently many years older than
herself, played with the grapes upon his plate, and
from time to time addressed a remark to his nephew,
the young Agrippa.

"Come, princeling," he said languidly, "drink with
me now to the health of the Emperor, Caius Cæsar,
who has bestowed upon thee all these good things."

"Gladly will I drink to the emperor," cried the boy
lifting his cup, "though truth to tell, I like him far off
better than near at hand. Yet by his grace I also
shall be king one day."

"Thinkest thou so?" said Herod Antipas with a
half sigh. "My father was a king, yet am I only a
governor."

"The more fool thou," murmured the woman at
his side, with an impatient toss of the head which set
all her jewels winking.

" Yet hast thou not failed of being queen—who art queen of my soul," whispered the man with an admiring glance at her beautiful face.

" Methinks the garland of pearls we sent thee adorneth the fair Herodias even as drops of dew adorn a royal rose," said Agrippa graciously, turning his flushed face upon the pair. " What sayest thou, my Antipas ?"

" Thou hast spoken golden words, as becometh a king and one favored by the king of kings—the great and glorious Cæsar ; a fairer jewel have I rarely seen ; 'tis worthy to adorn a queen of beauty."

Herodias raised her eyes slowly to the face of Agrippa. " I could believe that I dream, brother of mine," she said with a curl of her red lips, " Thou a king—who wert of late but a beggar, flying before thine enemies like a withered leaf before the blasts of winter !　Thou a giver of jewels, who—"

" Hold, daughter of my mother !" said Agrippa, his eyes flashing dangerously. " Beware lest thou speak words of which thou shalt hereafter repent. The past is dead—Ay, dead as that just man whose head was served up to thee in a platter at thine own request, a dainty dish for a dainty princess."

Herodias shrugged her fair shoulders with seeming indifference, but Antipas grew white to the lips as if stung by some unseen lash of remembrance. " The man was just," he cried, " but he had spoken words hard to be forgiven ; besides there was my oath, what could I do ?"

Herodias smiled evilly. "There was also my oath," she said, languidly adjusting the jewels upon her round arms. "But why fatigue ourselves by thinking of the fellow; he was a fool, and he perished in his folly; in like manner shall other fools lose the air from their nostrils and become for lack of it—carrion." She raised her eyes suddenly and fixed them insolently upon Agrippa. "Am I not right, my royal brother?"

"Thou art as ever entirely right, princess," replied Agrippa with a mocking laugh. "I drink to thee, charming being, blent of fire and snow, and endowed with all the wit, purity, and exalted goodness of a daughter of the gods."

"A pretty speech, by the immortals!" exclaimed Antipas complacently. "There is a subtile something in the air of Rome that refines the tongue, lends luster to the eye, and—"

"Adds perchance a coronet where none appeared before," whispered Herodias in his ear. "I pray thee try that air, my lord, that thou also mayst learn the trick by which a beggar may be made a king."

"I like not the air of Rome," observed Cypros, who had hitherto kept silence, albeit a look of anxiety had crept into her soft eyes. "'Tis heavy with dread; in this pure air of the mountains one can draw the breath of joy and freedom. Taste this conserve of pomegranates, my sister; 'twas made, they tell me, by the mountain maids, especially to grace this feast."

"Then beware lest it contain poison," said Herodias harshly. "These mountain folk are little used of late

to the glitter of a crown, and they love it perchance
no better than the Alexandrians when it rests upon the
head of a Jew."

Agrippa flushed scarlet. "Since when hast thou
kept a spy upon our movements?" he demanded.

"A spy, a spy?" repeated Herodias with a taunting
laugh, "there was no need of a spy, brother; all the
world knows how thou wast welcomed at Alexandria,
how they mocked thee, insulted thee, lampooned thee
in every square and theater. How they seized a foul
demoniac from the mud of the streets, clothed him
with a footcloth, crowned him with a papyrus leaf, and
bowed the knee before him crying, 'Hail Agrippa,
Agrippa, King of the Jews!'"

"They shall yet smart for it," hissed Agrippa from
betwixt his teeth. "So also shall the short-sighted
fool Flaccus, who permitted the outrages."

"Is it true that images of the emperor are being
erected in their synagogues?" said Herod Antipas
with a languid show of interest.

"The Alexandrians demanded it," replied Agrippa,
frowning, "only that they might accuse the Jews of
treason should they refuse."

"And what sayest thou, king, should these Jews
refuse or comply with the decree of the emperor concerning the worship of his image?" asked Herodias
suddenly, raising herself upon her elbow and fixing
her brilliant gaze upon the face of the speaker.

Agrippa glanced at the lady and opened his lips to
reply, then he looked again, and a scornful smile crept

into his eyes. "The emperor," he said deliberately, "is too truly god-like to look closely at the worms which crawl so far beneath him. What possible difference can it make to the illustrious Caius whether or not his image be adored by the Jews of Alexandria?"

"Thou hast not answered my question."

"I would the rather ask thee one—which also thou shouldst be able to answer; is it better to enjoy the little one possesses with a pure conscience, or to grasp at the unattainable and fail?"

"'Tis better to grasp at what is beyond," answered Herodias defiantly, "than to loll with empty hands in inglorious content. The beyond is seldom the unattainable." She arose from her place and with a low obeisance swept from the banqueting hall, superbly indifferent to the following eyes of the assembled courtiers.

"And is the son of the great Herod content to sit below the son of Aristobulus at meat?" she asked her husband an hour later, when the two were alone in their apartments.

"Nay, I care not," replied Antipas indifferently. "Agrippa's crown is but an empty bauble bestowed to recompense him for his chain."

"He is a king—a king, I tell thee, a favorite of the emperor of Rome, and he will yet snatch from thee the meagre power that thou hast if thou bestir not thyself sharply. Let us to Rome without delay, and there shalt thou demand thy rights at the hands of Caius."

" My rights ? "

" Thy rights—yes, a crown, and the extension of thy domain. Why shouldst thou not receive Judea ? "

Antipas frowned slightly and shook his head.

" Thou art afraid of the sea perchance," sneered Herodias, " or thou art thinking of the feast which king Agrippa may serve up to thee to-morrow."

" Thou art mad with envy, woman, and knowest not what thou art saying."

" Ay, mad enough to die by my own hand if thou be not king. What, can I endure to see yonder woman, who of late was a pensioner upon our bounty, a crowned queen, whilst I am nothing ? "

" A queen ! what is it to be such a queen as she ? What hath she that thou hast not, jewels, robes, palaces, a tribe of waiting women—which of all these things hast not thou ? "

" I have not a crown. I will have a crown."

" But the emperor gives not crowns for the asking, as thou wouldst give a farthing to a beggar. Come, be reasonable, sweet one, thou art the queen of my soul, crowned and anointed. Let us go hence and forget that Agrippa is other than a homeless disgraced wanderer."

" Think not to turn me from my purpose with hon-eyed words. Thou knowest me well, have I ever yet forgotten when I would fain remember ? "

" By the immortal gods, no ; nor yet remembered when thou wouldst forget. Thou art indeed queen of my destiny ; 'tis vain to contend against thy decrees."

"And if it be so, have I not held to thy lips a rich chalice of delights?" murmured Herodias, laying her delicate hand caressingly upon her husband's arm.

Antipas gazed at the beautiful face so near his own in silence for a moment, then he dropped his eyes to the floor. "For thee I have made a deadly enemy of my brother,"* he said in a smothered voice ; "for thee I thrust forth the daughter of a king who was also my lawful wife ; for thee I slew John Baptist, the man of God ; and shall I refuse thee this bauble ? Nay, I will go to Rome, that I may ask for thee a crown, and if the fates have willed that I return not—thou wilt still be beautiful and young—it will not matter."

---

* Matt. xiv. 3-11.

CHAPTER XV.

CAIUS, THE GOD.

"HE is asleep then, my Codrus?"

"For the moment, yes—thanks be to the gods—if thou canst call a drunken stupor sleep. He sleeps no more save as his eyelids fall for a moment from exhaustion."

"Since his illness he hath strangely altered, both in his temper and in his habits. Can it be that the envious gods have smitten him?"

Codrus shrugged his shoulders. "Were there gods in heaven, my Narcissus, think you that our illustrious master would be suffered to exist? He alone is god; he hath declared it; we must needs believe it. Yesterday he spit upon the image of Jupiter; the day before he smote Diana on the mouth; to-morrow he will himself be Apollo and receive the homage of the people. Of late his divinity hath grown too big for his mortal frame, hence these frenzied rollings of the eyes, these midnight mutterings, this strange thirst for blood which he bids stream from noble veins in his very presence."

"Thou wert at the banquet last night?"

"I stood behind his couch."

"And saw?"

"Strange sights, my Narcissus. It thundered while

the nightingale's tongues were being passed, the emperor leapt from his couch in a frenzy, and lifting his hand to heaven rebuked Jupiter for daring to hurl his thunderbolts whilst he, Caius, was supping."

" Did the storm cease ?"

" Did it cease ? Where wast thou, dullard, that thou dost ask the question ?"

" By my faith, I was asleep. A mortal must sometimes sleep."

" Even as he spoke another bolt fell with crashing and thunderous sound, seemingly in our very midst. The cups trembled on the board ; the women shrieked with fright. 'A libation ! a libation !' they cried, 'pour a libation to Jupiter that he slay us not in his wrath !' 'A libation shall be poured, fair ladies,' said the emperor. He beckoned to the officer who stood on guard, and whispered in his ear, afterward he bade me hand him his sandals, since he would eat no more till the sacrifice should be made ; the others commanded he to remain where they were. ' Especially the ladies,' he said, ' at whose request this libation is to be made.' He walked up and down the portico, laughing to himself and muttering, till presently the officer returned bringing with him three wretches bound hand and foot ; these crawled to the feet of the emperor shrieking for mercy ; he ordered the soldiers to tear from the robes of the women pieces large enough to gag the prisoners."

" And they suffered it ?"

" What else, my Narcissus ; the god had decreed

it ! The prisoners were gagged, as I have said, afterward they were beheaded before the whole company, the emperor standing so near that his feet were bathed in the rushing torrent of their blood."

" Hark ! I hear a sound from within ; he is awake."

" Yes, and the dawn is breaking ; order Cheridus to bring the posset."

The emperor lay upon his back staring up into the folds of the purple canopy above his head, he did not stir as Codrus entered on noiseless foot but he seemed nevertheless to be aware of his presence. " Is Macro without ?" he asked in a querulous voice.

" A vision of the night perchance yet lingers with the majesty of the universe," responded the chief officer of the bed-chamber. " Macro is indeed without, in that he no longer—"

" True, he is dead ; I killed him. I had forgotten, his wife Ennia also, and Marcus Silanus. Ha, ha! A merry conceit was that of last night. My brother, Jupiter, will be pleased with such honors. As for the silly sheep who bleated for a libation, their mouths will be shut another time. Come, I must be stirring ; quick, my robe, my sandals. But there is one thing, slave, that I will not bear, hear it ; I will not again endure the presence of that grinning fool, Tiberius Gemellus ; I always hated him. All night he hath been in my chamber, peeping from behind the curtains, staring and grimacing like the witless clown that he is. Let him be sought and plunged into the deepest dungeon of the Tullianum."

Codrus grew pale and glanced with an involuntary shudder at the voluminous folds of purple drapery which shaded the imperial couch. "The wine, perchance," he said hesitatingly, "which the supreme being of the world drank last night hath caused visions of unhappy import to visit the royal pillow. Surely a humble worshiper of the living deity may wish all enemies of Rome to be even as is the young man Tiberius Gemellus."

"Thou dost mean that he is already dead?" said Caius quickly, fixing his red eyes upon the cringing menial. "By my faith, I had supposed so, until last night. Well, it was a dream then. Let the immortals beware in future how they choose the night visions of the emperor of Rome.—Ah, stay, the merchant who furnished last night's wine, let him be drowned in a cask of his accursed dream-breeding liquor. See to it. And now command Helicon and Apelles to breakfast with us. They shall drive these foul visions of the night afar into oblivion and darkness."

Codrus bit his lip in silent anger. What, Helicon, a low Egyptain slave, and Apelles, a second-rate actor, to breakfast with the emperor where he must serve? For despite his freedom and his rapidly-growing wealth, it suited the emperor to employ him about his presence in the most menial capacities.

"What hast thou to tell me this morning concerning the Alexandrian riots?" demanded Caius, when the three were dallying with the spiced fish dressed with peacock's brains which formed one of the principal dishes at the morning meal. " Look you at my stockings," he added, suddenly thrusting out his mis-shapen legs, "gold thread embroidered with pearls ; a pretty conceit, say you not so ? I am minded to personate Venus to day."

"A glorious thought !" exclaimed Helicon, casting down his eyes.

"Ay, why not," pursued the emperor, "in a robe of silver gauze bound with a girdle of emeralds, shall I not be radiant—divine ? But Cerberus devour the gods and goddesses ! there is something more important on hand, these Alexandrian Jews now, what of them ?"

" They still refuse to pay divine honors to the lord of the whole earth," replied Apelles with an air of mingled grief and indignation. " They have suffered for their obstinacy, it is true, in that they have been driven from their possessions, burnt alive, tortured, compelled to eat swine's flesh, and—"

" I know all this," growled Caius frowning, "and it pleaseth me not : the Jews are peaceable and industrious, valuable as money-getters and traders ; the prosperity of the empire doth depend, perchance, on these same Jews. I have already commanded that Flaccus, who hath inflicted upon them these sufferings contrary to the law, shall be banished. Nay, he shall die, since if he live he may employ his breath in praying for my destruction—I have heard the like." He paused, his head sank forward upon his breast. His guests exchanged stealthy glances of terror and dismay

"I should not have spoken of these matters," ventured Helicon at length, "save for a horrible thing which came to my ears only this morning."

"A horrible thing? then relate it, by all means," said the emperor, bringing his wandering gaze to a standstill upon the speaker.

"The Jews of Jamnia, divine Caius, seeing an altar which the Romans had erected to thy honor and glory, tore it down and trampled the fragments under foot."

"What art thou saying!" shrieked Caius, springing to his feet. "Are the dogs not satisfied with refusing me the honors which are my due, that they also destroy the altars which pious hands have erected?"

"It is too true, alas!" sighed Helicon, rolling up his eyes sanctimoniously, and affecting not to notice that the emperor, finding words too feeble for his purpose, was smashing the delicate cups and crystal dishes which adorned the table.

"Fool!" shouted Caius, his eyes starting from his head, "why dost thou lie there like a sated beast whilst thy god is displeasured?" he followed this question with the contents of his brimming goblet, then seeing the sudden change which swept over the face of his victim as he gasped and spluttered helplessly he burst into a fit of discordant laughter.

"I was about to suggest, glorious majesty," said Helicon wiping his face with what composure he could muster, "that there is a way of punishing these vile Jews and at the same time of securing to thyself the rights of thy godhead, and that is to place within the shrine of their temple at Jerusalem a colossal image of thyself with the attributes of divinity. To Jerusalem all the tribes of the Jewish nation resort for worship, and continual sacrifices burn upon its altars."

" In Jerusalem—in the temple !" exclaimed Caius, with the malignant distortion of his visage which passed for a smile. " By the shades of my fathers ! it is an inspiration from Olympus. What have they in their shrine which must be removed to make room for my image ? It shall be destroyed at once, and the place thereof remain empty until the colossus be wrought."

" I am told that there is nothing in their shrine, divine majesty," replied the slave. " 'Tis an empty dark close-curtained cell in which they believe the invisible presence of their God resides ; to this emptiness they pay their vows, and before it smoke countless offerings."

" Poor fools !" cried Caius, striding up and down the apartment with long uneven steps. " We shall confer an actual benefit by giving them somewhat to worship. Ay, a golden colossus with face and hands of wrought ivory, seated on a lofty throne set with gems of every color, in the right hand shall be the thunderbolts of Jove and beneath the feet the emblems of every other god and king under heaven, to signify that I, Caius Cæsar, am god of gods, and king of kings. A glorious thought of mine ! Send quickly for Cassius Chaereas ; I will order the work begun in this self-same hour !"

"Whilst thou art waiting the presence of the tribune," said the royal chamberlain, advancing, "will it please your majesty to receive one Herod Antipas, tetrarch of Galilee, with Herodias his wife? They seek now for the third time an opportunity of paying their court to the majesty of the universe."

"Antipas? Ha, a Jew, I remember him; a son of that old fox Herod, and himself a sly and conscienceless rascal. 'Twas in Rome he carried off this Herodias; she was his brother's wife and a very wonder of beauty. Fetch them in and at once."

"They send you this with their humblest worship," said Codrus, presenting a case, which when opened displayed a heavy chain of gold, clasped with an engraved gem of great value.

"A pretty trifle," remarked the emperor, glancing at it carelessly. "Give it to Helicon here; 'twill serve to ease his vanity for the wine I wasted on him at breakfast."

"Here are also letters from the king Agrippa to the emperor of Rome, which came this morning by the hand of Fortunatus, a slave," continued Codrus.

"And what hath Agrippa to say?" exclaimed the emperor, who was apparently in high good humor for the moment. "The fellow hath already run through the gold I gave him I'll warrant me, and asks for more. Well, he shall have it, this kinsman of his who is without shall give it him.—What is this! scorpions and furies! Bring in the Jew, I say, and the woman."

"Will not the divine majesty receive these persons

in the audience-chamber?" suggested Codrus. "All
is prepared, and the court is in attendance."

"Perchance they hunger after their long journey
and would break their fast with the remains of our
morning's meal," sneered Caius, glancing at the disordered table.

"As ever thoughtful of the best good of others,
but the radiance of thy glory will scarce appear in
this guise to the eyes of strangers," ventured Narcissus, who had entered followed by two slaves laden with
gorgeous robes.

"That is true," assented Caius, looking down at his
untidy person. "Tire me quickly. I will receive
them in the audience-chamber."

To Herodias, who yet waited with her husband in
an ante-room of the palace, the moments lingered
leaden-footed; again and again she glanced impatiently into the great mirrors which hung upon the
walls, bidding her tire-woman make fresh changes in
the disposition of her veil, in the arrangement of her
jewels, in the folds of her richly-embroidered robe.

Antipas pale and silent, strode up and down the
apartment paying no heed to the curious glances of
the liveried pages, who whispered and tittered about
the great doors which shut off the audience-chamber
from view. He paused at length before the princess
and looked at her in silence, his burning eyes roving
with feverish impatience over every detail of her magnificent dress, and coming at last to a standstill on the
beautiful flushed face.

"Herodias," he murmured with a beseeching look, "it is not yet too late to draw back from this dangerous venture. Since we have come, let us pay our court to the emperor as befits our rank, but something warns me that this is not the time to beg for favors."

"Not the time!" exclaimed Herodias, with an impatient gesture, "and when will a better time arrive? Hast thou then consulted the auspices, that thou dost prate of times and seasons? At the worst, we shall but be refused—and I swear I fear it not. I only fear lest in our modesty we ask too little. But see, the doors are opened! They beckon us to advance!"

Caius Cæsar, seated on his lofty chair of wrought ivory, stared at the man and woman who now slowly and reverently approached, with a look to which those of his courtiers who stood about him were no strangers. His fierce yet dull eyes seemed to have withdrawn themselves beast-like beneath the bulging wrinkled forehead; his face, the color and apparent consistency of impure wax, was distorted by a frightful expression which, although it drew back the lips revealing the yellowish pointed teeth within, could by no stretch of the imagination be termed a smile.

The two knelt for an instant, then arose and stood with bowed heads, as if awaiting some token of recognition from the motionless form before them. The emperor continued to stare with unwinking eyes, but it was remarked that after the first glance he had fixed his gaze upon the woman, who with proud consciousness of her glorious beauty still allowed her long

11

lashes to shadow the smooth oval of her olive cheeks. "A handsome woman, I swear it by the immortals," he croaked at length. "What sayest thou, Asiaticus? Is she not handsomer than the empress of Rome?"

Herodias lifted her great black eyes, a spark of womanly indignation burning in their depths, and fixed them boldly upon the man in the ivory chair. "We have come," she said in a ringing voice, "to crave from thee a boon."

"A boon? Ay, of course, they all want something. Thou didst not answer my question, Valerius Asiaticus. Is not this woman handsomer than the empress of Rome?"

The man to whom he addressed the question grew pale. "'Tis impossible," he faltered at length, "that any woman can be more divinely beautiful than the consort of the emperor."

"Thou hast lied, Asiaticus," replied the emperor coolly, "yesterday also, thou didst lie to me twice, thrice concerning—well, no matter what. To-night after we have supped, we shall try thee by the rack to see if by any means we shall be able to draw out from thee the truth about certain matters concerning which we are in doubt. Do not forget the hour." Then he turned to Herodias, "Such is the manner in which we deal with these stubborn lying Romans, my pretty one; the cord, the rack, the plate, the fire, we try them all in turn—ay, one and all. A boon, saidst thou, now what is it?"

"The son of Herod, my husband, shall place the matter before thee," answered Herodias, indicating with a superb gesture the man at her side.

"Speak, son of Herod, what wilt thou?"

Antipas straightened himself, "As the son of that great Herod," he began resolutely, "who formerly held sway over all the nations of Israel under the empire of Rome, I would crave of thee the right to wear the crown of my father, and to add to my domain the province of Judea."

"A boon indeed—a pretty boon!" exclaimed Caius. "Canst thou show me any reason why I should grant thee this favor, son of Herod?"

"None, save that I am loyal to Rome, and that the crown I crave is mine by right of descent."

"Stay, not so fast, good Herod, thou art loyal to Rome, sayst thou? Then what meaneth this letter which came to my hand this very day? 'Tis writ by Agrippa, whom I made king because I had willed that he who had worn a chain for me should also wear a crown. Listen, while I shall read to thee from this same letter.

"'I am grieved to irk thee with tidings of evil, beloved friend—for so have I received permission to term thee, who art king of kings—but nevertheless it seemeth to be necessary for thy peace and the peace of Rome that thou shouldst be aware that Herod Antipas, tetrarch of Galilee, doth meditate treason against thy glorious majesty. To this end he hath conspired with Artabanus, king of Parthia, to overthrow the govern-

ment of Rome, and hath made ready in his armory
equipment sufficient for seventy thousand men.' What
sayest thou, son of Herod, to this accusation?"

The face of Antipas had gradually assumed the livid
hues of death as he listened to the reading of this
letter.   His head fell forward ; he seemed not to have
heard the emperor's question for he made no effort to
answer it.

"How now, Jew! art stricken dumb that thou canst
not answer a plain question?   Hast thou this armor,
as king Agrippa doth allege, or hast thou not?"

"My royal consort is unable to answer so terrible
and so false an accusation," said Herodias haughtily.
"Made moreover by a kinsman who was formerly but
a beggared outlaw, dependent upon our bounty for the
food which he ate.   We have warmed a viper in our
bosom and it has stung us, as is the fashion of such
deadly reptiles."

"Ay, stung thee to the death, fair one, unless thou
shalt shortly prove thine innocence of this treason.
Once more, Herod Antipas, hast thou the armor?"

"I have the armor," replied Antipas in a dull hollow tone, "but may not the governor of a province
maintain an armed force sufficient to preserve peace
within his domains, without incurring the charge of
treason?"

"Seventy thousand men can scarce be necessary to
preserve peace within the confines of Galilee, in addition to the Roman legions which are within ready call,"
said the emperor with biting emphasis.   "Hear now

the boon which thou shalt receive : the tetrachy of Galilee, with all the revenues and appurtenances thereof, I do hereby take from thee ; and I do bestow it, by virtue of my imperial authority, upon Agrippa. Moreover thou shalt be deprived of whatever private wealth thou hast acquired, and shalt in the future make thy residence in the province of Gaul, to which province thou art henceforth perpetually exiled. As for thee, fair lady, since thou art—as I further learn from this letter—own sister to Herod Agrippa, I do offer thee asylum and support in Rome, suitable to thy rank. Freed from this blundering knave whom thou hast called husband, thou shalt yet reign queen of beauty in a kindlier sphere. I, the emperor of Rome, have sworn it."

Herodias looked for an instant into the leering mask which bent toward her, then she turned away with a haughty gesture of refusal.

" Thou hast indeed, O emperor, extended to me a boon which is in accord with thy imperial magnificence, but the kindness which I have for my husband hinders me from partaking of the favor of thy gift ; for it is but just that I who have been made the partner of his prosperity, shall also cleave to him in the hour of his adversity."

Antipas raised his haggard eyes full of mute questionings, and fixed them upon the woman at his side. Something in the pallid unsmiling face answered him.

" I have received my crown !" he cried aloud.

But the emperor sprang to his feet in sudden fury.

"Go, woman!" he cried with a terrible execration, "and when lashed by the furies thou art perishing in squalor and misery, remember what thou hast lost."

* So the two went away into banishment and oblivion—for what befell them from that hour is known to no man. Yet who shall say that their last days were not their best days, since at the last love went with them.

---

* Josephus, Antiquities, B. XVIII., Chap. vii.

Paul—5

"SO THE TWO WENT AWAY INTO BANISHMENT."

CHAPTER XVI.

THE COLOSSUS OF SIDON.

A STRANGE, inarticulate, inhuman, maddening noise, a sound, now sinking to a low wailing like that of despairing disembodied souls, now swelling shrilly to a full throbbing note of agony, a thunderous myriad-voiced pean of woe, rising and falling, fainting, dying, only to burst out anew into more terrible crescendos.

Publius Petronius, the newly-made governor of Syria, arose from his couch at day-break with a curse, his usually fresh and ruddy countenance haggard and yellow.

"The seven and twentieth night," he muttered betwixt his teeth, "and I have not slept. Beasts!" He kicked the slave who had brought him his toga and sandals with such vigor and precision that the unfortunate menial landed upon the opposite side of the room. The man arose with commendable promptness and returned to the matter which he had in hand, namely that of investing his irascible master with the habiliments of civilization. Petronius meantime was engaged in roaring out divers great oaths, which comprehended creation in general, the gods, whom he held responsible for all his discomforts and miseries past, present, and to come, also and in particular his bed, which he compared to a certain choice locality in Hades.

" Beasts !" he growled savagely, striding to the window of his chamber, " I will show them that I am not to be trifled with. There are at the least ten thousand of the devils—Nay, by Apollo, I believe there are ten times ten thousand of them, and all howling like damned souls. And for what ? because a certain crack-brained imbecile, who wears the purple, will set up his trumpery image in their temple. Let him take the matter in hand himself, I say, since he calls himself the god of the universe. God? Pah ! He is inferior to the slave yonder whom I have kicked." He thrust his fingers into his ears as if to shut out for an instant the frightful clamor which arose from the multitude below.

" The master stone-cutter from Sidon, excellency !" announced the slave with some quite natural hesitation. " He wishes to consult your worshipful highness concerning the transportation of the statue."

" The furies fly away with the master stone-cutter from Sidon ! I have not breakfasted. Go tell him that I will not see him.—Nay, bring him hither and at once."

" Most worshipful, exalted, and revered—"

" Hold thy peace, man, I am no royal weakling, bloated nigh to bursting with impious folly, but a Roman soldier ; speak to me as such. What wilt thou ?"

"I have, excellency, well-nigh finished the work upon the colossal statue of the emperor, which is to be placed in Jerusalem. It will, I hope, be possible to erect it in the Holy of Holies before the next feast-day."

"Sanctissimi dei! what, finished already? Nay, thou art most diligent in the pursuit of thy calling, good stone-cutter."

"I am, in truth, diligent," replied the man complacently, "and at all times ; yet on this present occasion have I wrought day and night, as it were, employing the most skilled artists, and sparing neither labor nor expense—even as thou didst bid me."

"It must be very perfect, man," growled Petronius, staring hard at the stone-cutter and pulling at his short beard. "This is no fool's job which thou hast undertaken ; there must be no slighting of even the inferior parts ; the smallest imperfection of the littlest fold of the robe, or the deviation of a hair's breadth in the disposition of a single feature ; the—"

"Am I not the greatest artist in Sidon—nay, in all Phoenicia ?" interrupted the master stone-cutter with heat. "Do I need therefore to learn my business anew ?"

"Hold, my good stone-cutter, there are yet many things connected with thy business which thou wilt do well to consider," answered Petronius, leaning forward and staring yet more fixedly into the angry face before him. "Listen now for an instant, I pray thee. Canst thou hear the sounds from without ? Ay, thou canst hear; thou hast ears. It is for these good people without that thou art fashioning this statue of Caius Cæsar, the new Jupiter. It is to be their god. Now if it be set up in their shrine at Jerusalem, and they discover in it the smallest flaw, what, think you, will they do unto the man that hath wrought the same to the dishonor of their temple?"

The stone-cutter grew pale.

"Ay, thou mayst well tremble," pursued Petronius, lowering his voice almost to a whisper, "for they would not scruple to rend thee limb from limb; as for the statue—" He paused and shrugged his shoulders.

"But—thou hast legions at thy command," faltered the man, wiping the great beads of moisture from his face. "Surely thou couldst protect me."

Petronius smiled. "I could crucify a score or more of thy murderers after thou wert dead," he said coldly; "but the legions of Rome can scarce stand guard over the body of a paltry stone-cutter." Then his manner suddenly changed; he clapped his great hand down upon his knee as if a solution of the whole matter had occurred to him. "Come, come, my good fellow," he said heartily, "thou art still alive, and like enough to outlive by a score of years any one of these yelping dogs outside. Go back to thy stone-cutting, and fail not to refine thy handiwork to the last degree of perfection. Let the very hairs of the eyelash, the—hum—the texture of the robe, the sparkle of the eye—"

"'Tis impossible—impossible!" groaned the artist, wringing his hands in mingled indignation and despair. "Who can express the sparkle of the living eye in dull insensate ivory. Unless—" he added eagerly, "the eye be fashioned out of gems, the white of the eye from pearl, the iris from—"

"Yes, yes, that is what I mean," interrupted Petronius rubbing his hands genially, "exactly, let it be done in that way—by all means."

"But it may occasion a great delay," said the artist pursing up his mouth with a dubious expression. "Six months or more might be consumed in seeking out the proper materials ; perhaps after all the ivory—"

"The delay is no matter, sirrah," roared Petronius with an emphatic stamp of his foot. "The statue must be perfect. Do you understand me?"

"I—I understand, yes—assuredly, I comprehend perfectly," faltered the stone-cutter, stepping back a little in his alarm. "I will send at once for the gems, and with all possible speed ; but the—ah—the added expense, how is that to be met?"

"With gold, knave, with gold, how else? There is no lack of gold with the emperor of Rome—the gods be praised for that much. Now get thee gone ; the needed gold shall reach Sidon within the month."

The stone-cutter still lingered, shifting uneasily from one foot to the other. "If I had the gold to-day," he began at length, "or at the latest by to-morrow, it might save two months of time in the completion—"

But at this Petronius sprang to his feet, calling with

a mighty voice upon all the gods of the nether world to bear him witness that a more stupid, thick-skulled, addle-brained monstrosity than the stone-cutter from Sidon never existed, vowing moreover by all the divinities of Olympus and by the shades of his ancestors that he would take the commission from him and give it to the slave who trimmed his beard, since the slave was the better artist of the two.

The unlucky sculptor retreated open-mouthed to the door, reaching it with a sigh of relief, and disappearing therefrom with the celerity of a withered leaf before the impetuous blasts of the north wind.

Seeing that the man from Sidon was fairly gone, Petronius chuckled grimly to himself. "So far, good!" he growled. Then he rapped upon the table. "My breakfast! and tell Valerius Flaccus that I will see him at once."

"I purpose," he said, betwixt great mouthfuls of the porridge which he preferred to all other dishes for his morning repast, "I purpose to advance at once to Tiberias, that I may see whether this same state of affairs prevails over the entire country; also I shall send for Herod Agrippa and put the matter to him. He may perchance have some influence with these accursed blockheads. 'If they endeavor to prevent the worship of my statue,' says the emperor, 'put them down by force of arms.' Very good, I am ready to fight, but who can fight men who throw themselves flat upon their bellies howling like a lot of sick children?"

"Charge upon them with a legion, excellency, and the cowards will shortly get up and run away," advised Flaccus, drumming loudly on the edge of his chair with his closed fist. "That is how I should deal with the rascals ; give them something to howl for, say I."

"I have not asked your counsel, sir," growled Petronius. "No, they must be persuaded, though may the gods smite me, if I know how it is to be done. But come, we start without delay with one legion, the other shall remain here under command of Procullus."

Valerius Flaccus shrugged his shoulders, but he nevertheless prepared to carry out the commands of his superior.

That day Petronius at the head of his cohorts marched from Ptolemais to Tiberias, pursued all the way by the dark cloud of mourning Jews. Thousands upon thousands, and tens of thousands of them beset the stolidly-marching columns before and behind, in companies of old men, of young men, of matrons, of maidens, of young children ; gaunt and wasted with fasting, their voices hoarse with prolonged wailing.

"Hear us for the love of God!" they groaned. "Save yourselves from the wrath of Jehovah !—The Holiest of the Holies !—Thy Holy Place, oh God !— Woe, woe is come upon us—even the abomination of desolation !"

And "Woe ! Woe ! Woe !" sounded in the ears of the advancing legionaries in ever louder and more awful insistence, till even the hardened veterans of a

hundred bloody battles ground their teeth in superstitious terror, and called upon all the gods of Rome
to protect them.

In the empty palace of Herod Antipas at Tiberias,
Petronius received that night a deputation, consisting
of Aristobulus the brother of Agrippa, together with
Helcias the elder, and other chief men of the Herodian
family.

" Where is Agrippa, the emperor's friend ?" inquired
the governor abruptly, looking uneasily from one to
the other of the serious faces before him.

" King Agrippa sailed for Rome more than a month
since, being at the time unfortunately ignorant of this
decree of the emperor which hath brought about such
unhappy consequences," answered Aristobulus.

The governor received this piece of information with
a fierce but unintelligible exclamation.

" It must be evident by this time to your worshipful
excellency that prompt measures must be taken to
pacify the people," continued Aristobulus firmly.
" Not only is all business at a standstill in our cities,
but the peasants have forsaken their fields and vine-
yards ; already the time for sowing is far past, and
unless the populace can be persuaded to return at
once to their avocations, a frightful famine will follow,
tributes will be unpaid, and, in a word, the nation will
be destroyed."

" When a man is ailing," began Petronius frowning,
" so that by reason of the foul fever which burns in
his veins he is for the time mad and knoweth not what

he doeth, raging and tearing also like to a wild-beast, then doth the wise physician open his swollen veins that the distempered blood may flow therefrom ; so shall the sick man recover—if haply the gods be propitious. Listen now to the ravings of the sick man without, and bethink you if I shall straightway crucify certain of the chief men of Jerusalem, and of the others send a score or more into banishment, will not distempered Israel forthwith forget this trifling matter of the statue ? and peace and prosperity shall be restored to the many at the expense of the few."

" There is but one way in which thou mayst accomplish this infamous decree of the emperor," answered Helcias, his voice trembling with indignation.

" And what is that ?" inquired Petronius. " By my faith, I should rejoice to hear it, since I am under commands to accomplish the matter at hazard of my own life."

" Go forth with thy legions, and straightway put to the edge of the sword every one both great and small, in whose veins there courses a drop of Hebrew blood, then shalt thou unhindered set up in the Holiest Place of the temple the image of the Cæsar."

" But and if I shall put the nation to the edge of the sword, what profit to set up the colossus in a temple wherein there are no worshipers ? Nay, good Helcias, the physician may not slay the patient openly before the eyes of his family ; if he would slay him, he must accomplish the matter by stealth, else would his own neck be in peril. Listen again, if a man suffer pain in a certain member of his body it is likewise the custom of the leech to apply to another part a grievous blister or burn, so that in the greater anguish the lesser may be forgotten, and this also is a wholesome practice. Not long since, I am told, there was an uproar at Jerusalem because of a certain man called Christus, who was crucified for his crimes at the hands of Pontius Pilate, the procurator. Let now the minds of the people be skilfully stirred within them against the followers of this man, who assuredly will work greater mischief to their religion than a dead mass of stone and metal in whatsoever shape it be wrought or wheresoever it be set up."

"The followers of the man Jesus are indeed hated by all righteous and law-abiding Jews," replied Aristobulus thoughtfully, "and in some more peaceful time their destruction shall doubtless be compassed; but what is any heresy or schism, however foul, compared with this threatened profanation of their inner sanctuary? For the time being they have forgotten the whole matter.* There remains yet one other resource; lay this matter before the emperor without delay and with all wisdom, representing to him that not only will there come great loss and suffering upon the Jewish nation—who indeed are willing to die rather than to suffer their laws to be trodden under foot, but that general havoc, destruction and famine will certainly prevail throughout the whole region,

---

* Acts, ix. 31.

whereby all tributes and revenues will be lost to the coffers of Rome: if thou shalt represent the matter to him with due discretion, it may be that he will be turned from his purpose."

Petronius laughed aloud, " Thou knowest not our Caligula, it would seem," he said bitterly. " It is possible that the threatened loss of tribute-money might serve to move him—though to make that good were a simple enough matter, since there yet remain unslain a few rich citizens at Rome. As for the sufferings of the Jewish nation, the story will suffice to amuse the god as he sups his wine." His head sank forward upon his breast, and the weird unearthly wailing from without filled the silence like an agonized prayer. " I am an old man," he muttered as if to himself, " my tale of life is almost told ; what remains is scarce worth a thought, and yet—it is dear to me."

The men who stood in his presence watched him breathlessly ; the fate of Israel was trembling in the balance, they thought, not knowing that the fiat of the Eternal had already gone forth.

Petronius lifted his heavy eyes and fixed them upon the white faces before him ; he arose from his chair and solemnly raised his right hand high above his head. " I will do this thing that ye have asked of me," he said in a loud firm voice, " and if I perish, I perish. May the gods bear me witness !"

When he had said this, he went out of the palace and spoke to the people, who were crowded even about the doors.

"It is just, O Jews, that I, Publius Petronius, who have received honors and advancement at the hands of Caius Cæsar should endeavor to carry out his decrees with diligence, yet am I not unmoved at the sight of your anguish and by the misery which those decrees have wrought in your midst. I am therefore resolved, at peril of my own life, to intercede with the emperor in your behalf, to the end that you may be permitted to exercise your laws undisturbed, and to worship your God after your own customs. And since I am told by those eminent among you that your God is also a great God and very powerful, I do request and ask that you will beseech him to prosper me in this perilous venture which I undertake for you. And now do you depart every one of you, each to his own avocation, and fall to the cultivation of your ground with all diligence —since the time for planting is already far past, knowing that I have pledged myself to your service in this matter both with my honor and with my life."

No sooner had Petronius spoken these words, than there came down from the heavens copious showers of water with a great sound of thunder ; which truly the Jews regarded as the voice of God, for thus was broken a terrible drought which had lasted for more than a year. And this took they for a sign that God had heard their prayers, and that he would prosper the undertaking of Petronius. So they departed with cheerfulness each man to his own place, even as the governor had bidden them.

As for Petronius, he had now a serious task before

him, that of communicating to the emperor of Rome the thing which he had done.

"I am aware," he said, "that in writing this letter I am also writing my own death-warrant, which is surely a grievous thing for a man to do."

Yet did he set forth the matter very plainly, declaring how that many tens of thousands of the Jews had entreated him for forty days, thereby neglecting their business and the tillage of their land. Also he mentioned in particular the matter of the revenues, and added that should the emperor refuse to grant the request of the people that he would not fail of being publicly cursed by them for all future ages.

This letter he dispatched at once to Rome by the hand of a certain centurion called Cornelius.

CHAPTER XVII.

THE MEDIATOR.

THE centurion Cornelius, bearing the missive of Petronius, had no sooner arrived in Rome than he made haste to seek an interview with Herod Agrippa.

"For," said Petronius, "in that he is both a Jew and a favorite of Caius Cæsar, thou mayest hope through him to obtain audience of the emperor at a good and favorable season. Do thou therefore acquaint him with what hath taken place and with what I have done, and act according to his advice in the matter."

Now it happened that Agrippa had already heard what the emperor had determined concerning the temple at Jerusalem, and he was both sorry and afraid, for in his inmost heart he believed in the power and might of Jehovah, since he had not failed from his youth up to receive information concerning the marvelous things which had befallen the Jews in times past.

"If Jehovah depart from Israel," he said within himself, "how shall it profit me to be king of the Jews, since without their God, Israel shall be speedily brought to naught."

Because therefore he wished to be mighty, and to

enjoy power and riches and dominion, as had his grandfather Herod, he listened carefully to all that Cornelius had to say. And when the man had finished speaking he said to him, " How is it that thou being a Roman dost manifest such kindness towards the Jews ? for indeed thou hast spoken even as one who also fears this Jehovah."

" There is truly no god among all the nations of the earth like unto the God of the Jews," replied Cornelius gravely, " for while other gods be fashioned out of wood and stone and ivory—which also can be looked upon, touched and handled by man, the God of the Jews alone is unseen and invisible, yet he alone can hear the cry of man and regard it."

" How dost thou know this ?" asked Agrippa curiously. " Hast thou also worshiped in the temple— who art a Gentile ?"

" I have never visited the temple," replied the centurion, looking intently into the haughty face of the Herod," but I prayed to the God of the Jews in mine own house at Cæsarea, since I could no longer with an honest heart entreat the gods of Rome ; I gave alms also, according to the teaching of the Jews, to them which were in need. Not long since there befell me a wondrous thing—but I forget myself," he added in an altered tone. " Shall I to-day deliver this letter to the emperor ?"

Agrippa waved his hand impatiently, " I must yet consider that question with care, good centurion ; the delay is no matter, since at present all goes well with

the Jews. I am minded to know the wondrous thing
that befell thee at Cæsarea."

" I will tell thee what it was," answered the centurion, " and this the more gladly since thou thyself dost
believe on this Jehovah."

Agrippa shrugged his shoulders with a slight smile.
"Say on," he commanded briefly.

" I was praying in my house according to my custom," continued Cornelius, " it being about the ninth
hour of the day, when suddenly I saw an appearance
as of a young man clad in garments of dazzling white-
ness. He spoke to me, calling me by name; when I
had looked still further at him and perceived by the
radiance which streamed forth from his person that it
was no earthly being which had addressed me, I was
afraid. Yet I made shift to ask what he might want
with me. Then spake he these words unto me, ' Thy
prayers and thine alms are come up for a memorial
before God. And now send men to Joppa, and call
for one Simon, whose surname is Peter; he lodgeth
with one Simon, a tanner, whose house is by the sea-
side : he shall tell thee what thou oughtest to do.' "

" Wondrous, indeed !" remarked Agrippa, his lips
curling. " Thou didst dream, man, and thy slumbers
were perchance disturbed by an over-draught of new
wine."

" I had drunken nothing, king Agrippa. But now
hear what followed. I called straightway two of my
household servants, who were good men, likewise an
honest soldier of my guard, and to them I related the

vision; then I sent them to Joppa to search for the man Simon, whose surname was Peter."

"And did they find the—the tanner, was it not?" interrupted Agrippa languidly.

"They found the house of the tanner, and the man Simon, whose surname was Peter, and when they had told him the things which I bade them say, he readily consented to accompany them to Cæsarea; which also he did on the day following, bringing with him certain other Jews which abode in Joppa."

Agrippa raised his hand with a gesture of dissent. "I am but half a Jew," he said, "and I care nothing for the burdensome customs of the rabbis, yet do I know that Jews enter not into the houses of Gentiles lest they incur defilement."

"That is true," answered Cornelius gravely. "And thus did the man Peter say unto me and to those of my kinsfolk and acquaintance whom I had gathered to my house. 'Ye know,' he said, 'how that it is an unlawful thing for a man that is a Jew to keep company with one of another nation. Yet God hath showed me that I should not call any man common or unclean, therefore I came unto thee, without question, as soon as I was sent for.' He then asked me what I would have from him, whereupon I related to him the vision which I had seen; and I told him moreover, that all that he saw assembled in my house were come together that they might learn from his lips the commandments of the living God.

"'Of a truth,' he said, 'I perceive that God is no

respecter of persons, but in every nation he that fear-
eth him, and worketh righteousness is accepted with
him.'

"Then declared he unto us Jesus of Nazareth, a
man anointed with power and with the holy spirit, who
during his lifetime went about doing good, and healing all that were oppressed of the devil. 'And we are
witnesses,' he said, ' of all things which he did both
in the land of the Jews and in Jerusalem ; how also
that he was crucified of them ; but God raised him
from among the dead on the third day and showed
him openly, not to all the people, but unto witnesses
chosen before of God, even to us, who did eat and
drink with him after that he arose from the dead, and
he commanded us to preach to the people, and to
testify that it is he which was ordained of God to be
the judge of quick and dead.' "

Agrippa moved uneasily in his chair. This was not
the first time that he had heard of this man Jesus.
He remembered on a sudden a strange story which
had been told him in his boyhood concerning certain
wise men who had once come to Jerusalem seeking
for the king of the Jews. "We have seen," they declared, "his star in the East, and are come to worship
him." His grandfather Herod, the greatest of all his
race, was troubled when he heard of the thing, and all
Jerusalem was troubled with him, he therefore assembled all of the chief priests and scribes of the
people—so ran the story—and demanded of them
where Christ should be born. And they answered

that it had been foretold by the prophets that out of
Bethlehem should come a ruler who should reign
over Israel.   Forthwith the king sent secretly for the
wise men and instructed them to seek for the young
child in Bethlehem.   " When ye have found him," he
said, " bring me word, that I also may come and worship him."   But the wise men did not return to Jerusalem, and Herod in a fury immediately sent forth
executioners into Bethlehem with commands to slay
all of the children in that village and its vicinity of
two years old and under.   Again he remembered that
Pilate, the governor under whom this Jesus of Nazareth was put to death, had told him that the man
boldly declared himself to be the rightful king of the
Jews.   True he was dead, but what of this strange
story of his resurrection which so many of the Jews
persisted in believing ?   Agrippa straightened himself
and a baleful light flashed from his eyes.

" Where is this man from Galilee—who also arose
from the dead ?" he demanded.   " Do they keep him
hidden from the people that they may raise an insur-
rection in his name ?   Verily when the knaves lead
after them loyal soldiers of the empire, 'tis time that
the matter be looked to.   Come now, what say these
fellows concerning the threatened profanation of the
Holy of Holies ?   Are they also amongst them which
have piously fasted and entreated the legate Petronius
for the space of forty days ?"

Cornelius hesitated and looked down.   Despite the
joyous confidence of his new faith, which urged him

to witness to the truth whenever opportunity offered, he half regretted that he had spoken of the matter to this man. "The followers of the Christ," he said at length, "affirm that should the temple be razed to the ground, men would still have access to the Father through the mediation of his son Jesus, who hath ascended into heaven and sitteth on the right hand of God."

"They do not therefore care for any of these things?" questioned Agrippa sharply.

"The peace of God which passeth understanding abides with them, and shall abide, now and evermore," answered Cornelius solemnly.

"Enough, we will speak of the matter no more, yet wilt thou do well, good centurion, to offer sacrifices and libations to the gods of Rome after the pious customs of thy ancestors, that these mists of Jewish heresy which envelop thee may be scattered in honest daylight. To worship a crucified criminal is scarce meet for a man in authority like thyself. Methinks if the matter should come to the ears of the emperor there would be another centurion of the Italian band in Caesarea."

Cornelius flushed hotly over all his honest face. "Dost thou, who art a Jew, commend me to the gods which thou knowest to be false?" he demanded.

"By Apollo, man, thou dost weary me with thy cant! Know that I care not a denarius for any god on earth or in heaven; they be all alike perchance the vaporous imaginings of the credulous. But, look you, as to this matter which thou hast in hand for Petronius and the Jews, do nothing for seven days. At the end of that time thou shalt hear from me further."

Having thus dismissed the messenger of the governor, Agrippa set himself to make ready a great banquet in honor of Caius Cæsar. During six days his servants were employed in preparing the pastries and cooked meats. Strange and costly delicacies were procured from every place where such things were to be found. Rich wines also in abundance, garlands of roses and sweet-scented leaves to wreathe the ivory couches on which the guests were to recline, music of sweet and varied sorts, together with bands of beautiful youths who should chant in chorus the praises of this new Jupiter. All of these things did Agrippa set in order, and on the seventh day the emperor of Rome was feasted in the house of his friend. When he had eaten and drunken gluttonously, as was his custom, and while the choruses were being sung in his honor, he lay back upon the silken cushions of his couch and looked about him well pleased.

"There is no one," he said at length, fixing his unsteady eyes upon Agrippa, "in all Rome—nay in all the world, of whom I think more highly than of yourself, my Agrippa; and when it comes to my mind how that while I was without power thou didst cleave to me, despite the commands of that old dotard Tiberius—whom may the furies tear, even enduring because of thine exalted affection for my person the ignominy of chains and imprisonment, I am minded

to show thee still further of my kindness, since what
I have already done for thee by way of amends for
thy suffering is but little.   Know then, that anything
which thou shalt ask of me to the extent of my ability
shall be immediately granted to thee ; and this also I
swear by the great Jupiter, my brother, and by all the
inferior gods."

The guests fixed their eyes upon the king, expect-
ing that he would ask nothing less than the addition
of other provinces to his kingdom, or the revenues of
certain cities, but Agrippa made answer after this manner—exhibiting withal a noble humility and an honest
sincerity of countenance which did mightily affect
every one that heard him.

"I have loved thee, O most gracious and conde-
scending of all the divinities," he said, "but I have
loved thee for thyself alone, and not for any benefits
which I hoped to receive at thy hands ; thou hast
already heaped upon me gifts beyond the craving of
even the most grasping of men, and although these
gifts may be beneath thy power—who art all powerful, yet do they greatly transcend my worthiness as
well as my desires."

At this Caius professed to be greatly astonished, and
pressed him yet more strenuously to make of him at
least one request, since he would not be denied the
gratification of doing him some further honor.

"I would ask nothing for myself, divine majesty,"
replied Agrippa, "but I desire a boon which may render yet more glorious thy renowned piety, and which

also will confer upon me the honor of having never failed in my requests of thee. My petition is this, that thou wilt forbear to set up that statue of thyself in the temple at Jerusalem."

With which request, indeed, Caius was mightily taken aback, yet because he had so publicly urged Agrippa to ask a favor of him, and because he feared that he might be made a laughing stock of them that had witnessed the scene, should he now refuse, he declared that he should take pleasure in gratifying so unselfish a wish. Within the hour he had written a letter to Petronius, commending him for what he had already accomplished, and bidding him proceed no further in the matter of the colossus.

" If, therefore, (he wrote) thou hast already erected the statue, let it stand ; but if thou hast not yet dedicated it, do not trouble thyself further about it, but dismiss thy army, go back and take care of those affairs which I sent thee about at first, for I have changed my mind regarding the erection of the statue ; and this—be it understood, have I done out of favor to Agrippa."

The next day Agrippa sent for the centurion Cornelius, and told him to deliver the missive which he had brought from Petronius, since he had made the matter sure beyond a peradventure. Cornelius took the letter of Petronius, and himself gave it into the hand of the emperor, who had no sooner read it, than he fell into a furious rage, which indeed resembled that of a wild beast, since he straightway forgot his

oath to Agrippa and what he had already written to
Petronius.

"They have bribed the knave!" he roared, tearing
at his garments like a demoniac. "Fetch me parchment that I may write."

"Seeing that thou dost esteem the presents made
thee by the Jews to be of greater value than my commands (he wrote) and art grown insolent enough to
be subservient to their pleasure, I charge thee to become thine own judge, and to consider what thou shalt
do, who art under my displeasure ;* for I will make
thee an example to the present as well as to all future
ages, that men may not dare to contradict the commands of their emperor."

And this letter, which was equivalent to a death-
warrant, the emperor caused to be sent to Petronius
by the hand of one of his own slaves. Also he commanded a colossal statue of himself to be made at
Rome with all possible speed.

"I will go to Jerusalem," he said, "and myself see
to its erection in the inmost shrine of their temple."

---

* An intimation of this kind was equivalent to an order to
commit suicide, the recipient thereof being thus allowed to
escape the ignominy of a public execution.

CHAPTER XVIII.

THE END OF THE PLAY.

CASSIUS CHAEREAS, the tribune of the praetorian cohort, was in an evil mood.   It needed
but a single glance at his unhealthily pallid face and
sullen blood-shot eyes to assure his slaves of the fact,
yet these astute observers performed their customary
offices with none of the cringing humility which might
have been looked for under the circumstances ; they
even laughed and winked at one another knowingly
behind their master's back.   Something of this thinly-
veiled insolence became evident to Chaereas after a
time, for rousing himself from his grim abstraction he
ordered them out of his presence.

"I care no more than that for his frown," said one
of them, snapping his fingers contemptuously as they
filed out into the passage-way.   "Can I not give
curse for curse? and are there not gods in Egypt?
But let him lay so much as a finger's weight upon my
body—"

"Ay, let him !" assented his companion with a boast-
ful laugh.   "Moreover, he knows it ; who better?
And he fears us.   A year since we should have trembled like whipped curs in his presence ; now—ha ! ha !
he is forced to bite his lips to keep back the curses,

lest we denounce him. Ay! the emperor is a good father to the oppressed."

"Hark you," whispered another, thrusting his swarthy visage betwixt the pair. "Have we not had enough of this sport, amusing as it is? I am for casting off even the semblance of a chain—and to-day."

"But bethink you, is he not too high in power? We might perchance burn our fingers in the attempt, and fail of the morsel in the end."

"Yesterday Pollux, the slave of Claudius the emperor's kinsman, denounced his master," growled the Egyptian. "Claudius will be tried without delay, and I wager a week's victual that the prince dies and the slave receives his freedom."

The others stared open-mouthed at this piece of intelligence. "He is a bold fellow, that Pollux," said one of them enviously, "if Claudius dies he will receive a goodly sum of gold, I suppose."

"No less than an eighth of the entire property,' together with his freedom," said the Egyptian with relish. "Oh, but we be driveling fools to groan in slavery when we might be free and rich."

"Fools—yes, we be accursed fools to talk of such things," said an old man, who had not hitherto spoken. "Look at my grey hairs, comrades, sixty years have I lived in slavery; in my youth I was sentenced to death because I had broken a crystal dish at a banquet, my life was spared at the entreaty of my master's son, who had conceived an affection for me. Again, when my **noble** master was found dead in his bed, all the slaves in his dwelling were condemned to the sword, since the physician could find no reason for the sudden stoppage of his breath. We who had looked on at the banquet that night might have explained the matter, since the paunch of a noble contains no more than that of a slave. A second time I was spared at the entreaty of the lad, who though grown almost to manhood had not forgotten his early kindness. Look you, that lad was Chaereas, our master, and he is a good master to us all."

"The furies burn thee for a meddlesome old grey-beard!" cried the Egyptian loudly, "take that! may it remind thee to hold thy peace in the future," and he struck the old man full in the face with his clenched fist.

"Come, come, man, let be; old Gorpius hath spoken truly enough, Chaereas is not a bad master, moreover it must be remembered that he is not a rich man as men are accounted; and 'tis only men with plenty of gold in their coffers who may be safely denounced to our illustrious emperor."

"An eighth of what he hath would content me," muttered the other with a black scowl at Gorpius, who was meekly wiping his bloody face. "The bell, slave! art thou daft as well as stupid?"

"We must have a care what we say in his hearing in the future," he continued, as the old man hobbled away; "if our master be not rich enough to put to death, yet if we be nimble-witted we shall soon find cause for his undoing. Here comes Cornelius Sabinus. Watch him, I pray thee!"

13

"He also hath an angry and sullen look for so gay a gallant. Come, explain to me—since thou art somewhat of a philosopher, what profit may it be to a man to be softly bedded and daintily fed when he doth forget all in his hates and his loves, even as do we who are slaves?"

"I have a mind to listen at the door; there be mischiefs on foot."

"Ay, and lose thine ears for thy pains; be content with what thine eyes shall tell thee."

Behind the closed doors Chaereas greeted his visitor with a surly look and an inarticulate growl.

"Thou art in an unwholesome humor this morning, my friend," remarked the new-comer with a keen look at the tribune. "How go our matters?"

"How go our matters?" repeated Chaereas irritably. "Nay, thou knowest as well as I. The empty days slip by one after another, and we stand on the brink of liberty, and hesitate, and grimace, and falter, like puny boys who dread the plunge into the invigorating cisterna."

"The emperor starts to-morrow for Alexandria," said Sabinus, throwing himself back in his oaken chair, "and once out of Rome—"

"He starts to-morrow!" shrieked Chaereas springing to his feet. "Who says so?"

"No less a person than the royal chamberlain Codrus, who is one of us. 'Tis a sudden resolve taken because of something which occurred at the sacrifice yesterday."

Chaereas smote his hands together without a word, his haggard eyes fastened feverishly on the face opposite him.

"The beast turned from the altar and rushed into the crowd just as the priest lifted the sacrificial knife," continued Sabinus, "a bad omen, as all the world knows. Upon examining the entrails the augurs advised the emperor to leave Rome at once, since the air from the marshes might prove deadly to him in his present state of health."

Chaereas laughed aloud drearily. "Something sharper than the wandering winds of the marshes must needs be called to our aid to rid the world of this living and walking death," he said with bitter emphasis. "Are we men or are we sluggish brutes that we are content to be the instruments of his detestable vagaries? Listen, that you may know how low I have fallen, then spit upon me. Yesterday he commanded me to torture a woman on the rack, to the end that she might be forced to confess her lover guilty of treason. The man was innocent of the charge—I knew it, yet did I, the tribune of the prætorian cohort, descend to the office of a low-born executioner. May the gods forgive me, the wretched woman's shrieks echo in my ears without ceasing."

Sabinus ground his teeth. "Did the woman confess to the lie?"

"Not she; with the courage of a lioness, she refused even amid the most horrible tortures. Afterward, as I had been ordered, I caused her to be borne into the presence of the emperor. He stared at her exquisite body, twisted and torn by the rack, as one might look upon a bit of ruined pastry. 'A monstrous pity,' he grunted. 'She was a handsome woman.' Then he turned to me with an oath, 'Why did you rack her, fool?' 'I did it at thy command, royal master,' I made answer. He turned on his heel with another execration. 'Take her away,' he commanded, 'and give her a thousand talents—from thine own coffers, knave, since thou hast tortured her.' This I did gladly enough, though it well-nigh stripped me."

"Why didst thou not strike him dead upon the body of the woman?" demanded Sabinus, his eyes blazing. "She is but one out of a thousand who cry for justice upon this monster."

"Why did I not strike him dead?" repeated Chaereas bitterly. "O why—why? Who after all am I? Why not the senate, which he has scorned and outraged? Why not the nobles, whose wives and daughters he has insulted, and whose sons he has murdered? Why not the army, whole legions of which he has decimated? Why not the immortal gods, whose faces he has spit upon? Nay, why does not eternal Rome herself arise from her seven hills, seize this demon and thrust him down into the smoking pit of unending torment?"

Cornelius Sabinus arose to his feet. "The matter must be accomplished, and now," he said in cold even tones. "If thou who hast undertaken this matter dost hesitate longer, I swear that I will to-day strike the blow in the face of all Rome."

Chaereas seized him by the arm. "Look you," he whispered hoarsely, "this hand and no other shall strike that blow! So may the gods restore to me my lost honor."

In the theatre which the emperor had lately caused to be built in the garden connected with his palace, a tumultuous throng assembled on this the fifth and last day of the games. Men, women and children, from every rank of society poured into the enclosure in such multitudes that the ushers were unable to perform their duties.

Caius Cæsar, who was already in his place observed this. "By my faith," he said with unwonted geniality to Sabinus who stood at his right hand, "we see to-day a great sight. Men, women, nobles, senators, soldiers and slaves sitting together without regard to rank or station. See to it some of you that plenty of fruits be flung among them."

"The matter has already been attended to, according to custom," replied Sabinus bowing.

The emperor shivered. "I am cold," he whined fretfully, "where is my furred mantle?" He looked uneasily about him, at the marble benches ranged in semi-circular tiers, and crowded to the very roof with gaily-dressed people, at the stage where the play was already beginning, at the decorous faces of his attendants, at his own pallid hands loaded with gems. That strange sensation of cold, a heavy breathless chill like that from a newly-opened vault, still oppressed him; again he shivered. Chaereas, the tribune, stood at his

side, his face as blank and expressionless as one of the
carven masks above his head.

"My good Chaereas!" said the emperor softly,
leaning forward.

The tribune did not stir. The senator Asprenas
touched him upon the shoulder. "The emperor is
addressing you," he whispered. Chaereas raised his
eyes and fixed them upon his master; he did not move
from his place, and he spoke no word of apology or
explanation.

"My good Chaereas," continued the emperor
suavely, "hast thou paid the woman Quintilia the
thousand talents, as I bade thee?"

"The money has been paid," said Chaereas in a low
voice, his dull unwinking eyes still resting upon the
face of his royal questioner.

"'Twas scarce needful that I should ask, my brave
tribune; for me to command is for thee to obey. But
know that I now restore to thee the sum fourfold, in
token of my appreciation of thy distinguished services."

Chaereas raised his hand in a military salute, his
face contracting painfully; he opened his mouth as if
to speak, but no sound came forth; turning abruptly
he left the royal presence.

The emperor looked after him thoughtfully. "Our
brave tribune is overcome with gratitude," he said
aloud drily. Inwardly he was thinking, "The man
hates me; he is dangerous; he must die." Again he
looked down at his feeble nerveless hands, and a sud-

den sickening sense of his own helplessness overpowered him. "They all hate me," he muttered, "but how can I slay them, and alone? They hate me; and I—hate, hate, hate."

He raised his eyes and fixed them indifferently upon the stage. The play represented the fortunes of a wandering robber chieftain who in the course of the drama was to be crucified: the part of the robber had been taken by the actor Apelles, but now that the scene of the crucifixion was reached, a condemned criminal, tricked out in the properties of the actor, was dragged onto the stage, that the scene might be properly realistic. This being one of the emperor's own devices he was wont to watch the stage with delighted eagerness, but to-day there was something offensive in the shrieks of the wretch as they nailed him upon his cross.

"I am weary of all this," he muttered, as the theatre rang with wild applause.

"Why not visit the bath, royal master," suggested Codrus, who stood behind his chair. "Afterward dine, and return to the theatre rested and refreshed; when the play is finished the pantomimes must still be performed, and the choruses."

The emperor grasped the arms of his chair, "I will go," he said, looking vaguely and irresolutely about him.

Minucianus arose quietly as if to pass out.

"Whither art thou going, O brave senator?" said the emperor, laying a detaining hand upon his shoulder ; the man dropped into his place again without a word, but a moment later, with a whispered aside to Sabinus, who stood just behind him, he slipped away unnoticed.

Caius still sat in his place, his head dropped forward upon his breast, his lips moving as if he talked with himself.

" Thou art over-weary, gracious majesty," said Asprenas, bending deferentially over him. " Would it not be well to withdraw for rest and refreshment ?"

The emperor looked up, his dull eyes full of vague bewildered questionings like those of a tired child.

" Yes, my friend," he said slowly, passing his hand across his eyes. " I am weary. It has been a long day—a long, long day ; I will get me to my rest."

Then he arose and went out, Asprenas following.

CHAPTER XIX.

INTERREGNUM.

ROME, the mighty lioness, whipped into cowardice, starved into submission, arose and shook her tawny sides ; she had heard a cry, a strange wild cry, beginning with the feeble moan of a dying man, and swelling anon into a fierce jubilant pæan of triumph. " The Cæsar is dead ! Rome is free !" At the sound the yellow light in the eyes of the starving brute blazed into liquid flame ; with a thunderous roar of joy she leapt forth unhindered into the night, to tear, to rend, to devour.

At the imperial palace lights sparkled from every window. Great fires burned briskly on the marble pavements of the inclosed court-yards, lighting up luridly the faces of the mob which surged in and out of the open doorways. Now and again some one would fling upon the blazing heaps an armful of broken furniture.

" Look you, brave comrades !" yelled a drunken soldier, holding a carved and gilded cradle high above his head. " Here slept the child of the Cæsar ; my child lies upon rags !"

" Into the fire with it !" roared a dozen voices in reply.

" The babe will sleep sound enough without it, pretty dear," muttered an old woman, who was warming her shriveled fingers at the fire. "Ay, sound and long, all three, the gods be praised! Hast thou seen them, wench?" turning to a woman at her side, who held a crying baby in her arms.

" No," answered the woman eagerly, "where be they? I have but just come," she added fretfully; " my husband is here somewhere; he will get no plunder worth the having unless I look to it, he thinks only of the wine. Hush thee, hush thee, child—nay I am weary of thee, and that is the truth."

" Hegh, girl! 'tis an evil thing to say, and of thy first-born too; what wilt thou do when there are half a score of them, all hanging about thy skirts and crying for bread? Give the lad to me; I will wrap him from the cold in this bit of the emperor's tunic. Ay! thou mayst look and look, girl; I took it with my own hands, he will want it no more; it shall warm honest flesh to-night. But come, till I shall show thee a fine sight—a beautiful sight. Besides, I know where to find some pretty robes, fit to set off those black eyes and red cheeks, my girl."

" Where be the pretty things?" demanded the young woman, " I will go there first. I want a necklace of red stones—a mirror—a purple tunic broidered with gold, and—"

" Yes, yes! Thou shalt have them all and more; I know where to look for them. But come along first and see what my old eyes have ached to behold for many a long day. Ay, a merry sight—a goodly sight!"

"But they will get everything," whimpered the girl, glancing with longing eyes into the half-open doors, past which her guide was hurrying her. "Look! they are pulling out beautiful robes now—and veils, and tearing them to bits. Stop, I must have some!"

"Never fear, my beauty, I know where there are a plenty more, and a thousand times handsomer. Just a moment of time, girl, and thou shalt see what thou shalt not forget to thy dying day—be it near or far. Look there!"

"Give me the babe," said the young mother, in a low voice.

"Ay, take him; I will hold the torch. Now, canst thou see? Come nearer, wench. There is naught to hurt the feeblest life in Rome in this heap of dead flesh. The gods be praised for it!"

The other drew back from the formless motionless mass which lay upon the floor at her feet. "Look!" she whispered with a shudder, pointing to the dark pool which crept slowly and crookedly toward her across the marble pavement. "I must not stay," she added hurriedly; "'twill be ill luck for the child."

"Ill luck!" screamed the hag. "Ill luck! Fool! A better day never dawned for the child, and a merrier sight than this was never looked upon. It means freedom and plenty in place of chains and starvation. See, they are all here." And she lifted the smoking torch high above her head.

The younger woman stared for a long moment in fascinated silence, the child in her arms cooing and stretching out its little fingers toward the light.

"Why did they kill—the woman?" she faltered at length; "and—the babe? Surely the little one had done no harm."

"The woman was his wife. The child was his child. When they hunt the mad wolf of the fens and haply track him to his lair, do they spare the she-wolf and the whelp? Come, we will eat and drink, then shalt thou array thyself in her royal robes—who hath no need further save for a winding sheet."

In another part of the palace a group of soldiers were tramping noisily down one of the long corridors.

"Liberty is the watchword of the night, and liberty it shall be!" yelled the foremost, stopping before a closed door. "Locked, by Hercules! Let us see to this, comrades. Together! with a will!"

The door fell with a loud crash and the assailants rushed in. A lamp which burned upon a large oaken table in the centre of the room flickered wildly in the rushing draught. One of the soldiers caught it up, and shielding the flame with his broad palm looked keenly about him by the reviving light. "Parchments as thick as leaves in Autumn, pens, an inkhorn," he enumerated, "more parchments, a pile of scrolls, a—"

"Bah! We have blundered into the lair of a scrivener," roared another with an oath. "There is nothing here; come on!"

"Stay, what is this?" said a third, who had been exploring the apartment on his own account. "Hold the light!" he added impatiently.

"I see a pair of legs," quoth the man with the light, staring hard at a crimson curtain from beneath which the limbs in question protruded. "Our scrivener hath betaken him to his couch with such haste that he hath forgotten his nether appendages."

The soldiers greeted this sally with a roar of laughter; the legs in question twitched convulsively.

"He hath a rheum in his feet for it," said one, "what think you good Petrus, thou'rt somewhat of a leech, shall we bleed him?"

The legs trembled violently, and a stifled moan was heard from behind the curtain.

"Reach me thy sword, comrade, 'tis sharper than mine," replied the man who was called Petrus, with a wink. "I will even prick this scrivener at thy suggestion, that we may see whether his veins be not swollen with over-much application to the inkhorn."

At this the curtain was flung violently aside and a strange disheveled figure tumbled out upon the floor. "Mercy! have mercy!" it shrieked, clutching wildly at the knees of the soldiers. "I have done no harm —no harm at all—I swear it! Do not kill me! For the love of the gods, spare me! spare me!"

"Thou'rt too noisy by half, friend scrivener," said one of the soldiers coolly. "Come, I will make of thee a scrivener to his majesty, Caius Cæsar," and he drew his sword.

" Not so fast, comrade," remarked the soldier who
held the lamp, fixing his eyes thoughtfully upon the
man at his feet, who still poured forth a torrent of
prayers and entreaties, mixed with loud blubbering
like that of a whipped school-boy.

" Why not, good Gratus. We waste time," said
the other, impatiently brandishing his weapon. At the
sight the wretch on the floor burst out anew.

" Why shouldst thou kill me, good, sweet soldier ?
I swear I do no harm ! I want to live—to live—only
to live ! Oh, spare me—spare me—spare me !"

" Look you, comrades," said Gratus with much
seriousness ; " this man's life may be worth a thousand
talents apiece to us. Ay, and more, if we but play
our game aright. This is Germanicus."

" Germanicus !" cried the others. " Who is he ?"

" Claudius Cæsar Germanicus, the uncle of the late
emperor, and therefore next of kin and lawful heir to
the throne."

" Away with him then ! we want no more emperors !"

" Hold hard, comrades ; an emperor is as good as
a consul any day. What will it advantage us to fight
and starve under Chaereas, or Lepidus, or any one of
them ? they be all covetous knaves. Let us make
this Claudius emperor, then will he make us rich.
Hear now, Claudius, if we spare thee and make thee
emperor wilt thou swear to remember us ?"

But Claudius was past understanding, the horrors
of that awful night had quite swept away for the
moment the little wit that he possessed. He could

only moan and blubber, his fat pallid face, streaked
with tears and dirt, twisted into a ludicrous semblance
of a colicky baby's.

"The man is a fool!" said Petrus contemptuously.
"He could not be emperor."

"Better a fool than a madman," replied Gratus
coolly. "Nay, the more fool the better. Come, we
will take him to the camp."

In an upper room of his house Herod Agrippa sat
moodily contemplating the space of blank wall opposite his chair. The visions which he saw there must
needs have been unhappy ones, for his lips moved
angrily, and from time to time he dashed his closed
fist violently down upon the carven arm of his chair.
"Fool that I was," he muttered, rising and walking
restlessly up and down, "blinded by my own little
resentment I left him to fall a victim to this accursed
conspiracy, which will ruin me as it has slain him.
—Ah, Cypros, what wilt thou?"

"I would know what hath happened, my lord; the
most frightful rumors are abroad."

"Not more frightful than the reality," said Agrippa
gloomily. "The emperor is dead, and with him
Cesonia and the child."

"God in heaven!" exclaimed Cypros faintly. "Why
the empress and the babe?"

"I would have concealed his body at once and
feigned that he still lived; thus order might have been
maintained, the murderers apprehended, and the matter
of the succession duly arranged; and this course I

urged upon the empress, but she was quite mad and
distracted with horror—a weak woman at the best.
'I must go to him!' she shrieked; with that she
caught the child from the arms of its nurse and fled
wailing to the place where the body was lying. And
there Lupus and another of the accursed brood of conspirators came upon her crying out to heaven for
vengeance upon the murderers of her dear lord.
There was one speedy way to silence those shrieks,
that way the wretches chose. As for the child; it
was his child."

"What will happen now?"

"Thou mayst well ask that question, woman! We
are ruined—nothing less. A friend of Caius Cæsar's,
I shall be set down an enemy to Rome by these so-
called patriots. 'Rome is free! Rome is free!'
howl the mob; they are sacking the palace now.
The Senate has convened to consider the situation.
The murderers congratulate one another openly. I
see no hope—no hope."

"Listen!" exclaimed Cypros suddenly, "What is
it that they are shouting?"

Agrippa flung open the casement and thrust his
head out into the darkness. "Something has happened!" he said at length. "I must look to it!"

Something had indeed happened; the sounds which
reached them in that upper room, were the shouts of
the soldiers in the praetorian camp as they hailed
Claudius Cæsar, emperor of Rome!

CHAPTER XX.

CLAUDIUS CÆSAR.

THE conspirators had sent for Herod Agrippa that they might ask his opinion with regard to the disturbed state of affairs.

" He is a dangerous man," said Minucianus ; " we shall do well to enlist his sympathies upon our side." And this it appeared was surprisingly easy to do. Agrippa had asked gravely for full information regarding the events which had transpired, and of which he professed entire ignorance.

" It is true that Caius Cæsar was my friend," he said with becoming seriousness ; " he heaped upon me many benefits by way of requital for what I unjustly suffered at the hands of Tiberius ; but think not that therefore my eyes were blinded to his character. In slaying him ye have acted the part of noble patriots, nor shall ye lose your reward." He paused and looked impressively about him. " Now with regard to the pretensions of this Claudius ; he is harmless enough, and a good man, yet withal not fit to hold the reins of government, in that he is feeble in mind and infirm of purpose. He must be persuaded to retire from the camp of the praetorians, and at once."

" He shall be forced to retire," said Chaereas hotly. " Our course is clear ; a part of the army is with us,

14

and we can free the slaves, thus binding them to our interests."

"True, O wise tribune," replied Agrippa with a deferential air. "Yet to meet the disciplined legions of Rome with a horde of untrained freedmen would imply an issue by no means doubtful. If Claudius can but be persuaded to lay down his pretentions peaceably, the army will at once fall under the direction of the senate, the horrors of a civil war will be averted, and all will be well both with the country and its rulers."

"Thou hast spoken wisely." said one Brocchus, a senator, " but to persuade the man will not be an easy task, since he hath had already a taste of power."

"I offer myself as ambassador," cried Agrippa boldly. "If the man refuse to listen to justice and reason, then may we think of employing force."

This suggestion was approved ; three ambassadors, of whom one was Agrippa, were chosen to wait upon Claudius Cæsar, so-called emperor of Rome.

Claudius Cæsar, for half a century the unhappy butt of his royal kinsfolk, had come at last to be master of the civilized world.

" Claudius is too nearly an imbecile to be emperor," Tiberius had said scornfully, and had passed over his claims to the succession with no further comment.

" Claudius is a monstrosity, which nature began but never finished," his mother Antonia was wont to declare with a sneer.

" Claudius is the most amusing person at court,"

observed Caius, "when he is sober he is a historian; when drunk a clown, and whether drunk or sober, he is first, last, and always a fool."

Having recovered at length from his not unreasonable fears of assassination, he had received the intelligence of his good fortune with solemn joy. To the fact that the senate was almost in arms against him, that the city was torn with contending factions, that even the army to which he owed his precarious position was of two minds regarding his succession, he seemed entirely oblivious. "I must have a throne," he said seriously, "else how can I be emperor? also purple robes and jewels; I will not remain longer in the camp; if Caius be dead and I emperor, why should I not return to the palace at once?—Moreover there are my parchments to be attended to."

"It is impossible for your majesty to return to the palace until it be put in fit order for your reception," said Codrus. This astute personage had followed the soldiers from the palace to the camp on the memorable night in which they had discovered Claudius, and being familiar with the character of the new monarch had lost no time in establishing himself as one of his principal advisers. "They say," he added, lowering his voice, "that the spirit of the murdered man haunts the place, and that the cries of the child are heard at night from the corridor where it died."

Claudius grew pale. "Then by the immortal gods I will never return! But what then shall I do?" he whined fretfully, "this is no place for an emperor."

"There are many palaces in Rome, divine majesty," began Codrus soothingly, but Claudius interrupted him with a violent wave of the hand.

"Do not call me divine," he whispered, "'twas that that killed him; the gods were angry.—Nay, I am but a man—a feeble man," he added in a loud voice, as if to propitiate any jealous divinity who might be listening. "Yet am I also emperor of Rome," and he heaved a long sigh of satisfaction and looked about him complacently. "Why do not the senate send to me for orders?" he inquired after a pause.

"The senate has been thrown into great confusion by late events," began Codrus, his face growing suddenly dark as he perceived that Agrippa had just been admitted into the royal presence.

"Master of the world, I salute thee!" said the Jew, kneeling gracefully and kissing the fat flaccid hand which was extended to him. "I have matters of importance for thy royal ear. I would therefore request a short time alone with your majesty."

Claudius glanced timidly at the scowling face of his attendant, but did not speak.

"Out of the way, slave," said Agrippa with a haughty gesture of dismissal. "I have no time to waste."

Codrus burst into a loud derisive laugh, then slowly and deliberately he turned his back upon the pair and left the tent.

"Impudent dog!" said Agrippa, "Why dost thou tolerate the fellow about thy person?"

" He is a useful knave—a clever knave," said Claudius. " A pretty hand at the dice too ; I have already
lost to him more than I rightly know since I came to
this place ; a man must do something to pass away
the time."

" Your majesty will do well to employ these hours
in considering the very grave situation," said Agrippa
frowning. " If now there should be war—"

" War !" exclaimed Claudius starting from his chair.
" No, no, my friend, there will be no war—no killing
of any sort ; I will not hear of it." His heavy good-
natured face had grown quite pale ; he leaned forward
and seized Agrippa by the sleeve, " Look you, friend,"
he whispered, " I hate blood—I hate it, dost thou
hear ? I will have none of it. There shall be peace,
and—money, plenty of it, shall be given to the people.
I have said it ; I am emperor." He leaned back in
his chair after this outburst and looked about him
vaguely. " I am emperor, am I not ?" he faltered,
turning again to Agrippa. " The soldiers yonder are
not making sport of me ?"

" Assuredly thou art emperor," said Agrippa impatiently, " but beware, lest thou be torn from thy high
estate. I tell thee plainly that the senate are as one
man against thee, and that a part of the legionaries are
with them. They will liberate the slaves, furnish them
with weapons, and thus form a great army with which
to force compliance with their demands, unless thou
shalt yield peaceably."

" I yield ! I yield !" cried Claudius, rolling up his

eyes in manifest terror. " Tell them so, good Agrippa, at once. What is it that they want of me ?"

" They want of thee nothing less than a complete renunciation of the throne," said Agrippa, studying with deliberation the face of the man before him. " They demand that thou shalt cease to be emperor, and become again Claudius Germanicus, a citizen of Rome."

Claudius stared vacantly before him for a moment, then his chin quivered, his eyes overflowed with tears and he burst into loud sobs. " I will not cease to be emperor," he blubbered. " No, I will not ! Why, look you, good Agrippa, I have not even sat upon a throne as yet ; *they* said I should be emperor," with a feeble gesture in the direction of the guard which could be seen pacing slowly backward and forward before the door of the tent. "*They* promised it."

Agrippa smiled darkly. " Listen !" he said sternly. " This is no time for womanish tears ; thou hast said aright, the army—the imperial, all-powerful army, has willed that thou shalt be emperor, and emperor thou shalt be, despite the empty threats of the senate, if only thou shalt listen and heed what I shall presently say to thee."

" I am listening," said Claudius, rubbing his wet eyes with the backs of his pudgy hands. " What must I do ?"

" An embassy from the senate—of which I shall be one—will shortly wait upon thee," said Agrippa, speaking slowly and clearly as if to a child. " They will demand of thee that thou shalt utterly renounce all claims to the throne, that thou shalt at once leave the camp of the prætorians, and further that thou shalt yield thyself to them in due obedience as a simple citizen of Rome, in return for which concessions they will promise thee their gracious protection, together with means of sustenance and support. Yet do not forget that the hands which extend to thee this so-called protection are dripping with the blood of thy kinsman."

" I will not yield!" declared Claudius stoutly.

"Bravely spoken!" cried Agrippa, with flattering emphasis, "thou hast the spirit of the war-like emperors of old. Thou wilt not yield, and why? What can the senate, torn into a thousand factions and threatened with complete disruption, supported, moreover, by a mere fragment of the army, what, I say, can it do? Let them free the slaves, what then? Can a mass of raw, unorganized troops meet the disciplined legions of the empire?"

Claudius laughed aloud. "They will not try it," he said boastfully. "I will give the soldiers money, plenty of money; they like that. I will give them— five thousand drachmae apiece, what sayst thou?"

Agrippa raised his brows in astonishment. "'Tis an extravagant sum," he said, "yet, if it gain the balance of the army—yes, give it. 'Tis no ordinary game that we play."

Claudius comprehended this language perfectly, for he was a confirmed gambler. He nodded his big head knowingly and snapped his fingers with a gleeful laugh.

"Ha! ha! thou'rt a pretty fellow, Agrippa—a knowing fellow; if we win this game, thou and I, I swear that thou shalt lose nothing by it. Caius gave thee a kingdom, but I can make it a bigger kingdom."

Agrippa's eyes sparkled, he drew a long breath. "This man," he thought within himself, "is no fool after all." Aloud he said gravely, "Your majesty is more than generous; but believe me, I have allowed no selfish considerations to influence me in this matter, which is world-wide in its importance. I must leave thee now, but do not fail to answer the senate as becometh the master of the world, and the gods grant thee prosperity."

"Do not leave me, good Agrippa," implored Claudius, "first tell me what I must say to them, that I make no false move in the game."

An hour later the embassy from the senate was ushered into the presence of the emperor with all the pomp and circumstance of which the surroundings permitted. The ambassadors duly preferred their demands, and were met with a refusal couched in such dignified and uncompromising terms that they were smitten with amazement. Claudius displayed a surprising knowledge of the disrupted state of the senate, coupled with a clear and far-seeing understanding of the advantages of his own position, which they found it difficult to confront.

Their consternation and astonishment were betrayed

clearly enough in their faces, and Claudius perceiving
it bade them be of good cheer. " Do not fear, citizens of Rome," he said majestically, " any repetition
of the scenes of blood and tyranny which have hitherto oppressed you ; this rebellion of which the senate
has been guilty shall be freely forgiven, since their
reluctance to seeing another emperor on the throne of
Rome is most natural. Under Claudius Cæsar the
people shall taste of equitable government, and this I
pledge to you by everything which I hold sacred. I
shall be ruler but in name ; the authority shall be
shared with the senate and with the people." The
eyes of the speaker rested for an instant upon
Agrippa, while a slight triumphant smile played about
his lips.

" Thy message shall be given to the senate, O
Claudius," said Herod with well-simulated dismay,
and the embassy withdrew from the presence.

Twenty-four hours later Claudius was borne in
triumph from the camp to the imperial palace ; the
remnant of the army had come over to him with loud
acclamation and rejoicing, and the senate left without
any means of defense had sullenly surrendered to the
inevitable.

" In place of a madman we have a fool for emperor," said Chaereas with bitterness.

" Look you," cried Sabinus violently, " rather than
see another Cæsar master of Rome, I will slay myself
in his presence."

" Happy Asprenas who fell at the hands of the

imperial guard at the very moment when liberty seemed ours," groaned Lupus.

In the meantime Claudius sat upon the throne of the Cæsars, well pleased with himself and all the world.

"To be emperor is a good thing," he remarked to Codrus, who by reason of his manifold accomplishments had already become indispensable to the royal pleasure, "but I am weary of all this ceremonial. Come, what say you to a quiet game with the dice? Ay, and let them fetch some wine."

"With all the pleasure in life, royal master. But there is yet one thing to consider. The murderers of Caius Cæsar still live."

The emperor's ruddy face grew pale. "They can do me no mischief;" he said querulously. "Why dost thou mention the matter? I wish to forget it."

"They do not forget, gracious majesty, who performed the deed," said Codrus darkly, "as long as they live moreover, the ghost of thy dead kinsman will cry aloud for vengeance! as long as they live, red-handed murder holds the sword over thine own head."

Claudius gave vent to a smothered shriek and involuntarily looked upward. "What shall I do?" he cried in anguished tones.

"What justice demands," said Codrus, assuming the stern integrity of an outraged patriot. "What the peace and safety of the state demand."

Claudius groaned. "What must I do?" he repeated helplessly.

" Give orders to the guard to have them apprehended. As for their lands and moneys, give them to those who are in deed and in truth thy friends."

" Thou shalt have them !" cried Claudius, mightily pleased with this idea, " thou shalt have them—thou and Polybius and Narcissus ; only manage the thing for me, for I will not hear of blood," he shuddered violently at the word and relapsed into a gloomy silence.

" Gracious emperor," cried Codrus prostrating himself at the royal feet, " I am unworthy of thy condescension, yet have I a request to prefer in view of thy generosity."

"What is it ?" demanded Claudius rousing himself.

" Grant me leave to change the name which I bear, and which is bound up in my mind with naught but slavery and degradation. Let me from henceforth be Felix, the happy, since thou hast conferred upon me all the joys of existence."

"A pretty conceit, by the immortals !" cried Claudius in high good humor again. " Felix thou art from this moment. Felix Claudius—for thou shalt also bear my name in token of the kindness which I feel for thee. And now for our game of dice, good Felix, that we may forget all the care that hath irked us !"

Thus it happened that Chaereas and Lupus, and with them many other noble Romans who were concerned in the death of Caius, were shortly condemned to be beheaded.

" I pray you good executioner, grant me one last

request," said Chaereas when he was led forth. "Slay me with the sword with which I slew the Cæsar; for if it failed to free my country, it shall at least deliver an unhappy mortal from the thraldom of an existence which has become hateful." And so he fared him forth upon the eternal voyage.

"They died for Rome!" murmured the multitude who looked on, and they poured oblations into the fire, calling on the spirits of the departed to be merciful, and to forgive Rome for its ingratitude. As for Cornelius Sabinus, whose life and fortune had by some oversight been spared, he kept his word, for coming suddenly into the presence of the emperor, he cried with a loud voice, 'that he could live no longer since his companions were slain,' and with the words upon his lips, he fell upon his sword and perished at the very foot of the throne which he had so hated.

Shortly after these events Claudius Cæsar caused a proclamation to be made, setting forth the death of Caius and his own accession to the imperial power, which proclamation being dispatched by special and swift messengers to every part of the Roman dominions reached Jerusalem full eight and twenty days before the letter of Caius to Petronius, bidding him take his own life; which message was afterward found to have been delayed by storms and shipwreck.

"Truly the God of the Jews is a great god," declared Petronius, when he understood all that had happened. "There is no other god like him among all the nations!"

PART II

"'The Day is at Hand'"

CHAPTER XXI.

"LUCIUS of Cyrene and Simeon a Jew of Antioch, to the believers on Jesus the Christ which dwell at Jerusalem : Peace be unto you, even the peace of the master, which he giveth to his well-beloved in all plenteousness.

"Be it known unto you, brethren, that after the death of that holy and just man, Stephen, when it seemed possible unto us to remain no longer in Jerusalem, we came seeking peace and safety to the regions of Syria wherein we now dwell ; being indeed driven out from the holy city at the edge of the sword, as also ye know, because we believed on the name of him who was crucified.

"After long wandering and many sufferings we came at length to this place, cast down indeed but not forsaken, for the Lord was with us according to his promise. And here we comforted one another with the remembrance of those things which had happened at Jerusalem, even the death and resurrection of our Lord Jesus Christ, by whom we have the hope, exceeding glorious, that when the sufferings of this present life shall be overpast we shall enjoy another life and that an everlasting one in his presence, who also hath redeemed us from sin. And seeing about us on every hand men created in the image of God, even as ourselves, who yet lived as the beasts live and died as the beasts die, our hearts burned mightily within us, insomuch that we also spoke to them of him who said, ' Come unto me all ye that labor and are heavy laden and I will give you rest'; being not unmindful, brethren, that the Lord when he was about to be received up into heaven, charged us that we should witness to his grace both in Jerusalem and in all Judea, and in Samaria and unto the uttermost parts of the earth. And behold, when we had spoken in the name of Jesus to these Gentiles, great numbers of them turned to the Lord with rejoicing, for the hand of the Lord was with us.

"And now, brethren, we beseech of you, send to us speedily those who shall help us, for the work is too great for us alone.

" The grace and peace of our Lord be with you all. Farewell."

" Thou hast heard this epistle," said James, laying the parchment aside and looking about him, " what say ye to the things which are here written ? Is the salvation of the Lord to be cast even as pearls before swine into the midst of a filthy and froward people ? Shall we who are clean and holy, charged of God to be perfect in every good word and work, company with the uncircumcised, eaters of the unclean beast, idolaters, liars, adulterers, murderers ? If we have been persecuted even to the death whilst we walked uprightly, keeping the law of Moses, what think you shall befall us if we thus break down the partition-wall which God hath set up of old betwixt the chosen and the accursed?"

" But what of the vision which the Lord vouchsafed to me in Joppa?" said Peter earnestly. "What and if the four corners of the great sheet which was let down to me out of heaven signified the four corners of the earth; and the four-footed beasts, the wild beasts, the creeping things and the unclean fowls which were within signified the nations of the earth? Surely if God hath pronounced them clean, it is not for us to call them unclean."

"I pray you, brethren," said one Eleazar, a man who had formerly been a rigid Pharisee, "that ye consider this matter with all soberness; for I see clearly that the consequences thereof will be vast and far-reaching. Our Lord and Master verily bade us witness to the truth of his Messiahship in every nation, but in what nation may we not find multitudes of the chosen of Israel, exiled as it were from the fold, yet hungering and thirsting for the glad-tidings which we alone can give them. If we preach the gospel to the Jews alone, in every nation and place where they are to be found, is not the task a great one? Will it not call for all the energy and patience of which we are capable? Ye are not ignorant that there are multitudes of Jews in Antioch, why then do we find these brethren speaking to the Greeks, who if they live in misery and perish in hopelessness do but show forth the wrath of Jehovah, which he hath declared abideth thus upon the children of disobedience—ay, and shall abide unto the end. If now we admit these Gentile dogs into our number we shall all alike become unclean ; and the chosen will justly hate us and will refuse to listen to us."

" What say ye then, brethren," cried Peter, " to the fact that upon Cornelius and upon his household also, the spirit of God was poured out, insomuch that they spake with tongues and magnified God ? If these Gentiles receive the baptism of the Spirit from on high, then are they no longer aliens but sons of God and therefore brethren of the same household of faith as ourselves."

" What I have said remains not the less true," said Eleazer doggedly. " We must in effect choose between Israel and the heathen nations, who have ever been hated of Jehovah since the days of our fathers, as the prophets also bear us witness ; and can our God change, of whom it is written, he is the same yesterday, to-day and forever ?"

" ' The Lord is merciful and gracious,' " said Barnabas softly, " ' slow to anger and plenteous in mercy ; he will not always chide, neither will he keep his anger forever.' Moreover, forget not that Israel hath rejected their Messiah and hath refused our testimony of his resurrection as blasphemous and unholy. Haply the Father's heart hath gone out after the prodigal nations which have wasted all in far countries, and which now approach trembling and starving that they may beg the bread of life at his hand, who never yet offered a stone to a hungry child. Let me go, I pray you, that I may look into this matter."

"So they sent forth Barnabas to Antioch ; and when he had seen the grace of God, he was glad and exhorted them all, that with purpose of heart they should cleave unto the Lord. For he was a good man, and full of the Holy Ghost and of faith ; and much people was added unto the Lord. Then departed Barnabas to Tarsus that he might seek Saul."

CHAPTER XXII.

A BOATMAN OF ANTIOCH.

"IN the reign of Antiochus, king of Syria," began the man who rowed the two strangers in his boat, "it happened one day that an enemy came stealthily across the borders of the kingdom. The enemy came by way of the sea in a small mean vessel from Egypt. No one saw him when he landed, no one heard him when he fled away into the land on the wings of the wind, but wherever he went the death angel followed and gathered great sheaves of lives into his arms.

"King Antiochus heard after a while that the enemy was come, and also what he was doing, but he laughed aloud in the midst of his great beard.

"'What care I,' he said contemptuously, 'for such an enemy as this? Let him glut his maw with the bodies of my slaves if it please him; the birth-angel holds wide the gate of life to the poor, and there are already too many of them.' But the enemy smote the king's army and a thousand soldiers died in one day. Then Antiochus laughed no longer; he consulted his astrologers instead, and poured libations to the gods. The second day another thousand passed over the Styx to join the first thousand, and this happened also on the third day, and for many days. Then was there a cry heard in the city, an awful wailing cry which floated across the current of the broad Orontes and pierced the ears of the selfish king, where he sat in his island palace.

"'The plague is upon us! the plague is upon us!'

"And the people died by hundreds and by thousands, not on one day but on many days, and the dead lay unburied in the streets.

"'I will give from the gold of my treasury ten thousand talents,' groaned Antiochus, when one told him with bated breath that the pestilence had crossed the river and had slain his first-born son in the arms of its mother, 'ten thousand talents to the man who will appease the gods, that this death be stayed in my land.' And he caused a proclamation to be made of the same.

"On the third day after that this decree of the king was published, there came into his presence an old man, exceeding bent and wrinkled; he bowed himself before the king and said, 'O king, live forever! thou art sorrowful and afraid because of this enemy which hath come upon thee, who hath glutted his maw not with the bodies of thy slaves only but with the flesh of the rich and the mighty, not sparing flesh of thy flesh and bone of thy bone, O king. Now do thou give the ten thousand talents to ten wise and honest men, who shall thoroughly cleanse the city, and purge it from all death and uncleanness of whatsoever sort be in it. Let them cause moreover that the beds of them that have died, and their clothing and whatsoever they have handled be gathered into heaps, and let the heaps be burnt with fire, and the ashes that remain shall they cast into the river. Let them give also to every one of the inhabitants that suffereth hunger a portion of food of the best that is in the royal houses; let this be done during thrice seven days, so shall the plague be stayed.'

" And when he had spoken these words the old man departed and was seen no more of any one, save indeed of a woman who declared that she had seen him go away in a boat. 'He went that way,' she said, pointing down the river, 'and his long beard blew out far behind and spread and widened into a white mist which received him out of my sight.'

" Antiochus did straightway all that the strange old man had commanded; and it happened that when the city was thoroughly purged from death and uncleanness, and when the hungry were fed day by day with the best that was in the royal houses, that the plague was stayed, and Antiochus was glad at heart.

" ' Fetch me cunning sculptors,' he commanded, ' and let them go up into the mountain which overhangs the city and hew out from the crags thereof a likeness of this aged one, who by his counsels hath saved us from death; for I believe by my soul, and by the soul of my father, that it was no mortal that visited us in our affliction, but Charon himself, who conveys the souls of the dead in his boat across the chill river which divides the land of the living from the land of the departed, and because he grew weary of the multitudes which passed from hence he hath given us these good counsels.'

"So they wrought the crag which is called Silpius into the semblance of an aged man wearing a crown, and it is called the Charonium unto this day."

The garrulous boatman paused as the strangers lifted their eyes to the crag Silpius, which at the bend of the river turned toward them its rugged profile, scarred by the storms of two hundred years.

"The king did according to his will," said one of them in a low voice. "He exalted himself against the God of gods; but that which was determined was done; he came to his end and there was none to help him."*

"Thou also knowest the tale?" said the boatman looking somewhat abashed. "It is true that it is an old story," he added apologetically, "'tis in the mouth of every inhabitant of the city yonder."

The keen eyes of the stranger rested quietly upon the face of the man as he answered, "No son of Abraham is ignorant of the story of Antiochus since it was writ by the hand of the prophet Daniel before ever it came to pass."

"Ye are Jews!" cried the boatmen, allowing his boat to drift with the tide as he looked with manifest astonishment from one to the other of his two passengers. "Why then did ye offer me to drink from

---

* Daniel xi., 36–45.

your cup, and a morsel also of your loaf at the noon-
tide ? I am not ignorant of the ways of Jews," he
continued with a shrug, "they be plenty enough
yonder," with a gesture in the direction of the distant
city. "And by that great Charon, I swear that any
one of them would look upon a man of another nation dying with hunger and thirst—nor offer him bite
nor sup !"

"Nay, thou doest us injustice," said the second
stranger gravely, "there be those among the Jews of
Antioch who are merciful to all men. Look you,
good boatman, I also have heard this tale of the
plague, and there be some who say, that he who appeared in presence of the king was no other than an
aged Jew, who dwelt in solitude not far from Antioch
that he might give himself to prayer and fasting in
behalf of his afflicted people. And when he heard of
the pestilence which prevailed in the city, he came
within the walls that he might bring what succor he
was able to them which suffered. The counsels moreover which he gave the king were in accord with the
laws of the Jews, which laws also were given them of
God in days of old. As for Antiochus, it is told of
him further that knowing these things, he restored to
the Jews which were in Antioch the brazen spoils
which he had taken from their temple in Jerusalem,*
for he perceived that the God of the Jews was great
and mighty, and he was afraid because of the judg-

---

* Josephus, B. J., vii., 3, § 3.

ment of the plague. Yet after those days he gave himself again to idolatry and uncleanness and to all manner of wickedness, so that God cut him off suddenly in the twelfth year of his reign, even as had been foretold by the prophet."

The Greek spat upon his hands and once more gave himself vigorously to his oars. "What thou sayst may be true enough," he said indifferently; "but for myself I am what the Jewish dogs yonder—saving your presence, good sirs—call a Gentile, therefore I worship mine own gods and the gods of my fathers; I know no other."

"Dost thou indeed know thine own god, friend?" said the stranger, leaning forward and looking earnestly upon the face of the boatman. "Tell me what manner of god is he that thou dost worship, and how dost thou worship him; what doth he do for thee in this present life, and what will he do for thee after that thy body shall have perished? Then will I tell thee of the living God, who not only saves men from out the evil of this present world, but who is also able to raise from the dead them which believe on him."

The Greek stared into the face of his questioner, his bright dark eyes full of amazement, then he threw back his curly head and laughed aloud. "Thou art not only a Jew, but thou art a mad Jew," he said, when he had recovered himself. "Come with me to the groves of Daphne* when we have landed, and I

---

* Daphne (the laurel) was the celebrated grove and sanctuary of Apollo, established by Seleucus Nicator, the founder of

will show thee what manner of god I worship and how I worship him—it suffices the young and the merry. When my body shall have perished, why, I care not a denarius what becomes of me ; death is yet a long way off." He burst into a snatch of ribald song, looking sidewise at his two passengers, who had fixed their eyes somewhat sadly upon the city which was now near at hand.

"By Apollo!" he muttered to himself, "I must sweeten them up a bit before they leave me, else will my purse smart for it. Antioch is a merry place, good sirs," he said aloud in a conciliatory tone ; "not Rome itself nor Alexandria can furnish forth a better holiday—and I have seen both. If ye be not over-strict Jews, honored patrons—as indeed I have perceived by your condescension to a humble boatman, ye may enjoy yonder in a single week all the pleasures of the world. Look you," he added, warming with his subject, "there be races, games, dances, processions, festivals, shows of magic and sorcery, all manner of plays and entertainments ; and as for the gods, of which thou hast spoken, they dwell in the groves of Daphne yonder, a very paradise of pleasures, as thou shalt shortly see, for—"

"Hold!" interrupted the elder of the two men with an authoritative gesture, "thou mayst put us on shore at this point ; we will enter the city on foot. If thou

---

Antioch. It contained a magnificent temple and statue of the god, and was famous alike for its extreme beauty and the nameless vices which flourished unchecked amid its cool shadows.

wouldst know our business in Antioch," he added
with a shadowy smile, " come to the street Singon to-
night and thou shalt learn, if thou inquire diligently
for Saul of Tarsus and Barnabas of Jerusalem."

" Not only Jews but mad Jews, by Apollo!" said
the boatman to himself, gazing after the retreating
figures of the two men. He clinked the pieces of
money which he held in his hand. " They be sorcerers—Ay, that is it ! thou art a shrewd fellow, Onesimus.
I will go to the street Singon that I may see ; they
will tell me what I must do to avoid my master." He
jumped into his boat and floated away with the tide,
singing melodiously a very wicked song which was
the fashion of the hour in the wicked city of Antioch.

Onesimus did not go to the street Singon that night ;
the two strangers and all that they had said to him
speedily slipped out of his mind before the in-coming
tide of a new day. As for sorcerers and fortune-
tellers, there was no lack of them in the city, they
were to be found in every wine-shop, and upon the
corner of every street ; for a denarius a man might
know what would befall him upon the morrow ; where
to invest his money that it might be doubled speedily,
and whether his lady were true or false. There were
also charms, potions and magic rings of marvelous
efficacy to be obtained at all prices and for all pur-
poses, so that a man might provide himself against
every contingency of life for a meagre handful of copper farthings. And if sorcerers, fortune tellers and
magicians multiplied in Antioch like swarms of

noisome flies under the summer sun, so likewise did the dealers in darker commodities, with their retinues of skilled thieves, practiced cut-throats, and cunning poisoners, which these worthies confidently recommended to their patrons as the best and safest solvers of the desperate problems which were daily arising in gay Antioch ; and with these a vast army of strolling musicians, quacks, panders, dancing girls and acrobats, who plied their several avocations industriously all day long for the benefit of the throng of idle pleasure-seekers from every nation under heaven, which ebbed and flowed in a ceaseless tide of corruption through the thoroughfares of the city.

The Greek, Onesimus, knew his Antioch well by this time ; he had lived in it now for more than a year ; where he had dwelt previous to this time and what his life had been, concerned no one, apparently least of all Onesimus himself. Life was a long holiday with him now, he took his pleasure easily, with no inconvenient memories to dog his footsteps. Money for his small needs was easily gotten in any one of a dozen ways, for he was a handy fellow, and could sing a song, strum a lyre, relate a legend or row a boat with equal facility. He envied no one, not even the nobles who lived in the beautiful marble villas surrounded by gardens and groves, certainly not the frowning officials who drove their gilded chariots down the great central avenues of the city, and whose airs of pride and importance the facile Greek could imitate to the life, to the vast amusement of certain of his boon companions.

Onesimus was confessedly a fine, clever, brave young fellow, free with his tongue, his laugh and his money; as he strutted along the streets, his red boatman's cap very much on one side, his bold black eyes searching the windows for pretty faces, it is to be doubted if a merrier heart beat in Antioch.

As he walked thus one day, whistling cheerfully to himself and clinking some bits of money in his hand, with which he had the intent to purchase a bowl of pottage for his dinner, he presently became aware of two young Greeks of his acquaintance on the opposite side of the street.

"Hi there, comrades!" he cried loudly, "what cheer?"

The two immediately crossed over to him. "Come along with us," said one of them, who was called Stephanas, "there is something going on in the street Singon; we are going to see it."

"In the street Singon!" repeated Onesimus, scratching his curly head reflectively. "What is it, sorcerers, jugglers, dancing? I am in for it as soon as I have eaten a bit."

"Never mind the eating, munch a mouthful of bread as we go; 'tis neither sorcerers, jugglers, nor dancing girls this time, but something new."

"What then?"

"How shall we know till we see for ourselves; there be Jews there, strange fellows, who say and do wondrous things in the name of a certain Chrestos, their master."

" Magicians after all !" said Onesimus, snapping his
fingers triumphantly.   " I said it."

" Said what ?"

" I myself brought certain Jews up the river six
months ago, who were magicians ; they were civil fellows and asked me to look for them in the street Singon ; but, by Apollo, I forgot them till this moment."

They had reached the place in question by this time,
a narrow thoroughfare, as Onesimus saw at a glance,
and choked with people from end to end. By dint of
much struggling and pushing the three Greeks succeeded in making their way through the crowd to the
spot where, elevated somewhat above the heads of the
people, a man was standing. He was speaking in a
low-toned but powerful voice, and the stillness was
sufficient evidence that he was saying something which
the people were eager to hear.

" For, if ye believe on this Jesus whom I have
preached unto you," were the words which Onesimus heard, " then shall ye become sons of God and
joint heirs with us of his glorious promises, and he
that spared not his own Son for our sakes shall also
with him freely give us all things. And know further,
that he that raised up this Jesus from among the dead
shall quicken our mortal bodies in like manner ; for
to this end Christ both died and rose and revived that
he might be Lord both of the dead and the living.
But I would not have you ignorant, brethren, that all
wickedness and idolatry and filthiness must be put
away from among you ; for neither fornicators, nor

idolators, nor thieves, nor covetous, nor drunkards, nor revilers, nor extortioners shall inherit the kingdom of God, and such are some of you ; but ye must be thoroughly cleansed and sanctified from all sin in the name of the Lord Jesus, and by the spirit of our God."

At this a tumult arose among certain of them which stood near the speaker. "Away with this Jewish knave!" cried one. "He speaks with the tongue of a fool ; we be men and not gods !"

"A sign ! a sign !" bawled a score of his fellows blatantly. "Show us a sign !"

"A pest on this show !" muttered Onesimus impatiently. "There is nothing to be seen here ; these be the same mad Jews I brought to Antioch in my boat. Let us go." And he began to elbow his way once more through the crowd. Suddenly he stopped short, and looked hastily over his shoulder, his ruddy face assuming the color of death. A man who stood in the doorway of a house near by was endeavoring to calm the excited multitude. "I beseech you, good friends !" he said in a loud authoritative voice, "to hold your peace, that those of us who have come from a distance to hear these words may hear them !"

*"Christian ! Christian !" cried a derisive voice from the multitude. At this there was a great outburst of laughter, and the cry was repeated from half a hundred throats, "Christian ! Christian !" In the

---

* Acts xi., 26.

midst of the tumult Onesimus made good his escape out of the street Singon.

"Merciful Apollo!" he muttered, moistening his white lips, "What if he saw me!" He stood for an instant as if undecided, gazing about him with the furtive frightened look of a trapped animal, then turning down a dark and narrow street he sped like the wind towards the river, the derisive cries of "Christian! Christian!" pursuing him more and more faintly as he ran.

CHAPTER XXIII.

THE KING OF THE JEWS.

HEROD AGRIPPA had received at the hands of Claudius the greater kingdom which the latter had promised him, a promise which Agrippa had not been slow to bring to the attention of the emperor, when once he was seated securely upon his ancestral throne.

"I promised thee an addition to thy kingdom?" said Claudius, wrinkling his fat forehead into the multitudinous creases which with him indicated great mental effort. "By my faith, man, I had forgotten it. Moreover, I need thee at Rome; who so clever as Agrippa amongst all my counselors. Stay with me, thou shalt have money—palaces—anything that thou wilt."

"There be many wise men at Rome, imperial majesty," replied Agrippa, his hand upon his heart, "yet are there none wiser than the learned Claudius, whom the gods have but justly rewarded for his virtues by placing him at the head of human affairs; perchance I may serve the master of the world better amongst the turbulent Jews, over whom thou wilt do well to place a strong hand at present."

"By Hercules, thou art right!" cried Claudius,

16

vastly pleased with this delicate imputation of supreme wisdom. "To the Jews thou shalt go; and do thou keep a tight rein over the knaves, for they hate the Roman bit and bridle even as the wild asses of the desert," and the emperor nodded his big head knowingly. "Thou hast already—?"

"The tetrarchy of Trachonitis, royal master," said Agrippa bowing.

"Caius was a selfish dog," remarked Claudius with a comfortable air of superiority. "I said more than once that his end would be a bad one. By the immortals, he treated me—the emperor of Rome—worse than any clown. Ay, that he did; I remember me—"

"Do not, I beseech thee, allow the bitter memories of the past to mingle with the sweet streams of to-day's prosperity," hastily interposed Agrippa, who foresaw a long rambling dissertation on the vices of Caius, which was likely to lead the imperial historian far enough from the matter in hand. "Caius bestowed upon me the tetrarchy of Trachonitis, a meagre gift indeed, though perchance commensurable with my humble merits."

"Take it all," said Claudius briefly but decidedly, throwing himself back in his chair. "I decree it."

"What! Judaea, Samaria, Abilene and the district of Lebanon, beside what I already have?" exclaimed Agrippa, scarce daring to believe his ears. "That were a royal gift indeed!"

"I have said it," said Claudius, bringing down his

broad palm with a resounding thwack. " The emperor of Rome hath decreed it. Let them fetch parchment and the seals straightway."

And so it came to pass that Herod Agrippa sat upon the throne of his father's father, who was called Herod the Great, though truly he was great in nothing but wickedness and unhappiness. No such bitter though salutary reflections visited Agrippa as he entered with great pomp into the holy city of Jerusalem. His ears were filled with the acclamations of the people, who saw in this return of the Asmonean dynasty a restoration of at least a fraction of their ancient rights and privileges ; in his mind he was already revolving ambitious projects to throw off the Roman yoke altogether, that he might be in fact what he was already in name, King of the Jews.

After the gorgeous and imposing ceremonial which took place in the temple in accordance with the ancient custom, the king with his own royal hands hung up in a conspicuous place above the treasury the golden chain, which Caius had given him in place of that iron chain which he had worn for a season.*

" Let this chain," he said piously, " serve to remind the people that however great a mortal may be, God hath the power to put him down from his high estate ; and he that putteth down is also able to exalt, high above all enemies and mischance, him that doeth virtuously." Which indeed was a wholesome saying,

---

* Josephus, Antiq., B. xix., 6.

and one that the king would have done well to re-member.

"Great and exalted be the God of Israel, who hath remembered his people to bless them in the restoration of this their lawful prince!" chanted the priests.

And all the people answered with a loud voice, "Amen, and Amen!"

As for Agrippa, he wept aloud so deep were his emotions; and when the high priest asked him, "Why these tears, O king, on this the day of thy rejoicing?"

He made answer, "I am weeping, reverend and holy priest of the most high Jehovah, because there flow in my veins some foul drops of the accursed Gentile blood; would that I were indeed and in truth a prince of the chosen people of Israel, who alone shall receive prosperity and peace and honor at the hand of their God." With which words, together with the multitude of the sacrifices which he had purchased, he perhaps thought to gain favor in the eyes of that Jehovah, in whom he believed even as he believed in the Olympian Jupiter.

His words did not fail of their intended effect upon the newly-made high priest, who in due time reported them as a matter of solemn rejoicing to the Sanhedrim. "The time of our prosperity is at hand," he said, "for the king also declared to me this day that he hath interceded with the emperor of Rome in our behalf and in behalf of the Jews of every nation, to the end that the temple of the living God be no more

defiled with idolatrous images of any emperor or king.
Moreover we have his promise that hereafter we shall
worship Jehovah after the custom of our ancestors in
all holiness and peace."

"If these things be so," said Jonathan, one of the
sons of Annas, "then ought we to cleanse the holy
city from every hateful heresy and schism which doth
defile it, that Jerusalem may be pure and fair even as
a bride made ready for her husband. Ye cannot be
ignorant, sons of Abraham, that the sect of the Nazarenes, which in days past we endeavored to put down
and destroy by every means in our power, hath again
in the troublous times which have beset us reared its
ugly head in our midst, even as some noisome weed
which waxeth fat and flourishing and bespreads itself
over all the fair garden spaces, if ever the husbandman
neglect the due tilling of the soil. Now must we pursue the work with renewed vigor, since Jehovah hath
regarded our distresses to alleviate them."

And this matter they brought without delay to the
ear of Herod, who gave them willing attention, not-
withstanding the fact that he was on the eve of departing for Caesarea. "I will again hear you of this matter," he said to them suavely ; "and I promise you
that your holy zeal in the matter shall lack no necessary support from my royal authority." With which
vague promise the Sanhedrists were forced to content
themselves for the time being.

"I have long enough played the sanctimonious Jew,
my lady queen," said Agrippa in the privacy of his

palace. "At Caesarea we may hope for a little peace from these importunate long-bearded whining rabbis. By Apollo! they weary me almost beyond endurance."

But Cypros flushed over all her fair face. "I am resolved," she said in her clear low-toned voice, "to serve this Jehovah, who alone of all the gods is true and great. And I pray you, my lord, to observe and do according to all that these holy men, who serve him continually, advise thee; for only by so doing shalt thou continue and prosper in this thy high estate."

Agrippa burst into a loud laugh by way of answer. "Ah, little one," he said, dropping a careless kiss upon the white hand of his queen, "these cunning foxes have gained a point since they have enlisted the fairest champion in all the land upon their side; yet I pray thee, my royal consort, that thou wax not too holy on a sudden, lest thou become also sour and forbidding like to these withered and ancient hypocrites who would teach thee."

Cypros looked troubled. "They be holy men," she said firmly, "and thou wilt do well to heed their counsels, and to propitiate their God by acts of service, that thou mayst reign long and prosperously and thy son after thee."

"What have they been saying to thee, child?" asked Agrippa, a half-mocking, half-tender expression in his dark eyes, as he fixed them upon the fair flushed face of the queen.

"There be wicked men called Nazarenes, my lord the king," she answered, clasping her small hands nervously, "who also blaspheme the great God, and continually do stir up strifes in Jerusalem ; these worship a dead man—a malefactor who was crucified. They declare that he is alive, and that he will usurp thy throne."

"There is no usurper less to be feared than a crucified criminal," answered Agrippa lightly. "May all my enemies be even as is this perished Nazarene ; yet give thyself no uneasiness in the matter. I have the intent to crush out these knaves from my realm, if for no other reason than to please Jerusalem : 'tis a cheap and easy way into the good graces of these Sanhedrists."

But though he had dismissed the matter thus carelessly, Agrippa privily called his chamberlain, one Blastus, and sent him into those parts of Jerusalem where the Nazarenes were chiefly gathered. "Go quietly," he commanded him, "and in such garb that thou be not known as the king's servant, and find out what manner of men these Nazarenes be, what weapons they have, how strong they are in numbers ; and presently bring me word of what thou hast seen."

After two hours Blastus returned. "I have performed thy behests, O king," he said, "and I have accomplished thy commands."

"What then?" demanded Agrippa with an impatient frown. "Waste no words in the telling."

"The Nazarenes be a feeble folk," replied Blastus,

"few in number and unarmed; they differ in no way from the common people of their sort, save that they cherish the memory of a slain malefactor and worship him as a god."

"Didst thou come upon any traces of the man himself?" asked Agrippa. "They tell a wild story of his having survived his crucifixion."

"Nay rather, that he arose from the dead," answered Blastus with a malicious smile. "I sought out one of their principal men, a fellow called James, and asked him many questions concerning their beliefs, professing myself to be one who was ready to join them."

"Thou art a shrewd fellow," said Agrippa approvingly. "And he said—"

"He said that the man Jesus was the prince foretold of the prophets; that he had been rejected by Israel and crucified, despite the fact that he was the only holy and blameless person ever created; that he actually died and was buried, but on the third day he became alive again, and was seen of many of them during a month or more, after which he went up into the air and disappeared."

"A likely tale, by the immortals!" exclaimed Agrippa with a scornful laugh. "Do the knaves pretend to have seen him since?" he added sharply.

"I asked that question, sire," replied Blastus, who was sufficiently shrewd to perceive that some real uneasiness lurked in the breast of his royal questioner. "And the fellow assured me that they had not since

seen him ; but he claims that they are in constant communication with the man, and that he will return after
awhile in great power and glory to rule over the whole
earth."

"The furies fly away with them !" cried Agrippa in
a rage, "such babbling—mad though it be—is no less
than treason ; the knaves shall smart for it. I will
nail a score of them to Roman crosses—they may
follow their master thus far ; then shall we see if they
who remain forget not their folly right speedily, if not,
there is wood enough in my kingdom to furnish them
all."

"They are but visionary madmen, your majesty,"
said Blastus soothingly, "with neither influence nor
power ; while in Caesarea—if I may make bold to
suggest it—there be matters which require the royal
presence and oversight."

"Thou art right," said Agrippa. "After all it
would be a wearisome thing to attempt this matter
now ; let it wait till a more convenient season."

That same day the king departed to Caesarea,
where, amid the royal splendor and pagan pleasures
with which he surrounded himself, he speedily forgot
that such a man as Jesus of Nazareth had ever existed.
His visits to Jerusalem became few and far between,
and while there he chiefly concerned himself with the
massive fortifications which he had commenced, and
which bade fair to render Jerusalem impregnable in case
of an attack. Meanwhile the Sanhedrists bided their
time with what patience they could muster, though

occasional murmurings rose among them as vague reports of the heathen doings in the royal palace at
Caesarea reached their ears.

In the fourth year of the reign of Agrippa it was
currently reported at Jerusalem that the king not only
built theatres for the amusement of the heathen population of Berytus and Caesarea, but that he himself
frequented them in company with unclean Gentiles ;
and further that he had presided in person over a
Caesarean jubilee, at which sacrifices were offered to
the pagan gods in honor of Claudius.

" This is not to be borne, sons of Abraham," declared a zealous Pharisee named Simon, arising in the
midst of the Sanhedrim. " That this Herod is capable
of playing the law-observing Israelite at Jerusalem,
while at Caesarea he becomes a law-breaking and law-
defying Gentile we have long known, and in times
past we have winked at these abominations ; but there
be bounds to our forbearance, set not by ourselves indeed but by the unchanging laws of the eternal Jehovah,
which laws this king hath trodden underfoot. Let
him therefore be altogether a heathen, and let him
keep his foot from our holy temple lest he defile it."

This daring speech was received in silence by the
assembly, since no other man present dared own that
the truth had been spoken. Simon presently received
a summons to appear before the king at Caesarea.

" Sit now beside me," commanded Agrippa, when
he had brought the Jew into the theatre, " and do
thou look carefully upon what thou shalt see, then tell

me if there is aught here which transgresses the law
of Moses; for I have heard of thee that thou art a
very zealous man, and acquainted with what pertains
to the law above all that be at Jerusalem; I therefore
purpose to avail myself of thy wisdom."

Simon trembled exceedingly as he witnessed the
entertainment, which consisted of a battle to the death
between some hundreds of condemned criminals.

"Thou seest, friend, how that law and pleasure may
be justly combined," said Agrippa, with an agreeable
smile at the trembling and pallid Jew. "These men,
whom you observe to be slaying one another, are all
persons who have deserved death for various crimes,
some being murderers, others thieves and highway-
men, while others still are traitors, who have blas-
phemed against the majesty and power of the king.
Now, thinkest thou that Moses himself would object
to so worthy a spectacle, since the beholding of it
serves not only to gratify the innocent but also to warn
the unruly?"

And Simon replied as well as he was able for the
chattering of his teeth, that the king was above all
men wise, and that he saw nothing contrary to the law
in what he had witnessed. Whereupon Agrippa dismissed him graciously with a small present.*

"To behold the face of the knave was a greater
spectacle than the battle of the criminals," declared
Agrippa with a scornful laugh.

---

* Jos. Antiq. B. xix., 4.

But his wife Cypros, who still maintained her ascendancy over him, entreated him to return to Jerusalem and to be at peace with the Sanhedrists. "Thou hast prevailed indeed over this Simon," she said anxiously, "but beware of dealing falsely with these holy men, since I know right well that they be of an unyielding temper."

"I will make amends," declared Agrippa. He returned forthwith to Jerusalem, and sent for the chief men of the Sanhedrim that he might consult them on a matter of importance.

The next day Jerusalem was ringing with the startling news that James, one of the chief of the Nazarenes, had been seized and beheaded in the prison.

CHAPTER XXIV.

A STRONG DELIVERER.

PASSOVER week was almost ended in Jerusalem, yet the throngs of people which filled the holy city showed no disposition to depart.

" I shall remain in Jerusalem until after to-morrow," quoth a Jew from Cilicia to his neighbor from Lebanon, "since to-morrow the Nazarene, Peter, will be crucified."

" He will be crucified?" said the other, raising his brows.

"So they say, so they say, friend ; 'twill be almost as great a spectacle as the crucifixion of the Galilean himself. I witnessed that, thanks be to Jehovah."

" This will assuredly put an end to the Nazarenes," continued the man from Cilicia, stroking his beard complacently, "a good thing too. Not that I know any great evil of them beyond this teaching of the Gentiles, but that is evil enough ; we are a separate people—a holy people, and we must remain so or perish miserably off the face of the earth. Our separateness is the salvation ordained for us by Jehovah."

" Exalted and blessed be his name !" responded the other, closing his eyes with an expression of holy rapture. He opened them again after a proper interval

and fixed them with a steely glitter upon his neighbor.
"I agreed to sell fifty bags of grain to one of these
same Nazarenes yesterday ; he gave me no surety but
bade me come to him on the morrow."

"The more fool thou, son of Abraham," said the
other with a comfortable shrug of the shoulders. "If
thou hast the grain still in hand, thank God for it and
take it to the Gentile woman, Helena ;* she will give
thee double its value without question, for she hath
undertaken to relieve the famine which prevails in the
city, to the end that she may cover her sins and purchase favor with the Almighty—which thing, thank
God, it is impossible for a Gentile to do."

"The Lord hath spoken it, so let it be !"

In another part of Jerusalem the same words were
being uttered in that selfsame hour, yet with a far different meaning. In the house of Mary, the mother of
John, there was gathered on this last night of the
Passover a company of the disciples, and with them
Saul and Barnabas, bearers of good cheer to the
famine-stricken brethren, since they brought to them a
generous gift sent by the newly-converted Greeks at
Antioch to the suffering mother-church at Jerusalem.
Yet the famine which had lain so heavily upon them
for months had been altogether forgotten in the terrible occurrences of the past days. James, the brother

---

* Helena was the queen of Adiabene, a province of Assyria,
and at this time a resident of Jerusalem. She had become a
Jewish proselyte, and being possessed of great wealth took energetic measures to alleviate the prevailing famine.

of that disciple whom Jesus loved, one of the first to
be called by the Master, one of the first to follow, a
chosen witness of the heavenly transfiguration, and of
that not-less-sacred agony in Gethsemane, James had
been seized and put to death so suddenly that those
who remained behind could scarce realize that he was
gone. And now Peter was lying in prison waiting for
the morrow which was to bring him a shameful and
horrible death, unless there should come speedily from
the unseen regions beyond their longing vision some
real and tangible help.

During all the days of that sad Passover week—
only less sad than one other, the bitter-sweet memory
of which would never leave them—a cloud of passionate prayers had ascended without ceasing to their risen
Lord, who had assured them that not a hair should
fall from the head of any one of them without the
Father's notice.

"It is not that he hath forsaken us," said the be-
reaved John ; "for he told us plainly of these days at
that last passover supper when he said, ' Yea, the time
shall come that whosoever killeth you will think that
he doeth God service.' My brother is gone to the
Father's house ; it is well with him. And if that other
saying of our Lord's concerning Peter be about to be
fulfilled, ' Verily I say unto thee, when thou wast
young, thou didst gird thyself and thou didst walk
whither thou wouldst, but when thou shalt be old,
thou shalt stretch forth thy hands and another shall
gird thee and carry thee whither thou wouldst not,'

we must also endure this affliction, knowing that he doeth all things well."

Yet in all patient acceptance of these words they prayed none the less earnestly to God; for had not the Lord also said, " If ye ask anything in my name it shall be done unto you," and also, " Where two or three of you be gathered together in my name there am I in the midst," and again, "Where two of you be agreed on earth as touching anything that you shall ask, it shall be done for you of my Father which is in heaven."

While they thus entreated God for his life, Peter lay in the prison of Herod guarded by four quaternions of soldiers, made fast moreover with chains to the men who lay on either side of him. For the Jews had told Herod of the strange escape of Peter and John out of the prison on a former occasion, and how it was whispered about among the common people that an angel had delivered them.

" No angel intervened to save the neck of the man James from the headsman's sword," said Herod, his lips curling with a scornful smile, "and if angel or devil deliver this knave from the chains which bind him, his guards shall answer with their lives. I have said it."

Therefore the quaternions, which had been detailed for this purpose, watched with the diligence born of mortal fear the man who had been entrusted to their keeping; for the governor of the prison had not neglected to report this saying of Agrippa to his underlings.

As for Peter, he sojourned during seven days in the

valley of the shadow of death, and like many who have perforce tarried there, he found it a wondrous place, a place where the tranquil stream of that river of life which proceeds from out the throne of God and of the Lamb flows noiselessly, mingling its pure waters with that darker flood which divides the narrow valley from the limitless reaches of the celestial country. And so it happened that on the seventh night he slept quite peacefully betwixt his guards, knowing full well that if death awaited him on the morrow, there also awaited him the triumphant song of the redeemed, the robes made white in the blood of the Lamb, and beyond all and above all the rapturous vision of that face beloved, the face of his Lord. And as he slept, the thoughts of the day floated and mingled in cloudy yet glorious imaginings, forms of divine beauty, strains of unearthly melody, faint rustling of angelic pinions, ineffable radiances of heaven-lit spaces.

On a sudden the vision grew clearer; an angel stood by his side clad in the dazzling garb of the celestial city. And his voice was the voice of command. "Arise up quickly!"

Peter arose, and the fetters fell from off his limbs.

"Gird thyself, and bind on thy sandals," whispered the radiant presence. Again the man obeyed.

"Surely," he thought within himself, "I am solaced beyond measure by the glory of this vision; 'tis a foretaste of that beyond, which is now so near."

"Cast thy garment about thee," said the angel once more, turning as if to depart. "Follow me."

Peter followed, still marveling within himself. They were in the street now, the white lustre of the angelic presence casting a clear light upon the dusty pavement as it flitted noiselessly on before. Past familiar streets and squares, through squalid byways and alleys went the twain, and now through the darkness loomed up the massive iron gate which led into the inner city; it swung open noiselessly as the mysterious radiance smote it. The angel passed through; the man followed, still dazed with the wonder of it all.

"I sleep," he said half aloud, "surely I sleep. This is but a vision of the night. Yet I hear the sound of my footsteps on the stones of the street— and yonder a cock is crowing. My Lord, my Lord!" He bowed his face upon his hands in an agony of weeping.

The clarion summons rang out lustily once, twice, thrice; it was echoed faintly from afar, then the silence settled down once more. The man raised his haggard face wet with passionate tears and looked about him; the angelic presence had vanished, but the moon struggling amid a mass of clouds shed a pallid light upon the place where he was standing.

Yonder was the house of John, a faint light twinkled feebly behind its half-closed shutters. "Why do they wake?" he questioned, passing his hand across his eyes in vague bewilderment. "Someone is ill, perchance. Yet I sleep. No—no, this is no dream; the Lord hath sent his angel and hath delivered me out of the hand of Herod. I am saved—saved."

And with the tide of returning life flowing strongly in his veins, he knocked imperatively upon the outer portal of the house.

"It is I, open, I beseech thee!" he said softly, as he heard the sound of a light hesitating footstep within.

But the maid—for it was a young maid named Rhoda who had come to hearken at the door—ran back in haste and joy to those who were within.

"Peter is without!" she cried breathlessly, her pale cheeks glowing like two lamps of delight. "Peter is knocking at the door!"

But the others, more sadly wonted to life, shook their heads. "Nay, girl," they said, "thou art dazed with much wakefulness and sorrow; thou hast imagined it." And this said they, though for seven days they had besought this man's deliverance at the hands of a God whom they professed to believe all-powerful. Truly if the Father gave only in accordance with our faith, we should gather but meagre handfuls of his abundance; but he remembereth our frame.

"Nay, I tell thee it is Peter; I heard his voice, I know his voice! He is knocking—knocking loudly, do you not hear?"

"It is his angel then," said Mary, wiping her eyes, "they have slain him suddenly, even as they slew James."

But the sound of the loud insistent knocking had brought the others to their feet.

"Someone is there of a surety," said John, and he opened wide the door.

"It is I, fear not," said the familiar and well-loved voice. "I am safe; the Lord hath brought me out of the prison by the hand of his angel. But I must not tarry lest I be seized when the morning dawns. Tell James* and the others. Be of good cheer; the Lord is with us alway, even unto the end."

---

* The Lord's brother and Bishop of Jerusalem.

CHAPTER XXV.

RETRIBUTION.

" A DEPUTATION from the Jewish council awaits the king," announced the groom of the bed-chamber with an elaborate obeisance.

" A pest on the Jewish council !" muttered Agrippa scowling. "What do the fellows want at this hour in the morning ?"

" It hath to do with the Nazarene Peter," replied Blastus, who played the part of a judicious go-between betwixt his royal master and the troublesome world without the palace walls.

" And what of him ? The knave dies to-day, after-ward I shall return to Caesarea."

" They say that he hath escaped from the prison, excellent majesty," said Blastus, wrinkling his fore-head deprecatingly, " but if it be so, the man can easily be—"

" Show in the Jews at once," interrupted Agrippa with an imperious gesture.

" How now, my lords," he said in a tone of mani-fest displeasure, as the deputation from the Sanhedrim was ushered into his presence. " Ye have perhaps seen fit to interfere with my provisions for the safety of the prisoner, and by so doing have allowed the fel-low to escape."

"Not so, my lord the king," replied the son of Annas, "the man was bound betwixt two soldiers and guarded by four quaternions, even as thou didst command ; but this morning his fetters were found empty. If perchance the king's clemency hath been implored, and he hath taken this way to release the man, it is enough to say the word."

"Think ye then that I dare not openly release the knave, had I been minded so to do?" demanded Agrippa, the veins of his forehead swelling with rage. "By Apollo, man, thou hast mistaken me ; of whom should I be afraid ?"

The Sanhedrists looked at one another in silence ; no one ventured a reply.

"I undertook the matter for the glory of Jehovah and the peace of Israel," continued Agrippa in a milder tone. "If the man hath escaped the just reward of his iniquities, it only remains for us to punish his guards for their negligence ; which thing shall be done straightway. Let the dogs be fetched."

"Will not your royal highness take any steps towards the apprehension of the criminal?" asked Jonathan, with an air of displeasure, "the people have awaited this day with holy anxiety."

"The inhabitants of Jerusalem are noted for their holiness," said Agrippa, with an unpleasant smile. "We will give them sixteen crosses in place of one ; will not that appease them ? As for the cunning Nazarene, ye have my royal permission to make what search for him ye may see fit ; for ourselves we must be in Caesarea to-morrow to celebrate the safe return of the emperor from his expedition into Britain, a matter of greater moment than the whereabouts of this fellow."

"The guards, your majesty; will your highness examine them here, or—"

"Here and now, in presence of these honorable members of the most holy Council of Jerusalem. Captain of the guard, speak. How is it that the important prisoner committed to your charge hath escaped?"

The soldier to whom he addressed these words looked up; he seemed half paralyzed with terror. "I— I scarce know how it befell, great king," he stammered. "We had watched with all diligence during seven days, the quaternions relieving one another in due order. The prisoner was quiet and gave no trouble; he prayed much to his God. Last night he slept early; we—" The man stopped short.

"Speak on, fellow."

"I know not how it befell," repeated the unhappy wretch, wiping the great drops from his forehead, "but a singular stupor crept over us, and when we came to ourselves the—the prisoner was—gone."

"You slept at your posts!" said Agrippa in a terrible voice. "What then, out of sixteen men was there not one sober enough to observe the king's command?"

"We had drunken nothing, your majesty, save our ordinary allowance of sour wine," replied the soldier with the firmness born of despair. " I speak as a dying man ; I have not forgotten the word of the king. By the soul of my father, and by the immortal gods, I swear that the man was delivered from his bonds not by any agency of flesh and blood but by some intervention of that strange God to whom he prayed, and of this I am the more certain since his fetters showed no sign of violence. Moreover, he had taken time to bind on his sandals, and also to fetch his outer garment, which hung upon a peg seven paces from the spot where he lay bound."

" To what god did the fellow pray?" demanded Agrippa.

" To one Jesus," answered the man steadily. " To us who stood on guard about him, and to the two soldiers who bore his chain he also spoke of the man continually during the days of his captivity."

"What said he concerning this Jesus?"

" That he was the Prince of Peace, the son of the most high God, who so loved men that he gave to them his only son. He also declared that if we would believe on him we should receive everlasting life in place of death, since Jesus also was made alive again after being crucified."

Agrippa threw himself back in his chair, a malignant glitter in his black eyes. " I begin to understand this matter, my lords," he said, addressing the members of the Sanhedrim. " The Nazarene hath converted these dogs to his own interests ; they have therefore released him. They shall bear his punishment. Take them away and crucify them; let it be done before the going down of to-day's sun."

The captain of the guard threw himself at the feet of the king. "A boon, my lord the king!" he cried, "a boon! as thou thyself dost hope for mercy in thy last hour. Grant me, I pray thee, to bear the punishment which thou wouldst have laid upon that other, but spare thou these my comrades who are innocent of any misdeed."

But Agrippa seemed not to have heard; he did not even glance at the despairing faces of the doomed men. "Take them away," he repeated coldly, "and carry out my will upon them."

Which thing was done straightway.

Before the going down of the sun the chariot of the king passed by the spot where stood the sixteen crosses on which were stretched the bodies of the hapless guard.

At the sound of the clattering hoofs and ringing harness-bells which marked the approach of the royal equipage, the man who had vainly besought the lives of his comrades raised his drooping head.

"Death presses hard after thee, O king!" he cried in a loud and terrible voice. "In thy last hour thou also shalt beg for mercy, but it shall not be granted thee."

The royal cortège swept by without pause, the clouds of acrid dust cast up by myriads of hurrying hoof-beats wrapping the ghastly figures of the sufferers in a suffocating shroud, pierced through and through by agonized shrieks and curses, which pursued the retreating chariot, a black throng of avenging demons.

On the day following, that high and mighty personage, Blastus, chamberlain to his powerful majesty, Herod Agrippa, found himself entrusted with a serious and delicate undertaking.

The maritime cities of Tyre and Sidon had been unfortunate enough to offend the king in some question relating to the tribute, and now in the midst of the famine they found themselves confronted with absolute starvation unless friendly relations could be re-established betwixt them and Judaea. Deputies from these cities had therefore been sent to Caesarea that they might take advantage of the festal occasion to present their plea.

"We have come to thee, most excellent Blastus," said one of the deputies from Sidon, "to the end that thou mayst gain for us the royal ear, since it is well known in all the land that there is no one to whom the king listens more attentively than to the wise and prudent Blastus." To which politic address, agreeably prefaced by a large present of money, the king's chamberlain lent a willing ear.

"You have not over-rated the difficulties of your position, my lords," he replied with a solemn wag of the head, "but I am not disinclined to befriend you; not indeed because of your gift to me—which I have accepted as a matter of duty, but because I am sensible of your great misfortune in having fallen under the displeasure of one who is only less great and powerful than Claudius Cæsar himself, whom the gods have made the supreme head of human affairs. You may therefore send to me such gifts and moneys as you have prepared for this occasion, and I will await a favorable season for presenting the same with your petitions, to the end that I may secure you favor with the king."

On this occasion at least Blastus made good his promise, for on the evening of the first day of the festival, word came to the waiting ambassadors that Herod would receive them early the following morning in the theatre.

Long before dawn the place was crowded, men, women and children of every rank, soldiers, courtiers, officials and slaves jostled one another in their eagerness to secure good places for the day of pleasure which awaited them.

"There will be a wild beast show to-day besides the gladiatorial combats," said a woman to her neighbor, as she settled herself comfortably in her place. "A score of African lions will fight fifty condemned criminals to the death, a goodly show. I have fetched little Marcus to see it, though he is sure to give me a deal of trouble before the day is over ; he always cries at sight of blood."

"Oh shame—for a man child, too !" said the other woman, frowning at the little boy, who cuddled his curly head beneath a fold of his mother's robe in his embarrassment. "Look now at my Daphne, only half his years, yet she loves to see the gladiators tear each other. Thou wilt never make a brave soldier, boy, unless thou learn to look boldly upon scenes of blood."

"That's what I tell him," said the mother of the boy crossly.

"Hold up your head now, do! See, here is the king coming in."

"Diana save us!" cried the other, "look at his robe where the sun strikes it; it hath the look of a garment woven from the light itself."

But now the royal heralds were trumpeting forth the signal for silence; the king was seated upon his throne surrounded by all the splendors of his court, himself the most splendid figure of them all, crowned with gems and robed in a marvelous garment of tissued silver.

Again the blare of golden-throated trumpets, and the deputies from Tyre and Sidon, preceded by a detachment of the royal guard, advanced and bowed themselves before the dais.

Agrippa stared at their anxious faces with haughty coldness, as one after another they poured forth their entreaties for his clemency.

"Our lives and the lives of our little ones are in thy hand, O mighty king, for famine and death press hard upon us. To thee alone we look for succor in this our extremity, for if we find not favor in thy sight we shall perish off the face of the earth. Do thou, we beseech thee—whom the gods have raised up to a level with themselves, display a god-like generosity to us at this time, and grant us that peace which we covet."

"I have heard your entreaties, men of Tyre and Sidon," answered Agrippa, "and I have somewhat to say to you in reply." Whereupon he reviewed at length the circumstances which had led to their present distresses, bitterly denouncing their past stubbornness and insubordination.

"Famine-stricken and helpless," he continued, "ye have appealed to me as one whom the gods have raised high above common mortals : and now, since ye have humbled yourselves, and have promised to amend your conduct for the future, I hereby graciously accord you my permission to reopen commerce betwixt my kingdom and your famine-plagued cities, but do not forget that like the father of the gods, I grasp the lightning-bolts of wrath, which shall be loosed to the utter destruction of any city, principality or power which in future ventures to defy me." The king raised his right arm in an authoritative gesture as he spoke the last words ; a wandering sunbeam smote the shifting folds of silver tissue to a dazzling effulgence. For an instant the stately figure seemed to tower to an unearthly stature, robed with splendid light as with a garment.

"A god! A god!" cried a voice from the multitude. "A god and not a man hath spoken to us!"

The dazzled, awe-struck throng lifted up its myriad voice in one mighty cry. "A god! A god!"

Agrippa made no effort to stay the tumult.

"I know no god greater than myself," he said within his heart.

At that moment the death-angel stood beside the king, a glorious unseen presence. His sword was in his hand.

"There is no god greater than myself," said Agrippa, and he laughed aloud. The laugh ended in a shriek of agony; the invisible sword had descended, piercing through splendid robe and gemmed girdle deep to the guilty heart beneath.

"I am dying," moaned the king, as his frightened courtiers gathered about him. He lifted his anguished eyes as if in quest of some help outside that circle of horrified faces, then he threw up his hands with a gesture of despair.

"Take me away!" he wailed, "it is there—the bird of fate—the bird of death."

As they lifted him, a small brown owl which had been staring solemnly down at the scene flitted noiselessly away with a short sharp cry.

They carried the king to his palace, where he lived for full five days, tortured with pangs unutterable, crying for mercy to a heaven which seemed to him as brass, and to a God whom he knew at last to be greater than himself. Having learned this lesson, he was released from his body of death and fled away into that great silence whither we may not follow him.

CHAPTER XXVI.

SENT FORTH.

IN Antioch life was flowing in the old channels. Men still trafficked and fought, loved and hated, cursed and prayed. The strong yet trampled the weak under foot and stifled their wails of anguish in shallow paupers' graves. A never-ceasing babble of awful sounds, an ever-shifting phantasmagoria of frightful suffering and not less frightful gayety, into which as into a resistless whirlpool flowed a perpetual tide of white speechless souls from out the hither darkness, and out of which drifted a dark cloud of the lost—lost because unwittingly they had lived; such was Antioch.

To this Antioch returned the two men, who believed that God so loved the world that he gave his only begotten son for its salvation; who believed that a certain Jesus of Nazareth—a Jew like themselves, poor, obscure, despised, even by his own nation, and hounded at last to a shameful death—was the incarnate deity, drawn by pure love and pity down from the unimaginable reaches of an unseen heaven; who believed that in this God-man lay the eternal remedy for eternal woe, comfort for sorrow and bitter crying, healing for sickness and wounds, life more abundant for hopeless

death, a mighty, everlasting, unsearchable, unknowable love, strong enough to lift the wretched wailing
world in its arms as would a mother.   Like Moses
they had looked upon this love, and their faces shone.

In Antioch they gathered about them those who
had also seen.   "It is for you to spread the glad-
tidings in this place," they said, "but we must go
forth whither the spirit leads us."   Yet they tarried
awhile to fast and to pray, lest haply they might have
mistaken the yearning of their own hearts for the
word from on high.

"Separate me Barnabas and Saul for the work
whereunto I have called them," came the command.

So when the brethren had fasted and prayed they
laid their hands upon them, in token that thus were
they set apart for the work, as yet only dimly comprehended by any of them.

Three men—for they took with them the young
John Mark—against a world !   Three men, in the eyes
of that world a band too feeble, too utterly insignificant
to merit even a laugh of scorn, yet sent forth by the
Holy Spirit, girt about with power irresistible, attended
by legions of angels, led by the cloudy fiery pillar no
less truly than the Israelites of old.   Three men, and
with them walked yet another, "and the form of the
fourth was like the Son of God."

At Seleucia, sixteen miles from Antioch, the little
company took ship for the island of Cyprus, and there
in the city of Salamis tarried for a time that they might
preach the word of God in the synagogues of the Jews.

Sergius Paulus, the Roman governor of Cyprus, was universally acknowledged to be a prudent man; a brave man he unquestionably was, and by virtue of this quality he held sway over beautiful Cyprus, living like a petty king in his palace at Paphos, surrounded by lesser officials, courtiers and sycophants who vied with one another in fawning upon the great men of the country.

To this Paphian court there came one day a wretched half-starved Jew. "I am a wise-man, noble Roman," he whined coaxingly to the guard who interrogated him concerning his business in the neighborhood of the proconsular residence. "I can look far into the future and tell what will befall a man: for thyself, honorable sir, I see—ah, what enviable fortunes!"

The soldier nothing loath fetched him into camp, where all day long he plied his craft with sufficient industry to earn a share of the rude supper, of which indeed he seemed in sore need.

"By Bacchus!" exclaimed one of the centurions shrugging his shoulders. "The Jewish dog hath either a nimble wit or a compact with the powers of the nether world. He told me what I supposed no one save myself had ever thought of—the truth too."

"The furies love their own," replied his comrade sententiously, "but what might one expect from a Jew, whose nation also is said to venerate the ass and worship the pig? Dost thou deny it, fellow?" he added with a brutal laugh, seeing that the Jew had approached them and was listening.

18

A look of malignant hatred blazed for an instant in the black eyes of the soothsayer as he turned them upon his questioner, but his voice was smooth and persuasive as ever as he answered, " The noble lord is mistaken ; we do not worship the—the—other thing,"* an involuntary shudder ran over his thin figure, " nor do we venerate the ass. We worship—but why do I speak thus, it is no matter : the noble lord perhaps wishes to know—" here he stepped quite close and whispered something into the ear of the Roman.

" By the immortals !" cried the soldier, his face flushing hotly, " Who told thee that ?"

" The ass whom I am supposed to venerate hath perchance communicated it to thee his brother," answered the Jew with a wicked laugh, " and I can tell thee more."

" No, by Hades, I will hear no more ! Thou art a lying slave ; I will have thee scourged."

" Nay, not so, noble sir, lest the furies scourge thee," and the Jew turned his back upon the twain.

" The knave hath the better of thee there," cried the centurion with a huge laugh. " Who knows what he is ?" he added with a superstitious shiver, "and whether he be not lately 'scaped from the realms of death and night."

The other swore softly to himself as he looked after

---

* No Jew would so much as name the despised and forbidden swine, but referred to it when compelled to do so as " *the other thing.*"

the retreating figure of the soothsayer, but he made no effort to carry out his threat.

The fame of this strange being spread apace, and it was not many days before he was ordered to appear in the presence of the governor himself.

"What is thy name, sirrah?" questioned Sergius Paulus, staring hard into the yellow wizened face of the soothsayer.

"My name is Bar-jesus, may it please your excellency," replied the Jew, apparently unmoved by the magnificence of the official presence.

"Bar-jesus—Bar-jesus!" repeated the Roman looking perplexed. "Where have I heard that name of late? Surely there was something strange told me concerning it. Ah yes, there was a certain prophet, a wonder-worker bearing the name of Jesus; art thou he?"

"I am a prophet, verily," replied the Jew with an inscrutable smile. "And I am more. All things which have happened are known to me; likewise of all that shall come to pass is there nothing hid from my eyes. The stars in their courses, the flight of the mountain eagle, the foot of the wild beast in the trackless desert are not more strange than are the wanderings of the soul unfettered from the body by sleep, yet all of these things are plain and open unto me: for this reason I am called also Elymas, which is being interpreted, The Wise."

"I have heard the like before," said the governor, leaning back in his chair with a cynical smile. "Rome swarms with thy sort. If it be lies, or if it be truth that ye tell, what after all matters it ; there is naught that can befall a man which hath not already been experienced by myriads of his fellows, and the end is the same—death. Yet it may amuse our over-abundant leisure to hear thee in thy craft at times ; remain therefore, and be ready when I shall call for thee."

Thus it happened that the Jew, Bar-jesus, otherwise known as Elymas, was installed a member of the proconsular household at Paphos. Being in his way quite as prudent a man as Sergius Paulus, he was not slow to avail himself of the advantages of his position. Having presently acquired an almost unlimited power over the slaves and lesser officials, he was denied nothing in the way of the choicest meats, drinks and dainties which the palace afforded ; in addition to this a steady stream of gold, silver and copper coins— for your truly wise man despises not the small things of the earth—speedily found its way into his greedy palm. He grew sleek and flourishing apace ; the soft stealthy rustle of his silken robe, 'broidered all over with strange hieroglyphs, came at length to sound in the ears of the cringing menials like the dread pinions of the great reaper himself. Sergius Paulus, it was true, still laughed at his pretensions, but it was noticed that he was more and more often closeted with the Jew, and no secret was made of the fact that on more than one occasion he had conducted matters of importance according to his advice.

"There be new arrivals in town—also wise men,"

said the groom of the bed-chamber one day to the slave who had fetched the scented water for his lordship's hands.

" Of what nation ?"

" Jews, I am told, but not like—" The speaker paused and looked apprehensively over his shoulder. "One never knows," he added in a half whisper, "when our wizard is about, he is—"

" An evil spirit," put in the other boldly, "there is no doubt of it, and I will say it though I be burned a thousand years, as he is wont to threaten us."

" That thou shalt be, knave," said a sneering voice from behind, " but to discipline thy unruly tongue until the burning begin, I grant thee a present wholesome torment." The sorcerer laid a long skinny forefinger upon the forehead of the cringing slave ; the man started back with a shriek.

" Mercy, good wizard !" he howled, sinking upon his knees before his tormentor, " have mercy upon me, I meant no harm ; 'twas but a jest—I swear it !"

" Out of my way, dog !" said the Jew with a terrible imprecation, and he passed on into the presence of his patron, leaving the slave groveling upon the floor.

The governor, Sergius Paulus, was in a state of pleasurable anticipation. " I have sent for thy countrymen who are in our city, good Elymas," said the great man with unwonted geniality. " They are saying wondrous things, I am told, concerning their God ; I am minded to hear them."

"In an evil day hast thou sent for these men!" cried Elymas throwing up his hands with a tragic gesture. "As destroyers of thy peace they come; a sharp sword is betwixt their lips, and the poison of asps under their tongues! As thou lovest ease of body and health of bone admit not these knaves to thy presence!"

"I shall hear them of the matters whereof they speak," said the governor coldly, "even as I heard thee, when thou wast a starveling magic-monger among the soldiers of my camp.'

Elymas shrank back at this allusion to his former poverty, biting his nails and muttering darkly to himself. He did not speak again, and the strangers were presently shown into the presence.

Sergius Paulus stared at them curiously. "Jews, certainly," he said within himself. "In want of money," he added cynically—"empty leeches as are they all:" he determined not to allow the new-comers to fasten themselves upon him.

"Your name and business in Cyprus," he said at length, addressing the elder of the two men.

"My name is Joses," replied the stranger, with a respectful inclination of the head. "I am also called Barnabas. I am a Jew, born on this island, but for many years resident in Jerusalem. I have returned to my native Cyprus in company with my comrade Saul, a Jew also and native of Cilicia, that together we may make known the glad-tidings concerning one Jesus of Nazareth."

"Saulos!" repeated the governor with a sneering laugh, "Saulos!* truly the name of thy comrade hath an evil sound, yet for a sorcerer—if such ye be—"

"We are not sorcerers, most noble Sergius," said Saul, with the authoritative tone and gesture which compelled attention, and which was habitual with him. "As for my name, Saul, it is not dear unto me; I bear also another name by which henceforth I am minded to be called, since its signification suits me, who am least of them which believe; that name is Paulus."†

"By what right dost thou assume a Roman name, fellow?" said the proconsul haughtily.

"By right of birth," answered Saul steadily. "I am a Jew, but I am also a Roman citizen."

The face of the governor changed perceptibly. "I will hear thee of thy matters which thou hast been expounding to the Cyprians," he said graciously, "if thou art a Roman thou dost not herd with such as the fellow yonder."

Elymas started forward, his evil face white and threatening. "The knave hath lied!" he shrieked. "Can I not read his heart?"

"Silence!" thundered the governor, "or I have thee removed by the guard. Tell me, good Paulus, of this Jesus of Nazareth, for I have heard somewhat concerning him, and I would fain hear more."

So Saul beginning at the beginning preached to him

---

* Saulos, the Greek form of the Hebrew name Saul or Shaûl, signifies *wanton*.

† Paul or Paulus signifies *little*.

Jesus of Nazareth, Son of God and son of man, slain in his innocence, as a lamb without spot or blemish, for the salvation of a lost world. And Sergius Paulus listened, leaning forward in his chair as one who is deeply stirred.

"A newness of life!" he murmured, as the deep eloquent tones of the speaker ceased. "Can it be true then, that death does not end all?" He raised his eyes thoughtfully only to find the black snake-like gaze of Bar-Jesus riveted upon him. The Jew who had been watching the scene in an agony of impotent rage, again thrust himself betwixt the strangers and his erstwhile patron and believer.

"Wilt thou then allow thyself to be miserably deluded and led away by these hypocritical knaves," he cried in a choked voice; "all that they have said is most blasphemous wickedness, and lies—foul lies! I also am a Jew, and I am not ignorant concerning the Scriptures and prophecies of my race; if thou wilt learn concerning the great Jehovah, can not I teach thee, as also I have taught thee other things? Hast thou forgotten—" he stooped and whispered a word or two into the ear of the governor, who drew back visibly shaken.

Then Saul, who was also called Paul, filled with the Holy Spirit, set his eyes upon the man.

"O, full of all subtilty and all mischief, thou child of the devil, thou enemy of all righteousness, wilt thou not cease to pervert the right ways of the Lord? And now, behold, the hand of the Lord is upon thee, and thou shalt be blind, not seeing the sun for a season !"

Immediately there fell upon the sorcerer a mist and a darkness ; and he went about seeking some one to lead him by the hand.

As for Sergius Paulus, when he saw what was done, he was astonished, and he believed from that hour.

CHAPTER XXVII.

A LIGHT OF THE GENTILES.

"FOR myself I am resolved to go no further; I shall return to Jerusalem." The face of the speaker was pale and determined, though the hand which he laid on the rude table trembled visibly.

The three travelers had just arrived at Perga and had broken a long fast at the little inn near the wharf. The older men discussed plans for the future as they ate. They determined that since the greater part of the population of the city was about making its annual migration to the mountain uplands, it would be useless to tarry in Perga.

" We will follow the caravans, preaching wherever we have opportunity," Paul had said, looking thoughtfully at John, who sat opposite him. " We shall thus be able to make our way through regions otherwise inaccessible. Truly, all things work together for us when we are about our Master's business."

Then it was that the young man had announced his determination to return to Jerusalem. There was dead silence for a full moment after he had spoken; presently Barnabas asked—his voice full of anxiety:

" Art thou sick ?"

" Nay, cousin, I am well enough in body, but I am

sick at heart," said John, rising to his feet and pacing restlessly up and down. "Of what use is our labor? There are but three of us to face a world. These Gentiles to whom we preach profess to believe, it is true, but what will hinder them from returning to their false gods, once we have left them? The Roman, Sergius Paulus, listened to the Jew, Bar-Jesus, and believed; yesterday he heard us, beheld a miracle and—believed. To-morrow it may chance that a wandering Chaldean with his blasphemous magic will claim his ear; he will again believe. And for such trophies as this we are about to penetrate a wild mountain region of which we know nothing, save that famine and thirst and wild beasts abound there. Follow a caravan? Madness! We could not keep up with it. I tell you that we throw our lives away to attempt such a thing; and why, indeed, should we attempt it? is there not work in abundance lying ready to our hand at home? Are there no Gentiles in Judæa? As I have said, I am constrained to abandon the project here and now, and thou wilt do well, cousin, if thou shalt think twice before leaping into the darkness which is before thee."

"God hath blessed thee and kept thee in past days, my son," said Barnabas, his voice trembling, "surely he will not forsake thee now, who hast laid thy hand to the plow in the strength and vigor of thy youth."

"I am ready and willing to work," answered the young man sullenly; "but a prudent man must count the cost of his ventures."

The deep voice of Paul broke the silence that followed. "Thou hast said a true word, friend," he said. "A prudent man must count the cost of his ventures; but I count not my life as dear unto myself since Christ died for sinners, of whom I am chief. Thou shouldst be able to endure hardness, my brother, even as a good soldier of Jesus Christ. If a man would run in the arena he is not crowned except he finish the race. Yet go thy way—if thou canst not come with us willingly, and the Lord give thee a better mind."

So the young man turned back to Jerusalem, carrying a sore heart within his bosom. But Paul and Barnabas went on into the mountain-ranges of Taurus, traveling sometimes with a passing caravan, sometimes alone and on foot, toiling over well-nigh impassable tracts of desert country, parched with the glaring heat of cloudless noons, drenched by sudden storms, "in perils of waters, in perils of robbers, in perils in the wilderness, in weariness and painfulness, in watchings often, in hunger and thirst, in fastings often, in cold and nakedness," until at length after many days they came to the Roman colony of Antioch, just beyond the great pass into Pisidia.

In Antiochia Caesarea, as it was also called, they went to the synagogue of the Jews at the appointed time for worship, and when after the reading of the law and the prophets, the rulers of the synagogue sent to them as was the custom, saying, "If ye have any word of exhortation for the people, we pray you give it now." Paul stood up and began to speak.

"Men of Israel, and ye that fear God, pay good heed to what I shall say to you." All that were in the synagogue fixed their eyes eagerly upon him, for his message shone in his face. First the speaker reviewed briefly the wonderful history of Israel, chosen from among the nations, delivered out of Egypt, sustained in the wilderness during the long training time of forty years; brought with a strong arm into the land of promise. Passing on over the rule of the judges, prophets and kings of Israel, he spoke of David, of whom also God said, "I have found David, the son of Jesse, a man after mine own heart, which shall fulfill all my will.—Of this man's seed hath God according to his promise raised unto Israel a Saviour, Jesus."

Then in words plain, simple and easy to be understood he proclaimed unto them the marvelous life and death of Jesus, rejected and slain by the dwellers in Jerusalem, "because they knew him not, nor yet the voices of the prophets which are read every Sabbath day, which also they fulfilled in condemning him. And when they had accomplished all that was written of him, they took him down from the tree and laid him in a sepulchre. But God raised him from the dead!

"Be it known unto you, men and brethren, that through this man is preached unto you the forgiveness of sins; and by him all that believe are justified from all things, from which ye could not be justified by the law of Moses. Beware therefore, lest that come upon you which is spoken of in the prophets; Behold, ye despisers, and wonder, and perish; for I work a work in your days, a work which ye shall in no wise believe, though a man declare it unto you."

When the service was finished, the rulers of the synagogue and the chief men went away without further notice of the two strangers, for they were displeased with what had been spoken, but many of the humbler Jews, together with certain Gentiles who were proselytes, followed them and asked that the same words might be preached to them the next Sabbath; Paul and Barnabas talked with these further and persuaded them to continue in the grace of God.

The next Sabbath day came almost the whole city together to hear the word of God. And when the elders of the congregation looked forth over the mixed multitude which filled their quiet orderly place of worship full even to overflowing they were angry.

" Look you," said the ruler of the synagogue, who was called Eliphaz. " Here be blasphemers, eaters of the unclean beast, and idolaters, which these men have gathered from out the four corners of our city; our synagogue is defiled by them, the sanctity of the law is threatened; the peace of Israel is disturbed. So now let us withstand the man to his face as he shall speak, lest the walls of our Zion be broken down and we be left desolate."

Accordingly as Paul again proclaimed the glad-tidings of Jesus, a Saviour from sin, a holy and acceptable sacrifice made once for all, releasing man from the burden of the law—a Christ raised from among the dead into an eternity of glory, they broke in with loud denials, calling upon the people to pay no heed to the strangers.

" Who are these men ?" cried the ruler of the synagogue, beating the air with his hands, " who come unknown and unheralded into our midst ? Behold, they speak lies and blasphemies ! If this man Jesus, whom they proclaim, was condemned to death by the most holy council of Jerusalem, then are we satisfied that he deserved to die, for what higher or more sacred tribunal is there on earth than the Sanhedrim ? If he was crucified, you that are Romans will know that he must have been a great criminal, for Roman justice hath become a proverb even among us. Shall we who live holy lives after the law, suffer these loud-mouthed strangers to speak against the law ? Shall we who long for the coming of our promised King, listen without a protest to these blasphemous knaves as they proclaim in this holy place a criminal done to death on the accursed tree, as the Messiah of Israel ?"

An indescribable tumult followed this outburst, some crying out one thing, and some another. But Paul and Barnabas stood unmoved, silenced indeed by the uproar, but calm and evidently unafraid of the now furious Jews.

"Away with them ! Away with them !" shrieked some, " Stone the blasphemers !"

" Hear ! hear ! Let us hear what they will say !"

At length some measure of order having been

restored by the active interference of the officers of the synagogue, Paul turned to the man who had insulted them.

"It was necessary that the word of God should first be spoken to you," he said with no sign of anger in face or voice; "but seeing that ye thrust it from you, judging yourselves to be unworthy of eternal life, lo, we turn to the Gentiles. For so hath the Lord commanded us, saying: 'I have set thee to be a light of the Gentiles, that thou shouldst be for salvation unto the ends of the earth.'"

At this the Greeks and other foreigners who were in the synagogue raised a cry of joy and triumph; many of them also believed, and these carried word of the glad-tidings throughout all the country about Antioch.

But the Jews were not minded to let the matter rest. Among their proselytes were certain foreign women of high rank, who had embraced the Jewish faith with all the ardor of empty hearts. To these women they went, knowing full well that through them they might hope to enlist the co-operation of the authorities.

"Who knows, noble lady," said the wily Eliphaz to the wife of the Roman deputy, "but that, like the noble queen Esther of old, thou wast called to the kingdom for such a time as this; if thou shalt through thine influence rid our city of these noxious blasphemers, the blessing of Jehovah shall abide with thee In no small measure."

The lady straightway laid the matter before her husband.

"Turbulent strangers—created a disturbance in the synagogue—set the Jews by the ears. Not a hard thing to do; they are quarrelsome dogs," grumbled that official frowning. "Peaceable enough before, dost thou say? That is true; and the religion of the Jews is the only true religion? yes—so thou hast told me before. Well, and what dost thou want of me in the matter?"

"Put them to death, my lord!" cried the lady, an angry glitter in her blue eyes, "they are blasphemers!"

The Roman shrugged his shoulders, "Thou art an over-apt pupil, my Julia," he said filliping her pink ear betwixt his thumb and forefinger. "I must take thee back to Rome till thou shalt forget what these hypocritical knaves have taught thee, for, by Apollo, I like it not. Yet I will see to it that these beggars be sent about their business—and at once; there shall be no disturbances of any sort in the place, whilst I govern it."

So it happened that Paul and Barnabas received official notice that their presence in Antioch was no longer desired.

"If ye be found in the borders of the city after midday," ran the order, "we can no longer be answerable for your bodily safety."

"When they persecute you in one city flee ye to another," quoted Barnabas, handing the missive to his companion.

"We have kindled the fire," said Paul thoughtfully; "the opposition of the Jews is even as the empty wind which will serve to spread the flames far and wide. Come, let us be going."

CHAPTER XXVIII.

A MESSENGER OF THE MOST HIGH.

"WE have rid ourselves of the blasphemers it is true, but alas! I fear me that our duty hath been but poorly performed." Eliphaz, ruler of the synagogue in Pisidian Antioch, wagged his head gently from side to side as though his feelings were too deep for utterance.

"In what have we failed? Surely Israel hath triumphed gloriously. Our enemies have departed weighed down with defeat and humiliation, Jehovah be praised! I myself saw the men as they passed out from the city gates followed by a filthy rabble of dogs and Gentiles—who despite the driveling flattery of the knaves were not slow to pursue them with stones and curses."

"Would that they had stoned the life out of them!" cried Eliphaz with sudden energy. "Hear, sons of Abraham! We have sent forth this foul heresy, which is even as a deadly serpent, threatening to smother in its sinuous coils the body of suffering Israel, and in this have we sinned : we should rather have dealt with them according to the law, and the law is death."

"Impossible, my brother, without the Roman authority," objected one of the council mildly; "the

men had transgressed no law of Roman making—
which is the only law the accursed recognize."

Eliphaz rolled up his eyes to heaven. "How long,
O Lord, how long!" he wailed, wringing his bony
hands and beating upon his breast.

The councilors gazed at him with respectful admiration. "What zeal! what holy zeal!" they murmured. "Ah! what a godly man is our ruler,
Eliphaz, son of Eliud."

The son of Eliud ceased to beat upon his breast
after a time; he sat quite motionless with closed eyes.
His brother officials pulled at their venerable beards
in silence.

"I am going to the city of Iconium," said Eliphaz
presently, in the feeble voice of one exhausted by his
emotions. "The blasphemers have gone thither."

The councilors looked at one another in rapturous
surprise. What a wonderful man was this ruler of
theirs; truly was there any knowledge to which men
could attain that he had not already grasped.

"I shall expose them there," continued Eliphaz
slowly, opening his small grey eyes. "I shall—
accomplish their death."

"Jehovah be praised!" exclaimed the council in a
chorus.

Iconium in the midst of its green oasis, stands like
a sentinel on the border of that interminable waste of
bleak and dreary upland which stretches away to meet
the distant ranges of snow-clad mountains. A pleasant and peaceful spot was the little city, where life

flowed smoothly on most days of the year, yet within
the waxing and waning of a single moon the place had
become the scene of a strange warfare—carried on, it
is true, with only tongues for weapons ; but is it not
written, The tongue is a little member, but boasteth
great things. It came to pass at length in Iconium
that all the inhabitants of the city, as many as could
wield this small but mighty weapon, were divided into
two factions, betwixt which the battle raged unremit-
tingly. What then had happened ?

Two strangers, upon whose heads rested the mysterious flame of the Spirit, whose lips also had been
touched with a live coal from off the altar, had kindled
this fierce outburst with but a few plain and simple
utterances. Jesus of Nazareth is the son of the Most
High God—the Messiah ! He was slain upon the
cross, but God hath raised him from the dead. He
hath fulfilled the law. In him alone is forgiveness of
sins and life everlasting.

And those that would, took of the bread and water
of life and were healed forthwith of the maddening
pangs of soul-hunger ; but to them who would not,
the words sounded like the babbling of demoniacs.

"These men are true prophets !" cried one from out
the multitude. "Behold the wonders of healing
wrought by their hands !"

"O fools and blind !" wailed Eliphaz, from the steps
of the synagogue. "These men also led after them
a base rabble of the accursed in Antioch, and were
expelled from out our city, clad with shame as with a

garment. Children of the devil are they, and through the powers of darkness they work these seeming cures. Beware lest to-morrow these sick folk whom they have defiled with their touch perish in torments."

The mob, composed of Jews and the dregs of the foreign population, needed no urging ; stopping only to gather up the loose paving-stones from the street, they rushed with a howl toward the great central square of the city where the strangers had been wont to preach to the multitudes.

"Rend the wretches limb from limb ! Stone them ! Knive them !"

But the strangers were nowhere to be found ; warned of the murderous designs against them, they had quietly left the city some hours before and were well away on the road to Lystra, a small town forty miles distant.

There was no synagogue in the mountain village of Lystra, but a temple to Jupiter reared its walls just outside the gates, where the primitive inhabitants were wont to implore the favor of their guardian deity. After some consultation the travelers asked leave to speak to the people in the market-place : permission being readily granted, they proclaimed to the wondering villagers the glad-tidings of the cross.

Among those that listened eagerly once and again, the keen eye of Paul noticed a wretched cripple, who was fetched to the market-place day by day that he might ask alms of the passers-by.

As the beggar listened for the third time to the

wondrous story of Jesus, Paul perceived that singular
shining in his eyes which indeed cannot be hid, for it
is the light of heaven.

"The man hath faith to be healed," he thought
within himself, and fixing his compelling eyes upon
the cripple, he said with a loud voice, "Stand upright
on thy feet!"

Immediately the man leapt up and walked.

"A wondrous miracle!" cried one of the specta-
tors in the rustic speech of Lycaonia, "Behold the
gods are come down to us in the likeness of men!"

Paul and Barnabas perceiving that they could speak
no further with the people because of the uproar, yet
understanding nothing of what was being said, retired
to their lodging-place.*

"Was I not oppressed with awe when the venerable
stranger approached me?" said the chief man of the
village, gesticulating violently in his excitement. "Behold his majestic height, his flowing beard, his benig-
nant front. Lo, our guardian Zeus hath visited his
people in human form!"

"O wondrous day! O blessed day!" cried the
multitude in ecstacy.

"And the younger stranger," broke in another,
"with his fiery eyes, his eloquent tongue and his
small agile figure, who should this be save the mes-

---

* The Apostle's discourse to the Lycaonians was doubtless
delivered in the Greek tongue, which was universally understood
at that day, but the people in their excitement very naturally
lapsed into the native vernacular.

senger, Hermes, who ever attends the sovereign Zeus, and who hath graciously given from the divine power of his winged feet to the feet which never have walked."

"Let us do them honor straightway, lest they be offended and smite us in their wrath!" counseled the priest of Jupiter, who had been fetched with haste to the scene of the miracle.

Selecting from among their herds the snow-white bullocks, reserved for the great triennial festival of the Olympic deities, the priests brought them with solemn chanting before the gates, where was assembled a festive crowd of citizens, eager to do honor to the divine visitants. Quickly they formed into line, the priests walking in front leading the victims, wreathed and garlanded. Then followed in good order, citizens on foot, armed with spear and shield, with others on horseback; the old men of the village bearing olive branches, and the wives of the chief men laden with votive offerings; after these walked young virgins two by two, carrying baskets containing the sacred knives and vessels to be used in the forthcoming sacrifice; last came the humbler matrons and young children. Every face shone with joy, every voice was upraised in the sacred hymn of thanksgiving as the little procession wound through the village streets toward the house where lodged the two strangers.

"Hearest thou the sound of rejoicing, gracious divinity," said the man of the house, approaching his guests with deep reverence. "I pray thee, heaven-born stranger, who hast honored my humble roof with

thy presence, speak now with thine august companion
—before whose face I scarce venture to stand, and tell
him that the priests and the people are approaching
with sacrifices to do him honor."

Paul looked up in sudden consternation from the
parchment roll which he was studying. "Surely thou
dost mistake—" he began, then he stopped short; the
sounds of loud joyous voices and the lowing of oxen
floated in at the open window.

"Tell me," he said sternly, turning to his host, who
was staring at Barnabas with wide reverent eyes, "what
do the people take us to be?"

"Do not be angry with me, O Hermes, if the people
have discovered thy divinity, hidden though it be beneath the veil of flesh," wailed the man sinking to his
knees.

"Hermes!" cried Paul in amaze. "O foolish man,
what hath bewitched thee!" He grasped his companion by the arm. "They think us gods!" he said
hurriedly, "Come, let us go forth to them."

"Behold the gods!" cried the multitude, which had
gathered about the house; the cry was echoed by a
jubilant shout from the approaching procession.

"Sirs!" cried Paul in a loud voice, rending his garment as he ran among them, "why do ye these things?"

"They are not minded to reveal their divinity, my
children," said the priest of Jupiter solemnly, "nevertheless it is fitting that we do them sacrifice."

"Not so! I declare to you that we also are men
of like passions with you; we proclaim to you that

ye should turn from these vanities unto the living God, who made heaven, and earth, and the sea, and all things that are therein."

The priests had fallen back now, and were staring suspiciously at the speaker.

" God in times past suffered all nations to walk in their own ways ; yet he left not himself without witnesses, in that he did us good, and gave us rain from heaven, and fruitful seasons, filling our hearts with food and gladness."

The priests turned resolutely away, leading the votive offerings. " There is some strange mystery here," they said. " We will slay the beasts before the temple and consult the entrails."

" What hath happened in your city to-day ?" asked a bearded and turbaned stranger, politely accosting one of the inhabitants who was following the retreating priests, " for I perceive by the commotion in your streets that it is a matter of no small moment."

" A matter of no small moment indeed !" answered the man sullenly. " Two strangers who have tarried in our town for three days past—who have also spoken strange things and hard to be understood—performed a miracle in our midst, the like of which was never seen in these parts, but when we would have done them reverence — supposing them to be gods, they refused to listen to us, and proclaimed some strange deity, calling upon us to forsake the gods of our fathers, which have protected us from the days of old even until now."

At that the new-comer rent his clothes. "Alas!" he cried in a loud voice, "the deceivers who have wrought ruin in Iconium and in Antioch have come hither also! Know, unhappy Lystrians, that these men are foul blasphemers, children of the wicked one, who will assuredly lead you away into eternal death, if ye resist them not!"

"Blasphemers—sorcerers—murderers!" the blasting words ran like forked lightning amid the sullen disappointed crowd.

"If ye would save yourselves from the wrath of the great God," cried the stranger, "slay these men and cast them forth from your walls!"

As in Iconium the people needed no second bidding; arming themselves with stones, they rushed back to the spot where but an hour since they had stood with joyous faces, chanting their simple hymns of thanksgiving. Paul was still speaking to the few who had lingered behind, and upon him they fell savagely. A whirlwind of sticks, stones, and dust, a smothered groan, savage shouts and imprecations, frightened shrieks and sobs from the on-looking women and children, and all was over.

"The loud-mouthed liar will trouble Lystra no more!" said a brawny peasant with an oath, as he wiped the dust from his face.

"So perish all enemies of the law!" murmured the turbaned and bearded strangers. "But come, let us hasten, we be already grievously defiled by the touch of these idolaters." And having accomplished their pious purpose, they went their peaceful way to their own cities.

Outside the walls of Lystra in the dim twilight, a weeping group gathered about the motionless body of a man which lay upon the ground.

" It cannot be that he is dead !" wailed the beggar whom he had healed.   " It cannot—cannot be !"

" Let me try this fresh water," said a gentle voice in the ear of Barnabas, as he crouched quite bewildered with grief at the side of his stricken comrade. " It may be that he is only stunned.   Ah, see ! I am sure that he stirred !"

Presently the dim eyes opened, and the voice which no one of them had hoped to hear again murmured, " It is a faithful saying, if we die with him, we shall also live with him : if we suffer, we shall also reign with him."

CHAPTER XXIX.

THE CALLING OF TIMOTHY.

THE wife of the dead Andronicus dwelt in a small house near the gates of Lystra. She mingled little with her gayer neighbors, and was but seldom seen either at the fountain or in the market-place, never in the temple of Jupiter. "She is a Jewess," whispered her neighbors with a shrug, when the young Greek first brought his dark-eyed bride to dwell in the village. The whisper was repeated many times during the quiet years that followed, but it was never more than a whisper, for Andronicus was known to be a man with whom it was not safe to quarrel. In the third year of their marriage a child was born, and six months later the father died of fever. There was much rude sympathy expressed for the widow; she received it quietly.

"Thou shouldst fetch thy boy to the temple, or he will be unlucky," said one of these would-be comforters, fixing curious eyes upon the delicate tear-stained face; "the jealous gods have already punished thee by slaying thy husband, what if they also smite thy son and thou be left desolate, like the impious Niobe?"

At that the widow—she was called Eunice—cried out with a loud and bitter cry. "Lo, I am desolate! My God hath smitten me, because that I turned aside from the law of Israel. The curse hath come upon me, even as the priest of Jehovah said; but what could I do, for my heart flew out of my bosom like a dove and followed after my beloved? Spare thou my son, O Jehovah, who also art the God of the widow and the fatherless!"

"Thou wilt do well if thou pray no more to strange gods," persisted the woman. "Come now with me, and make an offering to the good Venus; the goddess will perchance send thee another husband—for indeed thou art comely enough in thy way."

Eunice arose from her place looking very tall and stately. "Thou shalt not repeat such words in my cars," she said quietly, but there was that in her eyes which caused her neighbor to hastily withdraw, muttering something about the week's baking.

A few days later an elderly woman was seen to enter the cottage by the gate, upon whose neck the young widow fell with tears and sobs.

They had dwelt there, all three, ever since, the quiet years bringing little change save to the babe, who despite the dismal prognostications of the townspeople had grown into a slender serious lad of fifteen.

Timothy—for so he was called—was not like the other boys of the town, for in his early childhood he had been seldom allowed outside the walls of his mother's little garden, and as he grew older he shrank timidly from the loud-mouthed quarrelsome urchins, who swarmed in the village streets.

Once, when he was in his sixth year, tempted by the
sound of music, he had stolen out from the gate. A
heathen procession was passing with solemn chanting
and the playing of pipes and lutes. The boy stood as
if spell-bound, his delicate face aglow, his yellow curls
shining in the sunlight like an aureole; but on a sudden his dream of delight was rudely broken, a rabble
of boys big and little, who brought up the rear of the
procession spied him standing there.

"Hi, Jew! Jew!" they cried derisively. "Get thee
out of sight, thou hast an evil eye! Get thee back to
thy witch-mother!"

The words smote the child like the blow of a brutal
fist, he scarce noticed the stinging smart of the pebbles which rattled about his ears.

"Mother! Mother!" he cried rushing back into
the garden. And "Mother, mother," was all he could
say for his weeping.

It was the wise grandmother, Lois, who took him
upon her knee, and after a time coaxed from him some
account of what had taken place.

"They called thee a Jew!" she said, her eyes kindling. "Thanks be to Jehovah, thou hast the blood
of Israel in thy veins! Daughter, we have done evil
in that we have kept the child thus long from his
birthright."

From that time the little Timothy was daily instructed in the wonderful history of his mother's
people.

"If the Messiah should come, mother," he said one

day thoughtfully, "how shall we know it in this place, so far from our own nation?"

"He will gather his elect from every nation, son of mine," she answered tenderly. Yet her heart misgave her as she looked into his face with its Greek forehead and mouth and the deep sad eyes of her own race. Would the haughty prince of Israel receive this son of an apostate Jewess and a heathen Greek? That he would be cast forth with loathing from any Jewish synagogue in the land she knew right well. She bemoaned herself because of these things to her mother, and the good Lois replied stoutly.

"There be more words than the law written in the Scriptures, my daughter, and all of them for our good. Behold in a market-place there be set forth many things for food, both of fish, of beasts, and of fowls; eggs also and fruits, corn, wheat, barley and green things from the gardens, honey from the hives; likewise the milk of herds, butter, and cheeses of goats' milk. Yet no man eateth of them all on a single day, but chooseth from among them such things as he hath stomach for; thus he is nourished and made strong for the labor of life. So in the Scriptures we have the law, which is the strong meat; but there be also loving and goodly sayings which nourish the fainting soul even as the dewy figs, the delicate honey and the fresh milk nourish the fainting body, whereas the strong meats would cause distemper. Listen now, whilst I read to thee from the words of David, who also sinned grievously in the eyes of the Lord, yet was forgiven.

" ' I love the Lord,
   Because he hath heard my supplications,
   Because he hath inclined his ear unto me,
   Therefore will I call upon him as long as I live;
   The sorrows of death compassed me,
   And the pains of death gat hold upon me.
       I found trouble and sorrow.
   Then called I upon the name of the Lord.
   O Lord, I beseech thee, deliver my soul !
   Gracious is the Lord, and righteous :
   Yea, our God is merciful.
   The Lord preserveth the helpless,
   I was brought low, and he helped me.'

" And again,

" ' If thou, O Lord, shouldst mark iniquities,
       Who should stand ?
   But there is forgiveness with thee.
   With the Lord there is mercy,
   With him there is plenteous redemption.'

" Canst thou not find comfort and satisfaction in such words, my daughter ?"

" Yes, truly, but—" and Eunice hung her head sadly. " My son is not—he is not of the chosen race."

The mother's faded cheek flushed. Her grandson, Timothy, was as the apple of her eye. " Tell me," she cried, " was not Ruth, the Moabitess also an alien —of whom the neighbor women said to Naomi, the Jewess, 'Behold, thy daughter-in-law which loveth thee is better to thee than seven sons '—whose son's son was also David, King of Israel ; of which lineage, it is written, shall come in the fullness of time the

Messiah. Thy son Timothy shall be blessed; with mine eyes also shall I see it."

Without waiting for an answer the good woman rose up from her place and wrapping herself in her veil went out to the market-place. "I will buy a choice fowl," she said in her heart, "that I may make a goodly dish for the lad and for his mother. I will dress it moreover with mine own hands that they may eat and be glad; surely savory meat maketh a merry heart, and there is overmuch sadness under our roof."

There was a crowd in the market-place that morning, at which Lois inwardly wondered, but she walked straight towards the poulterer's stall, intent only upon her errand.

"How much art thou asking for a choice fowl this morning?" she said; but the keeper of the stall was paying no heed. He was standing upon an upturned basket, mouth and eyes wide open, apparently engrossed with his efforts to hear something which was going on over against the fish market.

"Sluggard!" exclaimed Lois wrathfully. "Thou wouldst do well to attend to thy business; eyes that wander to and fro, and ears that hear not the call of duty, so shall poverty come upon thee as an armed man." She turned nevertheless to see what the man was looking at, and straightway forgot the poulterer and her errand with him.

Elevated slightly above the heads of the rustic crowd which gathered about him, stood a small dark man.

A fragment of what he was saying floated distinctly across the intervening space.

"And in this is the Son of God made manifest, that while we were yet sinners, Christ died for us. For the wages of sin is death ; but the gift of God is eternal life through Jesus Christ, our Lord."

"The Messiah !" gasped Lois, turning pale, "he speaks of the Messiah !"

Dropping her basket she hurried back to the little cottage by the gate. "Come," she cried breathlessly, seizing the startled Eunice by the arm. "Come quickly ; there be tidings of the Messiah ! The lad, too, where is he ?"

And so it came to pass that Lois and Eunice and the boy Timothy heard the story of Jesus from the lips of Paul. It never entered into their simple hearts to doubt either the man or his message. And while they wept much at the thought of the terrible cross, they also caught something of the triumphant joy of the inspired speaker, as he flung a halo of glory about the symbol of shame and death.

The three witnessed the healing of the lame man, but had withdrawn immediately afterward to the safe shelter of home, alarmed by the shouts and cries of the turbulent multitude. That he who had brought such joy and gladness into their souls was in any peril at the hands of the enthusiastic villagers, never occurred to them.

"Little wonder that yonder poor idolaters think the man Paul a god," Lois had remarked with a smile, as they sat in their little garden, the late afternoon sunshine lying warm and pleasant about them. "But he will teach them all things in the days to come."

An hour later they stood weeping about his motionless body, who was truly what the villagers had declared, a messenger of the Most High. "Bring him to my house," whispered Lois, as he began to show signs of life. "It is near the gate ; no one will see."

And there through the night they ministered to him, binding up his wounds, and pouring upon his bruised spirit the wine and oil of affection and sympathy, which he so sorely needed.

As the mists of pain cleared away from before his vision, he became conscious of the face of the lad Timothy, luminous with love as the face of an angel ; the soul of the lonely man went out toward him.

"My son," he said, calling him to his side, "dost thou believe on the Lord Jesus Christ who died upon the cross for our redemption, and for whose name I also have tasted death this day ?"

"I do believe, and with all my heart," replied the lad, sinking to his knees beside the couch.

"Then do thou lay fast hold on eternal life, whereunto thou art also called, and the Lord keep and bless thee in all thy ways from this time forth, even forever."

In the gray light of the early dawn, he called them all about him. "We must be going," he said, "for the day is at hand ; it must find us many miles from this place."

"But thou art not able to travel," cried Lois in

dismay. " Surely thou wilt tarry with us till thou art recovered of thy wounds."

" I can do all things through Christ that strengtheneth me," he replied gravely. Then he prayed with them and blessed them. " We shall be with you again before many days," he said as he bade them farewell, "for if God wills, we shall return to all the cities wherein we have preached the gospel, that we may comfort and confirm them which have believed."

The two women and the lad stood in the morning twilight, their wet eyes fixed upon the retreating figures of the travelers ; the wounded man limped painfully as he walked ; at the sight the tears of the women streamed forth afresh.

" Alas !" sobbed Eunice, " he will die by the wayside."

But Timothy's face shone. " I love him," he murmured. " I shall always love him."

CHAPTER XXX.

FROM JERUSALEM TO GALATIA.

MORE than three years have elapsed since the fickle inhabitants of Lystra first worshiped, then stoned the man who sought to turn them from death unto life. Three years of tireless labor, in Antioch first, where the church increased mightily from month to month, until there came into their midst certain men from Judaea who declared that the foreign converts must comply with the laws of Moses ; that they must become, in effect, Jews.

" Uncircumcised, unclean, eaters of the forbidden beast," they thundered, " unless ye obey the ceremonial laws, ye are accursed."

" Christ hath redeemed us from the curse of the law," answered Paul steadily. " No man is justified by the law in the sight of God. If righteousness come by the law, then Christ is dead in vain."

And when the discussion waxed hot between them, Paul and Barnabas went up to Jerusalem and there called that memorable council of the apostles and elders, in which it was determined, after much deliberation, that the heavy yoke of Judaism should not be laid upon the neck of the Gentiles, since if they were to be saved at all it must be through the grace of the

Lord Jesus. This was a decision fraught with the most tremendous consequences to all Christendom, a decision assailed again and again by the persistent adherents of Judaism, who even traveled about from place to place in the steps of the apostle, striving to quench the pure light of faith beneath the incubus of the law.

"False brethren," Paul calls them bitterly,* "who came in privily to spy out our liberty which we have in Christ Jesus, that they may bring us into bondage."

Even Peter, who was received by the church at Antioch with all gladness and singleness of heart, yielded to the subtle influence of these men.

"When Peter came to Antioch,"† wrote Paul afterward to the converts in Galatia—who had also been thrown into great distress and confusion by visits from these same Judaisers, "I withstood him to the face, because he was worthy of blame; for before the coming of certain brethren from James, he was in the habit of eating with the Gentiles, but after they came, he began to draw back and to separate himself from them for fear of these brethren. And he was joined in his dissimulation by the rest of the Jews in the church, so that even Barnabas was drawn away with them.

"But when I saw that they were walking in a crooked path, and forsaking the truth of the glad-tidings, I said to Peter before them all : If thou being born a Jew, art wont to live according to the customs of the Gentiles, how is it that thou wouldst compel

---

* Galatians ii., 4.   † Galatians ii., 11-17.

the Gentiles to keep the ordinances of the Jews? We are Jews by birth and not Gentiles; yet because we know that a man is not justified by the law, we have put our faith in Christ Jesus, that we might be justified by faith in Christ; for by the works of the law shall no flesh be justified."

Justified by faith in Christ. How the words must have smitten the proud impulsive heart of Peter. Surely the vision of that night in the palace of the high priest, and his blasphemous denials of the Master; of the look in the eyes of that Master, as "he turned and looked upon Peter," must have come back to him then, and with it the solemn memory of the thrice-repeated question, "Simon, son of Jonas, lovest thou me?" and the thrice-repeated admonition, "Feed my sheep."

Afterward we find him writing "to the strangers* scattered throughout Pontus, Galatia, Cappadocia, Asia and Bithynia" such words as these. "Blessed be the God and Father of our Lord Jesus Christ, which according to his abundant mercy hath begotten us again unto a lively hope by the resurrection of Jesus Christ from the dead, to an inheritance incorruptible, undefiled, that fadeth not away, reserved in heaven for you. That the trial of your faith, being much more precious than gold that perisheth, though it be tried with fire, might be found with praise and honor and glory at the appearing of Jesus Christ; whom having not seen, ye love, rejoicing with joy unspeakable and

---

* Strangers, *i.e.* Gentiles.

full of glory; receiving the end of your faith, even the salvation of your souls.

" Feed the flock of God which is among you, and when the chief shepherd shall appear, ye shall receive a crown of glory that fadeth not away. Be subject one to another, and be clothed with humility ; for God resisteth the proud, and giveth grace to the humble. And the God of all grace, who hath called us unto his eternal glory by Jesus Christ, after that ye have suffered awhile, make you perfect, establish, strengthen and confirm you. To him be glory and dominion for ever and ever. Amen."*

After those days Paul said to Barnabas, " Let us go again and visit our brethren in every city where we have preached the word of the Lord, and see how they do."

" I will go with thee gladly," Barnabas replied ; " and let us take with us, I pray thee, my kinsman Mark, since we shall have need of him in our labor."

" I think it not good to take him with us," said Paul decidedly, " since he left us in the midst of our work at Pamphylia." And to this opinion he adhered despite the arguments and entreaties of Barnabas. " Go thy way," he said at length, " since we may not agree in this matter, and I also will go mine."

So Barnabas took Mark, and sailed unto Cyprus, and Paul chose Silas and departed to Syria, being recommended by the brethren unto the grace of God.

As for John Mark, he was both sorry and ashamed

---

* Selections from I. Peter.

because that he had brought about a separation betwixt the two friends, a separation which proved to be a lasting one, since Paul and Barnabas never again labored together.

"I will prove to him—God helping me, that I am not altogether unprofitable in the Master's service," cried the young man, his face glowing with honest shame, as he heard the sentence pronounced upon him by the uncompromising apostle.

He kept his word; in after years we find him the energetic self-denying companion of Peter in his great work, the author of the gospel bearing his name, and Paul himself writes of him to the church at Colossae, "If Mark comes to you, receive him; he is one of my fellow-workers unto the kingdom of God, which has been a comfort unto me."—And again in his old age from the Roman prison, to Timothy, "Bring Mark with thee; for he is profitable to me for the ministry."

Through Syria and Cilicia Paul and Silas traveled, diligently confirming the churches. At Lystra they came once more to the house of Lois and Eunice. The lad Timothy was a lad no longer. He had grown in grace and in the knowledge of the Lord Jesus as well as in stature, and as Paul taught the people in the village market-place, he came upon more than one evidence of the work of the young disciple. At Derbe also, the neighboring town, and in Iconium forty miles away, he found Timothy "well reported of" by all the brethren.

"Wilt thou give this thy son to the ministry of the Lord?" he asked Eunice.

And the widow with wet eyes made answer. "If the Lord hath called my son, who am I that I should withstand him."

So Timothy was ordained before the whole church ;* the elders and Paul himself solemnly laying their hands upon his head. From that time he was to Paul the faithful companion of all his wanderings. "Mine own son in the faith," he calls him. "My dearly-beloved son," whom without ceasing he henceforth remembers in his prayers night and day.†

Not many days afterward the three set forth on their journey through the cities, making known to each church the decision of the apostles and elders at Jerusalem concerning the law of Moses.   .

In Galatia—through which they had purposed to pass without tarrying, they were forced to remain for several months because of a grievous sickness which befell Paul, a fresh piercing of his tortured flesh with that thorn of suffering, concerning which he once wrote to the Corinthians, "There was given me a thorn in the flesh, the messenger of Satan to buffet me, lest I should be exalted above measure. For this thing I besought the Lord thrice that it might depart from me. And he said to me, My grace is sufficient for thee ; for my strength is made perfect in weakness."

And to the Galatian church which he founded in the midst of his sufferings he wrote, "Ye have never

---

* I. Tim. iv. 14.   † II. Tim. i. 2-5.

wronged me ; on the contrary, although it was sickness as ye know—which caused me to preach the glad-
tidings to you at my first visit, yet ye neither scorned
nor loathed the bodily infirmity which was my trial ;
but ye welcomed me as an angel of God, yea, even,
as Jesus Christ himself. What blessedness was yours
then ; and I bear you witness that if it had been possible, ye would have plucked out your own eyes and
given them to me."*

Because of these words there be many who think
that this infirmity, this " thorn "—this " sharp stake,"
ever and anon driven deeper into the quivering flesh
of the sufferer, was that terrible inflammation and ulcer-
ation of the eyes, which is still the scourge of the countries wherein Paul labored.   Be this as it may, God's
grace was sufficient, and his strength was manifested
in the weakness of his servant, ' while he painted, as it
were, visibly and large the picture of Jesus Christ
crucified,' before the eyes of the heathen Galatians.†
Many, indeed, both of Jews and Greeks, men and
women, freedmen and slaves,‡ lifted their weary eyes
and, looking away from themselves and their sins to
Jesus the author and finisher of the faith, were saved.

---

* Gal. iv. 13–15.   † Gal. iii. 1.   ‡ Gal. iii. 27, 28.

CHAPTER XXXI.

IN PHILIPPI.

L EAVING Galatia, the travelers came at length to
the classic city of Troas; here Luke of Antioch, "the beloved physician," joined them; from
henceforth to be almost uninterruptedly the companion
of the great apostle, the chronicler of his journeys,
his labors, his sufferings and his imprisonments.

In Troas also as they tarried awhile—uncertain
which way they must go, since they had been prevented from carrying out their plan of preaching in
Asia and Bithynia—there came to Paul a vision in the
night. It seemed to him, lying upon his bed, that he
saw standing by his side the figure of a man, clad in
the full panoply of a Roman soldier, and as he looked
at the appearance in wonder, the figure raised its hands
beseechingly and cried out, " Come over into Macedonia and help us !"

" Assuredly gathering," writes Luke simply, "that
the Lord had called us to announce the glad-tidings
there, we immediately sought to go into Macedonia."

A vessel was found in the harbor of Troas on the
point of sailing for Neapolis, and upon this the party
of four, Paul, Silas, Timothy and Luke, embarked;
the south wind drove them rapidly upon their course

betwixt Tenedos and the mainland, past Imbros, till evening found them anchored for the night beneath the towering peaks of Samothrace; from thence on the morrow their course lay northwest to their destined port, Neapolis. Nine miles distant, and connected with Neapolis by a paved road, lay the Roman military colony of Philippi. And thither after some anxious consultation the travelers made their way, through the mountain-pass of Pangaeus, across the fertile rose-decked plains to "the place of fountains," where Philip, the father of Alexander, first set a garrison to protect his frontier against the Thracian mountaineers. Where Brutus and Cassius, their hands red with the blood of Cæsar, had marshaled their legions against Augustus, escaping his victorious sword only by ignominious flight into that dim land of shadows, whither no earthly vengeance may pursue its prey.

Amid the bustle and stir of this little city, which the colonists, proud of their Roman origin, had made as nearly as possible like the eternal Mother of Cities, with its theatres, baths, palaces, temples, and magnificent private dwellings, the new-comers passed a few quiet days. They found no synagogue dedicated to the worship of Jehovah among the marble temples of the heathen deities; in the busy market-places and on the street corners they came upon no faces bearing the sign manual of Israel.

"If there be any in this place who worship God," said Paul at length, "we shall find them by the river-side, where prayer is wont to be made."

So they passed out of the city through the massive gates, recently granted to the colony by Claudius, upon which the workmen were still busily employed, and turned their steps in the direction of the river Gangites, which rushed between its banks with all the headlong impetuosity of a mountain torrent. Not far from the paved causeway which led to the river, they found as they had hoped the little prayer-house, or proseucha, a temporary structure open to the sky and fronting directly upon the river.

A few women crouched within the humble walls of the place, their heads bowed, their somber mantles drawn closely about their faces ; if they prayed at all it was in silence and sadness, as indeed women are wont to pray. Something in the aspect of these lonely veiled figures touched the heart of Paul, "We will speak with them," he said.

So they sat down, all four, and Paul in the simplest language began to speak of the glad-tidings. As he told the story of the wonderful sinless life spent in far-away Judæa, of the yielding up of that life on the cross, of the mysterious resurrection and ascension, one by one the bowed heads were raised, the shrouding veils pushed aside, as if their wearers feared to lose a syllable of what was being spoken. And when at last the inspired speaker declared that through faith in this Jesus the sins of past years might be forgiven, that through his death the bitterness of the grave was overpast, and the pure fountain of life everlasting unsealed in the arid desert of this present life, that whosoever would might take freely, the silent lips broke forth into alleluias.

"O Lord, thou art my God!" cried a tall stately woman, springing to her feet. "I will exalt thee, I will praise thy name; for thou hast done wonderful things! Behold, I believe with joy the words that thou hast spoken, for my heart beareth me witness that they be true words."

So did it please God to send his messengers to a handful of faithful women, who alone in all the gay city of Philippi remembered the Sabbath; and so it came to pass that the first person to confess Christ on European soil was a woman, a humble seller of dye-stuffs.

"I am not a Jewess," she said meekly, when questioned by the apostle. "I was born in the city of Thyatira, in the province of Lydia, which name also I bear. Many years ago did I forsake the gods of my fathers, for I was persuaded that the Jehovah of the Jews was the only true God. Yet have I found the laws of their religion a grievous burden, since it hath seemed not possible to observe them all perfectly, and by reason of one failure all is lost—for so I was taught."

When all the fulness of the glorious glad-tidings had been explained to her, she gladly consented to be baptized.

"I and my household," she said simply, "for I have many hand-maids and slaves, who also labor in my house preparing the precious dye-stuffs of purple and crimson, these have I instructed in the fear of Jehovah, so that they worship no other god. If the Lord Jesus will receive me, he will surely receive them."

So the woman Lydia was baptized with her household, and afterward she asked of the strangers where they were lodging, and when they told her of the place—a humble one truly and in a mean part of the city, she urgently besought them, " If ye have judged me to be faithful to the Lord, come into my house and abide there."

And since Jesus himself had bidden his disciples abide with them that were worthy, in whatsoever town or city they might tarry to proclaim the glad-tidings, they went to the house of Lydia and remained there, and their "peace came upon it," according to the promise.

On this same Sabbath morning in quite another part of Philippi, a young girl sat flat upon the ground in one corner of a squalid courtyard. The sun shone hot upon her uncovered head, but she seemed not to notice it; her dull protruding black eyes were fixed upon a swarm of flies, which darted noiselessly back and forth in the dazzling light with the strange unceasing energy of shuttles thrown by viewless hands in some loom of fate. Now and again she waved her lean brown hands before her face with a short sharp cry.

From the low-ceiled room on the left of the yard came sounds of loud laughter and the clinking of cups and dishes; presently a woman bearing a platter heaped with food stepped out into the court.

"Mara!" she called sharply, "come and eat."

The girl did not stir, and with a muttered oath the woman strode up to her and shook her roughly. "Devil-possessed!" she said angrily. "Art thou also deaf and blind? come eat, I say."

With a deep sigh the unfortunate girl pushed back the tangled black hair which hung about her face, then her eyes fell upon the platter; without a word she snatched it out of the woman's hand and began to devour the contents greedily, moaning and snarling like an animal as she ate.

"Beast," grunted the woman, spurning her contemptuously with her bare foot.

A couple of red-faced men now sauntered out into the courtyard; one of them carried a short whip of braided thongs in his hand, he snapped it playfully in the air as he approached the girl. She sprang up shrieking.

"No, no, no, master! do not beat me, I will obey. I am coming—I am coming! Yes, I see—many— many things; I will tell thee all, good master—kind lady."

The man with the whip burst into a loud laugh. "Ah, thou young she-devil," he growled, "thou dost know thy master at last; come, bestir thyself, 'tis time we were moving; and mind thou speak up loud to-day, we'll have none of your dumb fiends."

The girl's eyes were blazing now. "Ay, come!"

she cried wildly. " No dumb fiends—but wheels that turn and turn, and waters that roar, and fire that burns —burns !"

" She hath a good spirit to-day !" said the second man, thrusting his tongue into his cheek and winking at the woman, who stood with her arms akimbo staring at the demoniac.

" Get you along with her then ; if she failed to bring in a good bit of gold, think you that I would have her about?—the filthy beast." The woman stooped and began to gather up the fragments of food which the girl had dropped in her fright, while the two men driving the hapless mad creature before them set off down the street at a good pace.

" Worshipful lords and beauteous ladies !" they bellowed as they tramped along. " Come one, come all, and learn the future from the lips of the divine prophetess, Mara ! More wonderful than the oracle at Delphi, the heaven-inspired Mara ! Hast thou lost anything ? Mara can reveal its hiding place ! Art thou in doubt about to-morrow's ventures ? Mara can counsel thee ! Art thou ill ? Mara can cure thee !"

And so for long hours they wandered up and down the streets, stopping now and again at the beck of the idle or credulous ; a sly flourish of the dreaded whip causing the demented girl to pour forth a torrent of ravings, which her masters cunningly interpreted to suit the case in hand. Toward evening as they passed through the main avenue of the town they came upon a group of men and women who were passing out at the river gate. Something that a tall woman in their midst was saying earnestly to her companion caught the quick ear of the demoniac.

"Servants of the Most High God!" she shrilled, "which show unto us the way of salvation! Servants of the most high God—which show unto us the way of salvation!" And this saying she repeated again and again, tearing at her streaming hair with frantic energy. A crowd quickly gathered to the spot, from which the unprincipled owners of the girl proceeded to reap a goodly harvest of copper and silver coins.

"By Bacchus!" growled one of them as they made their way homeward long after nightfall. "Fortuna hath favored us richly to-day; now that I bethink me, I have seen those fellows before; Jews clearly enough —cunning rogues, but not more cunning than our little treasure here, hey, Mara?"

The girl shuddered as the man laid his hand upon her shoulder, "Servants of the most high God," she muttered brokenly, "Servants of the most high God!"

"Yes, yes, my pretty, now remember that to-morrow and we shall do well."

Not only on the morrow but on many succeeding days, the wretched creature, driven by her masters, followed Paul and his company as they went to and from the place of prayer, crying out monotonously the words which seemed to have taken complete possession of her darkened mind. "These men are servants of the most high God! which show unto us the way of salvation." And the idle multitude that followed echoed the demoniac's cry with foul cursing and ribald laughter.

When Paul understood the matter he was stirred with pity because of the grievous condition of the slave ; turning suddenly he said, addressing the evil spirit with which the girl was thought to be possessed, " I command thee in the name of Jesus Christ to come out of her."

Immediately the strident voice faltered into silence, the frenzied gestures ceased, the staring eyes softened, a gentle rain of healing tears flowed down the burning cheeks.

" Mara, Mara !" shouted her master with an oath, snapping the dreaded whip. " What ails thee, wench ; never fear the whining Jew !"

The girl looked about her at the motley crowd, then into the brutal face of her owner. " How came I here ?" she said gently. " I must go home now."

" Ha, ha !" yelled a shrill voice from out the multitude. " The Jew is an exorcist ; he has spoiled your property, good masters. The girl is not worth a denarius for your business from now on."

" You lie !" shrieked the man with the whip. " I swear by the immortals that I will beat the wench till the spirit returns." And he brought down the braided lash again and again over the delicate neck and shoulders of the girl ; she moaned and wept piteously, but there was no outburst of the familiar ravings.

" She's done for assuredly," exclaimed his partner

with an execration. "Let be; better take thy vengeance out of the hide of yonder accursed Jew."

"Thou hast spoken!" cried a buxom woman who had pushed to the front, "Seize the mischief-makers, and let them taste of Roman law!"

With a fierce yell the owners of the slave girl rushed off in the direction of the prayer-house, the mob following.

Within the hour the market-place was filled with a turburlent excited multitude, all agog to learn the details of the hurried trial and punishment of the strangers.

"Jews? yes," said one of the owners of the demented slave girl, as he elbowed his way through the crowd with an important air—"accursed, meddlesome beggars! but they have had a lesson. They will think twice hereafter before they thrust their hooked noses into another man's business. A scourging, you say? A sound one, you may believe, my masters. Ah, but it pleased me to behold their blood! and now they be fast in the inner prison where they may rot for all I care." And he went his way, thinking to lay his hand upon the slave, who had been quite forgotten in the general excitement. "There be other uses to which she may be put if she has recovered her wits," he muttered to himself, "and property is property and must not be allowed to go to waste."

He did not find the girl, that day nor yet the day after. She had wandered dazed and weeping through the great gates that led out to the river, and attracted by the solemn unceasing chant of the waters had made her way to a small roofless enclosure on the very brink of the torrent, here she sank down with a sigh of relief and lifted her face to the pure distant heavens, a strange happiness swelling in her breast. "God—God!" she murmured smiling. "Servants of the most high God."

"Ah, it is thou?"

She started and looked about her, her breath coming faster in her fright. A young man with a very gentle yet sorrowful look in his face was steadfastly regarding her. "I am one of them that were with him when he healed thee," he said softly; then his eyes filled with sudden tears, "I—I fear that they have killed him."

The girl started to her feet, "I must go," she said with a return of her wild tone and gesture. "If they have killed him, I will die also."

"Nay, thou shalt come with me now—it will also please him best; the good Lydia sent me forth to find thee."

And so it was that the hapless Mara found a home, for her former masters were not unwilling to part with a piece of property which had so strangely become valueless in their hands, more especially since the charitable dealer in dye-stuffs offered a goodly sum for the girl.

These worthies found themselves in a most unpleasant situation the very day after they had brought

about the scourging and imprisonment of Paul and
Silas. The duumvirs had sent for them in hot haste.

"Those strangers," they said severely, "whom ye
falsely accused in our presence of being mischief-
making Jews have turned out to be Roman citizens,
whom it is not lawful to scourge, as ye well know :
now therefore it is meet that ye taste of punishment in
your own bodies, that your offence be not repeated."
So saying, the magistrates commanded them to be
thrust into the inner prison, where also their limbs
were made fast in the stocks, in the very spot where
Paul and Silas had sung their midnight praises.* And
in this plight the miscreants remained many days.
But Paul and Silas, after that they had comforted
them that believed, departed with Timothy on their
journey.

---

* Acts xvi., 25.

CHAPTER XXXII.

A STRANGER IN ATHENS.

IT was high noon in Athens. The wonderful water-clock which stood in the midst of the Agora declared it, so did the unerring finger of the sun-dial, which the builders and makers of the clock had discreetly placed on the outside of the beautiful little structure which enshrined the mechanism, either by way of providing against possible errors in the time-piece, or to prove to the doubtful-minded the perfection of their handiwork.

It being the proper and natural time to eat, Athens was hungry; the fruiterers were doing a driving business, slices of cool melon and clusters of early grapes being in especially brisk demand; before the stalls of the fleshers and pastry-cooks an impatient crowd was waiting, while even the humble dispensers of plain barley cakes—three for a farthing, emptied their flat baskets once and again.

A young man who wore his red cap very much on one side, and carried a kithera slung over his shoulder by a leathern strap, had eaten exactly nine of these cakes besides a slice of melon; it appeared however that he was still hungry, for he shook his head ruefully as he fingered his lean purse.

"A pest on my importunate belly," he muttered with a frown. "What then, I have no money it appears, therefore I can have no provender. But stay, there is more than one road to Rome."

He strode across to a flesher's stall whereon were displayed in tempting profusion roast fowls, great joints of beef and mutton, cutlets of veal and pork, heaps of succulent and dewy salads, interspersed with steaming bowls of soup thickened with vegetables. The greedy crowd it is true had wrought great havoc in this noble array of victuals, but there was still enough left to make a hungry man's mouth water.

"Look you, my good Cimon," quoth the man with the kithera, fixing his bold black eyes upon the merchant, "Onesimus, the bard, is assuredly not unknown to thee. Many a bowl of pottage have I eaten at thy stall. To-day I would also eat—for alas, the memory of yesterday's dinner serves but to whet to-day's appetite—but with a purse as empty as his belly, my excellent flesher, a man must needs bestir himself; if music fail to bring the silver, brawn and muscle must come into play. Give me a bowl of thy soup there—which will go to waste perchance if I eat it not, and in return take my kithera till this evening when I shall redeem it. The instrument is worth thy whole stock of victuals and a broad piece besides. 'Tis bound with wrought silver, mark you."

The flesher, who was after the manner of his craft a fat red-faced man, merely grunted by way of reply. He reached out his hand for the kithera, which his

would-be customer readily passed over to him.
"Hump!" he ejaculated, running his greasy fingers
over the strings, "'tis not Athenian-made plainly
enough, yet the tone is not bad." He lifted the instrument and scanned it more closely. "Colossae!"
he exclaimed, pursing up his lips. "Now, how might
you have come by this, my young sir?"

Onesimus flushed a deep angry crimson over all his
face and neck. "Give me back my kithera," he said
in a low tone, eyeing the flesher fiercely.

"Not so fast, not so fast, my good fellow; there
can be no harm in asking a civil question—nor yet in
answering the same. Take the soup; fetch me a
penny at sunset, and thou shalt have thy kithera, not
a whit the worse for my keeping." He laid the instrument aside with an air of decision, and arose to wait
upon another customer, who unquestionably had
money to spend, as the cheerful jingle of coin in his
wallet bore witness.

Onesimus stood for a moment as if undecided, then
drawing a bowl of the pottage toward him with a somewhat sullen air he emptied it in a trice. "I will return
at sunset," he said shortly, turning on his heel.

"As you like," replied the flesher indifferently. "A
pretty instrument that, good sir," he added, addressing his latest customer, who had glanced after the retreating figure of the musician with a faint show of
interest. "If yonder knave return not I shall lose
nothing by the transaction—which, indeed, was none
of my choosing."

Being presently left to himself, the excellent Cimon allowed his eye to wander idly to the glittering heights of the Acropolis, which towered in majestic grandeur high above the great irregular square of the market-place. The white wonder of the Parthenon was a familiar enough sight to the worthy flesher, who indeed had been born under its shadow; he yawned wide as he looked, and reaching out for the kithera proceeded to strum upon it unmelodiously.

Onesimus in the meantime was striding moodily along the busy street between the long walls which led down to the Piraeus; "If I can but get a couple of hours work at unlading," he muttered, looking anxiously at the clustered galleys which dotted the placid waters of the harbor. "If I cannot—what then? I am at all events no longer a slave." He threw back his head and laughed aloud, a harsh unmirthful laugh which caused more than one pair of eyes to follow him.

"Yonder knave hath a merry heart, it would seem," observed one enviously.

"He is mad, perchance," said another, who knew the world.

The object of their surmises still pursued his way and the unhappy tenor of his thoughts. "No longer a slave to one master, but a slave to a thousand necessities, anxieties, pains, fears and forebodings; a wretched fugitive without a friend, without a home, without a God." By which it may be seen that Onesimus had also been diligently studying the gloomy page of worldly experience, and that he had found little comfort therein.

He had reached the water's edge by this time, but instead of pressing forward into the busy throng about the wharves he leaned up against a pile of newly-unladen merchandise and continued to stare moodily at the incoming and outgoing vessels.

He was partly aroused from his abstraction by some words which were being spoken at his side in a deep resonant voice. " I have no further need of your good offices, my friends ; return ye therefore to Berea and bear my request to Silas and Timotheus, my fellow-laborers, that they come to me with all possible speed ; I will await them here."

Onesimus turned and fixed his eyes upon the three men who had paused near his side. They had evidently just landed from the vessel yonder and were strangers in the city. Moved by a sudden impulse, he started forward and bowed low before them, doffing his red cap respectfully. " You are newly arrived in Athens, noble sirs? Yes—it is so? You will perhaps have need of a guide to show you lodgings, shops, markets, also it may be the wondrous sights of the city? Shall not Onesimus offer you his services, to whom Athens is as a tale that is told ; there is no one better, I assure you, my lords."

The man who had first spoken, regarded him keenly for a full moment before replying. He was a small man, somewhat bent over, as if from age or infirmity, the impression of age being still further confirmed by the fact that the fringe of curling hair which mingled with his abundant beard was thickly sprinkled with white. The grey eyes beneath the bushy eyebrows were steady and kind, and the whole expression of the face genial and winning.* Onesimus involuntarily repeated his obeisance, although he had not failed to remark the fact that the stranger was wrapped from the searching sea wind in an ample cloak or dreadnaught which had unquestionably seen long and hard service.

"So thou didst not remain in Antioch," said the stranger quietly.

Onesimus started violently. "In Antioch?" he stammered reddening. "Where—how—"

"Didst thou not fetch me in thy boat up the Orontes some eight years ago?"

"Truly I did," said Onesimus, hanging his head as he recalled his last meeting with the man. "I heard thee speak in the street Singon," he added, "but I was not of those who threw stones and sticks because of what thou didst say; I left Antioch that same day because—well, because of my affairs. Yet I can show thee Athens as well as another."

"Stand thou here till I shall speak with my companions," said the stranger authoritatively. "Thou shalt show me lodgings presently, and I will pay thee a penny for thy pains."

---

* This description of the personal appearance of the apostle is taken from the traditional accounts of the third, fifth and sixth centuries. See also II. Cor. x., 10–16.

Half an hour later the strangely-assorted pair walked slowly up the long street which led from the Piraeus to the city of Athens. "There be lodgings near the shore," Onesimus remarked, pointing to a labyrinth of narrow streets which hemmed in the busy quarters of the shipping merchants, "cheap lodgings," he added, with a sly glance at the well-worn garments of his companion.

The heavy cloak had been removed now, and its owner carried it upon his arm. "I shall require cheap lodgings," he said tranquilly, "but I will go into the city."

Onesimus observed that he breathed heavily as they climbed the long ascent, and that his thin face had grown quite pallid.

"I will carry the cloak," he said bluntly. "Thou art perhaps ill."

"I have been ill," said the stranger, "but thanks be to God, I am recovered."

"Which god?" cried Onesimus, sneering openly. "'Tis easier, they say, to meet with a god than a man in Athens, yet can I thank neither god nor man for anything. I may starve, die, rot, and if my carcass be but thrust from out the walls before it plague the nostrils of my fellows, there is no one to waste so much as a thought upon me."

"If thou hast so learned this present world, my son," said his companion, laying a gentle hand upon his arm, "thou hast done well; and thou wilt haply pay the more diligent heed to what I shall say to thee concerning the God which is above all gods—the only wise God, eternal, immortal, invisible."

"To whom perhaps this altar was erected in times past," observed Onesimus, with a bitter laugh.

The two paused before an ancient shrine built of rough undressed stones, above which in characters but dimly discernible ran the inscription, "To an Unknown God."

"Unknown but not unknowable, thanks be to our Lord Jesus Christ, who hath revealed to us the unspeakable love of God through the power of his grace," murmured the stranger, bowing his head.

The young man did not venture for a time to break the silence in which his companion wrapped himself as in a garment. Once only did the new-comer arouse himself from his seeming abstraction; it was when they entered the famous street of Tripods, which sweeps boldly about the foot of the Acropolis. His eye kindled as they passed between the seemingly interminable lines of graceful statues, which stood like sentinels guarding the shrines and temples of the Olympian deities.

"Are they not divinely beautiful!" cried Onesimus, his heart swelling with all the pride of his race. "And look you, good sir, in the white temple yonder on the heights, stands the Phidian Pallas, wrought from pure ivory, and robed in virgin gold."

"Idols all!" exclaimed the stranger in a tone which echoed strangely amid the classic haunts of immortal beauty. "Idols all, and therefore accursed."

Onesimus bit his lip. "Not only a Jew," he muttered half scornfully, half pityingly, "but a mad Jew."

Neither spoke again till they reached a narrow and rather squalid street which lay near the river. "Here dwell thy countrymen, good sir," said the Greek coldly. "Yonder is their synagogue; thou wilt doubtless find good accommodations hereabouts."

He turned as if to go, but his companion detained him with a word. "Stay, my friend," he said, "there is somewhat that I owe thee," and he proffered a coin.

Onesimus stared at it in silence for a moment, then he shook his head. "No," he said decidedly, "I want no pay for what I have done. Farewell." And before the other could speak again, he was gone.

Within the space of three days the Agora was buzzing with a new bit of gossip. "What of this Jew— this madman—this proclaimer of strange gods? His own countrymen will have none of him, say they, yet he stands yonder haranguing the crowd with all the assurance of a philosopher." Such were some of the sayings concerning the 'shabby,' 'insignificant,' 'stoop-shouldered,' 'hook-nosed' Jew, who had recently come to Athens.

Certain of the learned professors, discoursers, lecturers and philosophers who were wont to air their vapid learning in the Stoa, shrugged their shoulders languidly at the mere mention of his name, "Paulus," said they, "we have heard somewhat of the man, a brawler, a barbarian Jew, akin to, or one with Christus —it matters not. Think you that he can have access to a secret hid from us? He writeth, doth he? Well, and he may write. O, the Jew findeth scholars! Certain slaves, perchance. His doctrines could be held by no sane man."*

"Look you," cried their rivals of the Epicurean school, "be he barbarian Jew or Greek—some call him Roman—'tis one to us. We will hear him of the matters whereof he babbles; there is no other breeze to stir the air to-day."

So half in earnest, half in mockery they led him up the rock-hewn steps of the Areopagus. "May we know," they said with thinly-veiled derision, "what this new doctrine whereof thou speakest is?"

Then Paul, standing upon the projecting platform which was known as the "Stone of Impudence," upon which Socrates once made his defence, spoke thus to the assembly.

"Ye men of Athens, I perceive that in all things ye are very religious. For as I passed through your city, and beheld the objects of your worship, I found among them an altar with this inscription, To an Un-known God. Him, therefore—whom ye worship though ye know him not—declare I unto you.

"The God who made the world and all things that are therein, being Lord of heaven and earth, dwelleth not in temples made with hands. Neither is he served by the hands of men, as though he needed anything; for it is he that giveth unto every creature life and breath, and all things. He made of one blood every

---

* Browning, *Men and Women.*

nation of mankind, to dwell upon the face of the whole
earth : and ordained to each the appointed seasons of
their existence, and the bounds of their habitation.
That they should seek God, if haply they might feel
after him and find him—though he be not far from every
one of us. For in him we live and move and have
our being, as certain of your own poets have said,

    " ' We are also his offspring.'

"Insomuch, then, as we are the offspring of God,
we ought not to suppose that that which is divine is
like unto a thing of gold, or silver, or stone, fashioned
by the art and imagination of man.

"Howbeit, those past times of ignorance God hath
overlooked ; but now commandeth he all men everywhere to repent, because he hath fixed a day wherein
he will judge the world in righteousness, by that
man whom he hath appointed, concerning whom he
gave proof unto all, in that he raised him from the
dead."*

"Hear, hear !" broke in a mocking voice. "This
unknown god is a marvel indeed ! He can raise the
dead ! He will also overlook our ignorance ! Let us
worship and bow down before his shrine !"

A burst of derisive laughter greeted this saying.
The assembly arose to its feet as one man ; the hearing was at an end.

"Impudent barbarian !" quoth a richly-dressed

---

* A translation from a careful comparison of various texts
and readings by eminent authorities.

Athenian, casting a look of withering scorn at the
stranger. " Look at him as he stands there ; it is
evident that he has more to say, but who would waste
precious time in listening to such babbling ? Come, let
us descend to the Stoa ; Apolonias will lecture there
this morning."

His companion regarded the speaker with cloudy
brows. " The man is no mere retailer of second-hand
learning, as is Apolonias," he said at length decidedly.
" I shall question him further concerning this matter ;
we have not given him a fair hearing."

The other threw back his head with a sneering
laugh. " Look you, my friend," he said with biting
emphasis, "yonder wench of a flower-girl is like-
minded with thyself ; the bold hussy is talking with
the fellow now. Go, join her by all means, and
Athens shall know by nightfall that Dionysius the
Areopagite and Damaris* the flower-girl are among the
converts of the Jew."

Dionysius did not reply ; he was already making
his way toward the " Stone of Impudence." His companion looked after him with a shrug of the shoulders.

" It appears that there be fools even in Athens !" he
remarked with a grimace. Which indeed was a true
word.

---

* Acts xvii., 34. The Athenian women of the better class
lived in the strictest seclusion ; it seems therefore not unreasonable to suppose that Damaris was one of the numerous flower-
girls that haunted the streets and market-places of the city.

Areopagite is equivalent to judge.

CHAPTER XXXIII.

THE TENT-MAKER.

THE tent-makers sat at their work in the open court-yard. There were three of them, a woman and two men. They had been at work since early dawn, but now the woman arose from her place and straightened her tall vigorous form. "Come," she said briskly, " let us rest for an hour ; our brother here is weary, if one may judge by his face. Two more seams to stitch and we shall be through with this piece of work." She pushed aside the coarse fabric of goat's hair as she spoke, thrust the great needle into a fold of her garment, and unwound the protecting bandages of linen from the palms of her hands.

One of the men speedily followed her example, giving vent to a long sigh of relief as he stretched his cramped limbs. "A mouthful of bread and cheese, my Priscilla," he began, "and—" But the woman had already disappeared. "She knows what I would say," he remarked with an air of content, his kind eyes resting upon his companion. "I tell thee, brother Paul, a good wife is assuredly from the Lord ; 'tis a pity that thou—" He stopped short, and glanced apprehensively in the direction of the house, whence issued a lively clatter of utensils. "She told me not to speak of this," he said cautiously, "but one cannot help his thoughts; what sayst thou, good brother?"

The man whom he addressed pulled his clumsy needle once and again through the stiff unyielding cloth before he replied. "It would ill become me to ask any woman to share the rigors of my lot, even were such a thing expedient for me. But thou art right to think with all affection of thy wife as a gift from God. Howbeit, fail not to think oftener of the Giver than of the gift, since the day of the Lord is at hand."

"Wilt thou continue to speak as heretofore in the synagogue on the Sabbath days?" said the other after a thoughtful pause.

"Assuredly," said the tent-maker looking up quickly, "and why dost thou ask, friend Aquila?"

"There be murmurings among certain of the Jews," said Aquila hesitatingly. "Nothing to speak of perhaps, and yet—"

Paul sighed wearily, "Necessity is laid upon me," he murmured—"yea, woe is unto me, if I proclaim not the glad-tidings."

"'Tis because of what thou didst say concerning the law," went on Aquila more boldly. "Thou mayst perchance make the matter right the next Sabbath day."

At this moment the woman Priscilla came out from the little scullery. "What, working yet?" she cried. "Nay, good brother, thou shouldst do no work at all with thy hands, if I had my say. There be many of us already who believe, and upon us should fall the burden of thy bodily maintenance—who hast also given to us of the bread of heaven, and that freely."

The sensitive face of the tent-maker reddened, "Thou hast spoken a sound word, my sister," he said quietly. "The Lord also appointed that they which preach the glad-tidings should live thereby; yet do I the rather labor with my hands that I may be free from the reproach of men—free, yet a servant unto all, that haply I may save some."

"The Lord reward thee!" said the woman, her clear brown eyes filling with sudden tears. "Ay, and he will reward thee. But come," she added briskly, "let us eat, since we must again labor; he that laboreth is assuredly worthy of his meat."

Six days out of the seven for more than a month the tent-makers had toiled at their needles from dawn until evening. "Work is not lacking in Corinth, thanks be to Jehovah!" said the good Aquila. And the stranger from Tarsus bowed his head in assent.

On Sabbath days all three passed through the busy streets of the great wicked city to the synagogue, where the tent-maker, Paul, became the impassioned proclaimer of wondrous sayings. On the first of these occasions people contented themselves by simply staring curiously. Later certain ones began the study of the prophecies; some were even convinced of the truth of the strange story of a crucified Messiah. Others shook their heads doubtfully. It was noticed with alarm by the wiseacres that an unusual number of Gentiles began to show their faces in the synagogue.

None of these offered themselves as proselytes. 'They had come,' they said, 'to hear the Jew Paulus tell of the strange god who could bring dead men to life again.'

Things were at this pass when one Ben Israel, a merchant of Athens, came to Corinth on business. He was known to be a reputable man, possessed moreover of much substance, and therefore not unreasonably a man of weight.

"Paul?" said Ben Israel, raising his eyebrows. "So the fellow hath come hither also."

"What dost thou know of the man?" asked one of the chief men of the synagogue, by name Sosthenes.

"Nothing good, son of Abraham," replied the merchant. "In Athens he fortunately gained no foothold among the chosen—nor indeed among the Gentiles; Athenians are not easily befooled." The speaker paused and drew his beard through his fingers with a well-satisfied air. "His object, do you ask? It seems not over-difficult to discover. Look you, the man is penniless, a fugitive, with a ready tongue and an impudent air. His so-called converts are what? Chiefly filthy Gentiles; with whom also he eats and sleeps, though he professes to be a Jew. In Philippi, I am told, after stirring up a tumult among the malcontents, proselytes and slaves, this fellow Paulus and another of the same sort who traveled with him, were seized by the authorities and soundly scourged. At Thessalonica—I have this information from kin of mine who dwell there—they fared little better, being forced to fly the city by night; so was it also at Berea."

The next day it was found by the now-thoroughly-aroused Jews that two coadjutors of the man Paul had arrived, both of whom set busily to work to spread the new and pernicious doctrine of a crucified and risen Messiah. A stormy scene followed in the synagogue. The tent-maker—as he was scornfully designated by the rich Jews—seemingly inspired to fresh zeal by the arrival of his companions, delivered a powerful discourse; the orthodox Jews replied to it on the spot, bringing all the thunders of the law to bear upon the bold apostate. The listeners were aroused to a frenzy of excitement, many weeping aloud and rending their garments, while others shouted "Alleluia !"

" Get thee hence, blasphemous liar," cried Sosthenes. " Thou hast defiled the house of Jehovah ; thou hast spoken abominable words in the habitation of the Most High !"

The eyes of the tent-maker flashed living fire. "Your blood be upon your own heads," he said, shaking his raiment with a gesture of appalling significance. "I am clean: from henceforth I will go unto the Gentiles."

The despised tent-maker went out indeed from that synagogue to enter it no more, but there followed him no less a person than its chief ruler, Crispus by name, who was straightway baptized with all his household, and with him many others, chiefly Gentiles. In the house of the proselyte Justus, who lived next door to the synagogue, these believers in a crucified carpenter met day by day, and the tent-maker taught them. They ate together—making no secret of it—meats clean and unclean, purchased in the heathen markets.

"Abomination of desolation!" wailed the orthodox Jews. "So doth the wicked flourish like the green bay! But he shall be cut down," they added, grinding their teeth.

The tent-maker was human. He was moreover feeble in body and worn with labor and suffering; his bent form staggered sometimes beneath the load of care and responsibility which seemed bound upon him. He slept little and prayed much. There were the other little companies of believers in distant cities, exposed to hatred and persecution, with no regular teachers, and no records of the blessed life. These lay heavily upon his heart; he must write to them. After the long day of exhausting toil, he pours out his heart to them, Timothy, the beloved, writing down the words as they fall from his lips.

*"Paul and Silvanus and Timotheus, to the church of the Thessalonians, in God our Father, and the Lord Jesus Christ: Grace be to you and peace.

"I give continual thanks to God for you all, and

---

* I. Thessalonians. From the translation from the original Greek by Rev. W. J. Conybeare. Conybeare and Howson's *Life and Epistles of St. Paul*.

make mention of you all in my prayers without ceasing; remembering, in the presence of our God and
Father, the working of your faith, the labors of your
love, and the steadfastness of your hope in our Lord
Jesus Christ.

"Brethren, beloved by God, I know how God hath
chosen you; for my glad-tidings came to you, not
only in word, but also in power, with the might of
the Holy Spirit, and with the full assurance of belief.
. . . . Others are telling what welcome you gave
me, how you forsook your idols, and turned to serve
God, the living and true; and to wait for his son from
the heavens, whom he raised from the dead, even Jesus
Christ our deliverer from the coming wrath.

"For, you know yourselves, brethren, that my
coming amongst you was not fruitless; but after I had
borne suffering and outrage, as you know, at Philippi,
I trusted in my God, and boldly declared to you God's
glad-tidings in the midst of great contention. For my
exhortations are not prompted by imposture, nor by
uncleanness, nor do I speak deceitfully.* But as God
hath proved my fitness for the charge of the glad-
tidings, so I speak, not seeking to please men, but
God, who proves our hearts. For never did I use

---

* In this place we have allusions to the outrageous accusations brought against St. Paul by his Jewish opponents, and by
some even in the church itself. He was charged with being
unprincipled, avaricious, impure. It is evident from the Acts
and the Epistles that among those in authority in the church,
Paul occupied no such position of influence as he holds with us
to-day.

flattering words, as you know ; nor hide covetousness under fair pretences, God is witness. . . . . Remember, brethren, my toilsome labours ; how I worked both night and day, that I might not be burdensome to any of you, while I proclaimed to you the message which I bore, the glad-tidings of God. . . . . You know how earnestly, as a father his own children, I exhorted, and entreated, and adjured each one among you to walk worthy of God, by whom you are called into his own kingdom and glory. . . . . For you, brethren, followed in the steps of the churches of God in Judæa, which are in Christ Jesus, inasmuch as you suffered the like persecution from your own countrymen, which they endured from the Jews, who also killed both the Lord Jesus and the prophets, and who have driven me forth from city to city ; a people displeasing to God, and enemies to all mankind, who would hinder me from speaking to the Gentiles for their salvation ; continuing always to fill up the measure of their sins. But the wrath of God has overtaken them.

" But I, brethren, having been torn from you for a short season in presence, not in heart, sought very earnestly to behold you again face to face. . . . . But Satan hindered me. For what is my hope or joy ? What is the crown wherein I glory ? What but your ownselves, in the presence of our Lord Jesus Christ at his appearing. Yes, you are my glory and my joy. Therefore, when I was no longer able to forbear, I determined willingly to be left at Athens alone, and I sent Timotheus, my brother, and God's fellow-worker in the glad-tidings of Christ, that he might strengthen your constancy, and exhort you concerning your faith, that none of you should waver in these afflictions. . . . . Fearing lest perchance the tempter had tempted you, and lest my labor should be in vain. But now that Timotheus hath returned from you to me, and hath brought me glad tidings of your faith and love, and that you still keep an affectionate remembrance of me, longing to see me, as I to see you—I have been comforted, brethren, on your behalf, and all my own tribulation and distress has been lightened by your faith."

And so to the end, with words of tenderest love, warning, exhortation, pleading, encouragement. Comforting them also with the comfort wherewith he had himself been comforted. "Be not afraid," the Lord had said to him in the night by a vision, "but speak, and hold not thy peace. Lo, I am with thee, and no man shall set on thee to hurt thee ; for I have much people in this city."

For more than a year he labored, gathering the elect of heaven from out the cesspools of iniquity, from out the dust-heaps of ignorance and superstition ; from among slaves, from among lost women, from among degraded idolaters of every class.

"For ye see your calling, brethren," he writes to them afterward from Ephesus, "how that not many wise after the flesh, not many mighty, not many noble, are called. But God hath chosen the foolish things of the world to confound the wise; and God hath chosen the weak things of the world to confound the mighty; and base things of the world, and things which are despised, hath God chosen—yea, and things which are not, to bring to nought things that are."

To Sosthenes also there came visions of a speedy triumph over the hated tent-maker. A new proconsul, one Gallio, was about to be installed over Achaia. He was the brother of the philosopher Seneca, reputed moreover to be a man of mild and easy disposition.

"The Roman will desire to stand well with us, since we represent no small share of the wealth of the province," argued Sosthenes. "We will therefore lose no time in laying this matter before him."

Accordingly, on the very day in which the new proconsul began his official duties, the Jews arose in a body, seized the tent-maker as he sat at his work, and dragged him before the judgment-seat of Gallio, which was set, as was the custom, on a square of tesselated pavement before the palace.

"Behold, O most excellent and righteous proconsul!" cried Sosthenes, "we have brought before thee this fellow that thou mayst pass judgment upon him. He teacheth men to worship God contrary to the law."*

---

* The Jewish religion was a *religio licita* : *i. e.*, it was licensed by the Roman government. The religion that Paul taught, in so much as it differed from the licensed Judaism, was therefore "contrary to the law."

Gallio surveyed the turbulent crowd with haughty disdain; like other noble Romans his feeling for all Jews was one of unmixed hatred and contempt. Pressing hard after the noisy complainants, he noticed a number of Greeks and other foreigners, whose faces and gestures expressed the strongest excitement and indignation. As for the accused, he was merely a shabby insignificant old man—a Jew also. It was evident that he would utter some sort of a defence if allowed to do so.

The proconsul frowned impatiently. "If this were a matter of civil wrong or moral outrage," he said with cold decisiveness, "it would be reasonable that I should listen to your accusation; but if it be merely a question of words and names, and of your law, look ye to it, for I will be no judge of such matters.— Lictors, clear the court!"

The accused at once withdrew with certain of his friends, who had awaited the decision with manifest trepidation. The lookers-on cheered them as they went away; then they turned their attention to Sosthenes and his fellows, who were elbowing their way through the crowd, muttering maledictions upon the head of the proconsul.

"Ha, Jews!" yelled a Greek, who wore a red cap very much at one side, and carried a kithera slung over his shoulder. "Jews—liars—thieves—unclean dogs! Go home and eat swine's flesh—Go!"

Sosthenes paused, and fixed his eyes burning with hate upon the bold Greek; he lifted one shaking hand high above his head. "May the curses of the living Jehovah—"

But the mob with a deafening howl rushed upon him. "Wilt thou also call down curses upon us?" they cried in a fury. "Nay, let thy God deliver thee if he will." And they beat him with their staves in full sight of the judgment-seat.

Gallio observed the proceedings with a shrug. He did not order his lictors to interfere. "The Jews of Corinth will beware how they trouble me in the future with their petty disputes," he said languidly to one of the officers of the guard, who stood behind his chair.

There be those who affirm that Sosthenes afterward went to Ephesus that he might avenge himself for that beating upon the tent-maker; and that there God opened his eyes to the truth. Certain it is that the first letter to the Corinthians begins thus:

"Paul, called to be an apostle of Jesus Christ through the will of God, and Sosthenes our brother, unto the church of God which is at Corinth, to them which are sanctified in Christ Jesus, called to be saints, with all that in every place call upon the name of Jesus Christ our Lord; Grace be unto you, and peace, from God the Father and from the Lord Jesus Christ."

CHAPTER XXXIV.

A BUSINESS MAN OF EPHESUS.

CLAUDIUS, emperor of Rome was dead ; poisoned—so ran the evil whisper, by his empress. There was no investigation of the suspicious circumstances which surrounded his death. The young Brittanicus, his lawful heir, with his sister Octavia, were, it is true, overwhelmed with grief and fear, but in the great palace with its fifteen hundred courtiers and retainers they were more desolate and helpless than the meanest slaves.

It was known that Agrippina Augusta,* sixth wife and niece of the emperor, had with her own fair hand taken a mushroom from the silver dish set before her at supper by Halotus, taster to his imperial highness, and with honeyed words of flattery had presented it to her husband. Shortly after eating it, the emperor was borne from the table in violent convulsions which terminated his life within a few hours. Those in high places merely shrugged their shoulders ; Lo-

---

* Agrippina was one of the daughters of Germanicus and therefore sister of Caius Cæsar ; she was recalled from banishment by Claudius, and became his wife after the death of the infamous Messelina. She was a woman of the most abandoned character.

custa, the most skilful poisoner of her time, yet lived
in a dungeon of the palace—too valuable an adjunct to
imperial power to be lightly thrust out of life.　It was
not the part of discretion to look at things too
closely, and why, after all, mourn for a man who
had quitted the palace of the Cæsars only to become
a god?

Agrippina herself officiated as priestess in the stately
ceremonial of deification ; and if the scarlet stola embroidered with pearls, which she wore, reminded the
beholders somewhat unpleasantly of blood, they had
only to raise their eyes to the beautiful haughty face
above it to be dazzled or awed into forgetfulness.
More than all, Nero was emperor.　Nero, young, gay,
genial, beautiful as one of the sculptured gods.　There
was no visible stain on the fair jeweled hands which
had lifted him to the throne, and therefore two hundred millions of mankind lifted their eyes and adored ;
adored Claudius dead—no matter how—and enthroned
amid the stately shades of Cæsars long-since departed,
adored Agrippina Augusta, the magnificent—the imperial empress-mother, adored Nero, her son, emperor
of Rome, and master of their future lives and happiness.

Reports of these ominous happenings reached the
provinces in due time.　Another emperor on the
throne ! this meant perhaps new governors, new legions, new taxations, new laws, better possibly—or
worse.　The people listened with commendable patience to the reading of the imperial proclamation,

raised a mighty shout in token of their loyal allegiance, then went about their business resignedly. Claudius was dead; Nero reigned; but bread must be eaten to-day and to-morrow, and bread was not easy to get.

In the shop of Demetrius, chief silver-smith of Ephesus, work was going on briskly, as usual; Demetrius himself, an undersized, yellow, grim-looking man of uncertain age was in a bad temper—also as usual; his eye traveled impatiently about the dark crowded room where a score or more of workmen sat bending over their tasks.

"Let the knaves look to the polishing more carefully than they have done of late," he growled, turning to the overseer who stood at his side. "And look you, there is no need to make the next lot quite so heavy; our pilgrims do not buy the image of the sacred Diana for the amount of silver that is in it, the gods be praised."

He picked up one of the finished pieces as he spoke and examined it carefully. It was a small but exact copy of the world-famous shrine and image of the Ephesian Diana, the original of which, shrouded from vulgar gaze, stood in the dark and awful adytum of the great temple; an image fashioned from some unknown substance by the fingers of the great father of the gods himself, and dropped down from unimaginable realms to the children of men for their comfort and healing—so at least ran the story of its origin, which had been implicitly believed for ages. The silver model at which Demetrius was looking, represented a hideous mis-shapen figure, swathed like a mummy and covered from head to foot with protuberances representing, it was thought, the all-bounteous breasts of nature. Upon the inverted pyramid which formed a base for the shapeless feet were inscribed certain words of mysterious import. 'The very words,' Demetrius was wont to assure his patrons, 'which rendered the sacred original of such wonderful efficacy for every human ill.'

"Askion — Kataskion—Lix—Tetras — Dammameneus—Aisia,"* he muttered to himself, his surly brow clearing.

The obtaining of these mystic words had turned out to be a wonderful piece of good luck, he reflected, superstitious awe and greed mingling on pretty even terms in his mind. It was a great sum assuredly which the rapacious priests yonder had forced him to pay for them — but well expended, as subsequent events had proven. At the forthcoming festival of the goddess he would sell hundreds—nay thousands—of these shrines. He was already a rich man ; he would speedily be richer.

"Who knows," he muttered, as he laid the image down, " I may be Asiarch yet."†

---

* See Farrar's *Life and Work of St. Paul,* page 360.

† Ten Asiarchs were chosen annually from among the wealthiest citizens of the chief cities of Asia. These presided over the great yearly festival held in Ephesus in honor of the goddess Diana, and upon them devolved the vast expenses of the occasion, but in return their names were recorded on coins

After finishing the inspection of his shops, the worthy silver-smith betook himself to the examination of his accounts, an occupation which proved on this occasion to be even more satisfactory. Profits were good, silver was plenty, labor was cheap; more than that, the worship of Diana was steadily increasing year by year. And he, Demetrius, the silver-smith, had helped to bring this about; he could see no limit to the dazzling possibilities of his pious industry; the more shrines he sold, the more pilgrims would flock to Ephesus the following year, attracted by the fame of the original heaven-wrought image—an image which Demetrius privately thought to be a very poor production compared with his own brand-new manufacture. Every worshiper would carry away some token of his pilgrimage, and what more desireable than one of these beautiful silver shrines, with the image of the goddess and the sacred words all complete.

"I shall certainly be an Asiarch," repeated Demetrius triumphantly, "and when that happens, let who will rule Rome!" He bestowed the parchments in his strong box, and putting on his conical cap strolled out into the Agora. The place was humming like a hive of bees, the shouts of the hucksters at their stalls, the shrill cries of itinerant venders, and the fitful blow-. ing of flutes which announced the presence of some beardless priest of Diana mingled confusedly with the

and in public inscriptions; they were robed in purple and crowned with garlands, and were henceforth regarded as persons of the highest distinction and honor.

clack of countless tongues. Demetrius surveyed the
scene loftily as if he already wore the purple robe and
laurel wreath of an Asiarch.

"And what say you, my good Demetrius, to the
news from Rome?" exclaimed a voice at his side.

The silver-smith turned and surveyed the speaker,
"My good Demetrius indeed!" he thought, "and
from a beggarly knave like Trophimus." Aloud he said
coldly, "The news from Rome does not concern me."

The man who had accosted him laid one finger at
the side of his nose, "O ho, my lord Demetrius, so
the wind sits in the wrong quarter to-day. Well then,
since the news from Rome does not concern thee, I
know something that does. In the school of Tyrannus
yonder, a learned traveler from Jerusalem is proclaiming a new and terrible god who will shortly destroy
the temple of Diana with all that worship her. How
many silver shrines think you will be sold when that
shall come to pass?"

"From Jerusalem!" exclaimed Demetrius scornfully, "What care I for the witless ravings of a filthy
Jew; I have heard of the man Sceva* and his tribe
before."

"This man's name is Paulus," said Trophimus,
dropping his voice; "by the heaven-born Artemis, I
am myself more than half convinced of the truth of
what he says."

Demetrius looked after him as he walked away.
"Blockhead!" he muttered comtemptuously.

---

* Acts xix., 13-17.

On the opposite side of the square stood a long low building with pillared front; it was called the school of Tyrannus after the famous Ephesian of that name who had once instructed a multitude of devout pupils within its walls. Of late it had been leased for longer or shorter periods to divers itinerant philosophers, astrologers and wonder-workers, who brimming over with real or imaginary learning had there harangued the gaping loafers of the Agora.

" Fool !" repeated Demetrius irritably. " Destroy the temple of Diana indeed !"

He lifted his eyes to the gleaming walls of the great building which was the crowning glory of Ephesus the magnificent, and one of the wonders of the habitable world, four times as great as the Athenian Parthenon, its peristyle consisting of one hundred and twenty Ionic pillars hewn from Parian marble, its roof of cedar supported by columns of jasper, its walls enriched by priceless statues and paintings by Praxiteles, Parhasius and Appelles, with its sacred shrine behind the awful curtain, where dwelt the heaven-wrought image, and its inestimable treasures of gold, of silver, of precious stones. Demetrius laughed aloud and rubbed his hands.

" There is nothing in heaven above or in the earth beneath that can shake the power of the eternal Diana," he muttered, " and praise be to the gods, my fortunes are linked with hers !" Nevertheless he turned his steps in the direction of the school of Tyrannus. " I will see for myself," he said, " what this thing may be."

There was a great crowd about the door of the place; Demetrius found himself unable to get in, but he could hear the tones of a man's voice, rising and falling as if in passionate exhortation; it was interrupted suddenly by a loud joyful cry, followed by a prolonged murmur of excitement from the multitude.

"For the love of the goddess, let me pass!" cried a ragged misshapen woman, wringing her lean hands piteously; "he has healed another—Nay, I must get in."

Demetrius had succeeded in forcing his way somewhat nearer the door by this time; he had made up his mind to see what was going on inside.

"For the love of the Christ, let me pass—that I also may be healed," repeated the beggar woman; in her desperation she pushed violently against the person of the wealthy silver-smith.

"Dog!" he cried, striking her full in the face with his clenched fist.

The woman fell back with a low moan, blood streaming from her mouth. The crowd burst into a loud jeering laugh.

"Ha, good silver-smith, I see that thou hast curiosity as well as another."

Demetrius turned and doffed his cap with respect. The man who had spoken was Plautius, the owner of rich silver mines, and thus connected with the craft of which Demetrius was master.

"Thou art a shrewd fellow, Demetrius, a shrewd fellow," said the other with a laugh, "but take my word for it there is no need; I have been within for a full hour and have heard all that I can stomach. The fellow is a Jew—and Diana alone knoweth what besides—an exorcist, magic-monger, proclaimer of a crucified malefactor, one Christus, who also arose from the dead. A mule teaching flies, say I. Come, a word with you on business."

Thus reassured by so wise a man as the wealthy Plautius, Demetrius straightway forgot the whole matter. There were thousands of chattering cheats plying their precarious avocations in Ephesus, but what did that matter to the head of a solid and highly-respectable industry. The time of the great yearly festival was moreover now close at hand, pilgrims were beginning to flock into the city from every part of Asia. The fortunate citizens who had been chosen to personate the gods in the great pageant, were already looked upon with that species of mock adoration which would be their portion for the month during which the Ephesia was in progress. The theatre and stadium were crowded daily with festive throngs, to witness the musical and oratorical contests, the chariot races, athletic exhibitions, gladiatorial battles, and the yet more terrible combats between men and wild beasts.*

While the city resounded day and night with the loud shrilling of flutes and jangling of timbrels from the gorgeous processions and spectacles which were constantly sweeping to the great temple of Diana,

---

* I. Cor. xv., 32.

while lust and murder stalked through the streets unveiled, while the herd of bloated and beardless priests with their attendant priestesses shamed the light of the sun with their nameless abominations, Paul, a servant of Jesus Christ, called to be an apostle, separated unto the glad-tidings of God, beheld in this sickening spectacle of debased humanity only "a great door and effectual which was opened unto him."

Toiling late into the night at his humble trade of tent-making, that he might support not only himself but those who were with him, by day he proclaimed the glad-tidings in the school of Tyrannus, in the streets and market-places, and from house to house, spit upon, reviled, greeted everywhere with hissings and maledictions, tortured by bodily sufferings, faint with hunger, parched with thirst, ragged and footsore, made as it were the filth and offscouring of the world, "pilloried on infamy's high stage," a spectacle to men and angels.*

"And this continued for the space of two years; so that all they which dwelt in Asia heard the word of the Lord Jesus, both Jews and Greeks."

During these years Demetrius has grown steadily richer; he no longer wears the conical cap of a master-smith, but affects the rich and sober garb of a wealthy citizen of leisure; he still visits his work-shops daily, and looks to the weight and finish of his silver images as carefully as ever. It is whispered that he is possessed of more treasure in the mysterious and invio-

---

* I. Cor. iv., 9–13.

lable stronghold behind the veiled shrine of Diana than
even Plautius, who was Asiarch last year. As he
stands in the door of his work-shop, occasionally
acknowledging with a haughty wave of the hand the
salutation of a passing acquaintance, it may be seen
that he has grown stouter and sleeker than of old.

" Demetrius, with his protuberant paunch and his
sour ugly little face "—Plautius had once observed
behind his back—" resembles nothing so much as one
of his own images." And this irreverent speech had
been whispered about with huge enjoyment amongst
his fellow-craftsmen.

On this pleasant spring morning the sour ugly little
face of the rich silversmith was sourer and uglier than
ever. He was looking at the crowd which had been
gathering for the last hour in the market-square in
front of the school of Tyrannus ; now and again he
muttered something unintelligible under his breath.
Suddenly a great shout broke forth from a thousand
throats, as a dense cloud of smoke pierced here and
there with darting tongues of flame rolled heavily
upward.

" Fools !" cried Demetrius aloud, grinding his teeth.
" Unspeakable asses ! they will be burning my shop
over my head next !"

" Ay, and so they will, friend Demetrius," said a
solemn voice at his side. " Repent and believe,
brother, repent and believe, else not only thy house
but thine own wretched body shall be burned with
unquenchable fire."

Demetrius spat venomously before him, his yellow countenance streaked and livid with rage. "And since when," he spluttered, "has Trophimus taken up the trade of the beggar Jew? I saw the wretch yesterday, ragged, bare-footed, sore-eyed, hooted by a crowd of gamins in the Agora."

"Nevertheless he hath prevailed, and that gloriously, over the powers of darkness which be at Ephesus," answered Trophimus steadily. "This burning of profane and wicked books which thou seest,* is but the token of that greater triumph over evil which shall speedily come to pass. Know ye not that the day of the living God is at hand? That in token thereof the sick are raised up, the blind see, the lame walk, and they that mourn rejoice in hope? Come, therefore, fetch forth thine idols and cast them also into the flames, and of the ill-gotten gains which thou hast heaped up to thyself give to the necessities of the poor; so shalt thou be saved from thy sins, and the blessing of the Lord shall rest upon thee and upon thy house."

Demetrius laughed aloud. "Ay! there's the point! 'Give of thy gold to the necessities of the poor.' How much will serve thee, my friend Trophimus? and how much will the false Jew, thy master, require? Name the sum.—Ay, do!"

Trophimus turned away. "The Lord have mercy upon thee, neighbor," he said sadly, "and bring thee to a knowledge of the truth as it is in Christ Jesus."

---

* Acts xix., 19.

With a sudden violent gesture Demetrius plucked the jeweled poinard from his girdle and hurled it after the departing figure of the man whom he had once called friend. The weapon fell short and clattered noisily upon the pavement. " The curses of Diana! —The curses of Diana light upon thee!" he shrieked. "Askion! Kataskion! Lix! Tetras! Damnameneus!"

But Trophimus went steadily on his way, and never so much as turned his head.

CHAPTER XXXV.

"GREAT DIANA OF THE EPHESIANS!"

"ASKION, Kataskion, Lix, Tet—" Demetrius stopped short with a snarl like that of an angry hyena, then he turned and darted into the shop. "How many shrines did we sell at the last Ephesia but one?" he demanded, glaring at his foreman as if he would tear him in twain.

"Diana be praised, we sold more than a score of thousands, gracious master," answered the craftsman with an uneasy smile.

"How many last year? Answer quickly, fellow."

"There were fewer pilgrims last year, as also thou knowest, honored sir," said the man, spreading out his hands apologetically, "fewer pilgrims and—"

"Yes, I do know," snarled Demetrius stamping his foot, "fewer pilgrims and only fifteen thousand shrines sold."

The foreman shrugged his shoulders, "Not a small number—fifteen thousand," he ventured. "Now this year—"

"Yes, and what of this year? Only a beggarly five thousand! Great Diana of the Ephesians! Askion, Kataskion, Lix!—Bah!"

"But the festival has but just commenced, honored—"

"Hold thy tongue, dog, till I bid thee bark. Go forth, say to the craftsmen who make images of the goddess—of whatever sort—come hither, and at once. Dost thou hear?"

"I hear, gracious sir," answered the man, staring at his master in amazement; "but surely thou dost not mean the makers of the miserable clay images, nor the fellow Helotus yonder who hath dared to imitate thy sacred production in copper bronze?"

Demetrius swallowed hard, the great veins on his forehead stood out like whip-cord. "Yes," he said fiercely. "Fetch them all—every one. Compel them to come. Tell them Demetrius hath a weighty matter to lay before them; a matter which hath to do with gold—ay, with gold."

Within the hour the square in front of the shop of Demetrius was thronged with brawny artisans, many of them bearing the implements of their labor. It was evident that these were in no mood to be trifled with.

"Where is Demetrius?" growled a great hulking fellow, who carried a brace of mighty hammers in his belt. "And what of the gold? By Artemis, I would have him understand that time is gold with me."

"Ay, where is he?" echoed a score of others. "If this be one of his scurvy tricks now, to lure us away from our shops—"

But Demetrius was already clambering upon a bench, which he had dragged with his own hands from the interior of the shop. His rich robes had been laid aside. He wore the conical cap of a master-smith and a shabby workman's blouse.

"What dost thou want with us, Demetrius?" cried the man with the hammers, stepping forward. This man was Helotus, the rival shrine-maker.

Demetrius surveyed him with an inscrutable smile, "I want much, brother craftsmen," he said.—"Ay, much. Yonder before the school of Tyrannus lies a heap of ashes; that heap of ashes was once worth fifty thousand pieces of silver—ay, fifty thousand pieces!"

"And what has that to do with us?" roared Helotus, advancing a step nearer.

"Much!" repeated Demetrius, his eyes flaming, "those costly books were burned at the instigation of one Paul, a knavish Jew, who hath dwelt in our city for a matter of three years now. So would he burn the images of the great Diana, which we fashion to her honor and glory."

A sullen growl of wrath greeted these words.

"'Tis a matter of gold," continued Demetrius, his shrill voice rising almost to a scream, "for, sirs, ye know that by this craft we have our wealth. Moreover ye see and hear, that not alone at Ephesus, but almost throughout all Asia, this Paul hath persuaded and turned away much people, saying that they be no gods which are made with hands. So that not only this our craft is in danger to be set at naught, but also that the temple of the great goddess Diana should be despised, and her magnificence destroyed, whom all Asia and the world worshipeth!"

"Great is Diana of the Ephesians! Great is Diana of the Ephesians!" burst forth a deep-throated roar.

Demetrius joined in the cry, waving his cap high above his head. From his elevated position he could see that people were running towards them from every direction. He laughed aloud.

"Great is Diana of the Ephesians! Great is Diana of the Ephesians!"

The hurrying crowds took up the cry with savage joy. And yonder was a score of long-haired priests, dancing, leaping, and shrieking forth the wild ululatus of the temple worship. "Great—Great Diana! Diana of the Ephesians! Great—great!"

"Ay, great Diana of the Ephesians!" screamed Demetrius, "and death to the man who hath dishonored her name!"

"Death! Death!" howled the mob. "Great is Diana of the Ephesians!"

"Follow where I lead!" cried Demetrius leaping into the midst of the crowd. "Death to the Jew! Death!"

Priscilla the tent-maker, busily at work with her husband in one of the squalid streets of the Jewish quarter, heard the sound of the tumult; she shook her head with a sigh. "They are shouting the praises of the idol louder than ever," she said with a quick impatient frown. "Nay I marvel at the forbearance of the living God. Surely this city is more noisome than Sodom of old which was burned with fire; it is more evil than Egypt which Jehovah

24

plagued with a sevenfold torment. And it is for such worthless wretches that our good Paulus doth live a life of toil and suffering, scarce taking time to sleep or to eat; spending himself like a copper farthing, who also is pure gold and worth a million souls of yonder screaming blasphemous besotted idolaters. Jehovah be praised, he is asleep now after toiling all night."

Aquila threaded his empty needle before he answered. "And how," said he slowly, "camest thou to possess such knowledge?"—setting two stitches firmly and deliberately—"Dost thou also hold the eternal balance in which men and cities are weighed for judgment?"

Priscilla did not answer; she was staring at the door of the courtyard. "What—what is it, my Gaius?" she faltered.

The man who had entered hastily locked and barred the door behind him. His face was white and his eyes stood out of his head with terror. "Is Paulus here?" he whispered.

"Yes—yes, asleep yonder, what is it?"

"We must hide him quick! The mob—dost thou not hear?"

Priscilla looked about her despairingly. "But—where?" she cried, wringing her hands.

"Great is Diana of the Ephesians! Death—death to the Jew!"

"They will tear him limb from limb," whispered Gaius, "but not whilst I live!—Aristarchus is without, he can hold them at the gate for a moment."

Paul—7.

"THE PLACE WAS FILLED IN A TWINKLING."

Now Priscilla was a woman of resources; some months before, finding herself hampered in her small house-keeping by the bulky masses of tent-cloth, she had caused a small square cellar to be excavated in the beaten floor of the courtyard, this place she had found most convenient for the storage of articles of food, fuel, and various utensils. It was provided with a close-fitting cover.

"Fetch him hither—on his bed," she whispered urgently: "do not waken him or he will face the mob—say what we will. Quickly, so!"

She dropped the cover softly, dragged the tent-cloth on which she was working across it, then coolly resumed her monotonous stitching. "Go out now into the street, both of you," she said, motioning to the two men. "I shall be best alone."

But there was no time for flight, even had Aquila and Gaius been so minded, the furious storm of blows which shook the door, mingled with deafening howls, "The Jew! the Jew! Open in the name of the great Diana!" announced the presence of Demetrius and his fellows.

Priscilla shrugged her shoulders, an angry light glittered in her brown eyes. "Curs!" she said contemptuously. "Open to them, my husband; the door is but wood."

The place was filled in a twinkling, so full that the first to enter were crowded against the further wall, and held there as in a vise.

"The Jew—the Jew!" yelled Demetrius, seizing

Priscilla by the wrist. "Where is the Jew, Paulus? Answer, wench !"

"And what might be your business with Paulus, sir ?" asked Priscilla, looking down at the puny silver-smith from the full height of her indignant womanhood.

For answer Demetrius reached up and struck her full across the face. "Where is the Jew?" he repeated with a vile execration.

Priscilla trembled ; the strength seemed to sink away from her limbs, a feeling of deadly nausea almost overpowered her. She looked wildly about for her husband and Gaius, they had disappeared ; she fancied she could hear their voices above the deafening tumult in the street. "Help, Lord !" she sighed ; and on the instant strength and courage came. She suddenly remembered that in the throng and tumult lay safety for the man she was striving to save. She smiled triumphantly. "He will be displeased with me," she said to herself, "but if I save him I can endure his frown."

"Thou hast led us on a wrong scent this time, Demetrius," shouted Helotus angrily. "The Jew is nowhere to be found. Come, let us go !"

"He was seen to enter this place not two hours since," snarled Demetrius, staring fixedly at Priscilla's white face. "He is not far away, and what is more the woman knows where. Fetch me a torch, some of you."

Helotus laughed savagely. "This will serve as

well," he said, holding up a brazier heaped with glowing charcoal. "The Jew's porridge may cool awhile."

"Ay, the brazier will do. Hold the wench from behind there—so. Now wilt thou answer? Where is the Jew? Tell me, or straightway I offer this right hand of thine a burnt sacrifice to great Diana of the Ephesians."

Priscilla threw back her head haughtily, her eyes blazed. "Thinkest thou to torture me unto confession," she cried. "Idolaters—cowards! I fear neither you nor the fire!" Snatching her hand from the grasp of Demetrius she plunged it into the brazier, seized a handful of the blazing charcoal and hurled it into the crowd.

"A witch! A witch! A fire-witch!" screamed a voice. "Run for your lives!"

With wild cries of terror the mob fought, bit, and tore each other in their frantic efforts to gain the street. There was a smell of burning, a thunder of trampling feet, a chorus of curses, yells, execrations, and the courtyard was empty. Priscilla looked anxiously about her. There was neither smoke nor flame, though the blackened holes in the tent-cloth showed plainly enough where the burning coals had fallen. The mob had trampled out the fire in their mad rush for the street.

"Thank God!" cried Priscilla, sinking to her knees. "Thank God!" Then she quietly fainted, her head falling back against the heap of tattered and ruined cloth. But Paul on his bed in the little cellar below still slept the death-like sleep of utter exhaustion. And so Aquila found them a few moments later, when torn and bleeding from his desperate struggle with the mob, he rushed into his dismantled house.

When Paul understood what had taken place, and how Priscilla and Aquila had stood between him and death in its most awful form,* he bowed his head. " Greater love hath no man than this," he murmured, "that a man lay down his life for his friend." After a pause he asked for Gaius and Aristarchus his companions in travel, and learning that they were still in the hands of the mob, he would have gone forth to their rescue straightway.

But Priscilla fell down at his knees. " By the burning anguish of my right hand," she cried, " which I endure with joy, knowing that it availed for thy life, I beseech thee to remain in safety."

And while she yet spake, there came others of the disciples who brought word from the chief men of the city, requesting that Paul should not adventure himself among the people. "The mob," said these, " have rushed into the theatre, where they are shouting as with one voice, ' Great is Diana of the Ephesians !' As for Gaius and Aristarchus, being Greeks, they are not likely to come to any harm."†

After the uproar was ceased, Paul called unto him the disciples, and when he had bade them farewell he

* Romans xvi., 3, 4. See also, Farrar's *Life and Work of St. Paul,* chap. xxxi.

† Acts xix., 29-41.

departed unto Macedonia,* where he visited the churches, exhorting and confirming them in the faith. From Macedonia he traveled into Greece and there remained for the space of three months, but being again in peril at the hands of the Jews, he returned to Macedonia and thence by ship to Miletus, for he desired if it were possible to be at Jerusalem on the day of Pentecost.

From Miletus he sent to Ephesus, and called the elders of the church. And when they were come he said to them,

"Brethren, ye know from the first day that I came to Asia, after what manner I have been with you at all seasons: serving the Lord with all lowliness of mind, and with many tears and trials which befell me through the plotting of the Jews. And how I kept back none of those things which are profitable for you, but declared them to you, and taught you publicly and from house to house ; testifying both to Jews and Gentiles their need of repentance towards God and faith in our Lord Jesus Christ.

"And now, behold, I go bound in the spirit unto Jerusalem, not knowing the things that shall befall me there, save that the Holy Spirit witnesseth in every city, saying that bonds and afflictions abide me. But none of these things move me, neither count I my life dear unto myself so that I might finish my course

---

* It is thought that II. Corinthians was written at Philippi at this time. Galatians and Romans also belong to this period, being written from Corinth a few months later.

with joy, and the ministry which I received from the Lord Jesus to testify the glad-tidings of the grace of God.

"And now I know that ye all, among whom I have gone from city to city proclaiming the kingdom of God, shall see my face no more. Wherefore I call you to witness this day that I am clean from the blood of all men. For I shrank not from declaring unto you the whole counsel of God. Take heed therefore unto yourselves, and to all the flock, over which the Holy Spirit hath set you as shepherds, to feed the church of God, which he purchased with his own blood. For this I know, that after my departure grievous wolves shall enter in among you, not sparing the flock. And from among your own selves shall men arise, speaking perverted words that they may draw away the disciples after them. Therefore be watchful, and remember that for the space of three years I ceased not to warn every one of you night and day with tears.

"And now brethren, I commend you to God, and to the word of his grace; even to him who is able to build you up and to give you an inheritance among all them that are sanctified. I have coveted no man's silver or gold, or apparel. Yea, ye yourselves know that these hands have ministered unto my necessities and to them that were with me. I have showed you all things, how that so laboring ye ought to support the weak, and to remember the words of the Lord Jesus, how he said, 'It is more blessed to give than to receive.' "

When he had thus spoken, he kneeled down and prayed with them all.　And they all wept sore, and fell on Paul's neck and kissed him, sorrowing most of all for the word which he had spoken, that they should see his face no more.

And they accompanied him to the ship.

PART III

"An Ambassador in Bonds"

CHAPTER XXXVI.

PAUL reached Jerusalem in time for the feast of Pentecost, as he had wished. What inward conviction urged him on can never be known. "Go not up to Jerusalem," said certain disciples at Tyre where the travelers tarried seven days ; and it is recorded of these that they "spake through the spirit." At Caesarea also came a second warning ; Agabus, on whom had fallen the mysterious gift of prophecy, took Paul's girdle and bound his own hands and feet, saying, "So shall the Jews at Jerusalem bind the man that owneth this girdle, and shall deliver him into the hands of the Gentiles."

At this both his host and the disciples of Caesarea who had gathered to meet him, with Timothy and Luke, Sopater, Aristarchus and Secundus, Gaius, Tychicus and Trophimus, his companions in travel, besought him with tears that he should not go up to Jerusalem.

But Paul answered them, " What mean ye to weep and break mine heart ? for I am ready not to be bound only, but also to die at Jerusalem for the name of the Lord Jesus."

" And when he could not be persuaded," writes Luke, "we ceased, saying, The will of the Lord be done."

The day of Pentecost passed quietly; and on the day following, Paul together with the delegates from the Gentile churches, bearing the contributions which were the fruit of untold sacrifices, of reverent and loving regard for the mother-church at Jerusalem, appeared before the council of elders. Paul had taught these men that there was neither Jew nor Greek in the sight of God, that all were one in Christ Jesus; he had encouraged them to rejoice in their freedom from the law, to beware lest they become entangled with the yoke of bondage, " In Jesus Christ neither circumcision availeth anything nor uncircumcision," he had declared, "but faith which worketh by love." Yet before the cold, almost hostile eyes of that conclave of rigid law-abiding Jewish presbyters, these ardent disciples must have felt some painful misgivings.

One by one the deputies came forward and laid their offerings at the feet of James, scarcely daring to lift their eyes to the mysterious white-robed presence· whence breathed an atmosphere of awful holiness.

The hands of the youthful Timothy trembled, his face was colorless, the rigid severe countenances of the presbyters, the unbending austere brow of the Lord's brother, that Nazarite for life, somehow awakened in his heart all the fears long since put to rest, but with a single look into the face of his beloved father in the faith a genial warmth stole into his chilled heart; he became conscious of that other and gentler presence, the presence of the Lord himself.

And now Paul began to speak of the wonderful ex-

periences of the past years ; as he unrolled the glorious
record of his labors, " showing one by one what things
God had wrought among the nations by his ministry,"
loud alleluias burst forth from the listening delegates,
and even the self-contained presbyters were roused
momentarily from their disapproving silence into a
murmur of dignified and cautious praise.

But this was all ; we are not informed that any gratitude was expressed for the generous tokens of love
and fealty sent by the struggling churches, nor does
the inspired chronicler record any word of encouragement or cheer spoken to the worn laborer.   There is
no mention of any plan whereby comfort and safety
might be secured to him whose life was avowedly in
danger even in Jerusalem.   What then happened ?

" You observe, brother," said one of the council,*
with a preliminary wave of the hand, "how many
myriads of the Jews there are which believe, and they
are all zealous of the law.   These have been positively
informed that thou teachest apostacy from Moses, telling the Jews among all nations not to circumcise their
children, and not to walk in obedience to the customs.
How then do we find ourselves ?   That a crowd will
assemble is quite certain ; for they will all hear that
thou art come.   Do therefore this, that we bid thee.
We have four men which have a vow upon them.
Take them, be purified with them, and pay their

---

* Some authorities attribute this speech to James.   Others as
positively affirm that it was spoken by some other member of
the Council.

charges that they may shave their heads. All persons
will then see that those things whereof they were informed concerning thee, are nothing; but that thou
thyself walkest orderly, keeping the law. But as re-
gards the Gentiles, which have embraced the faith, we
have already enjoined their exemption from anything
of this kind, save only that they keep themselves from
things offered to idols, and from blood, and from
strangled, and from fornication."

For a full moment there was silence in the place;
the great apostle to the Gentiles was looking down
upon the ground. Did he recognize in this unworthy
and humiliating proposition that spirit of hatred and
jealousy which had dogged his footsteps for so many
years? Did he feel that the eyes of the Gentile
churches were upon him; that they looked to see
whether he would bend his own neck to that galling
yoke of bondage from which he had labored so valiantly to set them free? Did he perceive that the
hand of the pharisaical Christian held out to him a cup
of appalling suffering and of certain death?

Yet nothing could avail to move him save that faith
which walketh by love. Truly, though he was free,
he was willing to become the servant of all that he
might gain the more, he was made all things to all
men that he might save some.*

He raised his eyes and looked his future full in the
face, and surely we may not doubt that there was the
ring of certain triumph in his voice as he said, " I will

* I. Cor. ix., 19-23; and John xiii., 14.

do the thing which ye have asked of me." Having said this he made no delay, but taking the four Nazarites entered at once upon the tedious ceremonial rites of purification.

For four days Paul lived in the chamber of the temple set apart for the Nazarites; for four days he submitted himself patiently to all the endless ceremonial which rabbinical pettiness had superimposed upon Mosaic ritual. The four he-lambs of the first year for the burnt-offering, the four ewe-lambs of the first year for the sin-offering, the four rams for the peace-offering, the six tenth-deals and the two-thirds of a tenth-deal of flour taken four times, from which were to be baked the four lots of twenty cakes, ten of which were to be leavened and ten unleavened, and which must further be anointed with the fourth part of a log of oil, and brought in four separate baskets for the wave-offering, all these had been duly provided. When the seven days should be completed, and all the sacrifices offered, the burnt-offerings, the sin-offerings, the peace-offerings, the wave-offerings, the meat-offerings, the drink-offerings and the free-will offerings, then the heads of the four men could be shaved, and their hair, roughened and tangled by more than a month of neglect,* burnt beneath the sacred cauldron wherein the peace-offerings were boiling.

---

* The duration of the vow was never less than thirty days. During this period the Nazarite was not permitted to comb his hair, lest some of it should be accidently torn out; he was allowed to smooth it with his hands.

How must the strong spirit of Paul have groaned during all this empty and tedious observance. In what is this better than the worship of Diana or of Jupiter? he must have asked himself; but if by means of this painful concession to the Jewish Christianity the spread of the glad-tidings might be hastened—as he had been assured, he was willing to endure it, even as he had endured stripes and imprisonment at the hands of his heathen enemies; he could endure all things through Christ who strengthened him.

On the morning of the fifth day among the crowds which surged through the temple enclosure, there came into the court of the women certain Jews from Asia. As their eyes roved about over the crowded space one of them caught sight of Paul and the four Nazarites standing oil-cakes in hand before the attendant priest.

"Look you," exclaimed Alexander* of Ephesus seizing one of his companions by the arm. "Yonder is the fellow Shaûl!"

"What, the mad apostate, who hath stirred up all Asia with his accursed heresies?"

"Ay, the very same," answered Alexander grinding his teeth. "Do you not see him yonder with the four Nazarites? Hypocrite! he would play the zealous law-abiding Jew in the temple after being excommunicated from every synagogue in Asia. His blood be upon his head!"

With that he rushed through the crowd and threw

---

* I. Tim. i., 20; and II. Tim. iv., 14.

himself like a tiger upon his prey, crying out, " Israelites, help ! This is the fellow that teacheth all men
everywhere against the people, and the law, and this
place ! Ay, and besides that, he brought Greeks into
the temple, and hath defiled this holy place !''

" He brought Greeks into the temple ! He hath
defiled the temple !" The blasting falsehood flew
from tongue to tongue and from court to court ; the
people cried aloud and ran crying and wailing to the
spot. Death was the penalty according to the law,
a penalty recognized by the Romans themselves.
" Death—death to the man who hath defiled the holy
temple !"

With wild howls and execrations the frantic Jews
dragged their victim by main force through the great
gate " Beautiful." It shut with a clang behind them,
impelled by the frightened Levites who had hurried
to the spot. Down the steps and into the spacious
court of the Gentiles rushed the infuriated crowd ; the
place was instantly filled with people, who ran together
from every direction yelling and howling with that
mad unreasoning fury which spreads from man to man
like lurid lightning flashes amid the flying cloud-rack
of an angry heaven. Above all the wild tumult of
trampling feet and strident voices sounded the dull
thud of furious blows.

Suddenly the harsh clang of shields and the measured thunder of mailed feet announced the approach
of a detachment of the Roman guard. It was useless
to resist ; at the Passover only a few months since

more than ten thousand of the Jews had been killed on this very spot, some falling beneath the swords of the Romans, others in their efforts to escape trampled and crushed to death. The people fell back on every side, stumbling over one another in their eagerness to avoid the merciless spear-points of their masters.

"Make way there!" and Lysias the commandant of Antonia, surrounded by his guards laid the authoritative hand of Rome on the half-insensible victim of Jewish intolerance. "Who is this man, and what is his offence?"

A wild tumult of voices answered him. "Apostate! Accursed! The Temple—The Temple—The Temple!"

Lysias frowned contemptuously; he was unhappily familiar with the senseless fanaticism of these mad Jews. "Bind him with two chains," he commanded briefly, "and take him to the castle."

But the mob, seeing their prey about to be carried out of their sight, set up a deafening howl, "Away with him—Away with him! Kill him!" hurling themselves upon the solid phalanx of armed men in unavailing fury. The fettered prisoner staggered and would have fallen before the shock of the assault, but the soldiers, obeying the command of their watchful superior, fairly lifted him off the ground and continued their steady retreat toward the stairs which led to the top of the cloisters, which in their turn communicated directly with the castle of Antonia. Now the stair was gained; a moment more and the prisoner

would be safe within the massive walls of the forti-
fication.

"May I speak a word with you?"

Lysias glanced at his prisoner with astonishment.
"Canst thou speak Greek?" he demanded; "art thou
not that Egyptian, who a short time ago made a disturbance, and led out into the wilderness those five
thousand assassins?"*

"I am a Jew of Tarsus, in Cilicia," replied the
prisoner, "and therefore a citizen of no mean city. I
beseech thee suffer me to speak to the people."

"Speak if thou wilt—and canst," said the Roman
with a shrug. But he stared in astonishment when
the battered, dusty, insignificant-looking man, his
clothing hanging in shreds about him, his face and
shoulders bleeding from countless wounds, succeeded
with an authoritative word and gesture in attracting
the attention of the furious multitude. A profound
silence followed in which the prisoner spoke rapidly,
urgently, persuasively, as the chief captain could make
out from his tone and gestures, although he understood nothing of what was being said.

---

* About two months previous to this time a certain Egyptian
created a great excitement in Jerusalem by announcing himself
as the promised Messiah. It is said that he succeeded in raising some 30,000 followers, promising them that he would lead
them to the Mount of Olives, and that the walls of Jerusalem
would then fall flat before them. Four thousand of his dupes
actually set out with him, but were surprised by Felix with his
troops; many of them were slain, and a host of others were
taken prisoners. The Egyptian himself made good his escape
and was never heard of again.

Two—five—ten minutes passed, and still the multitude listened in perfect silence, every eye fastened upon that chained figure in the midst of the Roman guard.

"What is the rascal saying to them?" growled Lysias to the centurion who stood at his side. "Must we stand here all day?"

But at that moment the tumult broke out afresh with furious shouts, yells, groans, execrations, and a whirlwind of flying stones, dust and shreds of torn garments.

"He said 'Gentiles' just then," answered the centurion with a grin, as they resumed their cautious retreat toward the barracks.

"Dogs!" exclaimed the commandant with an oath. With a fresh access of irritation he cast his eye upon the prisoner. He was also a Jew by his own confession. "Take the fellow and scourge him," he commanded, "that we may find out what this accursed tumult is about; there is no other way to get the truth out of the lying knaves."

But as they bound him with thongs to the low pillar, preparatory to the awful examination by torture, the prisoner said very quietly to the centurion who stood near,

"Is it lawful for you to scourge a man that is a Roman and uncondemned?"

The centurion started with amazement. "Hold," he said gruffly to the soldiers who were preparing to lay on the flagellum. "I must look to this."

He at once sought out his superior officer. "What are you about?" he demanded bluntly. "The man is a Roman."

Lysias brought down his hand heavily upon his knee. "A Roman, sayst thou? then, by Bacchus, we had no right to bind him! I will come out at once."

The prisoner was still bound to the torture post, and as Lysias stared at his back, made naked for the whips, he perceived from the livid scars which disfigured it that the man had already suffered more than once beneath the scourge.* "Tell me," he said with an incredulous smile, "art thou a Roman?"

"Yes."

Lysias shook his head doubtfully; the man was a Jew clearly enough, and a poor Jew; the franchise was a costly privilege. "I know how much it cost me to get the citizenship," he said boastfully.

"But I was born a citizen."

The commandant turned pale. "Take him away," he said irritably; "I will look into his case further."

With that he turned on his heel and strode away, muttering execrations on the whole Jewish nation, but more particularly on that Jew who threatened to make it very uncomfortable for the captain of Antonia with his claim of free-born citizenship.

"It is some matter of their infernal law," he determined at length. "I will let the pack of hair-splitting rabbis yonder take the case in hand."

---

* II. Cor. xi., 24.

CHAPTER XXXVII.

A PROMISE AND A VOW.

THE news had spread throughout Jerusalem that
Paul, the apostate Sanhedrist, the hated propa-
gator of hateful heresies, the mad fanatic who openly
declared that a Gentile could be as holy as a Jew, had
been captured in the very act of openly defiling the
temple. If James and his circle of Jewish presbyters
made any effort to set the matter right it is not mentioned in the inspired records. It would seem that
the man was abandoned to his fate, a fate which some
of the Jewish Christians no doubt thought well-
deserved. When the Sanhedrim received notice from
the commandant of the garrison that the prisoner
would be delivered over into their hands for trial,
there was a general expression of satisfaction. It was
felt that for once the Romans had shown a proper
deference toward the Jewish authorities.

On the day following the arrest every member of
the Sanhedrim was in his place ; every eye was fastened
upon the prisoner, as he was brought into the council-
chamber under the escort of a quaternion of soldiers.
In his turn the prisoner looked steadily about the
circle of frowning faces which confronted him, from
Nasi to Scribe, from Scribe to Pharisee, from Pharisee

to Sadducee. Did he remember the day when he himself was one of them, and the young man Stephen
with his angel face stood in the place of the accused?

The preliminary questions were asked and answered ;
then Paul, still gazing earnestly into the faces of his
old-time friends and associates, began his defence.
" Brethren, I have lived in all good conscience before
God until this day."

Something in the unflinching look of the prisoner,
and the air of quiet confidence with which these words
were uttered stung the high priest, Ananias, into sudden fury.

"Smite him on the mouth !" he snarled, motioning
authoritatively to one of the temple police who stood
near the accused.   The man obeyed.

"God shall smite thee, thou whited wall !" exclaimed
Paul, his pale face crimson, his eyes flaming with
righteous anger.   " Sittest thou to judge me according to the law, and in violation of the law dost thou
command me to be smitten ?"

The officers of the court closed in about the bold
prisoner with threatening looks.   " Revilest thou God's
high priest ?" demanded the man who had struck him.

" I did not consider that he is a high priest," answered
the accused with a singular smile, " it is written thou
shalt not revile the ruler of thy people."   His keen
eyes swept once more about the frowning circle.
" Brethren !" he cried out suddenly, " I am a Pharisee,
the son of a Pharisee ; of the hope and resurrection
of the dead I am called in question !"

Instantly a tumult of passionate voices arose. " The
man is innocent !" exclaimed certain of the Scribes
who with the Pharisaic party thoroughly detested the
Sadducean high priest, Ananias.

" Away with him !" howled the Sadducees.

" We find no evil in the man," returned their opponents, the Pharisees, instantly in arms.   " If a spirit
or an angel hath spoken to him, let us not fight
against God !"

"Away with such a fellow from the earth !" repeated
the Sadducees with savage emphasis ; then casting
aside every vestige of their dignified reserve they
rushed upon the defendant with howls of rage.

" To the rescue ! To the rescue !" cried the Scribes
and Pharisees, preparing to do valiant battle for their
favorite doctrine.

An indescribable uproar followed, in the midst of
which the Roman centurion sent a hasty message to
the commandant, to the effect that there was danger
of the prisoner being pulled in pieces betwixt the rival
factions.   A second time a rescue party under Lysias
removed this singular offender by main force to the
Roman stronghold.

" By all the gods of Rome !" exclaimed the chief
captain when he had heard a full account of the affair ;
" these Jews are past finding out ; first, they are all
for beating the man to death, then half of them turn
and fight the other half like a pack of curs. Ay, curs
they be, one and all ; but if this Jew be also a Roman
citizen they shall not rend him whilst this castle stands.

If he hath lied, Rome herself will make short work with him."

That night there passed unchallenged and unseen through the triple cordon of watchful sentinels a radiant presence, through massive wall and ponderous fast-locked door, through damp and gloomy corridors where echoed the mailed feet of the midnight guard, through ill-smelling barracks where sleeping soldiers lay by hundreds upon their shields, it came, straight to the spot where crouched the prisoner, wakeful and suffering in body and soul because of all that had befallen him, and because of the future which lay dark and threatening before him.

"Be of good cheer, Paul," said the voice that had once smitten the unbelieving Saul to the earth on the Damascus highway, "for as thou hast testified of me in Jerusalem, so must thou bear witness also at Rome."

Ananias, the high priest, was also wakeful and ill at ease on that night ; the occurrences of the morning had been peculiarly irritating, doubly so since he felt that in a measure he had precipitated the uproar by his own unwarranted order. Now that the hated apostate was removed beyond the reach of his vengeance, his anger burned all the more fiercely against him. "A Pharisee !" he muttered, "and the son of a Pharisee— accursed be all Pharisees with their driveling cant concerning the resurrection—the knave lied ; he is no more a Pharisee than was the Nazarene himself."

At dawn there came an urgent message from certain of the chief priests demanding his presence in the council-chamber. "There is a plan on foot," said these, "whereby we may outwit the Romans, humiliate the Pharisees, and at the same time rid the world of a dangerous apostate, who may otherwise escape our vengeance on the score of his Roman citizenship."

"Name it," said Ananias, his evil face lighting up. At a signal the door opened and a number of men were ushered into his presence. They were headed by the Ephesian Jew, Alexander, who the day before had started the uproar in the temple.

"Thou seest, my lord," began this worthy, bowing himself almost to the ground before the hierarch, "that there are here forty of us, law-abiding all, and zealous concerning the commandments of Moses. We hate with an unspeakable hatred the man Shaûl, who has taught abominable sayings against the temple, against the law, and concerning that Galilean who died the accursed death ; and this not only in Jerusalem, but among all nations. We have therefore bound ourselves with a most solemn vow that we will neither eat nor drink till we have accomplished his death. Now do you, in the name of the Sanhedrim, send word to the chief captain that he bring the man down unto you on the morrow, as though ye would make more accurate inquiry into his case, and we, or ever he comes near, are ready to kill him."

Ananias sprang to his feet. "A righteous vow, O son of Abraham !" he cried, "A holy vow. May Jehovah grant its speedy fulfillment. As for me, I will do as thou hast said ; by the veil of the temple I swear it !"

In a certain quiet street not far from the temple, there dwelt at this very time a Jewish lady to whom the news of the arrest and imprisonment of Paul came as a fresh disgrace and humiliation.

"God of Israel!" she wailed, "has not this man already humbled his kinsfolk and aquaintance to the dust, in that he hath allied himself with the hateful sect of the Nazarenes—he who was once a learned rabbi, a teacher and leader of the wise, a veritable 'remover of mountains;' and now, alas, he hath fallen to the lowest depths, a defiler of the temple, an eater of the unclean beast, having fellowship with the uncircumcised and accursed. Would that Jehovah had taken away his breath while he yet observed His commandments to do them. Yea, verily, I would that we both had gone down to the grave whilst we were innocent babes at our mother's knee!"

"He is no less thy brother," said her son, a lad of about thirteen years. "And he is sorely in need of help and succor; even the Nazarenes have forsaken him."

"What knowest thou of the Nazarenes?" cried the mother angrily. "Have I not forbidden thee to speak to one of them?"

"I heard it in the temple," answered the boy stoutly. "The Nazarenes also observe the law of Moses; and they are saying that my uncle declares that Gentiles as well as Jews can be saved in the resurrection through faith in the risen Jesus, and that the law no longer avails for either Jew or Gentile."

"Because he hath said such words he is no longer

brother of mine," said the lady coldly; "they are
even as a sharp sword before which the ties of blood
fall asunder and are no more. Soil not thy lips with
such wickedness, my son, lest the evil one gain thee
also, and I be left desolate."

The boy drew his brows together, "There be many
beliefs even among the rabbis, mother," he said argumentatively, "the Sadducees do not believe that there
is a resurrection, of either angel or spirit, but we
Pharisees confess both. What if—"

"Nay, child, thou art not yet a rabbi," interrupted
the mother with a shadowy smile. "Go now to thy
school and learn wisdom, that the Almighty may bless
thee, and save thee out of the pit which the froward
and the foolish dig for themselves."

The school was already called when the nephew of
Paul shyly took his place in the circle which sat about
the teacher, Simon Ben Gamaliel, in one of the cham-
bers of the temple. The boy saluted the great rabbi
with the prescribed obeisance and the courteous words
of morning greeting.

"Thou art late this morning, my son Jesse," said
the rabbi, shaking his head. "Fail not to remember
that the days of a man's life are fashioned from the small
moments of the hour; and that all the days and all the
hours and all the moments are too few in the which he
may gather that wisdom which is better than rubies."

The lad hung his head. "I pray thee to have me
excused for this once," he said; "I talked with my
mother, and the moments fled unaware."

The learned Simon smiled, " A wise son delighteth in the conversation of his mother ; as for her, her price is far above rubies, even as it is written.—Thou art pardoned."

The lessons in theology, philosophy, law and arithmetic were at last finished ; and now the pupils separated to the study of the different trades which had been chosen for them by their parents. All the great rabbis of the day were masters of a trade. " Learning, no matter of what kind," declared the wise Gamaliel, " if unaccompanied by a trade, ends in nothing, and leads to sin." And so Rabbi Ismael, the famous astronomer, was a needle-maker ; Rabbi Jochanan was a shoe-maker, Rabbi Simon a weaver, Rabbi Joseph a carpenter. The boy, Jesse, after the custom of his family for many generations, was learning to be a tent-maker. He did not like the work, but that made no difference, as he knew full well. As he threaded his great needle he became aware that the other boys were staring at him and whispering together ; some of them were laughing.

" Why dost thou laugh ?" he demanded, fixing his keen grey eyes on the boy who sat next him. " And what are Simon and Asa whispering about that I may not hear ?"

" They say that the apostate, Shaûl, who was seized in the temple yesterday is the brother of thy mother, and that to-morrow he will be killed," answered the boy with a malicious grin.

" He will not be killed to-morrow," retorted Jesse

promptly, drawing his needle through the coarse cloth with a jerk. "And he hath done nothing blameworthy."

"Hear that," cried the other, looking carefully about to be sure that the master tent-maker was out of hearing. "Young Jesse, here, says that the fellow Shaûl will not be killed to-morrow, and that he hath done nothing blameworthy!"

"He will be killed, young kinsman of a swine-eater; thou wilt see before the setting of another sun."

"The Romans will protect him!" cried Jesse, turning pale.

"Ay, and will they, boy? Let me tell thee that no less than forty law-abiding Jews have bound themselves with a curse that they will neither eat nor drink till they have slain the knave."

"Thou art telling lies, son of Abraham," said the nephew of Paul, indignant tears standing in his eyes, "and thou knowest the penalty of the law for that."

"And thou art near kin to a blasphemer, who also shall be killed with stones according to the law," retorted the other; "if I lie, then may Jehovah smite me where I stand. The forty will fulfil their cherem; one of them who fetches wine-skins to my father's house told our gate-keeper, and I heard it. They will send word to the chief captain of Antonia to bring down the prisoner again before the council, then in the court of the Gentiles they will fall upon him and slay him."

At this moment the master tent-maker re-entered

the room ; instantly every voice was hushed, and forty
shining needles flew in and out the long seams with
commendable alacrity.   Jesse worked as diligently as
any of them.   Not once during the hour did the stern
teacher chide him for inattention ; he was also thinking.   When the signal for dismissal came he hurried
away as fast as possible, scarcely hearing the derisive
whispers which buzzed about him.   He had resolved
on a course of action about which he hardly dared
think further, for fear his timid heart should fail him.

An hour later Claudius Lysias, commandant of
Antonia, received a call from one of the centurions
of the garrison.   "The prisoner Paul," said that
officer with a grimace, "asked me to fetch this young
man to you ; he has something to tell you."

Lysias surveyed his visitor curiously, then seeing
that he was hardly more than a child, and that he was
evidently terrified at his surroundings, good-naturedly
took him by the hand and led him out of ear-shot of
the soldiers.   "What is it that thou hast to tell me,
my child?" he said kindly.

"The Jews have agreed to desire thee that thou
wouldst bring down Paul to-morrow into the council,"
half-whispered the lad, fixing his eyes anxiously upon
the bronzed and bearded face of the soldier ; "but do
not thou yield unto them ; for there lie in wait for him
more than forty men, which have bound themselves
with an oath that they will neither eat nor drink till
they have killed him ; and now they are ready, looking for a promise from thee."

" By all the gods of the infernal regions !" began
the chief captain, then he stopped short.—" Thou
mayst go, my lad," he said shortly, " and make thyself easy concerning the man Paul; we shall find a
way to keep these agreeable compatriots of his hungry
and thirsty for some days yet.   But see that thou keep
a close tongue in thy head; tell no one what thou
hast told me."

At nine o'clock that same evening Lysias dispatched
the prisoner to Caesarea under an escort of nearly five
hundred men.

" See that ye deliver this man safe and uninjured
unto the governor," he charged the centurions whom
he placed in command of the troops.

CHAPTER XXXVIII.

PAUL AND FELIX.

FELIX CLAUDIUS, the worshipful procurator of Judaea, was apparently lost in thought. He sat motionless in his massive carven chair, quite oblivious it would seem, to the fact that one of his attendants had been kneeling before him for full five minutes, holding out at arm's length a salver upon which reposed a letter. The eyes of the great man were fixed stolidly upon the point of his gold-embossed sandal, and the expression of his heavy sensual face was a degree more savage and gloomy than was its wont. On either side stood four slaves, silent and rigid as the kneeling page, but not the less apprehensively-observant of the man in the chair.

After a time the central figure in this singular group raised his eyes to the face of the kneeling slave. As the moments dragged by it could be seen that the man was suffering slow torture under the merciless unwinking stare; his legs trembled beneath him, his hands clutched convulsively at the edges of the salver, great beads of moisture started out upon his livid forehead. Felix Claudius smiled evilly; he reached out and took the letter, which he proceeded to open and read with deliberation.

"Claudius Lysias to the most excellent governor Felix : Greeting. The prisoner whom I send you was seized by the Jews, and was on the point of being killed by them when I came down upon them with a guard and rescued him, for I learned that he was a Roman citizen. As I wished to know the offence which the Jews had to allege against him, I took him down to their Sanhedrim, and there I found that the accusations related to certain questions of their law, but that nothing worthy of death or imprisonment was charged against him. And now having received information that a plot has been made against the man's life, I forthwith send him to you ; at the same time I have notified his accusers to bring their charges before you. Farewell."

The procurator crumpled the parchment with a smothered oath. "Fetch in the prisoner and the centurions," he commanded briefly.

The slave who still knelt before him arose to his feet with a cringing obeisance and retreated backward to the door. The centurions were evidently waiting in the ante-room, for they entered at once, the prisoner walking between them. The contrast between the fine soldierly presence of the officers and the small, stoop-shouldered, shabby figure of the prisoner was strikingly apparent as the three advanced ; the procurator thrust out his under lip with a sneering smile.

"From what province art thou ?"

"I am a Jew of Tarsus, of Cilicia," replied the

prisoner looking calmly into the face of his judge. "I am—"

But Felix interrupted him with an arrogant gesture. "I will hear your case when your accusers are come. —Take the man away, and put him under guard in Herod's judgment hall."

Five days later the high priest Ananias, with a number of the Sanhedrists, and "a certain orator named Tertullus," whom they had employed to argue their side of the case, arrived in Caesarea. They lost no time in presenting themselves before the governor.

After the customary preliminaries, Tertullus was introduced. The lawyer prefaced his accusation with a fulsome eulogy upon the wisdom, discretion, and energy of the procurator. "Under whom," he declared unctuously "we have enjoyed great peace and prosperity. Seeing," he continued with a flourish of his hand, "that very worthy national reforms have been brought about through thy excellent wisdom, we are ready to accept the decrees of that wisdom always, and in all places, most noble Felix, with all thankfulness.* But in order that I be not further tedious unto thee, I beseech thee to hear us briefly of thy clemency. We have found this man a pestilent fellow, one that is continually stirring up insurrections

---

* The facts concerning the rule of Felix were of a widely different complexion; he had made use of his power from the beginning to oppress and impoverish the nation, and was therefore peculiarly detested and feared by all the Jews.

among the Jews throughout the habitable world; he is also a ringleader of the sect of the Nazarenes. More than this, he deliberately attempted to profane the temple; but when we seized him and were about to judge him according to our law, the chief captain Lysias came upon us, and with great violence took him out of our hands. He then commanded that the case should appear before thee, by whom also thou wilt be able to corroborate these charges, after having thyself examined the man."

From this speech it may be seen that there were three counts in the indictment against Paul : first, he was a dangerous disturber of the peace, an offence against the Roman government amounting to high treason ; second, he was a ringleader of the Nazarenes, which involved infringement of the laws of Moses ; third, he had attempted to profane the temple at Jerusalem, a capital offence according to the law of both nations, since Rome recognized thus far the Judaic code.

The complaint having been thus formally lodged, the members of the Sanhedrim who were present arose one after another and vehemently confirmed the same ; intimating that since Lysias had improperly exercised his powers in forcibly removing the prisoner during his ecclesiastical trial, it now remained for Felix to make the matter right by returning the offender into their hands.

Felix listened stolidly without question or comment. After the Jews had finished speaking he motioned to the prisoner to advance.

"Knowing that thou hast been judge over this nation for many years," began the defendant, "I answer for myself in the matters brought against me with the greater confidence. For it is in thy power to learn that only twelve days have passed since I went up to Jerusalem to worship. And neither in the temple, nor in the synagogues, nor in the streets, did these my accusers find me disputing with any man, or causing any disorderly concourse of people ; nor can they prove against me the things wherewith they now charge me. But this I acknowledge to thee, that after the way that they call sect, so I serve the God of my fathers, believing all things which are written in the law and in the prophets, and having a hope towards God—which they themselves entertain, that there will be a resurrection of the dead,* both of the just and of the unjust. Wherefore I strive earnestly to preserve a conscience always void of offence towards God and man.

"Now after many years I came hither to bring alms to my nation and offerings ; and they found me so doing in the temple after I had been purified, neither with multitude nor with tumult. But certain Jews from Asia came upon me—who should have appeared here before thee to accuse me, if they had aught against me. Or let these men who are present, say

---

* This shows that the Pharisees were the principal accusers of Paul, and that therefore the effect produced upon them by his speech before the Sanhedrim was only momentary.

whether they found me guilty of any offence when I
stood before the Sanhedrim, except it be for this one
word which I cried out as I stood in the midst of them :
Touching the resurrection of the dead I am called in
question by you this day !"

Felix had not lived six years among the Jews without learning something of their characteristics.   He
had had dealings on more than one occasion with these
slippery rabbins from Jerusalem, and while he thoroughly detested them, he was anxious for private rea-
sons of his own to remain on good terms with them
for the present at least.   Of the sect of the Nazarenes
he knew more than the Sanhedrists gave him credit
for ; this new religion had penetrated even among the
Roman troops which were stationed at Caesarea.*
Religion in general did not interest Felix, but these
soldiers were brave, obedient, easily controlled, further than that he neither knew nor cared.   As for the
prisoner, his interests were quite naturally considered
last, the man was evidently innocent, but it would
not do to say so ; moreover, there were two words
in his defence which possessed a deep interest for his
judge, those two words were "alms and offerings."
"If the Jew has resources," quoth Felix to himself,
"he shall pay me roundly for the trouble I have taken
before he tastes of liberty."

For some moments after the prisoner had finished
his defence this righteous arbitrator remained silent,
then with a show of great prudence and fairness, he

---

* See Acts x. 1–48.

announced that it would be impossible for him to arrive at any decision in the matter until he had collected further evidence. "When Lysias, the chief captain, shall come down," he said, "I will know the uttermost of your matter."

In pursuance of his plans he gave Paul in charge to one of his centurions, directing him to show the man due consideration, and more especially to allow him free communication with his friends. The prisoner was accordingly removed to the guard-house, where a long light chain was riveted about the wrist of his right hand ; the other end of the chain was fastened to the left hand of a common soldier, who became answerable with his life for the security of the prisoner. This chain was never to be loosed day or night, save when the soldiers relieved one another.*

It shortly transpired that the worthy governor had other and more agreeable business on hand than the trying of Jewish suspects. The very next day he departed from Caesarea with a large retinue of slaves and soldiers, leaving minute directions for the refitting and furnishing of certain apartments in the palace, known as the queen's wing. There was much anxious conjecture in all circles of Caesarean society as to what these things should portend, but all suspense was shortly put to an end by the return of the governor himself in the character of a triumphant bride-

---

* This form of imprisonment was known as the *costodia militaris ;* it is clearly indicated by the statement that Paul was given to a centurion to keep.

groom. The Roman matrons smiled and whispered behind their fans; while the discontented murmuring in the Jewish quarters grew loud and threatening. The bride, it appeared, was none other than the beautiful princess Drusilla, youngest daughter of Herod Agrippa, reared by her mother as a rigid Jewess. She had been enticed from the protection of her lawful husband, it was said, by the skillful machinations of the Cyprian sorcerer, Simon Magus,* who had been for some time an important member of the proconsular household. What subtle arts were employed to induce this beautiful girl of twenty to leave the young and handsome prince of Aziz for the elderly and cruel profligate who had once been the slave of her father, could only be guessed at. She took no one into her confidence, and met the polite innuendoes of the Roman courtiers with the same freezing hauteur which she displayed toward the infuriated hierarchs of her own nation.

Not many days after her installation in the Caesarean palace the princess learned from one of her attendants that Paul, the famous Nazarene, was imprisoned in one of the dungeons of the palace.

"I should like to see this Paul," she said languidly to the man whom she chose for the present to call husband. "They tell me that he can perform miracles, as did the Nazarene himself. It will amuse me; so far I do not find Caesarea amusing."

"Thou shalt see the man and at once," answered

* Josephus, Antiq., xx., 7, § 2. See also Acts viii., 9-24.

Felix promptly; "I will order him to be fetched to the judgment-hall."

"But if I choose to see him here?"

"Thou wilt not choose to see him here, light of my eyes."

The princess lifted her brows haughtily. "What didst thou swear to me?" she demanded.

"That thy word should be law, daughter of Agrippa. But from henceforth I am that word. Dost thou understand me?"

Drusilla's black eyes blazed; her scarlet lips trembled. "Slave!" she cried, springing to her feet, "was it for this I left the man who adored me? I will stay here no longer; I will go back to my husband!"

Felix took two steps across the room and caught her slim wrists in a grip of steel. "Look at me," he said in a low voice.

The girl slowly and sullenly raised her eyes.

"Go back to Aziz if thou wilt. Ay—go back to thy Jewish rabbis. Go where thou wilt and when thou wilt; thou art free as air."

The scarlet lips were white now. "I—I cannot. They would kill me—I—"

"Nay, princess, tears do not become thee;" and the man laughed mockingly. "We will go now to the judgment-hall, shall we not? And the prisoner shall entertain thee with his magic."

And so it happened that Paul was again summoned into the august presence of the governor of Judæa.

"Thou mayst expound to us this matter of the

crucified man," said Felix with an easy wave of the
hand. "This lady is curious concerning the matter."

Then did Paul preach unto those twain Christ crucified. And as he reasoned of righteousness, of temper-
ance and of judgment to come, Felix trembled, even
as he had once trembled beneath the lash. A strange
unearthly power streamed forth from the presence of
this chained prisoner; those searching grey eyes
seemed to pierce to the furthest limits of the darkened
and narrow soul of the man, and lust, murder, greed,
hatred and all the host of noisome things within writhed
and twisted in agony beneath the unwonted flood of
light which was suddenly poured in upon them.

"Hold!" cried out the tortured man at length,
wiping the great drops from his forehead, "Go thy
way for this time; when I have a convenient season I
will call for thee."

"What ailed thee when the man was talking?"
enquired Drusilla of her lord and master, after the
prisoner had been removed; "for myself I found him
very dull. Why didst thou not command him to perform a wonder for me?"

Felix answered her never a word. Yet after a
while he was ready to laugh and sneer as before. The
light had disappeared and all the brood of creatures
within his soul drowsed contentedly once more. "The
man hath an evil eye!" he cried with a great oath.
"I swear that I believe all that the Jews have said
of him."

Nevertheless he sent for him more than once in private, and intimated in no uncertain terms that if a sum of money sufficiently great were forthcoming, he should be at once liberated.

"If I have done no evil," said the prisoner on one of these occasions, "freedom is mine according to the law ; but if I am guilty, thou canst not lawfully sell me my liberty."

"I am the law !" cried Felix fiercely ; "thou shalt wear thy chain during my pleasure."

And so passed away two years. At the end of that time there was a great cry made in the streets of Caesarea. The never-ending feud between the Jews and Greeks had come at length to a head ; there was a fierce battle in the market-place, in which the Greeks were worsted at the hands of their antagonists. When suddenly the procurator at the head of his cohorts appeared on the scene and ordered the rioters to disperse. As his commands were not instantly obeyed, he let loose his soldiers upon them. A great slaughter of the insurgents ensued, and the massacre was followed by a general plundering of the houses of the wealthier Jews. This was not to be borne, the heads of the nation arose in their might and demanded the instant dismissal of the offending governor. He was at once recalled to Rome to answer to the charges against him before Nero.

"What of the prisoner, Paulus, your excellency?" asked one of the centurions on the eve of his departure. "Wilt thou that we release the man ?"

"Release him ? No," growled Felix. "Leave him

as he is. It may pacify those accursed Jews to know that I have left the man bound," he added ; "they will at all events have one less count against me."

On the following day he departed for Rome with the woman Drusilla and their son, who was called Agrippa.*

---

* Little further is known of the career of this man, except that he was compelled to disgorge the greater part of his ill-gotten wealth. He seems at once to have dropped back into the obscurity from which he emerged. Drusilla with her son is said to have perished at Herculaneum during an eruption of Vesuvius which took place some nineteen years later.

CHAPTER XXXIX.

" CÆSAREM APPELLO !"

JERUSALEM was in a ferment of excitement; people of every nationality, clad in every variety of holiday garb, jostled one another in the narrow streets, or overflowed the market-places. The temple courts were crowded ; all day long countless sacrifices smoked upon its altars. In the wider streets and squares and from the battlemented walls resounded the continuous blare of trumpets, the clash of arms, and the low thunder of marching cohorts. Everywhere glittered the Roman eagle, hated symbol of Gentile supremacy and national degradation. Porcius Festus, the new procurator of Judaea, had arrived, and Jerusalem bade him welcome.

While his excellency was busily occupied in reviewing the troops and inspecting the walls and fortifications of the city, the Sanhedrim held an important session. As the ecclesiastical heads of the nation it devolved upon them to formally recognize the newly-arrived official ; there were also certain matters to be laid before him, the settlement of which had already been too long delayed during the lax and disgraceful rule of Felix. A deputation was chosen to wait upon the procurator of which the high priest, Ishmael Ben

Phabi, recently appointed by Agrippa II., was the natural head.

At a set time these dignitaries presented themselves with great pomp and state in the audience-chamber of the Asmonean palace. The tedious formalities suitable to the occasion having been duly observed, the spokesman of the deputation proceeded to make known among other matters one of the principal objects of the interview. "There is a certain man named Paul who has been under bonds in Caesarea for two years past," began this person, who was no other than the ex-high priest, Ananias. "He is a mischievous person, most excellent Festus, and a transgressor of the law of Moses ; he was arrested by us in an attempt to profane our holy temple, an offense which thou knowest to be punishable with death. Moreover he hath been guilty of numerous and heinous offenses against the Roman government, having in times past stirred up insurrections against Caesar in many provinces, as also here in this holy city. We therefore unite in requesting that thou wilt cause this man to be fetched at once to Jerusalem, and that thou wilt deliver him into our hands that we may deal with him after our law."

Porcius Festus listened to this bold request with astonishment not unmingled with displeasure. "It is not the custom of Rome," he said haughtily, "to deliver any man to death by way of doing a favor ; but to place accused and accusers face to face, giving the accused a full opportunity for his defense. This prisoner of whom you speak shall remain in Caesarea, whither I myself propose shortly to return. Let those of you therefore who are able to do so, return with me and prefer the charges against him there."

The Sanhedrists withdrew from the presence of Festus full of rage and disappointment. They had made so sure of their request that they had already hired assassins to make way with their hated enemy on the road between Caesarea and Jerusalem. It was evident that this new procurator could not easily be intimidated, but they nevertheless resorted to their old plan of "stirring up the people."* During the few days that Festus remained in Jerusalem, crowds of turbulent Jews surrounded his palace night and day loudly demanding the death of Paul. And when he returned to the political capitol a noisy multitude of Caesarean Jews greeted him with the cry, "Away with Paul! Away with him! Away with such a fellow from the earth!"

Festus needed no further urging to prompt action in the matter; on the very next day after his arrival in Caesarea, he commanded that the hearing should take place.

The Sanhedrists were present in full force; on this occasion they had hired no lawyer to present their cause, but preferred their accusations themselves with all the vehemence and fury of rancorous hatred.

As at his first trial, the prisoner steadily asserted

---

* Mark xv., 11, Acts vi., 12; xiii., 50; xiv., 2.

his innocence of every charge. "Neither against the law of the Jews," he declared, "nor against the temple, nor yet against Cæsar, have I offended in any way whatsoever."

Scarcely were the words out of his mouth when the Jews cried out the more fiercely, demanding his death.

Festus surveyed the scene with manifest displeasure; to the dignified, just, order-loving Roman these bearded and turbaned rabbis with their fierce dark faces and strident voices afforded a strange and odious spectacle. At the same time he knew full well that it was necessary for him to ingratiate himself with them, since otherwise he could hope for nothing save a speedy and disgraceful recall to Rome. He saw as plainly that the case in hand had nothing to do with Roman law, that it was simply a matter of tedious and incomprehensible religious fanaticism, concerning which it would be impossible for him to judge. He turned to the prisoner, whose calm dignified demeanor in the face of his furious enemies had impressed him most favorably. "Wilt thou go up to Jerusalem," he said, "and there be judged of these matters under my protection?"

The prisoner straightened his bowed shoulders, his worn and pallid face glowing with indignation. "I stand at Cæsar's judgment seat," he said boldly, "and there ought my trial to be. To the Jews I have done no wrong, as thou knowest full well. If I am guilty of anything which is worthy of death, I refuse not to

die ; but if the things whereof these men accuse me
are false, no man can give me up to them.   I appeal
unto Cæsar !"

For an instant there was silence in the judgment
hall ; the two words " Cæsarem appello !" had
changed the whole aspect of affairs.   The Jews glared
at their intended victim in transports of unavailing
rage, those words of power had raised in an instant
between the man and their fury the impassable barrier
of Roman law.

Porcius Festus was also displeased by the appeal ;
to be thus reminded in the very beginning of his pro-
curatorship that he was but an underling of the emperor was, he thought, a bad omen for his future suc-
cess, besides he had meant well and fairly by the man ;
to appeal to Cæsar was not only unnecessary on the
part of the prisoner, but considering the complexion
of affairs at Rome it would assuredly prove disastrous
to his interests.   Festus, however, had now no choice
in the matter ; all future jurisdiction in the case was
out of his power ; it only remained for him to decide
whether or not the appeal was admissable ; on this
point it was evident that there could be no doubt, since
the accused was neither a pirate nor a bandit.

He turned to the prisoner, after the brief formalities
relating to the admission of the appeal had been finished, and pronounced the solemn words, " Cæsarem
appellasti, ad Cæsarem ibis."*

Two days later Agrippa II., the last of the Herods,

* " To Cæsar thou hast appealed ; to Cæsar thou shalt go."

came with his sister Berenice, to proffer their con-
gratulations to the newly-installed procurator; it
afforded these pseudo-royalties a fine opportunity of
flaunting their phantom magnificence, and at the same
time enabled them to bespeak the good-will of their
powerful neighbor. Agrippa had been trained from
youth in all the minutiae of Jewish law and theology;
he was legal custodian of the sacred robes and guardian of the temple, with the power to make and un-
make high priests at his royal pleasure.

Festus was, therefore, especially glad to see him at
this time; it gave him an opportunity of consulting a
wise authority concerning the strange prisoner whom
he was about to dispatch to Rome. The law required
that a full statement of the alleged offences must be
sent with the prisoner by the provincial official, and
Festus could make nothing of the extravagant state-
ments of the rabbis.

"There is a certain man left here in bonds by Felix,"
he said, drawing his heavy brows together, "concerning whom, when I was at Jerusalem, the chief men of
the nation informed me; they also demanded judgment
against him. Romans deliver no man to the death, I
answered them, until he has had opportunity to defend
himself face to face with his accusers. They came
therefore to Caesarea, and I called the case without
delay. But the accusations proved to be nothing but
certain questions having to do with their own super-
stitions, and of one Jesus, a man who died long since,
but whom Paul, the prisoner, declares to be alive.

Because I knew nothing of such matters, I asked the man whether he would go to Jerusalem for trial, whereupon he appealed unto the emperor, and I remanded him to the prison till such time as I could conveniently send him to Rome."

" I would also hear the man myself," said Agrippa.

" Thou shalt hear him to-morrow," declared Festus readily, seeing in this request a way out of his own perplexities. Accordingly on the day following, the proconsular court, the chief officers of the army and all the principal men of the city were invited to be present in the council-chamber of the palace. Festus appeared in the full splendor of his scarlet paludament, attended by his lictors and armed body-guard. On either side of his seat of state was placed a gilded chair for the chief guests of the occasion, to gratify whose pardonable curiosity this imposing function had been held. They entered presently in magnificent state, followed by an imposing retinue of attendants. The young Agrippa wearing the glittering crown and purple robes of royalty, and Berenice, regally beautiful in the trailing amplitude of her queenly garb.

At a given signal the door at the lower end of the hall was thrown open and the prisoner, chained to a soldier, and further guarded by a quaternion, advanced into the open space reserved in front of the dais. Every eye was at once eagerly fastened upon him. Many had never seen the famous captive. Could it be possible that this worn feeble old man was the hated apostate, the dangerous fanatic, the inciter of tumult and riots, of whom they had heard so much? He seemed unembarrassed and unafraid in the face of all that brilliant assembly; his face shone with a singular joy, as if his thoughts afforded him secret satisfaction.

"King Agrippa, and all who are here present," began Festus with stately formality, "ye behold this man about whom all the multitude of the Jews have dealt with me, both at Jerusalem and also here at Caesarea, crying out that he ought not to live any longer. When I found that he had done nothing worthy of death, and since he appealed to Cæsar, I determined to send him to Rome. But having no clear statement regarding the man to make to my lord the emperor, I have brought him forth before you, and especially before thee, O king Agrippa, that when thou hast examined him, I may have somewhat to write. For it seemeth to me unreasonable to send a prisoner to Rome without signifying the crimes alleged against him." Having thus introduced the prisoner, Festus with an easy wave of the hand signified that the man was now at the disposal of his royal guest.

Agrippa accordingly addressed the apostle with haughty condescension. "Thou art permitted," he said, "to speak for thyself."

"I think myself happy, king Agrippa," began Paul, stretching forth his manacled right hand in his own familiar way, "that I shall defend myself to-day before thee against all the charges of my Jewish accusers: especially because thou art expert in all Jewish cus-

toms and questions. Wherefore I pray thee to hear
me patiently.

" My manner of life from early youth—which was
passed among my own nation at Jerusalem—is known
to all the Jews. They know me from the first and
could testify, if they would, that according to the
strictest sect of our religion, I lived a Pharisee. And
now I stand here to be judged for the hope of the
promise made by God unto our fathers. Which
promise is the end whereto, in all their zealous worship
night and day, our twelve tribes hope to come. Yet
this hope, O king Agrippa, is charged against me as
a crime, and that by the Jews. What! is it judged
among you a thing incredible that God should raise
the dead?

" Now I myself determined in my own mind that I
ought strenuously to oppose the name of Jesus of
Nazareth. And this I did in Jerusalem, and many of
the saints I shut up in prison, having received from
the chief priests authority to do so ; and when they
were condemned to death, I gave my vote against
them. In every synagogue I continually punished
them, and endeavored to compel them to blaspheme ;
and being exceedingly mad against them, I pursued
them with persecutions even unto foreign cities.

" With this purpose I was on my way to Damascus,
bearing my authority and commission from the chief
priests ; when I saw in the way, O king, at midday, a
light from heaven above the brightness of the sun,
shining round about me and them which journeyed

with me. And when we were all fallen to the earth,
I heard a voice speaking to me, and saying in the Hebrew tongue, Saul, Saul, why persecutest thou me?
It is hard for thee to kick against the goad. And I
said, Who art thou, Lord? And the Lord said, I am
Jesus whom thou persecutest. But rise and stand
upon thy feet; for to this end I have appeared unto
thee, to ordain thee a minister and a witness both of
these things which thou hast seen, and of those things
wherein I shall appear unto thee. And thee have I
chosen from the house of Israel, and from among the
Gentiles; unto whom I now send thee, to open their
eyes, that they may turn from darkness to light, and
from the power of Satan unto God; that they may receive forgiveness of sins, and an inheritance among the
sanctified by faith in me.

" Wherefore, O king Agrippa, I was not disobedient
to the heavenly vision. But first to those at Damascus
and Jerusalem, and throughout all the land of Judaea,
and also to the Gentiles, I proclaimed the tidings that
they should repent and return to God, and do works
worthy of their repentance.

" For these causes the Jews, when they caught me
in the temple, endeavored to kill me.

" Having therefore obtained help of God, I stand
firm unto this day, and bear my testimony both to
small and great; but I declare nothing else than
what the prophets and Moses foretold, that the Messiah should suffer, and that he should be the first
to rise from the dead, and should be the messen-

ger of light to the house of Israel, and also to the Gentiles."*

At this allusion to the resurrection from the dead, which sounded like the wildest folly in the cars of the worldly Roman, Festus cried out loudly, "Paul, thou art beside thyself; much learning doth make thee mad!"

"I am not mad, most noble Festus," answered the prisoner steadily, "but I speak forth the words of truth and soberness. For the king hath knowledge of these matters; and moreover, I speak before him with boldness, since I am persuaded that nothing of all this is unknown to him, for this was not done in a corner. King Agrippa, believest thou the prophets? I know that thou believest."

The Jewish prince stirred uneasily in his chair, the light of those compelling eyes was fixed full upon him; he attempted to put down the look with his customary haughty stare, but his own eyes fell. He shrugged his shoulders with feigned indifference, exclaiming with a derisive smile, "Almost thou persuadest me to be a Christian!"

"I would to God," answered Paul with a pathetic movement of his chained right hand, "that not only thou, but also all that hear me this day, were both almost and altogether such as I am, except these bonds!"

The hearing was at an end; the governor, observing the embarrassment of Agrippa, had signaled to the cen-

---

* This rendering follows in the main that of Conybeare and Howson; see "Life and Epistles of St. Paul."

turion to remove the prisoner. Then rising he swept
from the judgment-hall with his guests, followed by all
the brilliant throng of soldiers, courtiers and lackeys.

There was much gay laughter and light jesting
among the ladies of Berenice, as they passed into the
more cheerful apartments of the palace; the princess
herself shrugged her fair shoulders with a frown.

"That dreadful old man has quite given me the
shivers," she said petulantly. "It was certainly most
insolent of him to address his royal highness, Agrippa,
in the bold manner that he did. As his excellency the
governor remarked, the man is doubtless mad; but it
seemeth to me it can hardly be a madness induced by
overmuch learning; 'tis more likely that the prison
walls have engendered strange and foolish fancies
within his brain. How horrible to be chained to an
odious soldier all the time." With that this amiable
and virtuous princess dismissed the subject from her
mind; there were so many other more interesting and
important questions relating to her jewels, her robes,
her lovers, her intrigues, and the care of her exquisite
body, that indeed she could scarcely be expected to
bestow very much of her royal attention upon a chained,
shabby, mad old fanatic.

Festus and Agrippa conversed of the matter more
seriously. "The man hath done nothing worthy of
death or of bonds," said the procurator decidedly.

Agrippa agreed to this. "The fellow might have
been set at liberty," he added with a suppressed yawn,
"if he had not appealed to Cæsar."

CHAPTER XL.

ON THE WAY TO ROME.

"FROM Fair Havens to Phenice is but four and thirty miles, sir," said the master of the Alexandrian wheat ship, *Artemis*, staring thoughtfully out to sea. "This is no place to winter in," he went on, glancing with a frown at the rocky headlands off their weather bow. "We get every wind that blows here, except the Etesians.* I am owner of this ship as well as master, and I am willing to risk her and the cargo as far as Phenice ; but it is for you to say, sir."

The Roman centurion, Julius, in command of a cohort and charged with certain prisoners of state on board the *Artemis*, followed the eye of the master. "I am no sailor, good Polybius," he said at length somewhat dubiously, "but if we must winter hereabouts, Phenice is surely preferable to yonder desolate place. If you think it safe, let us get under way at once."

"Sirs, I crave your attention."

The centurion turned, "Ah, Paulus," he said with a certain deference in his manner at which the sailor stared open-mouthed ; "what wilt thou?"

"If we loose from this harbor, I perceive that the

---

* The North-West winds.

voyage will be with hurt and much damage, not only to the lading and ship, but also to our lives."

The captain laughed contemptuously. "Who is this convict," he enquired with an oath, "who will also navigate the vessel for us?"

The centurion made him no answer, he was looking thoughtfully at the prisoner. "This harbor is most incommodious, even unsafe, good Paulus," he said argumentatively. "Surely it will be better to push on to Phenice, which is less than a day's sail."

Paul shook his head. "The day of Atonement is already past," he replied quietly; "the winds and the sea may not be safely trusted longer."

"The fellow is a Jew and therefore a coward!" roared the master of the vessel with a great oath. "Let him hold his tongue about matters concerning which he has not been asked. By the body of Bacchus, do I not sail the good *Artemis* every year for full two months after every beggarly Israelite has taken to the land?*   At this moment, sir, there is a south wind blowing fit to fan a lady's cheek; 'twill waft us to Phenice before sundown."

"Then let us loose and away at once," said the centurion, turning away with an air of decision.

The *Artemis* was a large staunchly-built vessel of about nine hundred tons burden, rigged after the

---

* It was now the last of September, and with the Jews navigation was considered at an end for the season; the Greeks and Romans however did not regard the sea as "closed" till about the middle of November.

fashion of the times with a stout but clumsy mast, to which was fastened the huge square main-sail on a yard as long as the vessel itself. From the bow projected a second mast, raking far forward over the water and rigged with a triangular fore-sail. The stem-post of the bow ended in a rudely-carven image of the goddess whose name the good ship bore, while below and on either side were painted two huge staring eyes, by means of which the vessel was supposed to be better able to "look the wind in the face." The *Artemis* sat deep in the water, for she carried a full cargo of wheat besides her two hundred and fifty passengers and a crew of twenty men.

At the lusty cry, "All hands ahoy!" the ample decks became a scene of the liveliest confusion; the anchors were weighed with much tugging and shouting, the great sails hoisted, and the unwieldly craft, slowly gathering headway in the light south wind, began to draw away from the land. Closely hugging the shore she sailed smoothly along, towing her boat a cable's length behind, it having been deemed unnecessary to hoist it into the davits for so short a run.

"How now, Jew," sneered Polybius, planting himself in front of the manacled prisoner who had ventured to challenge his wisdom, "does the goddess carry that precious chain of thine softly enough to please thee?"

Paul lifted his eyes thoughtfully to the heights of the Cretan Ida, beneath whose shelter they were now sailing. "A prudent man maketh no boast of his running until he hath laid his finger upon the goal," he said with a shadowy smile. "What make you, good master, of yonder cloud on the summit?"

"Body of Bacchus!" bawled the sailor, "may the furies—" But the imprecation was never finished; it seemed on a sudden as though the furies so lightly invoked had seized the luckless vessel in their grasp and were hurrying her on to certain destruction.

So swift and so fierce was the descent of the hurricane that there was no time to furl the great main-sail. Through a smother of blinding mist and boiling surge the hapless *Artemis* staggered onward, her heavy masts tugging and straining fearfully beneath the unwieldly mass of wet canvas.

"Fetch in the boat," shouted the master, perceiving from the momentary lull that the vessel had run under the lee of the island of Clauda. With the help of the less-terrified passengers this difficult task was at length accomplished. But now it was discovered that water was rising rapidly in the hold; it was too evident that the frightful straining of the masts had opened the seams.

"She must be undergirded," quoth the captain— "and may the gods be merciful!"

Twice, thrice, the great cables were passed under the leaking hull and knotted fast across the decks; then ensued a desperate struggle to lower the main-yard with its huge sail; this was happily successful, the ship was hove to with her right side to the wind, and thus secured, rapidly drifted beyond the danger most feared at the moment, the perilous quicksands of Syrtis.

The day was now far spent, and night, moonless and starless, shut down over the boiling sea. The prisoners were secured aft, while the soldiers and sailors huddled together in the waist of the ship. Many of them prayed wildly, invoking their favorite gods with noisy supplications and extravagant vows, but their futile clamor was swallowed up in the loud monotonous chanting of the shrieking winds and hurtling waters.

Towards midnight, one of the sailors crept from his place and made his way along the slippery decks to the place where the prisoners were crouched beneath the shelter of the bulwarks. Putting out his hand in the thick darkness he touched the rough wet cloak of the man he sought.

" Art thou afraid, Paulus ?"

" The spirit of God moveth upon the face of the waters," murmured the prisoner as if thinking aloud. " Who hath measured the waters also in the hollow of his hand ; who stretcheth out the heavens like a curtain ; who layeth the beams of his chamber in the waters ; who maketh the clouds his chariot ; who walketh upon the wings of the wind. O Lord, how manifest are thy works ! the earth is full of thy riches, as also is this great and wide sea. My meditation of him shall be sweet ; I will be glad in the Lord."

"And is this also the 'Unknown God' of whom thou didst speak in Athens?" asked the sailor.

" Who art thou ?"

" I am Onesimus, once a slave in Colossae. And look you, I escaped from my master, taking with me ten gold pieces which I stole from his strong box. I tell thee this because I know that thou art a holy man, and because death stares me in the face and I am afraid. Can thy God save ?"

Then Paul preached once again the message of the glad-tidings to the repentant slave and to the soldier who was chained to his right hand. The two hung upon his words, forgetting the night and the tempest and the yawning deeps below.

When the first faint beams of morning dawned, the slave Onesimus cried out with joy, " Lo, I believe !"

But the soldier shook his head. " A strange tale," he said ; " it hath helped to while away the night ; but I see not how it can help us in our present plight."

The day which had now fully dawned seemed half-smothered in the murky cloud-rack which scudded rapidly overhead ; as far as the eye could reach, the sea was rolling in immense surges white with foam. The ship still drifted west by north from Clauda, the water sweeping completely over her at times ; it was evident that she must soon founder unless something could be done to lighten her. All hands were accordingly called and a part of the cargo was heaved overboard.

On the third day, the situation appearing even more desperate, the great main-yard with its mass of torn canvass and tangled rigging was cut away. The fury of the storm abated slowly during the days which followed, but the vessel, now little better than a dismantled leaking hulk, drifted helplessly broadside on in the sweltering seas. A despairing apathetic silence gradually settled down over the doomed vessel; no attempt was made to navigate the wreck, no rations were served out, nor even asked for; no one spoke. For twelve days and nights the death-angel had hovered over the *Artemis*, and the three hundred famishing helpless wretches on her decks cowered dumb beneath the terror of his unseen eyes.

Yet there was one man among them who was calm and confident amid all the horror. After long fasting Paul stood forth in the midst of them and said, " Sirs, ye should have hearkened to my counsel and not have loosed from Crete : then would ye have been spared this harm and loss. And now, I exhort you to be of good cheer; for there shall be no loss of any man's life among you, but only of the ship. For there stood by me in the night the angel of God, whose I am and whom I serve, saying, Fear not Paul; thou must stand before Cæsar ; and lo ! God hath given thee all who sail with thee ; wherefore, sirs, be of good cheer ; for I believe God, that it shall be even as it was told me. Howbeit, we must be cast upon a certain island."

When they had heard these words the soldiers and sailors were not a little encouraged, for they were ready to grasp at any hope, even as a drowning man will clutch at a floating straw. Moreover there was something in the pale face and shining eyes of this man which inspired them with confidence. " He hath himself the look of an immortal," they whispered one to another.

As for Polybius he declared to Julius, the centurion, with one of his outlandish oaths, that he believed the man was an oracle. "Unless," he made haste to add, " he is a sorcerer, and hath raised this tempest because we refused to follow his words. If I thought that, by Bacchus, I would heave his carcase overboard in a twinkling! Ay, the skies would clear then, and the wind would fall. Look you, good centurion, if this man be a great criminal, the gods will follow us in anger till we shall appease their wrath by his sacrifice."

But the centurion frowned, " Thou art sadly lacking in wisdom and discretion, my master, and that in more things than in the sailing of thy vessel. I warn thee to let the man be, for he is under the protection of Rome."

About midnight of the fourteenth day, the keen ears of the sailors distinguished above the howling of the tempest the sullen roar of breakers dashing upon a rocky coast. Orders were at once given to heave the lead; the soundings were reported to be twenty fathoms.

"Heave again, my lads!" shouted the master, straining his eyes through the darkness.

"Fifteen fathoms, sir."

"Ay, ay, there be breakers! I see a smother of foam not a quarter of a mile ahead. Drop the stern anchors—all four of them—or we shall drift broadside on !"

At no time of this fearful voyage had their situation appeared so hopeless ; drenched with the driving rain and blinding spray, their ears filled with the thunder of the hungry breakers, in imminent danger— so they thought—of dragging their anchors, it is perhaps not strange that at this moment of frightful peril the brute rose uppermost in the breasts of the sailors. " Let us take the boat," muttered one of them, " and get us to the shore if we may ; there is no need that all perish, and yonder rascally soldiers will seize it in the morning."

In pursuance of this cowardly design they prepared to lower the boat into the sea, under cover of dropping the bow anchors.

But the keen ear of Paul had caught a word or two, and he at once comprehended their plans. Turning to the centurion he said quietly, " Unless these sailors remain in the ship, ye cannot be saved."

Without a word three or four of the soldiers who were standing near drew their short swords and cut the ropes ; the boat fell off into the sea with a great splash and drifted off to leeward in the darkness.

As the first faint beams of morning shone in the eastern heavens, Paul besought them all to take some food. " This is the fourteenth day," he said, " that ye have continued fasting. Wherefore I pray you to take some meat ; for this is for your health. Not a hair shall fall from the head of any of you."

When he had thus spoken he took bread, and gave thanks to God in presence of them all : and breaking it, he began to eat.

"Ay, ay, master," cried one of the sailors, "we will do even as thou sayest ; for if thy God save us not we be assuredly dead men."

After all had eaten they righted the ship by casting overboard what remained of her cargo, then hoisting the tattered remnant of the fore-sail and cutting the anchor cables they ran the ship toward the shore, intending if possible to thrust the vessel into a certain depression in the unknown coast, which they took to be a creek, but which was in reality the narrow channel which runs betwixt the island of Salmonetta and the mainland. When the disabled *Artemis* struck the rough water caused by the current of the channel meeting the inrolling waters of the bay, she ceased to answer to her rudders* and drove violently on to an adjacent sandbank ; here the hull soon began to go to pieces under the action of the waves.

"What of the prisoners, sir," said one of the soldiers, approaching his superior officer. "As thou knowest we are accountable for them with our lives. That they may not now escape us, nothing remains to be done save to put them at once to the edge of the sword."

"Not so," exclaimed the centurion, "do not we

---

* The steering of ancient vessels was accomplished by means of two long oars or paddles, which projected from either side of the stern, and which could be raised or lowered at pleasure.

owe our lives to the sagacity of one of them? Loose them, and let those that can swim fling themselves into the sea and so get to land if they are able."

"As for the rest," writes Luke, "some clung to spars, and others to pieces of the wreckage; and so it came to pass, that all escaped safe to land."

Drenched, bruised, faint, and chilled with the cutting blasts of the raw November wind, the shipwrecked company yet had abundant cause for thanksgiving, for not one of their number was missing. And now the inhabitants of the place, which proved to be the island of Melita, began to gather at the scene of the wreck. A "barbarous folk," Luke calls them, but not devoid of human sympathy, for they at once set to work to build fires, that the sufferers might warm their benumbed bodies. Paul, eager as ever to work for others, was among the most active in collecting drift-wood and dried furze roots for this purpose. As he cast an armful of fuel upon the flames a viper leapt out from the smoke and fastened upon his hand.

"Behold!" cried one of the islanders, catching his neighbor by the arm, "this fellow must be a murderer; he hath escaped the sea, but vengeance suffers him not to live."

They stared at the man with great eyes as he shook off the venomous beast into the fire. "Presently," one whispered, "he will be swollen; then he will drop dead."

But after they had watched a long time and neither of these things came to pass, they changed their

minds. "Assuredly, this viper-bitten is a god; for
no man hath suffered the like and lived—no, not
within the memory of the oldest of our tribe."

And of this they afterward became the more convinced, for it was told them how Paul healed the father
of the Roman governor of the island, one Publius, at
whose house the centurion Julius and the chief passengers were hospitably entertained.

"The Roman had lain desperately sick of this
fever for more than seven days," quoth their informant
who had himself witnessed the miracle; "those of us
who attended him thought verily that his last hour
had come, when this man—whom they call Paulus—
entered into the chamber. He first looked attentively
at the sick one, afterward he lifted up his eyes toward
heaven and uttered some words in a strange tongue,
next he laid his hands upon the man and bade him
rise up. Which thing also he did with ease, my
friends, for he was perfectly healed of his disease."

When the fame of this miracle had gone abroad
throughout the island, others who were sick came and
besought Paul, and he healed them every one.

Now when the winter had come to an end it became
necessary to continue the voyage, and this the centurion determined to accomplish by means of another
Alexandrian wheat-ship, the *Castor and Pollux*, which
had wintered at the island. All the inhabitants of
Malta, as many as had been healed by the hand of
Paul and those who had been taught by him, mourned
and wept when the day of parting came, especially

since they beheld him once more chained to a soldier of the guard. These good islanders brought gifts in abundance, clothing and food, and many other things which they hoped might prove a comfort to the prisoner in his captivity.

Thus the travelers set sail from Malta, followed by many prayers and tears. After a prosperous voyage they arrived at Syracuse, where they tarried three days. "From thence," writes the historian, "we fetched a compass, and came to Rhegium : and after one day the south wind blew, and we came the next day to Puteoli, where we found brethren, and were desired to tarry with them seven days. And so we went towards Rome."

It is interesting to note in connection with this chapter that every detail of the voyage and shipwreck as given in the inspired record has been amply proven by the researches and experience of modern times. For example, it has been ascertained that it would take just fourteen days for a vessel to drift from the island of Clauda to Malta. It is thought that the exact position of the wreck has been determined ; and the anchorage of tenacious clay, "the place where two seas meet," and all other features of the place are precisely as represented by Luke. For the technical details of this chapter I referred most frequently to that valuable authority, Smith's "Voyage and Shipwreck of St. Paul."

CHAPTER XLI.

" READY TO BE OFFERED."

THE little town of Appii Forum, twenty-seven miles from Rome, was crowded as was its wont with a motley throng of travelers, soldiers, hucksters, bargemen, and idlers of every nationality. Some stood about in the warm March sunshine gossiping and laughing over the latest scandal from the city, others crowded the wine-shops and places where hot victuals of all sorts were offered for sale, while others still anxiously watched the great highway, a triumph of human patience and skill, which stretched its broad and solid leagues away through the noisome Pomptine marshes.

Before a small tavern on the main road, among other persons who were eagerly awaiting the incoming cohort of Julius, stood a group of five men and two women, their eyes fixed upon a distant cloud of dust which evidenced the approach of a large body of foot and horse.

" Yes," cried one of the women, clasping her hands, while the tears streamed down her cheeks, " it must be that they are coming ; but how can we bear to see him in chains ?"

" Nay, my Priscilla," said her companion sooth-

ingly, "let him not find thee in tears; surely he
will need all the cheer and comfort which we can bestow."

"Thou art right, my Junia.—But see it is the cohort!" and the warm-hearted Priscilla started forward
as if she would have penetrated the serried ranks of
legionaries which now began to file past them. "Yes
—yes, there he is! See, my husband—riding on the
mule behind the two horsemen.—My God, the chain!
And ah, how old and worn!"

The cohort had come to a halt now and the prisoners, each manacled to a soldier and further guarded
by a quaternion, were marched into the shelter of a
shed near by.

Aquila lost no time in asking permission to speak
to the prisoner Paulus, and he was not a little
comforted at the readiness with which his request was
granted.

"Thou mayst speak with Paulus," said the centurion courteously, "and I will also give orders that he
be removed to a room in the inn, where he may further refresh himself in your good company."

When the worn prisoner found himself once more
among them that loved him, "he thanked God and
took courage." About ten miles further on, at a
place called The Three Taverns, a second group of
Christians was waiting to bid him welcome. And so
along the Appian Way, where many a mailed warrior
had ridden proudly with his conquering legions to
celebrate his triumphs in imperial Rome, came this

scarred and wearied veteran, clad in the whole armor
of God, the hero of the grandest triumph the world
had ever witnessed, to receive the glorious crown of
his reward. Past tombs and temples, past snug ham-
lets and marble palaces embosomed in trees, past the
storied Alban hills, across the famous viaduct of Ari-
cia, through long rows of suburban villas, through the
Porta Capena, with its vast arch perpetually dripping
with the waters of the aqueduct which flowed above,
under triumphal arches, Julius and his prisoners
marched on, till at length they reached the "Golden
Milestone" of the Forum, the heart of the civilized
world, the centre and source of all earthly power and
magnificence. From this "Golden Milestone" radi-
ated the shining roads which bound the distant provinces to the heart of the Eternal City, and about it
clustered the historic buildings of the republic, and the
glittering courts of the "Golden House," that wondrous palace of the Cæsars. Here Julius delivered
the persons of the prisoners into the charge of Burrus,
the prefect of praetorians. By his orders they were
at once marched into the barracks of the imperial
guard.

The centurion seemed in no haste to depart though
his duty was now ended. "A word with thee, most
noble Burrus," he said, "before I leave the prisoners
in thy charge. There is among them a certain aged
man called Paulus, who is innocent of any crime. I
myself heard his defense before Festus and Agrippa,
both of whom pronounced him not guilty; but be-

cause he appealed to Cæsar they had no choice but to send him to Rome. He was first imprisoned in the days of Felix, through the spite and malice of the Jews who hate him consumedly because he is what we call a Christian. But by all the immortals, I swear that he is not only guiltless of any misdemeanor but that he is also a wise, just and holy man." Whereupon he related all the circumstances of the voyage and shipwreck, and also concerning the miracles performed among the inhabitants of Malta. "Therefore I pray you," he said in conclusion, "show the man what favor you may, and give him all the liberty possible under the law; he will not abuse it, this I can promise thee."

Burrus nodded his head understandingly. "It shall be as thou hast said, my good Julius. I will look to it."

And so it came to pass that Paul was allowed to dwell in lodgings by himself near the barracks. The soldiers to whom he was chained also showed him such kindness as they were able, and best of all he was permitted to receive his friends freely. On the third day after his arrival he sent a message to the chief Jews of Rome asking them to assemble themselves at his house. They came to a man for they were curious to look upon the famous apostate.

"Brethren," began the prisoner regarding his countrymen with wistful eyes, "though I have committed no offense against Israel, nor against the customs of our fathers, yet was I delivered chained from Jerusalem

into the hands of the Romans.   And these when they
had examined me would have set me free, because I
had done nothing worthy of death.   But when the
Jews opposed this, I was forced to appeal unto Cæsar
—not that I had aught to accuse my nation of.   For
this reason therefore I sent for you, that I might see
and speak with you.   For the hope of Israel I am
bound with this chain."

"We have received no letters from Judæa concerning thee," said one Simon Ben Ishmael cautiously,
" nor have any of the brethren who have recently visited
us shown or spoken any evil of thee.   But we desire
to hear what thou hast to say concerning this new faith,
for we know this much that the sect is everywhere
spoken against."

A day was accordingly appointed, and the Jews
flocked in great numbers to the house of Paul that
they might hear him expound the Christian faith.   And
he preached to them from morning until evening concerning Jesus the Christ, backing up his words with
the solemn testimony of the law and of the prophets.
"And some believed the things which were spoken,
and some believed not."

At the last when the discussion waxed hot betwixt
them, many also mocking at the tale of the crucified
Christ, Paul dismissed them with that one weighty
word of warning and reproof once uttered by Jesus
himself.   "Well spake the Holy Spirit by Esaias the
prophet unto our fathers, saying, Go unto this people
and say, Hearing ye shall hear, and shall not under-

stand ; and seeing ye shall see, and not perceive : for
the heart of this people is waxed gross, and their ears
are dull of hearing, and their eyes have they closed ;
lest they should see with their eyes, and hear with
their ears, and understand with their heart, and should
be converted, and I should heal them.   Be it known
therefore unto you, that the salvation of God is sent
unto the Gentiles, and that they will hear it."

"And when he had said these words," writes Luke,
"the Jews departed and had great reasoning among
themselves."   Then he brings his chronicle to an end
with these significant words, "And Paul dwelt two whole
years in his own hired house, and received all that
came to him ; preaching the kingdom of God and
teaching those things which concern the Lord Jesus
Christ with all confidence, no man forbidding him."

Of those years in Rome there yet remains to us
some slight record in the Epistles written to his beloved
churches in Colossae, in Ephesus, and in Philippi.   If
he could not go to them himself there were yet willing
messengers ready to bear his words of love and wisdom
to "the faithful in Christ Jesus."   And so, though he
knew it not, this "ambassador in bonds" spoke to
the church of all the ages.

"Unto me," he writes, "who am less than the least
of all saints, is this grace given, that I should preach
among the Gentiles the unsearchable riches of Christ
Jesus our Lord.   For this cause I bend my knees
before the Father, of whom the whole family in heaven
and earth is named, that he may grant you, according

to the riches of his glory, to be strengthened with might by his spirit in the inner man ; that Christ may dwell in your hearts by faith ; that ye being rooted and grounded in love, may be able with all saints to comprehend the breadth and length, and depth and height thereof. And to know the love of Christ which passeth knowledge, that ye may be filled with all the fullness of God."

Seldom in these letters does he refer to his helpless condition, except by way of apology for his barely-decipherable signature, " which was the token in every epistle." Not once does he bewail the injustice of his imprisonment, nor ask that means shall be taken to bring about his release.

"Walk in wisdom toward them that are without," he writes to Colossae, " redeeming the time. Let your speech be always with grace, seasoned with salt, that ye may know how ye ought to answer every man. All that concerns me will be made known to you by Tychicus, who is a beloved brother, and a faithful minister and fellow-servant in the Lord : whom I have sent to you for this very end, that he might learn your state and comfort your hearts ; with Onesimus, the faithful and beloved brother, your fellow-countryman ; they will tell you all that has happened here. . . . . The salutation of me, Paul, with my own hand. Remember my chain. Grace be with you."

What then had happened ? Onesimus, the fugitive slave, was about to return to Colossae, to face the master from whom he had escaped so many years ago. He had followed Paul to Rome and had attached himself to his person in the capacity of a humble attendant. "If thou art a slave of the Lord Jesus," he said, "let me, I pray thee, be thy slave." And Paul had suffered him, that he might the more readily impart to this darkened soul the teachings of the Master.

But after a year had elapsed he spoke to him gently of his duty to the master whom he had so grievously wronged. "I will write," he said, "a letter to Philemon—who also received the glad-tidings with joy many years since; he will receive thee from my hand no longer as a slave but as a brother, which indeed thou hast been and art—even a brother faithful and beloved."

Onesimus raised his head; his face was white but determined, and his eyes shone with the radiance of a great love. "I will do this thing," he said in a low voice, "because thou hast bidden me; and if I perish, I perish."*

"Nay, my son," said Paul, laying his chained hand on the bowed head, "thy master will receive thee as he would receive me, in all love and honor, for the sake of him who both died and hath given himself for us, even Christ our Lord."

In his quarters near the barracks of the praetorian guard, under the very shadow of the "Golden House,"

---

* The law condemned the fugitive slave to death by crucifixion. See also the Epistle to Philemon.

the aged prisoner could not have failed to hear frequent mention of the shameful and horrible events daily transpiring in that abode of blood and lust. He must have heard of the fatal ascendancy of the adulteress, Poppaea, whom the Jews now proudly claimed as a proselyte ; of the banishment and murder of the innocent Octavia, the lawful wife of the emperor before whose tribunal he was soon to stand. But he makes no mention of these historic events in his letter to the Philippians, written at about this time ; nor does he allude, except in the most casual manner, to the threatening aspect which his own affairs had assumed, owing to the death of the kind and honest Burrus and the accession to power of the infamous Tigellinus. "Wherefore, my beloved," he writes, "as you have always obeyed me, not as in my presence only, but how much more in my absence, work out your own salvation with fear and trembling ; for it is God that worketh in you both to will and to do of his good pleasure. Do all things for the sake of goodwill, without murmurings and disputings, that you may be blameless and guiltless, the sons of God without rebuke in the midst of a crooked and perverse generation, among whom ye shine like stars in the world ; holding fast the word of life, so that I may rejoice in the day of Christ, that I have not run in vain neither labored in vain. Yea, and if my blood be poured forth, I rejoice for myself, and rejoice with you all. And do ye likewise rejoice both for yourselves and with me."

Toward the close of this epistle are found these significant words, "All the saints salute you, especially they that are of Cæsar's household."

"They of Cæsar's household," the fierce veterans to whom he was chained, but who also were chained to him during many weary yet blessed hours; the slaves who crept to his feet for comfort and solace, the lowliest of the lowly, despised and downtrodden beneath the iron heel of infamy, yet brothers beloved and saints of God.

Not many days after, the aged prisoner was called before the dread tribunal of Rome. Was he acquitted and released, or was he remanded to his prison there to languish for unknown months and years? We cannot tell. Volume after volume has been written on the subject; wise men of every creed and nationality have discussed the question in all its varied aspects, but to-day we can only repeat the words, We cannot tell.

To Timothy, his "dearly beloved son," Paul writes his last word.

"I adjure thee before God and Jesus Christ, who is about to judge the living and the dead, I adjure thee by his appearing and his kingdom—proclaim the tidings, be urgent in season and out of season, convince, rebuke, exhort, with all forbearance and perseverance in teaching. But watch thou in all things, endure afflictions, do the work of an evangelist, make full proof of thy ministry. For I am now ready to be offered, and the time of my departure is at hand. I have fought a good fight, I have finished my course, I have kept the faith. Henceforth there is laid up for me a crown of righteousness, which the Lord, the righteous judge, shall give me at that day; and not to me only, but unto all them who love his appearing.

"Do thy diligence to come to me speedily; for Demas hath forsaken me for love of this present world, and hath departed to Thessalonica; Crescens is gone to Galatia, Titus to Dalmatia. Only Luke is with me. Take Mark and bring him with thee, for he is profitable to me for the ministry.

"When thou comest, bring with thee the cloak that I left at Troas, and the books, but especially the parchments.

"At my first answer no man stood with me, but all forsook me. I pray God that it may not be laid to their charge. Nevertheless the Lord Jesus stood by me and strengthened my heart, that by me the heralding of the glad-tidings might be accomplished in full measure, and that all the Gentiles might hear; and I was delivered out of the lion's mouth."

For an instant the light shines full upon the heroic figure, then it disappears forever in the impenetrable mists of the years, but not before we catch the triumphant words of farewell. "And the Lord shall deliver me from every evil, and shall preserve me unto his heavenly kingdom. To Him be glory unto the ages of ages. Amen."

The QUEST *of* HAPPINESS

A Study of the Victory over Life's Troubles. By New-
ELL DWIGHT HILLIS, Pastor of Plymouth Congregational Church, Brooklyn. Cloth, Decorated Border,
75c., postpaid.

It is a consummate statement of the highest conception
of the nature of human life, and of the only methods by
which its meaning and possibilities can be attained. A
serene satisfaction with God's method of moral government breathes from every page and makes the teacher
trustworthy.—CHARLES FREDERICK GOSS.

"The Quest of Happiness" is Dr. Hillis' very best
book. It is strong, vivid, clear, and has a certain indefin-
able human quality which will be sure to give it a large
circulation and make it a source of great helpfulness.
—AMORY H. BRADFORD, Pastor of the First Congregational Church, Montclair, N. J.

I find "The Quest of Happiness" a very rich and
beautiful work. It is eminently a book for the home.—
PHILIP S. MOXON, Pastor of South Congregational
Church, Springfield, Mass.

HAPPINESS

Essays on the Meaning of Life. By CARL HILTY.
Translated by Francis Greenwood Peabody, Pro-
fessor of Christian Morals, Harvard University,
Cambridge. 12mo, cloth, 75 cents, postpaid.

Great numbers of thoughtful people are just now much
perplexed to know what to make of the facts of life, and
are looking around them for some reasonable interpreta-
tion of the modern world. To this state of mind the
reflections of Prof. Hilty have already brought much reas-
surance and composure.

GROSSET & DUNLAP, PUBLISHERS
52 DUANE STREET   ::   ::   ::   NEW YORK

BOOKS ON ART

POPULAR, AUTHORITATIVE, INEXPENSIVE

RENAISSANCE AND MODERN ART. By W.
H. GOODYEAR, M.A., Curator of Fine Arts in the
Museum of the Brooklyn Institute. Profusely illus-
trated. 12mo, cloth.

This volume aims to present in a popular and non-
technical form a history of the various periods of art from
the time of the Renaissance to the present day. Two
hundred and three reproductions of paintings and sculp-
ture add to the interest of the work.

ROMAN AND MEDIÆVAL ART. By W. H.
GOODYEAR, M.A. New edition, revised and en-
larged. Profusely illustrated. 12mo, cloth.

The epochs treated in this work, those of the Romans
and of the Middle Ages, make this work not so much a
history of the arts as a history of the civilization of the
period. One hundred and ninety-six reproductions illus-
trate the text.

A HISTORY OF GREEK ART. With an Intro-
ductory Chapter on Art in Egypt and Mesopotamia.
By PROF. T. B. TARBELL, of the University of
Chicago. Profusely illustrated. 12mo, cloth.

This book has been written in the conviction that the
greatest of all motives for studying art, the motive which
is and ought to be the strongest in most people, is the
desire to become acquainted with beautiful and noble
things, the things that " soothe the cares and lift the
thoughts of man." Illustrated with one hundred and
ninety-six reproductions.

Price per copy, 75 cents, postpaid.

G R O S S E T & D U N L A P
52 DUANE STREET   ::   ::   ::   NEW YORK